The Myrmidon Project

THE

MYRMIDON

Chuck Scarborough and

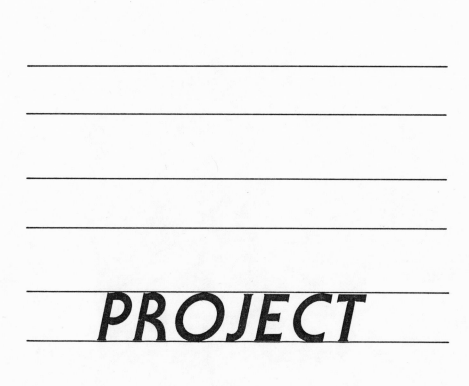

PROJECT

William Murray

Coward, McCann & Geoghegan/New York

Library of Congress Cataloging in Publication Data

Scarborough, Chuck.
The Myrmidon Project.

I. Murray, William, date. joint author.
II. Title.
PS3569.C32M9   1981   813′.54   80-20639
ISBN 0-698-11054-4

Printed in the United States of America

The world first saw it on July 20, 1976,
but few understood its implications
for the future of mankind.

A MAN-MADE CRAFT called Viking One had joined the Martian moons, Phoebos and Deimos, in orbit. It lingered awhile after its long voyage, then dropped through the thin Martian atmosphere to the surface of the red planet. With people all over the world waiting to witness this momentous event, a tiny television camera poked out of the Mars probe, aimed itself at the horizon, converted what it saw into electromagnetic impulses and propelled them earthward. Traveling at the speed of light, each signal took no more than five minutes to traverse the dark void in which Viking One had been traveling for months. months.

At Space Flight Operations, in Building 230 of the Jet Propulsion Laboratory in Pasadena, California, a large television screen displaying the mindless, snowy patterns of electronic noise was itself being photographed by cameras of the four major American TV networks waiting to feed the first pictures of Mars into millions of homes all over the U.S. and, by satellite, to the rest of the world.

Mankind's first glimpse of a planet whose odd color and mysterious features had haunted the imagination for eons was an enormous disappointment, an indistinct blur of shapes suggesting a shadowy, almost abstract watercolor. The scientists and technicians sitting at their electronic consoles in Building 230, however, seemed unconcerned. Poised over control boards whose transparent buttons glowed dull-white, these men and women calmly passed on the electronic signals from space to the Image Processing Laboratory in Building 168, only three hundred meters to the east. It was the home of an electronic mind far more advanced than theirs, a computer the scientists had pushed beyond their own human limits—the cutting edge of a technological rush already beyond the understanding of most men. Soundlessly, incandescently, the computer absorbed and incorporated the blurred images from Mars, dissected them into separate components, assigned numbers to each tiny element, examined the results, adjusted each one a thousand times a second, then sent these now processed images back to Space Flight Operations. The snowy blur from the Mars probe suddenly, miraculously, metamorphosed into razor-sharp depictions of a moonlike desolation, pocked and cratered not in red, but in lifeless shades of sand and gold.

The sight amazed and enraptured all who saw it. The larger significance of the process eluded all but a few. . . .

1

THE CHAIRMAN couldn't believe what he thought he had just heard. "What?" he asked, leaning forward in his chair, the fingers of his right hand brushing the edge of his ear, his head turning slightly as if to hear better. "What was that?"

Harvey Grunwald smiled and leaned comfortably back in his seat across the desk from the old man; he was enjoying this particular moment immensely. "You heard me, Larry," he said, smiling pleasantly at his boss. "I want half the gate."

The Chairman seemed puzzled. The late-afternoon sun angling in through the smoke-gray Thermopane windows of his forty-fourth-floor office brilliantly outlined the contours of his large head and shadowed his face, so that Harvey couldn't quite make out his expression. From where Harvey sat, in fact, the Chairman, even in his seventy-fifth year, looked as formidable and mysterious as ever, all the more so for the halo cast around him by the fading sunlight. A deliberate tactic? Of course. Harvey had been here before, many times, and his thirty years in the business had toughened him to deal even with Larry Hoenig, better known to everyone in his world as the Chairman. Harvey waited. He had plenty of time and he knew he was holding good cards.

"What was that, Harvey?" the Chairman asked. "My hearing, they tell me, is getting a little shaky."

"I'm sorry about that," Harvey said. "I guess neither of us is getting any younger."

The Chairman chuckled and leaned confidently back, his slightly gnarled but deeply tanned fingers drumming their familiar rhythm against the arms of his oak-and-leather swivel chair. "No," he said, "no, that's certainly true, Harvey. We're a couple of old bird dogs, you and I. We've been in the hunt a long time, haven't we?"

"That's exactly my point, Larry," Harvey said, thrusting himself forward now and speaking with the precision his thirty years in front of the cameras had given him. "I'm sixty years old. My contract is up in six months, and this next five years will be my last deal. You do understand, Larry?"

The Chairman understood, but he also knew how to negotiate. He sat quietly and steepled his fingers as he looked intently at his anchorman. He offered no immediate comment, but waited for Harvey to finish. Larry Hoenig had built a communications empire not merely through aggressiveness but also because he had the talent to wait and listen.

"I'll make it simple for you," Harvey Grunwald said, standing up and putting both his hands on the polished surface of the Chairman's burled-walnut desk, his face no more than a couple of feet from the Chairman's icy blue-gray eyes. Harvey spoke his next words slowly, enunciating every syllable. "I want half the gate, no more and no less."

"Half the gate? What do you mean, half the gate?"

Harvey smiled and began pacing about the room, pleasurably conscious of the fact that the Chairman's impassive stare now followed his every move. "I'll lay it all out for you, Larry," Harvey said. "My newscast is number one in the nation. It generates roughly one hundred fifty million dollars in revenue annually for the American Communications Network. CBS and NBC currently make about one hundred forty million each from their evening news programs. ABC, number four, makes one hundred thirty million. Approximate figures, Larry, but close enough, right?" Harvey stopped pacing and again leaned over the Chairman's desk. "Without me, where would you be? ACN would be number four, that's where. Without me in that anchor chair, you'd be pulling in one hundred thirty million instead of one hundred fifty million bucks. If you want me to stay on, Larry, it's going to cost you half the difference. I flunked math at school, but even I can figure out what half of twenty million is, Larry. It comes to ten million a year, give or take a hundred thousand. Am I getting through to you now, Larry?"

The Chairman did not answer right away. Slowly his hands dropped into his lap. He studied Harvey carefully, evidently unsure whether he was to take him seriously or not. "Is this a joke, Harvey?"

"No joke. Sorry."

The Chairman smiled faintly, though his eyes, half hidden under slightly drooping lids, remained intensely serious. "Aren't you being just a tiny bit greedy, my friend?"

"Greedy!" Harvey suddenly shouted at him. "If I were being greedy, I'd demand reparations!"

"I'm afraid I don't follow you there."

"Larry, I've been number one or tied for first place for twenty years—"

"Wait a minute, Harvey," the Chairman corrected him, holding up one hand, "that's not quite accurate. There was the time—"

"I remember it, I remember it very well," Harvey said. "You don't have to remind me, Larry. And you fired me."

"Not exactly, Harvey," the Chairman said, his voice mild and low. "We had to reassign you for a time."

"Yes, and it took one good year out of my life," Harvey said. "One good year out of twenty. So let's say it's been nineteen years, all right?"

"That one good year away from it," the Chairman continued smoothly, "that so-called lost year of yours saved you, Harvey."

"I'm not going to argue the point with you now, Larry," the anchorman said. "The point is that in these twenty years you've made a quarter of a billion dollars more off my newscast than if we'd been number four in the ratings. That's two hundred and fifty million dollars, Larry. And in those twenty years you've paid me a little over five million. Total."

"Not exactly poverty wages, Harvey," the Chairman said, still unruffled.

"It's all relative, Larry," Harvey said. "What you paid me was a lousy two percent of the take. Two percent, Larry. If I were a greedy man, I'd ask for a retroactive cut. Fifty percent from the day we hit the top of the ratings."

The Chairman chuckled mirthlessly. "Not really practical, Harvey, is it?"

"I know that. That's why all I'm asking now is a new deal for the next five years."

The Chairman seemed unshaken. He regarded his top employee with the benevolent look he might have lavished on him if the man had come into his office to thank him for all the good years instead of making such an extraordinary demand. The Chairman sighed, as if only slightly disappointed in the ingratitude by which he was clearly surrounded. He passed his carefully manicured fingers lightly over his full head of silver hair, still parted, as always, on the left, and blinked thoughtfully at his anchorman. "You are serious, aren't you?" he asked, in a mildly bemused tone.

"You're damn right I'm serious," Harvey said, flinging himself angrily back into his chair.

"Harvey," the Chairman said, "you know we admire and respect you. We realize very well what you're worth to this network and we certainly want to make you happy. But within reason. You know we have stockholders and—"

Harvey again thrust forward in his chair and rapped one hand on the edge of the desk. "You know what you can do with the stockholders, Larry? Stuff 'em."

The Chairman chuckled. "I wish we could, Harvey," he said. "I'd like to stuff them and mount them on my wall, but I can't. And you can't ask me to. There's no way I could justify what you ask to them or anybody, Harvey. Be reasonable. Now, what would it really take to keep you happy for the next five years?"

"What would it really take?" Harvey echoed him, then sat back and stared at the Chairman for a full minute. When he finally did choose to answer him, he spoke slowly and carefully, as if explaining a complicated adult problem to a very small child. "Reasonable, you say. You think that fifty percent of what I earn for this company is unreasonable. It is not unreasonable, Larry. It is very reasonable indeed. Muhammad Ali took eighty percent of the gate and they were glad to give it to him. On a fight that grossed five million, Ali got four. That was reasonable, Larry, very reasonable, because without him the promoters had nothing to offer the public. Twenty percent of something is better than a hundred percent of nothing. In Las Vegas, in the movies, in rock music, any proven box-office draw gets more than half the gate, Larry. And they're glad, they're anxious to give it to him. That's what I call being reasonable, Larry."

The smile below the Chairman's icy gaze froze as Harvey spoke, then faded slowly from his face. "I don't think you're making an especially good case for yourself, Harvey," the Chairman said. "You're not a sports hero and you're not a rock star."

"Right, Larry, you're right," Harvey quickly agreed, "which is why I'm not asking for more. I only want what I'm worth, that's all."

"It occurs to me," the Chairman observed in his calm, even voice, "that there's a difference of opinion about that."

"You bet your ass there is," Harvey snapped. "For a long time the news divisions of the networks were costly money-losers, but you needed them and you needed us because of the prestige we brought you. We cleaned up your lousy act for you. You could always point to us, when the going got heavy with the FCC or consumer advocate groups or with the Congress, and crow about how much money the news operations cost you, about what a great public service you were doing. Well, that all changed in the sixties, didn't it? Only nobody noticed. Suddenly the news divisions became big money-earners for you and they grew and they created their own stars. Like me, for instance. Only you guys continued to treat us like news hacks and you paid us accordingly."

"We paid you pretty well, Harvey," the Chairman cut in.

Harvey was not to be deterred. He brushed aside the Chairman's almost parenthetical observation with a careless wave of one hand. "I'm not finished, Larry," he said, leaning in closer to the old man. "You bastards have made exorbitant profits off our backs long enough. If you want the use of my talents for another five years, it'll cost you fifty percent of the gate. Fifty percent, not a dime less. Ten million dollars a year. If you don't, I'll go to ABC, where they're dying to have me, and within a year they'll be grossing one hundred fifty million from the news and you'll be sitting in fourth place with one hundred thirty million. That's just easy arithmetic, Larry, even for me. It costs you ten to keep me, twenty to lose me. That's what *I* call reasonable."

The Chairman sat very still; he had long ago learned to contain his rage. "Well, you've certainly made your point," he said matter-of-factly. "And you've given me quite a bit to think about. Why don't we both sleep on it for a couple of days?"

"You've got six months to sleep on it, if you want, Larry," the anchorman said. "But it's cut and dried from my end and I can assure you there's no room to negotiate."

"There's always room to negotiate, Harvey."

"Not this time, Larry. Just keep the simple figures in mind and we'll be all right. Ten to keep me, twenty to lose me. Simple arithmetic." And with a final wave of his hand Harvey Grunwald turned his back on the Chairman and walked swiftly out of the room.

For a long time the Chairman sat silently behind his desk, his fingers drumming lightly on the arms of his chair. He had just felt the communications empire he had built over a lifetime of hard work totter. The Chairman did not like the feeling. He swiveled away from his desk and gazed out the window at the New York skyline, where the battlements of the city's tallest buildings testified eloquently to his position in the world. Out of absolutely nothing but guts and talent and a genius for manipulating people and events to his own advantage, Lawrence Hoenig had risen in the world and he was not about to let one greedy employee sabotage this achievement. No way. Why couldn't they understand? Why couldn't they place their ultimate trust in him? Didn't they know what he had achieved and what he had to defend, even if it cost him his life? The Chairman sighed, turned back toward his desk and reached for the phone.

Shirley Boyd's cool, efficient voice responded immediately. "Yes, sir?"

"Get me Sarah Anderson, Shirley."

"Do you wish to see her?"

"I'll talk to her first."

"Yes, sir."

The Chairman hung up and sat back to wait. He was a patient man and during his long career he had outwaited and outwitted opponents far more formidable than Harvey Grunwald, who was, after all, merely another in a long line of misguided adventurers who had mistaken the achievement of a popular success for a position of real power. The Harvey Grunwalds of this ungrateful world were legion and the Chairman had always known how to deal with them in the past. Never directly, of course. No, that small privilege he had always delegated to others and always successfully. Harvey could prove to be more of a problem than most, but—

The Chairman's musings were interrupted by the buzz of his phone. He picked up the receiver. "Sarah? . . . Yes. Yes, I think we'd better talk. Harvey was just here." He paused to hear her out, then sighed. "Yes, I'm afraid so. I suppose we'd better meet in person. Tomorrow morning? Ten o'clock? . . . Fine."

After he'd hung up, the Chairman again turned to face the city he had conquered. The setting sun now bathed the skyscrapers in a golden glow. It was a glorious sight, one he never tired of, and it was a real shame that the glory this view symbolized for him had to be periodically sullied by the likes of Harvey Grunwald, that ungrateful exploiter of the Chairman's trust and generosity of spirit.

* * *

Ann Grunwald was a tall, slim woman whose figure belied her age. From a distance she could still be mistaken for the beauty she had once been, though she'd spent too much of her early life outdoors on her family's Texas ranch, and her deeply tanned, leathery features were crisscrossed by a network of deep wrinkles. Her hair was gray, too, but she did move well, with the elegant grace of an ex-athlete, and her smile was still radiant, a great flashing of large, strong teeth framed by full sculptured lips. Too bad, Harvey thought once again, as he saw her hurrying toward him across their large living room, too bad she wouldn't get a face lift. Harvey hadn't insisted, but he had mentioned it once or twice. After all, he *was* a celebrity and she should have realized that her appearance, at his side in public and private functions, would inevitably reflect on him as well. It couldn't be helped, though; that was the way she'd always been—unpretentious, honest, the same open personality he'd fallen in love with nearly forty years ago when they'd met as students at Colorado. God, that was a long time ago. Harvey set his briefcase down and took her in his arms.

"How'd it go?" she asked.

"A slow evening," he answered. "Not much going on in the great wide world today."

"I thought Gene's special from the Philippines was interesting."

"The Philippines, *that's* how slow things were," he commented, with a laugh. "Anyway, I thought it was only so-so. And badly written. Somebody goofed."

"Gene?"

"Probably. Half the time he doesn't even look at the copy they hand him before he goes on the air." Harvey sighed and shook his head sadly. "This new crop of so-called newsmen we've got, these young punks with no background in print, they think all they have to do is look authoritative and pretty in front of the camera and talk sincerely."

"Gene's just another pretty face, huh?" she said, smiling and leading him by the hand out toward the kitchen, where she had laid out their light supper. Harvey always came home still tense from his broadcast and, unless they were going out somewhere, he ate only light, uncomplicated meals that she had always prepared herself. Also, she had learned over the years to have it ready for him by the time the network limousine deposited him in front of their apartment-house entrance every working evening; Harvey was sometimes so ravenous from his chores that he'd dispense with drinks and get right to the food. She knew him better, far better, than anyone else. "How about a drink?"

"Tonight, yes," he said. "Tonight we're going to celebrate."

"Oh? What's the occasion?"

"I'm the occasion," he announced, with a laugh. "I saw Larry today."

"About your contract?"

"Yep. I really told him."

She did not answer immediately, but opened the refrigerator door and took out the ice-cold bottle of imported Polish vodka Harvey favored. She poured him a good shot over the rocks, handed it to him and looked around for the sweet vermouth she had earlier deposited somewhere on the cluttered counter between the kitchen area and the breakfast nook where Harvey sat. She splashed a generous portion of the amber liquid into a glass for herself. "Cheers."

"Don't you want to know how it came out?"

"What do you think?"

"Then sit down a moment."

"I've got a quiche in the oven. Hold on a sec," she said, turning her attention to her cooking.

"Boy, you're funny." He laughed again, feeling the tension of the day begin to drain out of him in the glow of the vodka and her comforting presence. "I'm talking millions and you're worried about your quiche. You're a riot, my darling."

"I'm glad you think so," she answered, a bit grimly, "but you won't be laughing if this turns out like a rock. There, that's it," she concluded, slamming the oven door shut. "Now, then."

"I hit him with it," Harvey said, "caught him completely off guard."

"Harvey—" she began.

"No, listen to me," he continued, waving her into silence. "I told him what I wanted and why. And he couldn't believe it."

"Does that surprise you?"

"Yes, I guess so. I just didn't figure that a guy as sharp as Larry Hoenig would be so surprised, that's all," Harvey said. "Especially, come to think of it, when you realize that I'm all he's got. Me and Gene Blanton, for God's sake."

"Then it is Gene they want to succeed you."

"Sure. But he doesn't have it. He's another of these bland, faceless nice guys, like Bill James. Jesus, the woods are full of them," Harvey said. "You know what happens if I walk away from ACN? They've had it, as far as the news is concerned. I'm the man who makes us number one and they know it. I'm the best any network's had since Cronkite retired, and they know that, too. Gene Blanton certainly can't cut it alone."

"He's pretty charming, though."

"That and twenty bucks will buy you a good cheeseburger these days," Harvey observed, smiling. "That's all the guy's got, Ann. That and a great mane of hair."

"Don't be jealous, darling."

Harvey grinned and ran a hand quickly over his own thinning locks. "I'm distinguished-looking," he said. "That's what they like about me. I'm like old Uncle Walt. Comforting, avuncular."

"Don't use that word on the air," she interrupted. "No one will know what it means."

Harvey chuckled. "Come on," he said, "let's sit out in the living room and enjoy our drinks."

From where they sat beside each other in the center of the huge room, on a long couch at right angles to the fireplace, they could gaze out their hermetically sealed windows across the rooftops of the city, peppered here and there by the brightly illuminated shafts of skyscrapers and tall blocks of office buildings packed side by side along the hub's major arteries. A view for the gods, Harvey had told her, but only for the very rich ones. When they had first decided to buy this luxurious penthouse at the top of Manhattan's Olympic Tower, the town's most prestigious co-op apartment house, Ann had been apprehensive. The huge rooms had seemed so empty and cold to her now that the children had long since grown up and moved out, but her first sight of the place at night had won her over. The view was breathtaking, a Peter-Pan ride among the stars. And so they had gone ahead and bought the place, and she'd spent the better part of a year simply trying to make it livable. But then, after all, they did have to do a lot of entertaining and Harvey had an image to keep up. When they wanted to be cozy and alone, they could always retreat into their kitchen breakfast nook or take refuge in their bedroom, which Ann had decorated in warm colors and enclosed in drapes to achieve the intimacy she required, but then—

"No," Harvey was saying, "Larry knows it as well as I do. Gene Blanton's just another pretty face. Harvey Grunwald is what keeps ACN up there. For that eminence, Harvey Grunwald is worth every penny of the money."

"How much money do we need, really?"

"I want to be paid what I'm *worth*, Ann."

"A million dollars a year ain't bad, as they'd say down home."

He was not amused. For weeks now she had been trying to kid him out of this crazy scheme, but without success. She hadn't realized how deeply he'd been wounded, all those years ago, and how the injury must have festered. It wasn't a question of the money. No, they surely didn't need the money. It was something else, perhaps revenge, but something she couldn't deal with on a rational plane with him. Ann knew her husband well, very well, and she knew that when that Teutonic will of his locked on a point there was no budging him. She would not argue about it anymore, either, but the scope of his ambition frightened her. Because Ann knew what Larry Hoenig was capable of when he was crossed. On his way to the top he had broken bigger and stronger men than her husband. Didn't Harvey realize that? My God, she thought, we're five years away from retirement and our last good years together and he's risking everything now just to get even. It's crazy.

"I proved it to them back in '73, when they fired me and sent me out on what they thought was a cockamamie field job that would make me quit," he was saying, pacing the room as he had earlier the Chairman's office. "I shoved it down their throats. And look what happened to their ratings when they tried to replace me."

"That was Brennan's idea, wasn't it?"

"Partly, sure. But every decision ultimately gets made in Larry's office, you know that."

"What does Sarah say?" Ann asked. "Have you discussed it with her?"

Harvey grinned. "No," he said. "She'll probably wet her queenly pants when she finds out, as she will, of course. Larry will have to discuss it with her. I wish I could be there, hon. I'd give anything to hear what their reaction is going to be."

"Larry and Sarah?"

"All of them," Harvey said, "all the moneyed fatcats on the corporate floor. Jesus, I love it! I've waited a long time for this day."

He went and stood by the window and gazed happily out over the gleaming lights of the city. Ann admired him at such moments, because he was so full of life, so vibrantly in touch with everything. At times like this her husband seemed so much younger, as full of ambition and idealism as when she had first been introduced to him at that fraternity party so long ago, when all he could talk about was becoming a great American novelist, the best since Dreiser or since Lewis, the two authors he most admired. Harvey had been an extraordinary man even then and she had fallen in love with him on that first day and had never regretted it, never doubted their capacity for shared happiness. And though he'd never become a great writer, had never, in fact, even written a novel, no one could deny his success, now capped by two Pulitzer Prizes for reportage and the esteem and affection of millions of his fellow citizens. Harvey Grunwald was the best anchorman television news had ever produced, more accurate than Murrow, wittier than Brinkley, better loved even than Cronkite.

"No, it's not the money, Ann," he said now. "It's a lifetime they owe me for, a lifetime of achievement out of which this network has made a killing. They owe me. And they're going to pay me what they owe, every last penny of it, or I walk."

She stared at him, seeing in that instant not the kindly face of the man she'd loved and lived with and whose children she had borne and raised, but the face of anger, of retribution, of hard, cold ambition. She shivered.

"You all right?" he asked. "You looked funny there for a moment."

"It's nothing," she said. "My nerves, a chill. Maybe I've got a cold coming on or something."

He walked over and kissed her. "Come on," he said, "I've got plans for you tonight, lady."

She held him in her arms, and for a minute or two the fear passed and they were safe, alone together, as they had been from the start.

2

SARAH ANDERSON took her time getting to the meeting. She had, of course, thought about nothing else since the Chairman's phone call, but she had guessed it would be coming and she had prepared herself for it. She had known all along, ever since she had first contemplated the possibility, that it would be Harvey she would eventually have to cope with, but she could have used a little more time, that's all. She wasn't absolutely confident yet that she could deal with such a delicate issue exactly as they had planned. It took not only money, but time, lots of time, to work these programs out, to make them absolutely fail-safe.

The appointment with the Chairman was for ten o'clock, but she left her office on the fortieth floor of the ACN Building a half hour early. She sometimes found it helpful in her job, as president of *ACN News*, to make a tour of her small, self-contained kingdom before arriving at any final decision that concerned it and herself. The tour reassured her, because it always comforted her to be able to stroll casually from section to section, to see with her own eyes how supremely well it was functioning. And, she had always correctly assumed, her occasional presence in the working areas of the newsrooms kept her close to her people, made them aware of her concern and involvement with their day-to-day achievements and problems. Like a good general, she knew that personal contact bound subordinates to her more closely, more creatively than an invisible presence behind closed doors. That was the only important thing she had learned from Ted Brennan, her otherwise unlamented predecessor. Brennan had always been a newsman and he knew by experience what built and maintained the morale of a good staff. Sarah had been smart enough to copy him in that at least.

Sarah Anderson was now in her early fifties, still striking, with soft reddish-brown hair streaked with gray, vivid green eyes, a complexion glowing with health and vitality, and a tall, strong-looking body. She radiated concern, intelligence and femininity. The positive impression she made on nearly everyone who met her had proved to be an enormous asset. Probably the most powerful female executive in the industry, Sarah also had a reputation for being nearly as tough as her boss, and her past contained some dark professional and personal secrets, sometimes gossiped about by the people who had known her longest, but which caused her to be feared as well as respected. She was in every way formidable, impossible to dismiss from one's mind after meeting her and clearly a personality of depth and consequence.

It was much too early in the day, of course, for one of Sarah's more formal tours, but she took the time anyway. Because the premises of network news, which occupied a string of quiet, elegant offices on her own floor, held no surprises for her, she descended the stairs to the landing below and let herself into the local newsroom, where the hurly-burly of constant activity had never failed to delight her. She liked most of all the feverish air of the command post, with its cluttered desks, clattering typewriters and ringing phones below the TV monitors and the wall clocks with their big, silently spinning second hands. It was here that the day's work spun itself out and ultimately came together, for this was the very heart of the news operation. Sarah, who had come late to her career, still loved the smell, the sound, the sight of it, every aspect of it. Even at her present eminence, she considered herself a vital part of it and it lifted her spirits to be there.

Mario Bellucci, just settling into his post at the assignment desk, below his board of blinking lights, the bright-red lines of the scanners monitoring the police frequencies, was the first to spot her. He was obviously surprised. "Hey, boss," he said, grinning at her, "come to see how the lowly half lives?"

Sarah laughed. "That's right, Mario, just checking up. What are you doing in so early?"

"Windom's out sick today, so I'm working a double shift. See the sacrifices I make for the team?"

"You're a jewel, Mario, we've always known that."

"Yeah? So how come I don't get promoted?"

"You're invaluable right where you are," Sarah said, laughing.

"Oh, yeah, I guess I knew that," the dark-eyed, heavyset man said, suddenly plugging into his board. "Hey, I think we've got a good bloody killing up in the South Bronx this morning. Some guy raped and murdered an old lady and stuck her inside a Laundromat machine. Want to hear the gory details?"

"No, thank you," she answered, with a grimace. "See you, Mario."

"Sure thing, boss. But you're missing all the fun."

She ignored the man's characteristic crudeness and moved on, nodding and smiling to the people already at work around their desks, then past the editing rooms, the labs, the reporters' cubicles, the larger offices of Bill James and Karen Lowe, the station's best anchor team, finally on to the corner office of Dwight McCarron.

The producer was sitting behind his desk, but immediately stood up when he saw her. "Hello, Sarah," he said, startled. "What's up? Anything wrong?"

"No, no, Dwight," she said quickly, "just killing a little time before I go up and see Mr. Hoenig."

"Come in. Some coffee?"

"No, thanks."

"Want to sit in on the ten-o'clock meeting? It looks like we may have a busy day, what with the transit strike looming."

"Sorry, Dwight, I haven't time. I've got my own meeting at ten. How are things going?"

"Pretty well," the producer said. "We had some real nice film on that crash out at La Guardia last night. Did you happen to see it?"

"Yes, I did. It was spectacular footage."

"Yeah, that was Jeff Campbell and Moss Johnson again. They're the best team we've got. Best in the business, I'd say. Sure you haven't time for some coffee?"

"No, really. But thanks again." She glanced at her watch now, then smiled at the producer. "I really have to go. I'm glad things are in such good shape with you, Dwight. You're doing a fine job."

"Thanks. I appreciate that, Sarah."

Sarah, reassured that the Swiss watch that was her news operation was functioning perfectly, waited calmly by the elevators. It was five minutes of the hour; she would arrive in the Chairman's office exactly on time, as always.

"That's nice," Jeff Campbell said as he draped himself casually into a chair beside Bellucci's desk. "Really nice."

"What is?" the editor asked.

"That new production assistant you've got in here," the cameraman explained. "She moves like a young doe. Really sweet stuff."

Bellucci swung around to have a look at the young woman in question, who walked briskly past them, presumably on her way to McCarron's office. He grunted noncommittally.

"Come on, Mario," Jeff said, "you've got to admit she's an improvement. The last six months it's been a regular Bay of Pigs in here."

The editor laughed. "Jesus, Campbell, don't you ever quit?"

"Nope," Jeff said. "And the day I do, I'll be dead."

"You're a sex maniac."

"Just because you're too old and chewed out. Hell, that wife of yours could turn the Washington Monument to jelly."

Bellucci grinned. "Ah, shit, who needs to get laid? The old woman can cook."

"I figured you weren't starving to death."

"Hey, where's Johnson?"

"In there, getting the gear together."

"I think we've got a busy day."

"Another one? Listen, I've got tickets for the ball game tonight. Have a heart, Mario."

"Tough," Bellucci said, "real tough."

"Well, I'm just a poor working stiff—"

"Sure you are. And speaking of stiff, you can forget about her," Bellucci said, cocking a hairy thumb in the direction of the girl, who stood now, with her back to them, looking in through the open doorway of McCarron's office. "She's taken."

"Ah, a challenge. You know that never stopped me, Mario. Who is it? Not McCarron. He's married, isn't he?"

"Sure. No, it's some corporate whiz-kid VP producer named Bridgeford."

"Don't know him."

"And he don't know you," Bellucci said. "Those network sharks in their dark suits don't come down into the pit with us poor working folks, you know that, Campbell. We're unclean."

"Compared to you, Mario, I'm Snow White. If I've ever seen a commercial for ground-in dirt, it's you, baby."

"Hey," Moss Johnson said, coming around the corner with Jeff's camera rig draped over his shoulder, "slavery went out with the last rerun of *Roots*. What's happening, man?" Moss hoisted the camera rig onto the desk and grinned at his partner. "We're a little late getting started, aren't we?"

"Yeah," Jeff said. "I was really just admiring the improvement in the view around here."

Moss caught sight of the girl in McCarron's doorway and smiled. "She's a real sweet kid," he said.

"You know her?"

"Sure," the black man said. "She came up to me yesterday, after she saw the tape on the crash. I guess you were still in there watching Vicki edit the last of it or something. Anyway, she asked all about you."

Jeff looked slightly dazed. "No kidding?"

"So help me. She wants to go out on assignment with us, when she can get an OK from McCarron. She wants to be a reporter."

"Who is she?"

"Tracy something. You dig her, huh?"

"Don't you?"

"No, man. I likes them with a little more chocolate and cinnamon in them. That's a little bland for my style, man."

"So what else do you know about her?" Jeff asked.

"Not much. She told me she started out here as a page, like everyone. Then she worked upstairs for a while."

"Where?"

"Mrs. Anderson's office. And now they've assigned her to the local news, poor kid. Legwork. She's a very ambitious chick, man. Not your kind at all."

"No? Why not? I thought you said she was sweet."

"Yeah, too sweet. You're poor white trash, Mistah Campbell," Moss answered, on the edge of another routine.

"Spare me, Moss."

"These nice Eastern chicks, man, they don't mess with no rednecks."

"Hey, Moss, you're pretty cute," Jeff observed, "pretty nifty, you know that?"

"I do my best," Moss said, laughing.

Later, after the ten-o'clock staff meeting, Jeff caught up to the girl by the hallway bulletin board, where she was idly scanning the personal notices. She was a beauty, all right, he decided, a tall, leggy brunette with an open, strong-jawed face, hazel eyes and a quick, intelligent-looking smile. "Hi," Jeff said, "can I help?"

"I don't know," she answered. "I'm looking for another place to live. Know of an apartment?"

"Sure," Jeff said, turning on his best smile, "Move into mine. I'm hardly ever there."

Tracy looked at Jeff for a moment. It's true what they say about him, she thought. A bit of a swordsman, this cameraman. She could see why. He was a rugged sort, deeply tanned, with tousled light-brown hair and pale-blue eyes with squint lines at the corners from years of peering at the world through viewfinders, his chest exposed by the open neck of his short-sleeved khaki bush jacket. She guessed him to be just under six feet tall, a little huskier and hairier than she liked, but still interesting. Tracy decided, however, to ignore his flirtation, and looked back at the bulletin board without responding.

"Only kidding," Jeff said, sensing he had moved too quickly. "I don't know of any places available right now, but I'll ask around. What can you afford?"

"Not much. I'm sharing a loft in Soho with two girl friends, but one of them's getting married and anyway I want my own place. By the way, I'm Tracy Phillips." She held out her hand and he shook it.

"Jeff Campbell," he said.

"I know. I've heard about you."

"Good things, I hope," Jeff responded with a suggestive smile, still holding her hand.

"Yes." Tracy pulled her hand away. "They tell me you're a terrific cameraman." Jeff's smile faded. "In fact," Tracy continued, "I've asked Mr. Johnson if I could go out on stories with—"

"Yeah. Say, call him Moss. We don't want any uppity niggers around here. We've got our full quota as it is."

"I don't think that's in the least amusing," Tracy snapped. "You'll forgive me, but I have strong feelings about that kind of racist talk."

"Hey, just kidding," Jeff said, realizing that things were beginning to deteriorate. He suddenly began to feel annoyed, as much with himself, he guessed, as with this young woman he found so attractive.

"Kidding or not," Tracy said, "that sort of talk is unacceptable."

Jeff groaned. "Oh, God, we've been saddled with a limousine liberal."

"Mr. Campbell—"

He smiled brightly. "You can call me Jeff."

"Look, I didn't mean to make a thing out of this," she said. "I don't really know you at all and—"

"We can fix that. What about dinner?"

"I'm sorry, but I'm tied up."

"Forever?"

She shook her head. "Look, somehow we've both gotten the wrong idea about each other. All I asked Mr. Johnson—Moss—was whether I could come out on some assignments with you. On my own time, of course. You shoot terrific pictures and I'm trying to learn to be a reporter."

"Why? It's low-life monkey business."

"Because it interests me, that's all. I'd like to think I can write a little."

Jeff groaned again. "God, another lady writer. Don't get married."

She stepped back in astonishment. "Why not, if I want to?"

"Because then you'll have three names," Jeff said. "Most lady writers wind up with three names. I don't know any good writers with three names, do you?"

"This is ridiculous," she said.

"Well, how about a date? Or is that ridiculous too?"

"Mr. Campbell, I hardly know you."

"As I said, that's easily fixed." He grinned and leaned against the wall between her and the bulletin board. "I'm a very charming person, really."

"I've seen no evidence of it so far," she said quietly. "Look, I appreciate your obvious interest in me. But I *am* involved with somebody right now."

"I sure hope he's worthy of you."

"What do you mean by that?"

"Well, I just meant somebody from your own class."

"And what class would that be?"

"Upper-middle East Coast WASP, with aristocratic overtones," he said, trying to keep the remark on the level of banter but realizing that he was failing miserably. What was it about this girl that managed to bring out the worst in him? "Listen," he corrected himself, "this isn't coming out the way I meant it—"

"Are you sure? It sounded loud and clear to me, Mr. Campbell. You're a snob."

"I'm a what?"

"A snob of the worst kind—a reverse snob. I'm sure you don't mean any harm, but frankly I find you insufferable. Now, if you'll excuse me . . ."

"Hey," he said, bewildered, "I'm sorry. Look, you can come along anytime—"

"I appreciate that," she said quietly. "As long as the relationship is strictly professional. Excuse me, but I have work to do." She stepped around him and headed back toward the newsroom.

Moss, who had apparently been listening, stuck his head around the corner from the entrance to the men's room. "Man, you sure handled that smoothly. You got the lady really turned on to your irresistible appeal."

"Hey, Moss," Jeff said, "don't you know it's bad form to crow over a man's agony? Where's your *savoir faire*, my good man?"

"Never had none of that stuff, Dad. It gives me the vapors."

Jeff stared unhappily after Tracy, whom he could see in conversation now with Bucky Santini, his chief professional rival. "Damn," he mumbled, "I sure blew that one."

As the Chairman droned on, Sarah sat quietly, presumably intent on his every word. Actually, she was thinking less about what he was saying than about how much the man had deteriorated in the past few months. Age seemed to have caught up to him at last. His face was changing, the flesh sagging. His eyes were still hard and clear, but she sensed that the mind behind them was failing. The Chairman personified habit without purpose now, an empty harshness, his memory a burial ground for old ideas and ancient victories of which he spoke more and more now. Yes, soon the torch would pass . . .

"So you see, Sarah, we can't give in to Harvey's demands,"

the Chairman was saying. "It would open the floodgates. The man's ingratitude is incredible."

Sarah nodded patiently. "It's no surprise, of course."

The Chairman blinked in disbelief. "What?"

"Well, we've known for some time that Harvey would try to negotiate a tough contract this time around," she began.

"But, really—"

"Yes, you're right, Larry," she continued smoothly. "Still, he's never forgiven us."

"You mean for that time we fired him back in '72 after he did so badly covering the conventions?"

"I wouldn't say 'fired' exactly. 'Reassigned' is more like it."

"Well, whatever. That was Brennan's decision, anyway, wasn't it?"

My God, his memory's going, she thought. It was *his* idea from the start. We'll have to monitor him more carefully. These self-made tycoons never know when to step down. "More or less," she replied. "You'll recall we all agreed Harvey had slipped badly. The ratings made that obvious."

"Oh, yes, of course," the Chairman agreed. "But Brennan overreacted to what proved to be a temporary fluctuation in the ratings."

Did he really think Brennan was entirely to blame for that disastrous decision to pull Harvey off the anchor desk in '73, Sarah wondered, or was he still hiding privately behind his public scapegoat? Was he being clever or simply aging? Whatever, it was obvious to Sarah that the Chairman would not go willingly into the darkness, no indeed. "I think even ABC beat us on the '72 convention coverage," she said. "And that was when they were in real trouble, too."

"Well, naturally we had to do something," the Chairman said. "We were all agreed about that."

The firm, authoritative tone of his voice warned her not to underrate him too soon. "I remember that both of us cautioned Ted not to move so quickly," she said, "but he wouldn't listen."

Actually, it made sense now to lay that responsibility off on Ted Brennan, who was no longer around to defend himself. And it had been Ted and Ted alone who had thought up the concept of a triple anchor team. It had cost him his job and led directly to Sarah's own promotion, but then, Sarah recalled, his inability to handle alcohol had already just about guaranteed his departure, even if the Grunwald debacle hadn't occurred.

Who but Ted Brennan, Sarah reasoned, could have imagined that Bill James, Rosemary Winkler and Wib Eikenberry would work well together? Bill was smooth-looking and slick on the air, but far too pale a personality ever to make it as a national TV figure. Rosemary Winkler, whisked off the women's pages of *The New York Times*, where she had been first a top fashion reporter and then a catty commentator on the social doings of the superrich, had been a disaster. She froze on camera and came across as an icy bitch. Wib Eikenberry, with his loose-jointed manner and locker-room wit, had functioned as comic relief, but made himself, his race, all of them look bad by becoming a kind of TV stereotype of the cheery black. Not only had this unlikely new anchor team been flayed in the press, but *ACN News* had plummeted, in less than three months, to the bottom of the ratings, where it languished for another half year.

Meanwhile, Harvey Grunwald, unceremoniously yanked off the air and dispatched on "special assignment" back to Vietnam, then later to the Middle East to cover the 1973 war there, had turned his demotion and potential eclipse into a personal triumph. Rejuvenated and inspired by the challenge of his assignments, Harvey had again proved himself to be, at his best, a skilled, compassionate and literate newsman. His series of half-hour specials, stunningly photographed by Jeff Campbell and others, had aired in prime time, thrust fortuitously against weak competition in the form of several witless sitcoms. The series had been phenomenally successful. Harvey had come home to find himself a media hero, the biggest since Ed Murrow back in the fifties, and he had been awarded a Pulitzer. Hastily reinstated at his old anchor spot on the evening news, he had quickly rescued ACN and established himself again as Walter Cronkite's only serious rival at the top of the ratings. No wonder Harvey intended to make them pay now, Sarah reflected. The man knew what he was worth to the network and he had an old score to settle, in the only terms the network could understand—dollars and cents.

"What Harvey's asking is unthinkable," the Chairman said. "We must find a way to bring him to his senses."

"You're right, of course, Larry, and we can."

"We haven't much time, Sarah."

"Nearly six months."

"Harvey seemed adamant."

"I know," she said. "I've already spoken to him."

"Then what—I mean, how . . ."

"There are some considerations Harvey hasn't really taken into account, Larry," Sarah said, calmly smoothing out the wrinkles of her elegant silk Calvin Klein. "I think we have a chance to get together. I really do."

The Chairman sighed. "Have you spoken to Crawford yet?"

Sarah shook her head. "Not yet, Larry, but we've kept him informed from the beginning."

The Chairman nodded approvingly. "A first-rate man," he said. "He has my complete confidence, as you know."

"I expect we'll be working together on this."

The Chairman nodded again, but without answering this time. Again Sarah was struck by how old he looked, as if his momentary outburst of vitality had exhausted him.

Sarah smiled and stood up to go. "I'd better get going, Larry, unless there's anything else . . ."

"No," the Chairman mumbled, his eyes clouding over and his head sinking slightly forward. "No, not now."

"I'll keep you informed day to day," she said, moving from his desk. "I appreciate your confidence in me, Larry."

She hesitated a moment, waiting for his answer, but he seemed frozen in position. She could no longer quite make out his face, but she smiled and, with a little wave, quickly and quietly let herself out.

Five minutes later, within the privacy of her own office, Sarah picked up the phone and dialed a number. "Hello," she said, without wasting time on preliminaries. "This is Sarah Anderson. We are activating Myrmidon. Immediately." Without waiting for an answer, she hung up and buzzed for her secretary, whose round, cheerful face almost immediately appeared in the doorway. "Paul," she said, "cancel all my appointments for the next three days. I'll be out of town."

REFERENCE: MYRMIDON—The new facility is everything I had dreamed it would be. As I look around I occasionally wonder if it could really be that I have a sponsor whose faith in my theories and whose financial resources seem limitless.

In any case, we've reached an important milestone today. The data from the newest tests are more revealing than even my earlier projections indicated. I feel it's due to the new facial electromyography probes we've devised. A few more tests should yield the answer on that one.

Master program nearing preliminary completion.

—From the Journal of Dr. Jerome Lillienthal

3

WHEN THE CALL about the fire came in, Bellucci was plugged into one of his police lines and trying to decide whether a chase involving a runaway mugger on the West Side might turn out to be a story, so Tom Meegan, one of his assistants, picked up the phone. He was a short, pale young man who, unlike his boss, never seemed to become excited about anything. It was a quality in him that sometimes exasperated Bellucci, but would make him an excellent successor, when and if the time ever came for Mario to retire.

"Well?" Bellucci asked him, when the younger man volunteered no information.

"Sounds routine to me," Meegan said. "A two-alarmer up in the Bronx."

"Any crispies?"

"Don't know yet." He raised the receiver to his ear again, just as Tracy Phillips came by with a stack of Teletype copy and dropped it on his desk. "Yeah? OK, I got you." Meegan looked at Bellucci again. "NNE," he said.

"How many?" Mario asked.

"Only three so far, but it might turn out to be a big one."

"Where is it?"

"The Grand Concourse, where else," Meegan said.

"Well, nothing else is going on," Bellucci growled. "Where's Campbell?"

Meegan cocked a thumb in the direction of the reporters' desks. "Slumming, as usual."

"Hey, Campbell!" the editor called out. "We got one for you."

"Is it a fire?" Tracy asked, still lingering in the area.

"Yeah," Meegan said. "Maybe a big one. Sounds like it, anyway."

"I'll ask Mr. McCarron if I can go along." And she hurried off toward the producer's office, stepping around a long row of desks to avoid Campbell, who was sauntering toward them. The cameraman watched her hurry by and smiled faintly, but she ignored him.

"Jeff, you ready to go?" Bellucci asked.

"Yeah, we're all loaded."

"Where's Johnson?"

"In the crew lounge, where else?"

"What's he do in there?" Meegan asked.

"Cleans up at pinochle," Jeff explained. "Or hearts. Or darts. Whatever's going on, old Moss sticks it to 'em."

"Get him and move on out," the editor said, turning to his assistant for confirmation.

"Twelve twenty-two Grand Concourse," Meegan said. "You know where that is?"

Jeff nodded. "Sure thing. Say, who's my mike stand on this one?"

"Williams," the editor answered, as Tracy came running up the aisle toward them. "He's down at City Hall, but we can spring him from there."

"Mr. Campbell," the girl said, joining them, "do you mind if I come along? Mr. McCarron said it was OK."

Jeff shrugged and smiled. "Sure, why not? I thought you'd picked somebody else for your maiden voyage."

She colored slightly. "I've been too busy till now. Today I've got an OK. If the call had come for Mr. Santini or anyone else, I'd have asked to go along. It's nothing personal, Mr. Campbell. This is work."

"Yeah," Jeff said, "only one thing . . ."

"Yes?"

"Let's cut out the Mr. and Miss or Ms. crap and go on first names, all right? All this formality doesn't sit too well with me on a job."

"If you insist."

"I do insist, Tracy."

She didn't answer him, only nodded. "Let's go," she said tersely.

"I hope you can keep up."

"I can keep up, all right."

They picked up Johnson and took the elevator down to the garage, where their company-owned sleek-looking Chevy Newscruiser awaited them, the gear already stored in the trunk. Jeff slipped the plastic computer card into its slot, and the doors of the turbodiesel sedan swung noiselessly open. Once inside, he touched his right index finger to the tiny screen above and to the right of the steering wheel. The car purred to life and Jeff drove quickly away, threading uptown through the city's heavy traffic. It would be twenty minutes at least before they could arrive at the scene of the fire, which made it more than likely that one of Golden's crews would already be there when they arrived. Any day he could beat Golden to the scene was a good day, Jeff reflected, but then he had learned not to let that aspect of his work disturb him too much. Golden had to live, too, didn't he? Even the jackals have to eat.

"Man, you sure did me out of a good hand," Moss complained as Jeff now picked up the West Side Highway and began to make fast time heading north. "I was cleaning up, man. That Santini, he can't play cards for shit."

"But it doesn't keep him from trying, does it?" Jeff observed, smiling.

"How big a fire do you think this will be?" Tracy asked, leaning forward eagerly from her rear seat. "It sounded like a big one."

"You measure them in crispies." Jeff explained. "I'd say if we had five or six, we got a good story."

"Crispies?"

"Dead folks," Moss explained. "That's what we call fire victims, Tracy."

"Oh, no," the girl said. "I had no idea . . ." She sank back in her seat.

"Maybe we'd better stop and let you out," Jeff said. "I wouldn't want you throwing up all over the back of my car."

"It wasn't a personal comment," Tracy insisted grimly.

"Hey, man," Moss said, "ease up. She's just asking. Didn't you ever ask questions when you started out?"

"Thank you, Moss," Tracy said. "The terminology is a little startling to me, that's all. What did Tom Meegan mean when he said 'NNE' to Mr. Bellucci?"

"'Not nearly enough,'" Jeff explained. "The more victims, the better the story. In this town one or two corpses out of a burning building is hardly news anymore."

"How fresh was the tip, man?" Moss asked. "Are we going to get there before the meat wagon?"

"I sure hope so. The call came in from some buddy of Meegan's who also monitors the emergency frequencies."

"Where?" Tracy asked.

"For the phone company, who else?" Jeff answered. "In this business we need all the help we can get. For one thing, we need shots of the bodies being carried away. If we don't get them, Golden will and the station will have to buy tape from him."

"I'm sorry," Tracy said, "but I'm a bit lost. Who's Golden?"

"Honey, you *are* green," Jeff said.

"I never said I wasn't," the girl answered quietly. "That's what I'm doing here, isn't it?"

"I guess you'd know the answer to that one."

Moss swung around in his seat and smiled at her. "Golden is a free-lancer with his own cars and camera crews who makes a specialty of agony stories. He shoots fast and crude and he's on the scene of every bad thing that happens all over this town. He sucks, baby."

"What's so different about what he does?" Tracy asked. "It seems to me we're in the same business, aren't we?"

"Sure," Jeff answered, "only Golden hires nonunion real cheap and sells cheap, which means all the stations know they can buy footage from him for less than it would take if they had to send out their own crews every time. Golden is a bloodsucker who keeps a lot of good people unemployed, because without him the stations would have to hire more union crews, get it?"

"Yes, I see," Tracy said.

"He's the worst of the ghouls in this town," Jeff continued, "so I figure that anytime we can beat him out of a sale we've scored some points for the good guys."

"Oh, my God," Tracy said a few minutes later, as Jeff suddenly swung the car down an off ramp and gunned it through a maze of side streets he seemed to know like the back of his hand. A great cloud of oily black smoke fouled the clear morning air above the rooftops of the South Bronx.

"Yeah, it looks like a goodie," Moss hummed, craning forward to see better. "Golden couldn't miss a fire this big unless somebody stuck him in the throat this morning, man."

Jeff grunted noncommittally and concentrated on easing their big car through the now thickening traffic to get as close as they could to the scene. "I hope the mike stand gets here, that's all," Jeff murmured. "Otherwise we might have to put you on the air, Tracy."

"The mike stand?"

"He means the reporter," Moss explained, smiling faintly. "That's old Jeff's friendly term for them. Spencer Williams is on his way up here by cab, but he has to come all the way from City Hall."

To Jeff's visible disgust, one of Golden's panel trucks was already present and its two-man crew was scrambling around inside the vehicle assembling its crude equipment. Jeff triple-parked behind a hastily thrown-up police barricade manned by four harried officers in blue and pressed another of his complicated array of dashboard buttons. A long, slender antenna fingered the air as Jeff activated the microprocessor in the car that established his audiovisual link to the microwave receivers mounted on top of the World Trade Center towers. Once established, the two-way link would enable them to feed back as well as receive information, while putting them in permanent audio contact with EJ Reception back at the station. This was a large complex of rooms filled with videotape machines, where engineers and editors routed the stuff coming in from crews in the field, either to run live or to be taped for editing and later viewing. In this case, both men knew, their shots would be taped for the six-o'clock news, then, in all probability, to be rerun at eleven, perhaps in truncated form, though much would depend on what other stories, national as well as local, happened to break in the interim.

"OK," Jeff said, "let's go. Stick close to us, Tracy, but try not to get in the way."

"You see Spence anywhere?" Moss asked as they opened the trunk of the car and began to rig themselves for action.

"Nope," Jeff snapped. "Let's go get 'em."

Swiftly Jeff hoisted his lightweight TK-100 camera to his shoulder as Moss slipped on his headset and put his arms through the straps of his backpack containing the miniature transmitter linking them to the car and the backup video recorder. Then, working smoothly and precisely, linked to each other by an umbilical cord of electric cable, both men ran toward the fire. Tracy, wide-eyed and breathless with excitement, hurried after them.

They reached the edge of the burning building, a dingy six-story apartment house that had once, many years ago, been an elegant small hotel, and began to scramble around taking pictures. Tracy noted that they had reached the actual scene even before Golden's crew, two fat men in short-sleeved shirts, who came panting up behind them five minutes after Jeff had begun shooting. The Golden outfit worked in silence, shooting everything in sight, while Jeff and Moss, skipping like ballet dancers through the smoke and the carnage, seemed to know exactly where the story would be and what would happen. A skinny black kid of about twelve suddenly hurled himself from the roof and landed, with a sickening crunch, not fifty feet from them. Jeff's camera had caught him in flight, whereas Golden's men had to content themselves with shots of the crumpled corpse, too bloody even for the late news. A woman leaned out of a top-story window, screaming and waving her arms, then collapsed inside before the firemen could reach her. Jeff had caught it all, while Golden's men had been concentrating on the building's main entrance, where a small knot of firemen was leading out several of the older tenants, sad-looking victims in torn, smoke-stained clothing, their eyes dazed by the catastrophe that had suddenly overwhelmed them.

When she tried to remember later exactly what had happened, Tracy realized that time seemed to have stood still for her. She saw Jeff and Moss moving efficiently, quickly, through the disaster as if she had been watching it all the time on a movie screen, the unfolding of an event entirely divorced from any personal involvement on her part, even though she had been there, her own face, hands and clothing stained by the filth of the fire, her feet soaked with the overflow of sooty water from the hoses of the fire trucks. She saw it all as a kind of mental collage. How much time had passed? She could not actually recall, but surely it had been hours. So it was even more of a shock to her to realize, after the last of the survivors had been evacuated from the building and the flames from the upper stories had been watered down into oily smudges of black smoke, that the whole event had consumed not more than forty minutes, from the time they had headed from their car toward the building to the sudden appearance on the scene of Spencer Williams, who came loping up the street toward them from the corner of the block.

"About time," Jeff snapped as Williams reached them.

"I was at City Hall," the reporter said. "Fucking traffic. OK, so what have you got?"

"At least six dead, maybe more," Jeff said.

"They been dragged out yet?"

"No. We'll get all that. Some kid jumped from the roof and I got it."

"Great," Williams said. "What else?"

"The usual footage. Oh, yeah, a good shot of a woman screaming from a window up there."

"She must be gone, man," Moss said.

"Good stuff," the reporter said, as he spotted a group of the building's surviving tenants huddled across the street from the main entrance. "Now let's get some interviews with the survivors. Did you talk to any of the firemen or the cops?"

"No time to," Jeff answered. "Anyway, you're here now, aren't you?"

"You bet," the reporter said. "Let's go."

Tracy tagged along and watched as Williams walked up to the group and began methodically to question the survivors. One middle-aged woman began to cry as she recalled being unable to save an elderly neighbor who had presumably perished in the blaze, and one young housewife became hysterical when told that her best friend's two children, aged five and seven, had also apparently died. The stunned and grieving parents had already been removed from the scene. No one knew exactly how the fire had started, but evidently it had begun in the basement and had rapidly engulfed the tenement, the flames having been sucked up the ancient stairwells as if through chimneys.

During his interviewing and questioning of the tenants, then later with two firemen and a police captain, Williams remained cool and thoroughly professional. When he confronted Jeff's camera for the closing stand-upper, however, Tracy sensed a touch of the ham in him. She noted that his tie was askew, his hair rumpled and his clothes slightly wrinkled, as if he himself had been in the thick of the carnage instead of merely a late arrival. "This is Spencer Williams for *WACN News*, at the scene of today's fire in the South Bronx," the reporter intoned in closing, his veteran newsman's face a study in grim compassion.

No sooner was he off camera, however, than Williams' entire manner changed. "OK, as soon as we have shots of the bodies being carried out," he said cheerfully, "let's wrap it up. I'm starving."

As Jeff and Moss positioned themselves in front of the

entrance to the building, Tracy came up beside Williams, who now noticed her presence for the first time. "Hey, Tracy, what are you doing here?"

"I got permission to come along," she said. "It's my first on-the-spot story. I guess I picked a pretty horrible one."

"Naw, strictly a routine torching," the reporter said.

"You mean somebody *set* this fire?"

"Sure."

"But why? Who'd do such a thing?"

"Maybe some nut," Williams explained. "There are a lot of those running around. But it's more likely to be the landlord."

"For the insurance?"

"You got it. The guy's got a run-down building full of welfare deadbeats using their checks for everything *except* the rent, and he can't evict them. So what else is he going to do?"

"But the victims—"

"Oh, these guys don't give a damn about victims. What they care about is making a buck out of their property."

"What if they prove somebody set the fire?"

"Easy to prove, maybe," the reporter said, "but hard to pin it on the right party. Everybody will get into the act. This is a typical story up here, Tracy. The truth will get lost in the usual bureaucratic morass."

Tracy didn't answer, but watched now as Jeff and Moss took shots of the bodies being removed from the still smoldering building, while overhead a fine spray of dirty water from the firemen's hoses chilled the morning air. A crowd of silent gawkers pressed against the police barriers, their eyes on the row of covered corpses being laid out side by side along the sidewalk. Tracy counted ten bodies, then, suddenly sickened by the sight, she turned away. Safely out of view behind the bulk of a fire truck, she doubled over and heaved the remains of her breakfast into the gutter.

Half an hour later, as they headed back downtown, Jeff grinned wickedly at her in the rearview mirror. "You look a little pale, Tracy," he said cheerfully. "Something wrong?"

"I suppose I'll get used to it," she said. "So many dead."

"Hey, man, why don't you lay off her?" Moss asked his partner. "You wasn't always so cool, you know?"

"I wasn't ever that green," Jeff answered. "But maybe that's because I didn't lead such a sheltered life."

"Mr. Campbell—"

"Ah-ah, what did I say?"

"Never mind, then," the girl said.

Spencer Williams leaned back in his seat with a contented sigh. "Thank God," he observed, "at least it got me out of that City Hall beat. Jesus, was that something! They drone on and on and on and you sit around for hours waiting for a little nugget of information you can make into some kind of story that nobody cares about anyway. There hasn't been a good story out of City Hall since that ex-cop went crazy last year and tried to shoot the mayor. Now *that* was a story."

Tracy sighed. "Anyway," she said, "I guess we got a scoop, didn't we? I mean, I didn't see anybody but us and the Golden crew till that last few minutes, when the others finally showed up."

"A scoop?" Jeff echoed her. "A scoop? You've been reading too many books or looking at old movies on TV, honey. We'll be lucky to get a minute and a half of this on the air."

"With all those people dead?" Tracy asked, incredulous.

"They didn't die on Park Avenue, Tracy," Moss said.

"Boy, I guess I do have a lot to learn," the girl observed.

Jeff laughed. "You said it, honey, not me."

As they headed into midtown, Jeff got Bellucci on the two-way radio, told him what they had and suggested they stop off for lunch somewhere, then come on in. "Ten-four. I saw your feed coming in and it's pretty good. You could have gotten in tighter on the kid who jumped," the editor barked. "If Williams is with you, tell him to get back down to City Hall. They've got a vote on the sanitation budget coming up sometime after four."

The reporter groaned. "Oh, shit," he said. "Hey, pull over. I'll grab a cab."

Jeff halted at Broadway and Fiftieth long enough for Williams to scramble out of the car and flag a taxi, then nosed the big sedan toward their home garage. "Hey, honey," he said, "you don't look well."

"I'll be all right," Tracy answered. "Just one thing . . ."

"What?"

"My name is Tracy, not honey." She leaned forward in her seat. "Please, would you let me out here? I am feeling sick."

Jeff pulled over to the curb, and Tracy quickly climbed out of the car and walked unsteadily away from them.

"She all right?" Moss asked.

Jeff grinned. "I think so. This was a rough one for her. But she's gutsy, huh?"

"Yeah, she sure is," Moss answered. "Hey, man, why don't you give her a break?"

"Moss, my good chap, this is a tough racket," the cameraman said. "Maybe too tough for little girls with big ambitions. Let's let her find it out the hard way."

"What's she done to you, man? Just 'cause she won't give you the time of day. Maybe she doesn't like you."

"That was beginning to come through. You did notice, huh?"

"Aw, shit, man," Moss said, "you are one arrogant dude. She's a nice kid."

"Yeah," Jeff said, smiling faintly, "but she's got a weak stomach."

4

"I APPRECIATE THIS, Sarah," Harvey Grunwald said. "I value your support and I'm glad you understand my position. Frankly, I had no idea why you wanted to see me here today. I thought maybe Larry might have told you to seduce me or something."

She laughed. "My God, at my age! I wish he had." She raised her glass to him. "To the next five years. I know they're going to be the best."

They sipped the cold wine in silence for a couple of minutes. "You really think you can bring Larry around?" Harvey asked again.

"I'll have to," she answered. "We can't afford to lose you. And there are ways. I have my secrets, too."

"I'm not going to compromise, you know."

"I know. All I'm asking, really, is that you be a bit flexible about the timing. It may take a while longer than you think."

Harvey shook his head, more in sorrow than in anger. "It's too bad, isn't it? He just can't see it, even after all these years and all those hundreds of millions he's made."

She sighed. "Oh, you know, it's also a question of pride with him. And he's getting old, Harvey. I think we all tend to forget just how long he's been around. You have to admire him. He built this network out of nothing but the bits and pieces the other three networks left him. ACN had to crawl before he could make it walk, never mind fly. Now we're number one and Larry, like a lot of self-made millionaires, tends to believe that he did it all himself. And that maybe, just maybe, somebody's going to come along one of these days and try to take it all away from him again." She threw her head back and laughed. "That really sets him off, Harvey. The idea of a mere newsman actually being paid what he's worth in proportion to what he earns for this network is not the Chairman's concept of how the game ought to be played. After all, he's the one who made the rules and now you're trying to change them."

"It's high time somebody did," Harvey said. "Of course, show-biz celebrities have been earning this kind of loot for years. That's all I'm asking, Sarah—the same deal any rock star can demand and get. In my own way, I guess, I'm worth it."

"I'll drink to that." She gracefully raised her glass to him and drank. "How's Ann?"

"Fine. She sends her best. We're really looking forward to getting away for a few days next week." He glanced at his watch. "Which reminds me, we do have opera tickets."

She got up. "Give me a minute, Harvey, and I'll come down with you. I'm going to a dinner party in the East Sixties. Can you drop me off? Taxis are a problem at this hour."

"Sure. Or maybe I'll let you drop me. I'm meeting Ann with our friends, the Millers. They have a box, old opera buffs. It's *Bohème*, thank God, not Wagner, so we'll be home early tonight."

She laughed again, set her glass down and walked swiftly out of the room. Harvey gazed admiringly after her, then, glass in hand, strolled across the huge living room and looked out the window at the city. Her view was almost as spectacular as his own. From this height, seventeen high-ceilinged stories up over Fifth Avenue, you could see across all of the park, then south to the luxury hotels and apartment houses lining Central Park South. It was a clear early-summer evening, and the sun flashed off windows, dazzling Harvey. He turned his back to the view now and gazed into the room, sparely but elegantly and comfortably furnished. A large authentic-looking Klee was mounted over the mantelpiece; two huge Mondrians dominated the far wall. The view in here, Harvey suddenly realized, was even more impressive than the one outside. In all these years, he'd been in her home only three or four times and always for large, semiofficial cocktail parties; he'd never had an opportunity before to get a true feel of the place.

What did he really know about Sarah? Harvey asked himself. What did this impressive room convey about the woman who lived in it? That it belonged to an ordered, disciplined personality, one that eliminated the frivolities to concentrate on the essentials. There was nothing unnecessary here, nothing that didn't have its specific function, its precise place in this woman's private universe. It spoke to Harvey of a methodically achieved success that trumpeted itself off her walls in her choice of art, but also told the viewer that the owner believed in discipline, in not flaunting success, but in quietly, firmly understating it. Sarah Anderson had made it to the very top of her profession and had begun her drive to her present eminence late, at an age when other, more ordinary people had already achieved comfort and a degree of success.

Harvey couldn't remember now when he had first become aware of Sarah; suddenly she was simply there and in charge. She had left a bad marriage to a bisexual society type back in Virginia, he'd learned later, using her social leverage to land herself a job as a researcher for the ACN Washington bureau. From that modest beginning she had swiftly worked her way up, first to news writer, then to field producer and eventually to bureau chief. As far as Harvey knew, she hadn't used her sex to move up, either, and that too had earned her the respect of her colleagues; she had made it on sheer talent and hard work. The only gossip Harvey had ever heard about her had been about a love affair with a younger man, a reporter in the New York office, but otherwise he couldn't think of a single derogatory thing about her.

When the network had, in effect, fired him from the evening-news anchor chair and shunted him off to do those specials, Sarah, he remembered, had been particularly supportive. She had never, so far as he knew, bad-mouthed him to anyone, and she had seemed genuinely delighted by his triumphant come-back. Since then she had always been one of his strongest allies within the corporation. When Ted Brennan had been fired and Sarah appointed to succeed him, the ACN news operation, with Harvey back at the anchor spot, had really taken off. Yes, he owed a lot to Sarah Anderson, Harvey reflected, and he intended to cooperate with her as much as he could, though he certainly wasn't going to back down in any way in his financial demands. But he would try to protect Sarah, yes, he would. After all, she'd been his ally, if not his close friend, for a long time now.

But what was it about this woman that had always made him slightly uneasy? Harvey had never been able to puzzle that out. She was a beautiful woman still, with that nearly unlined face, those startlingly clear green eyes, that full, handsome figure, and he should have responded to her in some way. He had always— well, almost always—been faithful to Ann, but he'd never been immune to the attractions of the opposite sex. Sarah was not unlike Ann physically (they were both big, strong-looking women), but she had never turned him on at all. He'd wondered about that, of course, not because he'd ever intended to have an affair or even a casual fling with her, but only because nothing about her seemed to connect to him sexually. God, the last thing he had ever wanted, Harvey thought, was an office affair, but it wasn't only that. Basically, Sarah Anderson struck him as a cold fish, absolutely calculating beneath all that surface charm, so he had kept his distance, even as a friend. Now, however . . . But his musings were interrupted by her return.

"I'm sorry," she said, hurrying into the room. "I hope I'm not going to make you late."

"No chance," he said. "And I wouldn't complain if I were. I'm a philistine when it comes to opera, though I don't mind Puccini. He wrote good tunes at least."

"Why do you go? Trapped into it?"

"Bill and Kitty Miller are two of our closest friends and they're both nuts about the opera, so we've struck a bargain with them. We go to the opera with them and they come sailing with us."

Sarah laughed and patted his arm. "Let's go. By the way, like the new suit?" She spun about to give him a full look at the tailored black silk outfit she had changed into.

"It's very nice, Sarah. Very becoming."

"Not too masculine?"

"Nope. Just the kind of thing Ann would like, too," he said. "It's elegant."

"Valentino," she whispered. "My major luxury purchase this year."

In the taxi, on their way downtown, she asked him again about his plans for his week off. "The Millers going with you?"

"Oh, sure. They always do. And Dave and Miriam Goldberg. The six of us do a lot of traveling together."

"Yes, so I gather."

"Well, it's a big boat," he explained. "We can sleep ten comfortably and we carry a three-man crew as well as a good cook. I like to sail her a lot myself, but not this trip. I need a rest. We're going to cruise up the coast, then head for Nantucket, spend a couple of days fishing and come back the following weekend."

"Sounds marvelous!"

"Maybe you'd like to come along sometime?"

"I'd love to."

"If you don't get seasick. It can get pretty rough under sail sometimes."

"Well, I never have been. Aren't there pills you can take?"

"Oh, sure, but they can make you sleepy."

"I could use the rest." She laughed, then looked at him thoughtfully. "You really love it, don't you?"

"Sailing? Yes, always have," he said. "I read *Mutiny on the Bounty* when I was twelve and it struck a deep chord. I couldn't get over how Bligh and those men in that open boat sailed alone all that way and made it back. My parents had a motorboat when I was a kid, and I used to take it out on the lake back in

Michigan, but I always wanted my own sailboat after that and I got my first one when I was fifteen. I've been at it ever since."

"I'll bet you are Captain Bligh, too!"

"I can be," he admitted with a smile. "I'm just naturally bossy anyway, and on board my own ship I can give all the orders I want. That's why, when we're with friends, Ann makes me hire a crew. Otherwise I'm impossible."

"I think I'm having second thoughts about sailing with you."

"Don't. I promise to be kind," he said, "a regular Spencer Tracy and not Charles Laughton. Wasn't he great as Bligh in the first movie version? God, I loved that picture when I was a kid! I must have seen it twenty times."

"Driver, I'll get off at the next corner," Sarah said, putting her hand on Harvey's arm to forestall any possible protest. "I can walk. It's only four blocks."

"You sure? I can catch a crosstown—"

"At this hour?" She laughed. "You'll be signing autographs on the bus all the way to Lincoln Center."

He grinned. "Silly, isn't it? I mean, I guess I'll never get used to being a celebrity. An old news hawk like me."

"Who are you kidding? It's getting you the ten million, isn't it?"

"There have to be some compensations for this lofty status," he teased her. As the car pulled up to the curb and Sarah started to get out, he squeezed her hand. "Seriously, I appreciate your support, Sarah."

"I'll do what I can. I don't want to lose you. With you gone for a week and Gene on in your spot every night, watch what happens to our ratings. It never fails."

"I hope Larry notices."

"He will. He always does. And I'll make certain this time."

When the taxi turned west into the park, Harvey glanced out the rear window. Sarah was standing on the corner, gazing after him, her face pale and serene in the twilight. He smiled and waved to her, but she did not wave back; she simply stood there on the corner of Fifth Avenue and Sixty-sixth as if unsure of her next move. A very beautiful woman, he thought, sinking back into his seat and feeling satisfied with himself. Perhaps I should have made a move in her direction. Well, never too late, is it? Oh damn, the opera . . .

"I don't get it," Tracy said.

"What?"

"Well, for a day or two you're nice to me and treat me like a human being, and then you revert to your usual m.o."

"Let's say it's all part of life's rich pageant, kid," Jeff said. "Want some more wine?"

"No, thanks. Look, Jeff, what is it? What's wrong? You invite me up here for a drink. I accept. Then, for a while . . ." She paused, as if groping for exactly the right way to put it.

"Yes?" he prompted her.

"Well, for a while you're really charming," she resumed. "You ask all about me, as if you care, and I open up and tell you all about my dreams and ambitions, but for some reason that annoys you. What did I do wrong?"

"I don't know," he said, keeping an absolutely straight face. "I guess there's just something about you, kid, that pisses me off."

"And now, for two days, you're calling me 'kid.'"

"You didn't like 'honey.'"

"I don't like 'kid' either."

"You're tough to please, lady."

"My name is Tracy," she said. "Why can't you call me Tracy?"

He shrugged. "I don't know. Like I say, there's something about you—"

"You really are infuriating."

"Then why do you stick around?"

"Because you're very good at what you do," she explained, "and I'm learning a great deal."

"You could learn just as much by tagging around after Bucky Santini."

"Ah," she objected, with a smile, "but you're the best, even if you do say so yourself."

"I guess I am, and I do say so."

"Modesty is not one of your more endearing qualities."

He laughed. "You're all right, kid. Here, let me get you some more wine."

"No, please. Whit's picking me up for dinner."

"Here?"

"Sure, why not? I called him while you were in the bathroom. He lives on Tenth, just west of Fifth."

Jeff grimaced with distaste and headed for the kitchen. "Tracy, Tracy," he sighed, "you're a terrible tease."

"I am not. I only agreed to come up here because I had a dinner date in the Village anyway. You knew that this morning. You're only being difficult out of your enlarged male ego."

"Another of my not-so-endearing qualities."

"You said it, I didn't."

She listened to him rummage in his refrigerator for another beer and smiled. It was true, he did irritate her with his assumed prole ways, but in the four times that she had been out on assignments with him and Moss she had begun grudgingly to like him. She wasn't quite sure why. Perhaps it was because she couldn't help admiring his skills; he was a superb cameraman, instinctively in the right place at the right time and absolutely fearless. She even understood his contempt for the run-of-the-mill reporters, whom he called "mike stands"; after all, he had explained, it was he and Moss who got the story. The mike stands just stood there and spouted lines into the camera, as if they'd shot the pictures.

Jeff Campbell, Tracy realized now, was wedded to his job, as committed to it as an artist to his muse. Shooting videotape was his life, an obsession that made him odd and difficult to work with, especially if you happened to get in the way of his taking the right shots, but which elevated him over every other photographer she'd ever known. Jeff took pictures and made movies with the same ferocious dedication to quality, to getting it on tape just right, that a good print reporter would devote to chasing a story down, or a fine painter might bring to a blank canvas. How could she fail to respect that in him? And so out of respect had come this liking, because Tracy had never been able not to like anything or anyone she admired. If only the man wouldn't be so deliberately rude to her. Just because they had equally consuming ambitions . . .

"So," he asked, reappearing, beer can in hand, and flinging himself down in his only armchair, "where are you and wonderful Whitford having dinner?"

"Whitner," she corrected him, "Whitner Bridgeford."

"What a name," he said, shaking his head. "I'll bet he's a junior, too."

"The Third. Whitner Bridgeford the Third."

Jeff groaned. "Tracy, Tracy, why?"

"You don't even know him."

"I don't have to. I know the type. What can you possibly see in this guy?"

"He's a nice man with good manners and he's very sweet."

"Very sweet."

"Yes, very. And handsome too."

"That part of it doesn't bother me."

"No?"

"No. In that area I can hold my own."

"Oh, my God," she exclaimed, falling back among his pillows, "you are the absolute end!"

"I'm an acquired taste, see, like good country whisky and mustard greens." He grinned wolfishly at her. "Listen, kid, why don't you ditch Whitford and stay here? I'll send out for a pizza."

"Absolutely not. Whit and I are involved."

"You're not living with him?"

"You know I'm not."

"Oh, that's right. Your new apartment. Say, is Whitford good in the sack?"

"That does it," she said, standing up again. "That really does it. Goodbye, Jeff, thanks for the wine. And for letting me come along today. I shouldn't have come up here. You have some insane fixation that it's important to shock me, and it makes you behave like a cad."

"A cad? What have you been watching lately? *Masterpiece Theatre?*"

"'Cad' is a literary word. I got it first out of books. It's also a very appropriate term for a man who behaves to a woman the way you do, Mr. Campbell."

"Oh, shit, Tracy, sit down. I don't *do* anything. I just talk."

"No. Whit's never late and I might as well wait for him downstairs. God knows what you'll say to him if he comes up here."

She waved a quick goodbye and briskly let herself out of the apartment as he slumped unhappily into his chair, cradling the half-empty beer can on his lap. He listened to her footsteps on the stairs, then the dull thud of his front door banging shut. Suddenly tired from his long working day and mildly remorseful over his continued needling of her, he heaved himself with a grunt to his feet, went to the nearest window and looked down.

Tracy was standing on the front stoop of his brownstone, one of a dozen or so lining the north side of his street, just off Hudson in the West Village. Jeff thought about joining her, but before he could make up his mind a sparkling brown Jaguar XJS turned the corner of Hudson Street and glided to a purring stop in front of his house and directly behind his own car, a battered dirty-green VW of ancient vintage. Whitner Bridgeford III, a smooth-looking young dude in a beard, a razor-cut hairdo and a sporty outfit from the windows of Paul Stuart, stepped out and opened the car door for her. Tracy ran down the steps, got in, and they drove away. Shit, she didn't even wave goodbye, he thought, turning back from the window and slumping morosely down into his chair again. His two-room apartment, with its slapdash array of favorite blow ups on his scuffed white walls, had never seemed quite so dismal to him. She was right to be angry at him. Why shouldn't her hopes and plans be as legitimate as his own?

Quietly, methodically, with awesome efficiency, Crawford completed the last of his daily isometric exercises, then paused briefly to survey himself in the full-length mirror opposite his bed. What he saw did not entirely displease him. True, with age he was having increasing trouble controlling the thickening flesh around his waistline, but otherwise he saw himself in fairly good shape. At two hundred and thirty-five pounds, he felt in fighting trim, still able to operate, he surmised, almost as effectively as in his younger days. What he'd lost in agility and stamina, he figured, he could make up for in experience, in jungle cunning. There hadn't been much real action lately, that was the only trouble, but now, with Myrmidon being activated, who knew? He grinned at his naked self in the mirror, tensed his big hands against each other one last time and saw with pleasure the bulge of muscle spring out across his huge chest, the ripple of flesh over his arms as they strained against each other. With one final grunting effort, he broke away and headed for the shower.

After ten minutes under the hot jet stream of his massage nozzle, he toweled himself off, slipped into a terrycloth robe and thong sandals, then went to the bar in his living room and poured himself a double slug of Glenfiddich. Humming softly, he pressed a hidden panel behind his stereo. Noiselessly the bookcases lining the far wall swung open to reveal a floor-to-ceiling cache of tape cassettes, all neatly, if cryptically, catalogued. Still humming tunelessly, he fished out a favorite, slipped it into the playback slot on his stereo, switched the machine on and fitted earphones to his head. Whisky in hand, he sat down to enjoy himself.

It had been a fine afternoon's work, that climactic little meeting with Ted Brennan. As Hoenig's vice-president in charge of special projects, Crawford took a great deal of pride in his achievements on behalf of the company. He listened now to Ted's story again, as if he had never heard it. The poor bastard was so desperate. Ever since he'd been fired from the network he'd had a pretty rough time—two newspaper jobs out in the Midwest, then that stint as news editor with a second-rate local station on the Coast, after that the final collapse into drink and the long months of recovery in that dry-out clinic in Oakland. He'd said this book of reminiscences he wanted to write was his only chance to reestablish himself. Doubleday was going to pay him a solid advance and he wanted to write a really first-rate book. Surely Crawford could understand?

Crawford did understand, but under no circumstances was Ted to write about his years at ACN, not unless the manuscript was submitted to him first. Crawford would go over it with the Chairman and they would make any deletions or changes they thought necessary. The integrity of the entire ACN operation could not be jeopardized.

"I'm—I'm afraid I can't do that." Brennan's voice. "It would compromise the whole book. I've got to write about what I know and as well as I can, Crawford. You and the Chairman have to understand that. Some chips may have to fall."

"No, we can't allow that," Crawford heard himself say. "I'm sorry, Ted."

"I don't really see how you can stop me."

"You don't? Well, of course we *can't*, if you're bound to do it. But I think you should know that we would take steps."

"Steps? What steps?"

"Whatever has to be done, Ted, we'll do."

"OK, I hear you. Now if you'll excuse me—"

"Just a minute, Ted. I have something for you."

Crawford listened smilingly to the sound of himself opening the attaché case and producing the bulky manila envelope, then the soft swishing noise of Ted Brennan riffling quickly through the pictures.

A gasp, then in a hoarse voice, barely audible on the tape: "Where'd you get these?"

"Does it matter? We have them."

"But how— Christ . . ."

Crawford had then quietly, gently filled him in. "We have it all, Ted. You see, you were drinking quite a bit there, toward the end. We figured you might someday become a hazard to us. We arranged to take a few photographs, make some tapes—"

"Tapes? What tapes?"

"Well, of this business here, for instance. That one and the second session in your office late that night, after the Christmas party. The girl you raped in this series."

"What? I didn't—"

"She says you did. And we have her testimony, too. You'll

remember that we had to settle with her for a very considerable sum."

"But . . . I didn't . . . I mean, you said—"

"Expediency, Ted. Surely you see the need for that? You were going downhill pretty fast by then. You do remember?"

Silence on the tape, but Crawford closed his eyes and recalled how it had been; how satisfactory to watch Ted Brennan's newly acquired composure crumble. I wonder if he's drinking again by now, he thought. I sure as hell wouldn't be surprised.

Crawford's voice: "So you see, Ted, we also have your best interests at heart." And then again, after a long pause: "We're not telling you not to *write* the book, Ted. All we're asking is a chance to see it when you've finished and to make any suggestions for alterations or deletions of any material that could reflect badly on the network. That's not unreasonable, is it?"

Ted Brennan's voice, at last, tight, angry: "You sonofabitch, Crawford! And I suppose you're recording this conversation as well!"

"Ted, old man, of course. Someday, maybe, I'll get around to doing a book of my own. You'd be a very colorful character in it."

The telephone on the end table beside him now rang and Crawford saw its blinking red light. He turned off the tape, slipped the earphones off and picked up the receiver. He knew what it had to be about, since only two people had access to this particular line. "Yes?" he said, then listened without saying another word for several minutes, before hanging up.

They didn't give me much time, he thought, as he headed back to his bedroom to get dressed. They call me this late and expect me to organize this whole complicated operation in a matter of hours. They must think I'm a goddam miracle worker. Well, he told himself, recalling Brennan with a dreamy grim, I guess I am at that.

REFERENCE: MYRMIDON—How can I describe my feelings tonight? Exhilaration. Trepidation. These and more. How strange it is to know that what I have worked on all these years in the laboratory will finally be applied to the outside world. Research is certainly its own reward, but this notion that I will soon see an industrial application of my work I find uniquely stimulating. So much so that I could almost forgo my daily medication.

Regarding the data from the new test series, we've determined it was the new facial electromyography probes that provided additional insights.

Master program complete and ready for periodic updating.

—From the Journal of Dr. Jerome Lillienthal

5

In the year and a half that he'd been in this job at the network, Whit Bridgeford had never known his boss to be so insistent. Sarah Anderson, he had quickly realized soon after coming to ACN from CBS, was a strong personality; she was used to getting her own way, but ordinarily Whit had found her open to suggestions and more than willing to listen to the ideas of her subordinates. On the question of the Colombian special, however, she had clearly made up her mind; she had decided, for some reason, that the project was of paramount importance, though for the life of him Whit couldn't understand why it couldn't wait a week. He fidgeted uncomfortably in his chair and decided to make one last attempt to talk her into a short delay.

"Sarah, I can't see what we lose by waiting one week," he urged. "I have both crews out on assignments now, in Africa. I can't get either of them back in time for this deal. And we're fully committed to both projects. We all agreed the Nigerian oil story was essential and, of course, we have to cover the South African border war. You don't want me to bring either of the crews back, do you?"

"No, Whit, I didn't say that."

"Corrigan and his team are due in on Friday," Whit continued. "I can send them out again on two days' notice, if necessary. They're my best documentary team. If the Colombian story is that important, I can postpone the production work on the Nigerian deal, which can hold a couple of weeks at least, and dispatch them back to Bogotá. We only lose about five working days."

"Not good enough, Whit," Sarah said. "I want a team put together and out of here by tomorrow night. Hire some free-lancers, if you have to. We're on top of a very big story down there and I want us to get it first."

"I haven't heard a thing about it anywhere."

"I told you, Whit, this story was leaked to us by some top people in drug enforcement," Sarah explained. "Washington is deeply involved. The raids now being coordinated out of Bogotá are joint ventures with the Peruvians, both financed secretly by us, and they're intended to wipe out the cocaine traffic from there literally overnight. This means that eighty percent of the coke now coming into the market in this country dries up. There's bound to be a good deal of violence, amounting, I'm told, practically to a full-scale war. The cocaine plantations are a big industry, with private capital heavily invested and the whole economy of that interior region dependent on it. It'll make a terrific instant special, and we'll have an exclusive. By the time any of our competitors hear about it, we'll have our tape and we'll be ready to go on the air. I figure we can get it on by next Monday, a week from now. We'll preempt time for it, too, but we'll need Harvey for that."

"Where is he?"

"Sailing up the coast of Connecticut about now, I guess."

"How do we locate him?"

"His boat is called *Average Annie*. She sails out of the big marina in Montauk Lake, at the end of Long Island," Sarah said. "They'll have information for you. They're heading for Nantucket. We can make radio contact with him and arrange to get him off by seaplane. I want Harvey here by Friday night. Your crew should be back by then, with everything we need. Harvey will work on it over the weekend in edit and we'll go on the air with it next Monday, the day it hits the headlines."

Whit sighed. "Well, boss," he said, "I guess we can do it."

"You *know* we can," Sarah snapped. "When I hired you away from CBS and made you a VP, Whit, it was because I was told you were the best producer of instant specials around. Don't let me down."

"We haven't much time—"

"We're in the news business, Whit," Sarah reminded him, "not Hollywood documentaries. Get on it and get on it *now*."

Whit stood up. "OK. Now, about Harvey—I'm not about to be the one to tell him he's going to have to cut his vacation short."

"I don't blame you, Whit," Sarah said. "We'll give him a couple of more days to enjoy himself. Just make sure we know where he is. Then I'll call him myself."

"We could use Gene."

"No, we can't," Sarah answered. "If we're going to preempt two of our top sitcoms for a special on the Colombian drug raids that no one has yet read a word about, we're going to need Harvey to narrate. It's what he does best and what we pay him all that money for. Get busy, Whit."

"Sure. I'll keep you abreast of developments. I can go outside my operating budget on this one? I presume you want the best outside crew I can put together, and I may have to bring in Smalley from London for this job."

"Of course. Do what you have to." She dismissed him by picking up the phone on her desk and asking for her secretary to come in for dictation.

Slightly dazed, Whit walked slowly back to his office, called in his assistant and began scrambling to put a good crew together. It wasn't until early evening that he realized he'd forgotten to call Tracy. He quickly dialed her number and explained the situation to her.

"It sounds as if she's expecting a war down there," Tracy said.

"Yes, I've never seen her quite so adamant. I think it's a little mad, don't you?"

"Yours not to reason why, Whit."

He laughed. "Mine but to do and die, Tracy. I'll call you back in an hour or so. Can you wait?"

"I'm famished, but I have a jar of olives to munch on."

"Munch away. Or, better still, why don't you come down here? As soon as I can take a break, we can sneak out for a bite. I'm expecting Smalley to call me from London, so I'd better hang up."

"All right, darling," she said. "Listen, I have a better idea. Unless I hear from you, I'll be at the bar of the Casa Margherita in an hour. How's that?"

"Fine." He hung up just as the call from Smalley came in, and he was so busy for the next hour and a half that he again forgot to call Tracy back to warn her he'd be delayed. He comforted himself by imagining she would understand, since clearly she was committed to being in the same business one day. He also made two calls to Washington, to sources he had cultivated inside the State Department, but, to his surprise, no one there had heard anything about the Colombian operation. Was it possible Sarah could be wrong? Could they have embarked on some kind of wild-goose chase? He wavered about bringing the matter up again with her, then decided not to. Better just to do his job and worry about the possibility of a fiasco later. After all, this was her show, not his.

From where he sat in his corner of the room, at an angle that provided him a clear view of one end of the bar, Crawford had plenty of time to speculate on how he might amuse himself with the girl. She had just the sort of looks—innocent, unspoiled, with long limbs and a slender figure—that could arouse him to frenzies of inventiveness. It was pleasant to be able to sit there, safely out of sight, and indulge himself; also, it helped kill the time. Morgan, his contact on this job, was late, and Crawford, who was always made uneasy by tardiness, had welcomed this unexpected small diversion.

Jeff Campbell also noticed her. He and Moss had no sooner walked into the Casa Margherita than he spotted her. He sauntered over to where she sat perched like a delicate bird on her bar stool, and smiled. "Hello, Tracy," he said. "I didn't come to apologize."

"Do you owe me one?"

"I thought maybe you'd expect one, after the other night."

"I never imagined it would occur to you."

"Hey, Tracy," Moss said, coming up beside his colleague and reaching out a long arm to pat her affectionately on the shoulder, "how you doin'?"

"I'm fine, Moss."

"Oh, you should have come along today, Tracy," Moss said. "We had a case!"

"A young high-school girl," Jeff explained. "Some maniac pushed her off a subway platform in the IRT station at East Eighty-sixth. The train took her arm off just below the elbow."

"Oh, my God, how awful!"

"They caught the guy who did it," Moss said.

"Yeah, four brewery workers on their way to a ball game," Jeff continued. "They ran him down and beat him into a pulp before the cops came."

"The guy who did it is the same nut they picked up five years ago for doing it to another girl," Moss said, "the one who lost her hand and had it sewn back on."

"Oh, God." Tracy was white-faced. "You mean he escaped?"

"No, they let him out last month," Jeff said. "He did his time and was supposed to be cured. You'll love the late news tonight. We got shots of blood all over the station walls and—"

"Stop it!"

"Sorry, Tracy," Moss said. "Hey, we didn't mean to scare you or anything."

"God, no, Tracy," Jeff said. "But we thought you wanted to be a mike stand. You should have seen old Spence in his glory there, knee deep in bone shards."

"What's the matter, Tracy?" Moss asked solicitously. "You're looking a little pale, girl."

"I didn't invent the story," Jeff said. "We shot just what we told you. The good parts won't get on the air, but I can show you unedited tape if you want to see it."

"I don't have to," she said quietly. "I believe you, Jeff."

"You know, Moss," the cameraman observed, turning to his

partner, "I think Tracy might actually make it in this business."

"Actually, if you must know, I *am* glad to see you," Tracy said. "Some man sitting over there in the corner has been staring at me for half an hour. I feel decidedly unnerved."

Jeff glanced toward the back of the room, but saw no one sitting alone. "I think he's gone," he said. "I don't blame him for staring at you."

"It was creepy," she said. "And I had a feeling I'd seen him before somewhere."

"What did he look like?"

"I couldn't really tell. Middle-aged, husky-looking. But it was too dark in here to make him out."

"How do you know he was staring at you?" Moss said.

"I caught him a couple of times. And I could sense it. I don't know. It was strange."

"Town's full of weirdos," Moss observed.

"What's weird about staring at Tracy?" Jeff wanted to know. "I stare at her a lot myself."

"Jeff, you're a sexist."

"Ah, but not a pervert," the cameraman said. "Just a good old-fashioned American macho sex maniac."

"If we don't talk about something else," Tracy said, "I'm leaving you two."

"Where's Whitley? I assume you're waiting for him."

"Working. And his name is Whitner."

"I guess I'm never going to get that right," Jeff said.

"Don't mind him, Tracy," Moss chimed in. "He's got soul under all that feckless surface charm."

"I'd have to accept that assessment on faith," she said, "and I stopped doing that when I lost my belief in God as an old man with a beard sitting on a cloud."

"You did?" Jeff answered, in mock amazement. "I still believe in that. Woman, you're shocking the hell out of me."

"I doubt that very much," Tracy said, "but it would be a welcome change."

Outside in the street, hidden from immediate view by a row of concrete plant stands flanking the entrance, Crawford slouched against the west corner of the building. He saw Morgan, a slight, hunched-over figure, coming toward him from the direction of Seventh Avenue, and he waited for the man to reach him. That was a close thing, he was thinking. The girl probably worked at ACN and she could have noticed him. He had realized she'd become aware of him five minutes before, when she glanced up at him as he was on his way back from the men's room. Then, when the cameraman and his buddy had appeared, she surely would have told them and one of them might have recognized him. It was nearly a year since Crawford had even been inside the ACN Building, but he was not unknown to the older hands there. It had been stupid to arrange this meeting so close to home. Crawford was a careful man, but his one liability, he knew, was his sheer physical bulk. People who had met him or seen him only once tended not to forget him, so he had felt certain that that cameraman could have at least placed him. Luckily, he'd gotten out of there unseen while they were bantering with the girl at the bar. Who was she, anyway? He intended to find out. Nothing he could do about her, of course, but she did feed his almost infinite capacity for complicated fantasy.

Morgan, heading for the Casa Margherita, did not see him, but Crawford fell into step with him and guided him quickly past the entrance. "Keep walking east," he said.

"Sorry," Morgan muttered, without looking up at him. "It took some doing."

"Where am I meeting them?" Crawford asked.

"They'll pick you up as you come off the plane in Boston tomorrow."

"All right."

"We're all set to go at that end. You should be in the target area by early Friday morning, if the weather holds."

"Right. And L.A.?"

"A problem there. We can't be sure what flight they'll be on."

"They have to be on the same one. It simplifies the whole operation."

"I know."

"Otherwise we have to arrange a third event. It's too risky, too coincidental. There would be questions."

"No other choices?"

"None. We're on a tight schedule here."

"We have taps into both home lines. We'll know right away."

"Yeah."

"We have to assume they'll take the same flight. One of them lives in Santa Monica, the other one in Orange County. That's not too far away."

"There's no sure payoff in assuming anything," Crawford said. "We have to have a contingency plan. I'll let you know."

"Right."

"What else?"

"Nothing." Morgan reached into his side pocket and produced Crawford's airplane ticket. "You get in at ten."

The big man pocketed the documents without looking at them. "It's a tight operation from beginning to end," he said. "It has to go off exactly as scheduled. I want you to double-check everything at this end."

"I have."

"Who's in California?"

"Quinn."

"Stay on top of him."

"I will."

Without another word, Crawford stepped out into Sixth Avenue and waved for a taxi heading uptown. Morgan turned and walked back the way he'd come. In his head he had already begun to review every arrangement made, down to the minutest detail. He'd worked for Crawford long enough to know that the man would never tolerate an avoidable miscalculation and that the consequences for mistakes could be high, even fatal. This was their most ambitious operation by far in over five years. It was a cool night, but Morgan was sweating heavily by the time he reached the garage, west of Broadway, where he had parked his rented car.

The small seaplane, a single-engine Cessna 210 with Edo floats that Sarah had dispatched to pick up Harvey Grunwald, spotted *Average Annie* shortly after two o'clock on Friday afternoon. Fortunately, the good weather that had graced their week at sea from the first day held. The pilot had no trouble landing on a smooth surface undulating only slightly from the long tidal swells moving landward. To make the operation easier, Harvey's hired captain had maneuvered the ship closer to the island, within a few hours' sail of the harbor, in case the weather turned bad and made it essential to put Harvey ashore. Sarah Anderson had been adamant about the necessity of getting Harvey back to the city by Friday night or very early Saturday morning at the latest. Never before in their relationship had Sarah been so insistent, and she had stood firm against Harvey's outraged protests. The anchorman, in fact, had been astonished by her intransigence.

"There must be something else behind it," Ann had said soon after Harvey emerged, red-faced and angry, the previous evening from the captain's cabin. "I think there must be more to it that she can't tell you over the air."

"There'd *better* be," Harvey had answered. "My God, we're not invading Colombia and Peru, are we? This sounds like some sort of large drug bust, like the one on the Mexican poppy fields a few years back. I think Sarah's having a breakdown. Blanton could narrate this show. There's no need to screw up our vacation this way."

The matter had been discussed at length that evening over dinner in the main cabin with their guests, the Millers and the Goldbergs. It had become clear to all of them that Harvey had no choice; he'd have to interrupt his cruise and go back to New York the next morning as Sarah had demanded. "They've got you by the short and curlies, Harvey," Bill Miller had said. "If Sarah's onto a big story nobody else knows about, you've got an exclusive. By the way, is it OK if I contact my office from here?"

Harvey grinned. "Not a chance," he said. "*Newsweek* will have to wait in line for this one, especially if it's going to screw up my vacation. And to make sure of my scoop I'm giving the captain orders to keep you all on the high seas till Monday noon."

Bill Miller had laughed. "Piracy! I'll sue!"

Harvey had known from the first that Sarah could force him to accede to her wishes. Quite apart from the consideration that she was likely to be his strongest ally in his forthcoming negotiations with the Chairman, his present agreement clearly stipulated that he had to make himself available for just such instant specials, though he had always imagined that only the outbreak of war or the death of an American President could be reason enough to dispatch seaplanes in pursuit of his yacht. Evidently Bill Miller was right: somehow the news division was onto a really big story that only Harvey Grunwald could handle for the network.

The pilot of the Cessna had no trouble maneuvering his craft in close enough to make Harvey's transfer by skiff an easy operation. The anchorman settled himself comfortably in his seat beside the pilot and waved to his wife and their guests, all cheerfully lined up against the rail of *Average Annie's* main deck. Within minutes the plane was airborne and Harvey found himself gazing wistfully down at his boat as they circled above it once, then headed south, gaining altitude. He hadn't even noticed the speck bobbing in the water a few miles astern of the yacht, and if he had he would not have known what it was.

No one on *Average Annie* had noticed anything amiss. By nightfall the yacht, quietly adrift on the surface of the calm sea thirty miles off Nantucket, was alive with lights and the sound of music from the stereo. Ann Grunwald, Bill and Kitty Miller, and Dave and Miriam Goldberg had gathered, after-dinner drinks in hand, on the upper deck, from where they could look out over the water as they chatted. It was a clear but moonless night, with only the stars in an empty sky over the black surface of the Atlantic. Aristides Karopoulos, the Greek sailor then at the wheel, was the only person on board to become aware of another boat in the vicinity. To make certain he had not merely imagined its presence, he squinted through the glass; all he had been able to make out in the glow of *Annie's* own lights had been a dim, low shape, perhaps a small fishing boat, briefly outlined by a flash of heat lightning to the west. The small cruiser seemed to be directly parallel to their position and holding, but the seaman couldn't be sure. He wondered whether he should alert the captain to her presence, but decided simply to ignore it.

At about the time that Karopoulos became aware of the other boat, Dave Goldberg decided to go to bed. He kissed his wife, stood up and stretched, then turned to say good night to his hostess. As he did so, he glanced out over the water. He was the only one on board to see the twin phosphorescent streaks of the torpedoes slicing swiftly toward the *Average Annie*. He had no time even to cry out before they hit.

6

THE GRINDING ROAR of a garbage truck mangling cans directly below his windows woke Jeff up. It happened every Saturday morning, but this time the sanitation men seemed especially vindictive, as if directing their noisy energies specifically at him. He sat up with a groan, rubbed his eyes and then walked painfully into the kitchen, where he opened his refrigerator door and fished out the orange juice. He poured himself a tall glassful and sank with a sigh into the straight-backed wooden chair by his kitchen table. He was going to have to stop doing this to himself, he realized, because his capacity was limited and he suffered acutely from hangovers. This one hadn't made him sick yet, but his head throbbed and his mouth felt as if it had been scoured by a large cotton swab.

He winced as the crew beneath his windows began to clash garbage lids together and roll the empty cans along the sidewalk. It was Tracy's fault, really, he told himself. Or was it? Certainly, as she had pointed out to him more than once, it was always Jeff who started with the provocative stuff, as if determined to offend and shock her. Why? Well, because something about that cool assurance of hers rubbed him raw; he took potshots at her out of a determination to make her human. Wasn't that it? Sure it was.

But then who was he to judge? How did he know she wasn't

putting him on at all but was simply being herself? It intimidated him, so what? Whose fault was that? And the hell of it was that he really liked her, quite apart from her sensational looks; he admired her cool determination to make a professional out of herself, her willingness to learn. And—yes!—her genuine admiration for his own work. So why couldn't he just be nice to her for once? Why couldn't he just shut up? Did he feel competitive with her—sense that her determination might someday carry her higher than his own? He didn't know, and, at this very moment, he didn't care. He closed his eyes briefly and tried to count all the bars he and Moss had been to the night before, not including the White Horse, where they'd wound up at 3 A.M. for the regular last rounds. Moss had disappeared at some point and Jeff had closed the place. Oh, God, what a mistake, and now the whole day of agony ahead and half the long weekend shot. He groaned, put his head in his hands and sat there until at last the noisy band in the street moved away in a great howl of revved-up engines.

After finishing about a quart of juice and when he felt strong enough to move, Jeff pushed himself to his feet and went back to bed. He lay flat on his back and reached out behind his head to punch his radio awake at its customary station, WCBS news. At first nothing the announcer said made any sense to him, but suddenly that mellifluous, faceless male voice jolted him to a sitting position and transfixed him like an insect on a pin.

"The Coast Guard is still searching for the *Average Annie*, the yacht owned by ACN anchorman Harvey Grunwald, which vanished last night after an explosion off Nantucket Island," the voice was saying, as if reciting the latest stock exchange quotations. "The captain of a Liberian oil tanker reported seeing a flash at about eleven P.M. last night and alerted the Coast Guard to investigate. Apparently, Harvey Grunwald himself was not on board. He had been taken off some hours earlier and flown back to New York. But his wife, Ann, and eight other passengers and crew members were on board, including William Miller, a senior editor at *Newsweek* magazine, his wife, Katherine, investment banker David Goldberg and his wife,

Miriam. The ship was on a pleasure cruise out of Montauk, Long Island, and had reported no difficulties of any kind. The weather had been mild and the ocean calm. To date one Coast Guard search plane has reported seeing floating debris in the general area of the explosion, but authorities won't say yet whether it came from Grunwald's yacht."

Jeff banged the radio off and reached for the phone. Nick Windom was on the assignment desk, but he was nearly as much in the dark about events as Jeff himself. "We've heard nothing definite, Jeff," the editor said.

"But what the hell happened?"

"Nobody knows for sure, but things don't look too good."

"And Harvey?"

"He flew out of here early this morning, in the same plane that picked him up yesterday," Windom said. "I guess he went up there to help in the search or to identify whatever they find."

"I don't get it," Jeff said. "How come he wasn't on board?"

"You got me," the editor answered. "Mrs. Anderson pulled him back here for some instant special they've been very hush-hush about."

"Bridgeford's project?"

"You got me."

"It must be a hot one for them to bring Harvey back."

"He was damn lucky, I guess," Windom said. "It sounds like the boat just blew up."

"Christ," Jeff said. "Listen, Nick . . ."

"Yeah?"

"If you hear anything at all, anything, give me a call, will you?"

"You home?"

"Yeah."

"Sure thing."

"Just blew up?"

"Yeah."

"God. I guess he *was* lucky. But, Christ, Ann . . ."

"I hear she was a real nice lady."

"The nicest, Nick," Jeff said, "the very best."

"It's a bitch, ain't it? You just never know, do you?"

After hanging up, Jeff sprang to his feet, but the move made his head spin and doubled him over with sudden nausea. He made it to the bathroom just in time. Afterward he forced himself into the shower and stood there for ten minutes under a cascade of cold water as he waited for the phone to ring. He then toweled himself off, made coffee and dry toast, turned the radio back on and settled down to wait.

At four o'clock, Windom called and told him Harvey was on his way back, after which Jeff telephoned Moss. His partner had heard the news only an hour earlier and was clearly shaken. "I'm going uptown," Jeff told him.

"What for?"

"I've got to do something," the cameraman said. "I figure if Harvey gets back and the news is bad, I'm going to see him. He's going to need a friend. He's just lost the best ones he had outside of the network."

"No kids?"

"A couple. They're in California, last I heard."

"I guess that leaves you."

"Yeah, I guess it does."

"Want me to come with you?"

"No, that's OK, Moss."

"I don't really know the cat, except through you. I guess you were real close, huh?"

"Yeah, we were. You get close to people in places like Vietnam."

"I can dig that."

"OK, Moss, I'm off, then."

"Yeah. Give me a shout if I can do anything."

"I will. Thanks, Moss."

By the time Jeff headed uptown toward the ACN Building, a bank of huge thunder clouds lay in a black mass over the Hudson River, and a scattering of fat raindrops spattered the sidewalks. Jeff leaned his head back against the seat of the cab and shut his eyes. He wasn't at all sure what, if anything, he could do now for Harvey, but he did know that he wanted to make himself available. It was the least he could do for the old man, the best reporter and newsman Jeff had ever worked with, in Vietnam or anywhere. When you go through experiences like those together, the bonds they create last a lifetime, or at least that was the way Jeff had always felt about it and, he felt sure, Harvey must feel the same way. Sonofabitch, Jeff thought, all that time in a war zone and not so much as a scratch, and now this. . . .

"Well, it's pretty ordinary stuff," Sarah Anderson said, drumming a pencil lightly against the edge of her desk. "That's all we have?"

Whit nodded. "Some of it is pretty good, I thought. The raid on the village is dramatic enough."

Sarah nodded. "Yes, I suppose we can edit it into some kind of shape."

"Smalley was lucky to get even this much," Whit explained. "There apparently was no big concerted effort of the kind you were told about. The Peruvians had no part in these raids. The one we have on tape here is a regular operation by Colombian forces against their own people."

"It's incredible," Sarah said. "You have no idea, Whit, what they told me from Washington. I thought we were onto a terrific story."

"Well, a lot of this is usable, of course. We haven't had much on the cocaine traffic." He paused a second or two, as if debating with himself. "I do think we ought to wait on it," he resumed. "The crew is still in Bogotá and I can send Smalley back there today. With enough time, I'm sure we can come up with a lot more good stuff, including interviews with drug-enforcement people as well as dealers and maybe another good look at the outback where they grow all this stuff. I think, if we can take our time, that we can probably salvage a pretty good special out of this."

Sarah nodded. "I agree. Anyway, there's no rush now. And this business about Harvey—" She broke off in midsentence and frowned. "It's just an awful situation."

"So I gather. Does Harvey have any idea what could have happened?"

She shook her head. "No."

"The boat just blew up in the water?"

"So it seems."

"My God."

"Yes. Listen, Whit, I really don't want to talk about it."

"I understand." He stood up. "Well, I'll put this stuff on hold and send Smalley back to Bogotá tonight. Another couple of weeks and I'm sure we'll have a pretty good program."

"I hope so, Whit. It's costing us enough."

He turned to go, but before he reached the door the phone rang and Sarah answered it. He saw her face go ashen and her lower lip begin to tremble.

"Yes, yes, I'll tell him," she said, hanging up.

"What is it?" Whit asked.

"They've found some bodies washed up on a beach in Nantucket," Sarah told him, her voice as dead as her eyes.

"They've been identified?"

"They're pretty sure," she said. "My God, I've got to tell him!"

"Do you want me to come with you?"

"No, it's all right," she said. "It's just that I've got to tell him myself." She moved quickly out from behind her desk toward the door and he stepped aside for her. He was struck again by her pallor. She looked sick. "My God," she murmured as she passed him, "I had no idea . . ."

"Want a drink?" Harvey asked.

"No, I couldn't," Jeff said. "Last night . . ."

"You never could hold your liquor, I remember."

Jeff grinned at the older man. "I could never become a drunk," he explained. "I have this early warning system that cuts me off at the pass line. If I go over it, I pay a heavy price the next day."

"I wish I had it," Harvey said. "Tonight I feel like getting drunk, but I won't. I can't." He was dressed in gray slacks and a sports shirt that bulged out over his belt. He hadn't shaved and he looked old and worn, a parody of the confident, benign, avuncular figure that five nights a week graced the nation's viewing screens. He sat down heavily on his sofa and slumped there, staring out over the city. The light had begun to fade and the long day was ending quietly in shadows cast over the empty canyons of midtown. The city seemed to be pausing, retreating, preparing itself for the evening tidal flow toward restaurants and theaters. In Harvey's apartment silence hung in the air like a sword.

"Listen, Harvey, maybe it will be all right," Jeff said. "Maybe they got off in time."

The older man shook his head glumly. "They'd have found them by now."

"You're sure?"

"Pretty sure, Jeff."

"You remember that time in Nam?"

"What time?"

"The time we got lost upriver?"

"Yeah, I remember. That would have been pretty hard to forget."

They had been shooting film on the river patrols and had come under fire. The captain of their boat, a wild kid from some fishing town on the coast of Maine, had swooped in tight under the river bank and skimmed the shallows like a water bug. He had been a gentle, loving, freckle-faced kid the war had turned into a maniac, the Ahab of the rivers, riding his motorized White Whale like a bronco buster. They lay flat on the bottom of the boat, hearing the thick crackle of bullets burying themselves in the jungle foliage over their heads. The boy took the boat suddenly out into the stream, zigzagging to avoid the hidden enemy sharpshooters, then spun it up a tight little estuary where he could coast to safety around long, meandering bends hidden overhead by the crush of jungle green that formed a canopy over them. He had cut the engine and they had sat there in silence, waiting for darkness, waiting for the helicopters, waiting finally for the planes to come in and free them. They had waited for nearly three days. The choppers had come in on the second day and missed them. The planes had not come at all. Finally they had made a run for it and come home intact, no one on board even slightly wounded, the hull a mess from the shattering impact of the bullets.

The whole episode had further fueled the legend of Harvey's exploits on the spot in Vietnam. It had provided eight minutes of terrific film, as tense, as dramatic as the wait in any thriller for the unseen menace to appear. Harvey's quiet, appraising, courageous voice, so ably documented by Jeff's camera eye—the silent walls of the jungle, the thin deadly lines of the tracers overhead, the ecstasy of recklessness on the boy's face as he spun the boat through the rhythm of death in the water around him. Memorable film, memorable days. Jeff relived them now with Harvey, hoping somehow that the recollection of that time could bring comfort.

But Harvey was a man now holding a single five-dollar chip and about to make one last try at breaking the bank. "Whatever happened to that crazy kid?" he asked.

"I don't know," Jeff lied. "I never heard." He had heard. Charlie had blown the boy out of the water two months later with a single, well-placed mine, but this was hardly the time to remember that event. Jeff realized he could have done better by Harvey than put him back on a boat in peril, even in casual reminiscence. War stories, they were all the same, anyway, but Harvey seemed to be deriving some comfort from them.

"What ever happened to that maniac sniper you vanished into the jungle with," Harvey asked, "that fellow, Norton, I believe?"

"Nolan," Jeff corrected. "Wade Nolan. Last I heard he was down South someplace still free-lancing for the government."

"God, what sensational footage you got with him," Harvey recalled. "One of my best reports, Nolan picking off those poor bastards like ducks in a shooting gallery."

"Yeah, well, one of those 'poor bastards' nearly picked off your friendly cameraman, you'll recall, while you were amusing yourself in Saigon."

"Research," Harvey quipped, smiling as he remembered for a moment how exquisite ordinary pleasures became when embraced by war, the heightened senses the living enjoyed when

surrounded by the dying. His smile suddenly faded. "Journalistic research," he added absently.

They went on talking. What else was there to do? Jeff sat most
of the time, while the older man moved about, fetching drinks
and bits of cheese and crumbly little crackers to put them on. He
looked older by the minute as the sky outside his windows
darkened. From time to time the phone rang. Reports of no
progress, the comforting voices of old acquaintances and colleagues, the madly incongruous concerns of strangers riding the
airwaves to put themselves in contact with celebrity. Star-
fuckers. Harvey at last gave up and allowed Jeff to begin
screening the calls while he sat and stared glumly out of the
windows. Catastrophe enclosed them in this room like the
heavy walls of a tomb.

At dusk Sarah came. Jeff opened the door and she stared right
through him, her face a gray mask. She brushed past him into
the living room, Jeff right behind her, and Harvey rose to greet
her. He did not need to be told, but she told him anyway. They
had found four bodies, she explained, at the water's edge in the
middle of a stretch of public beach. One of them was Ann's.
There were apparently no survivors. The cause of the accident
was still unknown.

Harvey stood alone in the middle of the room. He was like a
fighter out on his feet, but numb to pain. He moved toward the
phone. "I've got to call the children," he said hoarsely.

"Let me do it," Jeff said.

"No, it's all right," Harvey insisted. "I want to tell them
myself. I'll call from the bedroom, if you don't mind."

Sarah took a step in toward him. She apparently wanted to
take him in her arms. She was a woman, perhaps it would help.
But Harvey was beyond help, armored in his grief. He walked
softly past her, his footsteps soundless on the carpeting. The
click of a door closing. Sarah turned, saw Jeff as if for the first
time and gazed at him in mild curiosity. "You're. . .?"

"Jeff Campbell. WACN News."

"Oh . . . yes. They sent you?"

"Sent me?"

"I mean, Harvey . . ."

"We've known each other a long time," Jeff said. "We worked together in Vietnam."

"Oh. Yes, of course. I see. I'm sorry to be so out of it."

"I understand, it's OK."

"This is really horrible. How could it have happened?" She sat down abruptly, as if someone had hammered her into place.

"I don't know. Can I get you a drink?"

"Please."

"What? Scotch? Vodka?"

"Anything. Scotch, I guess. And a little water."

He got her the drink and she took it from him without a word. Most of it remained in her glass, even after three sips. She didn't seem anxious to lose her self-control, because, Jeff thought, some sort of hidden conflict raged within her and she was frightened.

"Should we go in there?" she asked as the minutes continued to slip away and darkness enclosed the room. "Is he all right, do you think?"

"I think so. But I'll check, if you want me to."

He started for the bedroom, but Harvey met him halfway. "It's OK," he said. "My daughter's taking it pretty hard."

Sarah rose to her feet, suddenly full of resolution. "Do you want them to come?" she asked.

Harvey nodded. "They want to," he said. "They live in different parts of the L.A. basin. They said they'd call me back."

"Let me make the arrangements," Sarah suggested. "I could help."

Harvey's son, Walter, lived in Santa Monica. He was thirty-five, still unmarried but living with a girl, and he worked as a reporter on the Santa Monica *Outlook*. Jane was twenty-seven. She was married to a real-estate developer in Palos Verdes and was four months pregnant with their first child. According to what they told Harvey, they were planning to take the same plane. One of them would call him back within the hour and let him know the flight number.

"Yes, that's sensible," Sarah said. "If they take the same flight, we can handle all the VIP arrangements, pick them up and get them into town quickly."

"I want to go to Nantucket," Harvey said. "We have to see her. I guess the Goldbergs and the Millers . . . everybody will have people . . ."

"Of course," Sarah agreed. "You can meet the kids at the airport. We can arrange for a private plane. You can fly out directly with them."

"Yes," Harvey said, "that makes sense."

"Harvey, dear, you'll be all right?"

"Yes," he lied, "I'll be all right, Sarah. Thanks for your help."

"I'd better get on my horse," she said. "I have calls to make. I'll ring you back to find out what flight they're on. All right?"

"Of course."

She put a hand on his cheek and kissed him quickly on her way out. She left swiftly, without so much as a glance at Jeff, who was startled at her haste.

"That's a woman with a lot on her mind," he said after she had gone.

"Sarah?" Harvey stared dumbly at Jeff. "Oh, yeah. She's a terrific lady."

"So I hear. Is it OK if I stay, Harvey?"

"Sure. Make yourself a drink."

"No, it's OK. I can't use one."

"I sure can."

Jeff moved toward the kitchen for ice. As he passed the phone on his way back, it rang. He picked it up. "Just a minute, please," he said, holding out the receiver. "They've booked their flight."

"Good," Harvey said, moving heavily toward him, like a diver walking on the bottom of the sea. "Good. That was fast."

He looks terrible, Jeff thought, he looks half dead; he's clutching the pieces of himself together, but he's in danger of coming apart. Jeff made up his mind to spend the night there, to stay with Harvey until no longer needed.

7

WHITNER BRIDGEFORD made love like a man running for a train.
His major concern was to get on board and get comfortable.
Once inside, he left the traveling to others and waited impatiently for the journey to end so he could go about his business,
which was the business of himself and his immediate concerns.
No one had ever told him he was a poor lover. Most of the
women he had slept with had been fooled by his good looks into
blaming themselves for the inadequacy of the performance. Or
perhaps it was his serenity, his self-confidence, that betrayed
them. How could anyone question the authenticity of anything
quite that beautiful? Whit was a morning glory, a racehorse that
burns up the track in dawn workouts but won't put out the extra
effort needed in the afternoons.

Tracy knew something was wrong, even though she was
relatively inexperienced for her age. At Bennington she had
allowed her drama coach to seduce her a couple of times, and
later, during her senior year, she fell in love with a willowy,
dreamy-eyed poet who carried inspiratory drugs around in a
worn-leather toilet kit slung from his belt. When the drugs were
working, he performed some astonishing convolutions on her
behalf, but most of the time he existed in a dreamy limbo of
unexpressed, passive desire that left her weak, as if on the verge
of a revelation that never came. The affair ended in June, when

her poet wandered into a grove of redwoods north of San Francisco and disappeared into a ground fog, never to return. Since then there had been a few others, none of them very satisfactory. Luckily, Tracy was too sensible, too sure of her own womanliness, to worry about what was wrong with her. Nothing was wrong with her. The world was askew, that was all. Someday it would right itself for her.

She lay now flat on her back, naked, spreadeagled on the wide golden expanse of Whitner Bridgeford's king-sized brass bed and open to his rabbity pelvic thrusts. She felt like an object. His hands were on her shoulders, pressing her down. Twice she whimpered, because he'd hurt her in his haste, but he mistook her reaction for one of ecstasy and thrust even harder. When he had finished, he lay on her utterly spent and she held him in her arms. It was then that she loved him best, because he seemed so vulnerable.

After a few minutes, he rolled away from her and lay on his side, gazing at her in the faint dawn glow from the overhead skylight. "You all right?" he whispered.

"I'm fine."

"Was it all right?"

"Yes."

"You didn't come, though."

"No, but it doesn't matter."

"Well, sure it does." He propped himself up on one elbow. "I'm sorry, Tracy."

"What for?"

"I guess I rushed everything. I don't know . . . I woke up—you were there . . ."

"Whit, it was fine, really."

"You looked so terrific." He grinned at her. "You should never wear any clothes."

"Never?"

"Never."

"I don't think that would go over big at the office."

"You never know," he said. "Don't knock it till you've tried it."

"Come to think of it, one or two of my colleagues . . ."

"Yes?"

"Skip it."

"I know what you mean. That photographer—Jeff, isn't it?"

"He's not alone. You'd better be nice to me."

"I guess. What *is* his name?"

"Campbell, Jeff Campbell. He has trouble with your name, too."

"Well, we don't have much in common, do we?"

"No."

"I hear he's very good."

"I wouldn't know about that."

He laughed. "I don't mean in bed. I mean he's a good cameraman."

"The best."

"Is he?"

"Yes. And unappreciated. Like all of them, good, bad or indifferent."

"They just take pictures, Tracy."

"You think that's easy?"

"Sure, if you shoot enough tape."

"Well, I don't know much about it."

"No, you really don't. But you're learning. Want some coffee?"

"What time is it?"

"Nearly seven."

"It's awfully early."

"I'm going to make some coffee."

He rolled out of bed, slipped into a pair of shorts and skipped down the stairs toward the kitchen. From her perch on the sleeping balcony of his duplex, she watched him go. He was beautiful. Oiled, he'd have looked like a statue of an ancient Greek athlete. She longed to freeze him forever into a golden posture, his body shaped permanently to one small, perfect, effortful moment. She wondered what he did to keep so fit. She had never seen him exercise or heard of him doing so, though he had once hinted to her that he'd worked at one time to achieve such muscular grace. When he came back with the coffee—two mugs, cream, sugar, on a tray—she asked him.

"My father was an All-American at Purdue," he explained obliquely. "My mother was a balletomane. Between the two of them I had a lifetime of exercise packed into what seemed a very brief childhood."

"You danced?" she asked, amazed.

He laughed. "Oh, no. I ran. The track team. The four-forty, the eight hundred meters. In winter I swam. Breaststroke, mostly. Spring and summers, tennis and golf. And more swimming. That's it."

She leaned over and kissed him. "It becomes you," she said.

"And you, Tracy. You're wonderful."

She was not wonderful, she knew that. She was just a long-legged, trim brunette who was trying to make something significant of herself. When she succeeded, she'd be worthy of him. She'd make demands. No more running for trains. For now, it didn't matter to her. The best part of her life was what she would one day do with it, what she would become. Her real love these days was the work, the learning, the stimulation of the person she aspired to be. Tracy Phillips was a talent, a person. Couldn't Whit see that? But, my God, he was staggeringly beautiful. . . .

"Why so early?" she asked an hour later as he dressed and she watched him from the safety of his bed.

"Because I've got a lot of tape to look at again," he explained. "Sarah Anderson and I went over most of it yesterday, but her mind really wasn't on it."

"I can see why."

"I wish I could. She dreamed up this whole caper."

"She must have been upset for Mr. Grunwald."

"I guess, but, darn it—I mean, we spent a hell of a lot of money on what was supposed to be a terrific instant special that turns out to be nothing. I sent Smalley back to Bogotá last night. He's calling in today and I have to be sure I know what he should go for. So far I've got maybe ten or eleven good minutes.

The rest of it is routine. Boring interviews with politicians and policemen. What we've got, really, is nothing."

"That's not your fault, Whit."

"So they tell me now. But you know what? At the end of the year, when they go over the budgets, I'll be way out on a limb on this one, even if we can salvage it. And do you know whose fault that will be? Mine."

"Mrs. Anderson will back you."

"I wouldn't bet on it, Tracy."

"I thought you liked her."

"I do, but that has nothing to do with it. This is dollars and cents we're talking about, and my contract will be up for renewal."

"Are you frightened?"

Startled by the question, he looked up at her from the chair where he sat pulling on his socks. "What do you mean by that?"

She shrugged and pulled the sheet up to her chin. She perched among his pillows like a bird on a high wire. She looked adorable, but at the moment he was beyond seeing how adorable she could be. His fate hung in the balance, riding on a crazy project that he hadn't originated or believed in and that now threatened his whole career. "I'm not frightened, Tracy," he said. "I can always get another job. I've got a good track record."

"You have. You've won prizes."

"Yes, I have."

"Well, then?"

He smiled, like an ad salesman late for a meeting with a client, a smile of gray-flanneled bravado. "You don't know about corporate decisions," he told her. "It's not what you do, darling. It's what you've done and it's measured in black and white. ROI, return on investment—*that's* the name of the game. Know what I mean?"

"I guess so."

She shrank back into his pillows, only her small dark head visible to his preparations across the long room from where she lay, immobilized, rendered speechless by his continuing self-absorption. Before leaving, he came over and kissed her. His lips were chill, his mouth antiseptic with remnants of a Swedish toothpaste he favored.

"Goodbye, love," he said. "I'll call you from the office later. Dinner tonight?"

"I can't," she murmured. "I'm driving out to Southampton to see my parents."

"Oh, yeah, I forgot." He bolted for the stairs. "I'll talk to you tomorrow."

And he was gone. She lay alone in his big bed, in this cold, empty room, and some small bit of her died. She didn't know what part or why, but the taste of his mouth lingered unpleasantly and she got up at last to get herself a second cup of coffee and the Sunday paper, which he had left, pristinely intact, just inside the front door. Harvey Grunwald's troubled face loomed up at her from the front page.

The Chairman had not slept all night, though he had dozed fitfully. When Louise came in with his tea at seven-thirty he was sitting up in bed, hands folded placidly on his stomach, his gaze fixed unwaveringly on the doorway.

"Good," he said. "I've been expecting you."

She seemed surprised. "I'm not late, am I?"

"No, but I've been awake."

"Are you feeling all right?"

"Fine, just fine."

She set the tray down over his knees and poured him a cup, exactly as he liked it, dark with a wedge of lemon and no sugar. He sipped it slowly, his hand trembling only slightly.

His wife regarded him fondly and patted his head. "Your hair, darling," she said. "You must have your barber in next week."

"I know," he grumbled. "I've been busy."

"You certainly have. I've hardly seen you."

"Lots going on."

She smiled. "Oh, I know," she said. "There always is. We're at home tonight, thank goodness."

"No guests?"

"No. Just the two of us. I've given Clara and Henry the day off."

"You're not cooking?" He looked mildly alarmed.

"Good Lord, no, Lawrence! When was the last time I did that?"

"Can't remember now. Two years ago, I think."

"Don't worry. We have a fresh seafood salad tonight. Clara fixed it yesterday."

"Good. Any calls?"

"This early, on a weekend? Good heavens, no."

"This Grunwald business—"

"It's dreadful. I'm so sorry. I sent flowers yesterday."

"Good."

She stood up. "Anything else, dear?"

"No, I'm fine."

"The papers?"

"I'll read them later."

She started for the door, and he watched her, wondering, not for the first time, what kept her going. The woman had no interests, apart from the busy social life of their home, in this elegant town house on East Seventieth Street between Park and Lexington. They'd lived in it now for thirty-five years and it was her whole life. He'd allowed her to spend a fortune redesigning and furnishing it. She had taste, he had to concede that, and they lived here now like Oriental despots. She had crowded his walls with masterpieces—several Renoirs, a Degas, two Matisses, a small Rembrandt over the living-room fireplace— and furnished his room with antiques, delicate sculptures, many other precious art objects. She had created a palace for an emperor and his consort; they lived together in it but apart. She was his gracious hostess, efficient housekeeper, the elegant façade behind which the Chairman could pursue his private concerns, which essentially were those of conquest. His self-absorption was awesome in its totality. She fronted for it with the glitter and panache appropriate to her elevated social standing, abetted by her impeccable taste in furnishings and art. It compensated for everything else that was missing in her life, including children.

An invitation to the Hoenigs' was much coveted in New York

establishment circles, but what visitors were admitted to was a stage set. The Chairman's real life at home, the only one that mattered to him, was lived upstairs, in his third-floor study. There, seated at his small antique desk and hemmed in by TV monitors, videotape machines, recorders, filing cabinets and private phone, he could continue to dominate and manipulate his world as easily as from his office suite in the ACN Building. Furthermore, from where he sat he could look down over a small but elaborate garden in which a graveled walk meandered through thick hedges and rosebushes around an Italian marble fountain and sundial to a latched iron gate, hidden from view at ground level by a greenhouse sheltering a tiny forest of exotic tropical plants. Beyond this gate, always kept locked and unknown to anyone else in the house, even Louise, a narrow alley sandwiched between two large apartment houses led through the basement of a third one, owned by the Chairman, to provide direct access to Seventy-first Street.

"Did you hear me, Lawrence? I'll be in the kitchen, if you should need anything." She was standing in the bedroom doorway, waiting to be dismissed.

"Fine. I'll be in the study."

"I thought so," she said. "Lawrence, you must stop driving yourself. You must try to relax more on the weekends."

"Don't lecture me, Louise," he snapped. "I have work to do."

"I understand. Ring if you need anything."

"Yes, I will. Goodbye, Louise."

She waved tentatively, a little dip of cool, manicured fingers, and swept grandly back to her well-ordered domain.

The Chairman got up and went into the bedroom to brush his teeth, massage his gums, shave, and comb his hair. By eight-thirty he was seated behind his desk in the study, where he made a pretense of reading the morning paper even as he watched the silent screen of his ACN monitor.

At exactly nine o'clock, the iron gate behind the greenhouse swung open and Crawford appeared. The Chairman looked down at the big man, who filled all of the space between the garden hedges. Crawford glanced up and saw him. The two men stared at each other unsmilingly, and Crawford contented himself with nodding, but only once, a barely perceptible tilt of the head. After which he turned and left unhurriedly the way he had come. The Chairman sighed and relaxed in his chair. On the TV screen, a middle-aged woman smilingly peddled a brand of coffee the Chairman detested. It was going well so far, he reflected. The complicated pieces continued to fall precisely, cleanly and logically into place. The Chairman was at peace with himself.

Sarah Anderson had arranged everything with her customary efficiency. The hired limousine had picked Harvey up at his house at precisely 3 P.M. and whisked him out to Kennedy, where he had been deposited directly in front of the arrival gates at the Trans-American Airlines terminal. There two young, neatly dressed men from the airline whisked Harvey through security and up to the VIP lounge overlooking the runways. The flight his children were on, Trans-American Airlines Flight 2 out of Los Angeles, was due in at 4:35 P.M. It had left ten minutes late, one of the young men had informed Harvey, but had made up the time due to a favorable tail wind, and would arrive on schedule. It was now just four o'clock, half an hour to go.

"Is there anything we can get you, Mr. Grunwald?" the same young man asked. "A drink? Some coffee?"

"No, thanks," Harvey said, "I'm fine."

"Good. If you want anything, please call us. Just pick up that extension over there. Also, if you wish to make any outside telephone calls, the courtesy phones are available. For long distance, just ask for the operator."

"I appreciate it," Harvey said. "I'm all right, thank you."

The young men, faceless, as indistinguishable to him as robots, left, and Harvey sat down to wait. He was alone. Jeff had departed earlier for the office, and the rest of the morning had been spent making long-distance calls to confirm the arrangements Sarah's office had made on his behalf regarding the return of Ann's body from Nantucket. There had also been four calls from the children of the Millers and two from Miriam Goldberg's sister, an abrasive woman who had enraged him, even as she pretended to sympathize with him, by hinting that Harvey himself had been careless, that he was in some way to blame for the accident.

Harvey had managed to survive those calls with his stoicism intact, but he was worried now about having to face his children and how they would react. Walter would handle it all right, but Jane had always been an emotional child, quick to shed tears. She would run off the plane and into his arms and probably give way to her grief. Harvey would find that tough to handle. He had already cried enough, he had told himself. Ann was gone and tears would not bring her back. It didn't matter, either, why the thing had happened—the question Walter had kept asking. They would have to pick up the pieces of their lives and forge ahead. That was what life required of them. Harvey's time for grieving was past, he had told himself. He hoped he would be able to make his kids, especially Jane, understand that. After all, she carried another life now. It was her duty to herself and her child to go on. Oh, yes, let her shed her tears, but let's still go on. It was what Ann herself would have wanted; she had always been the most sensible, down-to-earth person of all of them. *My God, I'll miss her. . . .* He sat alone, very still and straight in his seat, and watched the planes come in and take off.

At precisely 4:31 P.M., a Trans-American Airlines DC-10 wide-bodied jet appeared in the cloudless blue sky approaching Kennedy's Runway 4-R. Harvey saw the big plane and assumed, from the time of its arrival, that it was Flight 2. He stood up, walked over to the window and watched glumly, hands thrust into his trouser pockets. Flaps and wheels down, nose up, the DC-10 coasted in for what looked sure to be a perfect landing. To Harvey, insulated from the noise behind thick plate glass, the plane looked unreal, suspended on an invisible cushion as it coasted soundlessly in.

Suddenly, for no reason anyone could immediately discern, at about five hundred feet from the runway the big jet inexplicably began to roll to the left. The wings tilted nearly to a vertical position, and the nose dropped. Someone in the room behind Harvey screamed. A man shouted, "Oh, my God!" and ran, the sound of his feet like thunderclaps in this glass-enclosed cocoon. The plane hit the end of the runway nose-first. A huge flash of fire, followed by a massive black cloud, billowed out into the empty sky. Almost immediately, two fire trucks and an ambulance, red lights whirling and flashing, shot out from under the building and roared off toward the site, hidden now in the enshrouding smoke of disaster.

Behind where he stood, Harvey heard the shouts and the sound of more running footsteps. All around him people crowded to the window. Outside, in utter silence, as if on a huge drive-in movie screen, the terrible drama played itself out in an explosion that now wrenched the big plane apart, sending scattered fragments of metal lurching through the sky like bits of torn paper whirling in a breeze.

Transfixed by the sight, Harvey did not move. He stood there until, as if from a great distance, he heard the cool, metallic voice of the P.A. system, a communication from some serene corner of outer space: "Attention, please. All those expecting arrival of Trans-American Airlines Flight Two out of Los Angeles, please report to the VIP lounge next to Gate Forty-three." Over and over the lunar voice proclaimed this oblique confirmation of disaster. Harvey heard it, but still did not move.

"Mr. Grunwald? Mr. Grunwald!"

Harvey turned and found himself facing the pale, sweating face of one of his escorts. "Mr. Grunwald! Oh, Christ . . ."

Harvey screamed, a dull, hoarse cry of primal grief and rage. He pushed the young man aside and began to run, where, he didn't know. Who stopped him and exactly what happened next he was never to be able to recall, though he did remember later that night having glimpsed an unidentified but vaguely familiar face—one he may have seen before, somewhere, sometime. But perhaps it was all in his imagination; too much was going on and too quickly.

All around him, fluttering noisily within this room like frantic birds in a glass cage, a crowd of people now surged helplessly back and forth. Beyond the outer wall of their prison, the oily, black smoke of death rose to obliterate the late-afternoon sun.

8

THE CEREMONY was relatively brief but seemed longer, because it had no formal structure. The chapel had been rented for the occasion from an exclusive Madison Avenue funeral home in upper Manhattan, and by the time most of the mourners had arrived, the hired string quartet, four intense young men from Juilliard, had launched itself into Mozart with an élan that belied the nature of the occasion. From where he sat, along the left aisle about halfway up, Jeff could see the backs of the heads of the ACN brass, massed together as tightly as the banks of flowers that crushed against each other and overflowed along both walls. The private security people, working with funeral-home personnel, had managed to keep out the curiosity seekers, but even so the hall, which could comfortably hold about five hundred people, was packed. Standees lined the aisles, where they shifted uneasily to the cheerful strains of Ann Grunwald's favorite composer.

The guy seemed suddenly to have a lot of friends, Jeff thought, realizing for the first time that he had never associated Harvey with such a swarm of people. The anchorman had always been a loner, rarely observed at big gatherings, hardly ever a participant in public events with which he was not directly concerned professionally. Although he hadn't seen very much of Harvey these past few years, Jeff realized that it was only because Harvey hadn't ever seen very much of anyone but his wife, his very close old friends, now dead, and, of course, his immediate colleagues in the news division. He'd had his wife and his boat, and that had always been enough for him; a private man, essentially. Now, in grief, isolated by the twin disasters that had overwhelmed him, he sat surrounded by people. Strangers, however, not friends, Jeff reflected. Harvey Grunwald was now truly alone in the world.

Jeff sat up straight and peered over the heads in front of him. He was trying to spot Harvey, but couldn't seem to find him.

"What's up?" Moss whispered beside him.

"Can't see Harvey, can you, Moss?"

"I saw him come in," Moss said. "He was surrounded by security. Man, he looked bad."

"Yeah, I guess he would."

Bellucci turned around from the row directly in front of them and fixed them with a hostile eye. "Knock it off," he growled. "This is a service."

Jeff leaned forward. "Mario," he whispered in the editor's ear, "this here is *not* a religious service. It's just a way to say goodbye, *capish?* We're here for Harvey's sake, not the Pope's."

The editor shuddered, but refused to acknowledge Jeff's insult. It was his dismal fate, after all, to be saddled forever with the uncouth riffraff of the newsroom. Before either he or Jeff could resume this conversation, the quartet, in a flourish of rippling notes, came to a halt, Mozart's final chords seeming to hang in the air like hummingbirds over the massed banks of flowers.

Sarah Anderson, looking beautiful and chic in a simple black silk dress, her luminous eyes half hidden by a delicate veil, rose to speak. As she moved toward the podium, the musicians picked up their folding chairs and stands and exited into a small room at the rear, behind the organ. The crowd stirred uneasily and waited. Sarah reached the podium, adjusted the microphone to accommodate her height and looked directly down into the front rows.

"We are here today to honor the missing and to grieve for them as we would for members of our own family," she began. "And we are here, most of all, because we cherish the man whose terrible loss we share, both as colleagues and as friends . . ."

Someone sobbed, a woman somewhere, but Jeff had no idea who it was or why. He had spotted Harvey. The anchorman was sitting in the second row on the right, wedged in between two men Jeff didn't recognize and directly across the aisle from Louise and Lawrence Hoenig, who dominated their contingent as securely as royalty in the presence of its court. No one moved. Harvey seemed made of straw, propped up between his companions like a doll, his head slumped forward, his shoulders as motionless as if he too had joined the ranks of the dead they had all gathered here to mourn.

Jeff wished he were sitting with the old man at that moment. Harvey might indeed have wanted him there, but events had moved too fast, too devastatingly, for all of them. Jeff's repeated phone calls had gone unanswered except once, by a cleaning woman who had told him that Harvey had been in the hospital, which one she didn't know. It made sense; Jeff should have realized it on his own. Poor Harvey had reportedly gone berserk at the airport and had needed immediate medical attention. Understandable, of course. Sarah hadn't seen him, either, her secretary had informed him. Harvey would be at the service, that was all he knew.

"There are some people whose deaths we mourn more than others," Sarah was saying in a calm, resonant voice. "There are some people whose dying diminishes all of us permanently, because they are unique and because we know they will not come our way again. Ann Grunwald was just such a person. . . ."

She spoke for twelve minutes, mainly about Harvey Grunwald's many outstanding characteristics. In fact, Jeff realized, the eulogy hardly mentioned the dead. It was Harvey whom Sarah had come to mourn, which probably made sense, after all. Harvey was alive, he was a valuable human being, and it was his welfare, his survival, they should all be concerned with. Certainly the network brass, including Sarah herself, had every reason to cherish him: Harvey was a multimillion-dollar asset.

The Chairman took note of this fact when he succeeded Sarah at the podium. A short man, he was forced to grasp the lectern with both hands and thrust his face forward toward the microphone, but his presence dominated the room. He was a poor speaker, who slurred his words and plunged ahead in a sonorous monotone, and nothing he had to say was in any way significant. Harvey Grunwald had always been like a son to him, the Chairman informed the assembled mourners, ever since, as a bright young news hawk, he had come to work at ACN, which had nurtured and cherished his career. Harvey's losses were their losses, the Chairman continued, his griefs were theirs as well. But, Jeff noticed, everyone listened attentively, or pretended to. In the presence of emperors, courtiers knew better than to yawn.

The Chairman rambled on for nearly twenty minutes, then finally departed in one last burst of baritonal clichés, during which he also managed to forget Ann Grunwald's name and merely referred to her as "Harvey's beloved wife, mother of his dear departed kin." Still, this boring speech was not to be laughed at, if only because, Jeff realized, it had been entirely improvised. The Chairman had spoken without notes and without once faltering in his stately progression toward a close, in which one of his business chattels was portrayed as a prime mover not more than a notch or two below the eminence he himself occupied. Impressive, damned impressive, Jeff thought; the old bastard would never die, he'd just gradually wear away, like the eroded face of Mount Rushmore. It was quite a performance.

The service concluded with the return of the musicians and another burst of Mozart. As the quartet played, the crowd rose to leave. Outside it had begun to rain, a swirl of fine drops that speckled the conclave of press photographers and curiosity seekers gathered around the chapel's main entrance. Jeff allowed himself to flow with the emerging stream of mourners, then stepped aside to witness the last of the proceedings from the safety of a short flight of steps leading up into an adjoining brownstone. Moss, on his way downtown to a dental appointment, waved a quick goodbye and fought his way up toward Fifth and the possibility of a taxi. Jeff waited, unsure of his motives for lingering, and watched.

Tracy, clinging tightly to Whit's arm in the crush below, looked up and saw him. She waved and Jeff waved back. "Hey," she said to Whit, "there's Jeff."

Whit hardly glanced at her. "Tracy, I'm late."

"Wait a minute, I want to speak to him."

"What for?"

"He looks upset. He's a friend of Mr. Grunwald's, you know."

"Really?"

"Yes, really."

"Well, look, I have a lot to do. Do you want a lift?"

"No, thanks," she said. "You go ahead. I just want to say hello."

"See you tonight?"

"Yes."

"Call me later," he said. "I'll be in my office. I think I can get out early tonight."

She let him go with a quick peck on the cheek and then maneuvered herself up the steps toward Jeff. "Hi," she said, finally coming up beside him.

"Hello, Tracy."

"You OK?"

"Sure. Why, don't I look it?"

"No."

He smiled. "I guess I'm not too good at funerals."

"Did you know his wife and children as well?"

"Not at all, really." He paused, groping in his head for something meaningful to say and finding nothing. "I—I guess I just can't get over what's happened. I mean, it's incredible. His wife and best friends gone, then his kids and two hundred other people, all in the space of a few days. I thought I knew about disaster."

"Nobody knows, I suppose, until it hits him personally."

"You're right. We covered worse things in Vietnam, but they didn't happen to us. That's the difference. I've never lost anybody, really. My dad, but he took a long time to go and we were ready for it. Nothing like this."

"Anything new on what caused the crash?"

He shook his head. "Rumors about an explosion inside the plane," Jeff said. "But it was probably a mechanical failure of some kind, most likely. They just don't know. They're still investigating."

"I guess it takes a while."

"Yeah, it does."

"It was a nice service, I guess," she said, after a pause during which they watched the lingering crowd eddying gently about the chapel entrance. The people were waiting for the star attraction, and it reminded Jeff of the mobs that gathered outside stage doors or around the marquees of movie premieres, autograph books and flash cameras in hand. He had seen that sight a thousand times before, but this version of it made him slightly nauseous. "Nice service?" he echoed her words.

"The music, at least."

"Yeah, I guess. Where I come from, they know how to mourn. I'd have preferred a good Irish wake."

"Yes, there's something to be said for a formal service, isn't there? I mean, it has a structure, and the form sort of dictates events. This one just kind of petered out. It was a little odd. Ann must have been a wonderful woman."

"Harvey always thought so, she never did. She always called herself just an average person, so he named the boat after her, *Average Annie*."

"I wondered about that."

"Yeah, that was it."

A tightly knit phalanx of dark-suited security men now pushed out into the street, scattering a brushfire of photographers as it advanced. From where they stood, Jeff and Tracy glimpsed the Chairman's white head disappearing into a waiting Rolls Royce. Then they saw his pale, drawn face between the heavy shoulders and bull necks of the guards and watched him being swiftly hustled into a long black Cadillac limousine that seemed moored to the curb. The anchorman vanished inside it, and the machine drifted soundlessly out into the street. Tracy gasped.

"What is it?" Jeff asked.

"That man," she said. "The one who got into the car with Mr. Grunwald."

"What man?"

"You didn't see him?"

"No. Or if I did, I didn't notice him."

Tracy looked puzzled, as if surprised by her own spontaneous reaction. "I've seen him before."

"Where?"

"That night at the Casa Margherita, with you and Moss?"

"Yeah? What about it?"

"He was the one who—I told you, didn't I? The one who was being so strange."

Jeff smiled wanly. "You mean looking at you. That's not strange. You're lovely to look at, Tracy."

"It was more than that, Jeff. It was . . . sick."

The limousine had vanished across Madison Avenue, and the crowd below had begun to break up, its more impatient members already out into the middle of the avenue or heading over toward Fifth in search of taxis. "Where are you going?" Jeff asked.

"The office, but later."

"Me too. Want some lunch?"

"All right. Lead the way. Actually, I'm starved."

The stone steps were worn and uneven and she was wearing high heels. He took her by the arm to steady her as they descended toward the street. The feel of her went right to his core and made him tremble for her.

Crawford stood impassively on the corner of Fifty-ninth and Broadway, staring at the disappearing bulk of the long black limousine. The urge had grown very strong in him by now, but he had learned to discipline himself. He waited until the car had disappeared in the heavy traffic; then, oblivious of the rain pelting down and beginning to soak through the shoulders of his navy-blue pin-striped suit, he turned and began to walk briskly uptown. It had been easy, he told himself. It had all gone very well. Time now for a little R and R. He glanced at his watch and noted with satisfaction that he had at least an hour to prepare. Still, it wouldn't do to take chances. He hurried along, keeping close to the buildings.

At Eighty-eighth, he turned west toward the river. About halfway up the second block he glanced around, then ducked swiftly into a side entrance below the crumbling stone steps of a faded brownstone. Two sets of doors separated by a small barren foyer swung open to the touch of an electric beam from a pencil-thin flashlight. He stood for a moment in darkness, listening, after which he walked across the empty room to the closet where that morning he had left his makeup kit. Nothing moved in that heavy silence. Through the gloom he could make out the fourposter bed, but nothing else. He paused at the closet door and listened. He was safe here.

He picked up the small leather bag and eased himself back along the wall toward the bathroom door. Once inside at last, he turned on the light and stared at himself in the small cracked mirror. He smiled. Twenty minutes to go, plenty of time. He set the bag down on the stool under the towel rack, opened it, took out the yellow wig first and combed it, making sure the worst of the stray hairs had been realigned, then hung it from the radiator knob. He took off his jacket, shirt and necktie, then leaned forward, No. 8 pancake and sponge in hand, to begin the transformation necessary to the complicated routine he had in mind. The rage surged inside his head, beat against the back of his eyes. It threatened to crash through, but, sweating slightly, he was able to keep it in check. Even so, his fingers shook as he began the long careful strokes across his brow. . . .

"Ridley's ass!" Jeff exclaimed as he knocked over the coffee cup and the liquid spilled across the table. With wads of paper napkins, he and Tracy finally managed to soak up most of it. "Damn!"

She laughed. "It's all right," she said, "really."

He looked forlorn, a small boy caught again with mud on his shoes. "I sure am clumsy, what my Jewish friends call a regular klutz."

She leaned across the table and brushed crumbs from the lapels of his brown leather jacket. "You do need dusting occasionally," she observed. "If I had a vacuum cleaner, I'd run it over you a couple of times a day."

He grinned at her. "You're too nice to me, Tracy."

"Well, I think that probably, underneath that often difficult exterior," she said. "beats a heart of pure platinum."

"Hey, how you do talk, lady!"

They were sitting at a corner table by the window of a coffee shop on Madison and Eighty-second. They had been there for an hour, sipping coffee and talking. Or, rather, he had been talking and she listening. He had told her all about his time in Vietnam with Harvey and what it had meant to both of them and what Jeff felt now about his colleague. He had told her of his most recent hours spent in the company of his old friend and how badly it made him feel that he could do nothing more to help. It was frustrating and painful. As he talked, the rain outside had become heavier and water flowed down the city's dirty gutters in torrents. Pedestrians huddled in doorways or raced along the sidewalks, shielding themselves under newspapers, magazines, briefcases, handbags. The storm had come up suddenly, unpredicted by the forecasters, and it had caught everyone by surprise.

Tracy glanced at her watch. "Goodness, I've got to get to work!"

"This will die down in a few minutes," he said. "Let me get you a fresh cup." He signaled at the waiter, a sour gnome under an orange toupee that listed over one ear, and looked at Tracy. "I really enjoy talking to you, Tracy. You're a terrific listener. And I guess I owe you an apology for being such a shit. I guess you intimidated me or something."

She blushed, not knowing how to deal with his unexpected surrender. She was saved by the arrival of the surly gnome, who splashed coffee into their cups and shuffled back to his stand by the radio over the cash register, where he had been listening to what sounded like a German soap opera. "By the way, I wanted to ask you . . ."

"What?"

"This expression I've heard you use several times concerning someone's donkey."

"Ridley's ass?" Jeff laughed. "Oh, that goes back a ways. To my first job, in fact."

"Who was Ridley?"

"An old man who used to have a half-hour show every week on the local station up in Eureka, where I was sort of running things," Jeff explained. "I did everything, from emceeing to reporting to producing to sweeping up when we went off the air at midnight. It was great training. I learned just about all there was to learn about running a TV station and how the cameras worked, the whole thing. Anyway, we had this weekend fishing show where Ridley would come in and sit down at a desk and talk about fishing and what equipment to use and read his mail aloud, hot stuff like that. Ridley was his first name, Ridley Dunning. One day I had this medium close-up on him and I'd drifted off somewhere else, I forget why, but I was paying no attention. The old man decided to show a lure so he stood up, turned around and bent over. He was looking for this lure, see. The camera was focused on his butt. The director started screaming for me. And all the time we had this tremendous close-up of Ridley's ass. Ever since then, every time I screw up some way, I shout, 'Ridley's ass!'"

"So you really started behind a camera, didn't you?"

"No, I started as a reporter. After I found out about taking pictures, though, that was it for me. I didn't want to do anything else. It was a mistake, I guess."

"A mistake? Why? You're a wonderful cameraman. You're an artist. I've seen what you can do, Jeff. It's super, really."

"Nice of you to praise the peons, ma'am," he said, relapsing briefly into his standard defensive posture with her. "We sure do appreciate a kind word from the top every now and then."

"You're embarrassed by praise, aren't you? Why?" she asked.

"Why?"

"Yes," she continued, determined now to get to the bottom of the trouble between them. "Why? I know you're an artist and that you're more sensitive, I think, than most of the men I know. Why are you always so prickly with me?"

He hesitated before answering. Could he tell her the truth? That he felt himself to be a victim, like Moss, of social bigotry? He decided to try. He explained to Tracy, very matter-of-factly, very calmly, that in the world of TV, network news cameramen were very low in the pecking order. "We're blue-collar," he told her. "We don't get invited to the fancy parties, at least not through the front door. We're just assembly-line cogs in the corporate machine, Tracy." He told her about how, during the 1977 peace negotiations in the Mideast, he and Moss had shuttled back and forth between two cities in Egypt. "The network used two correspondents but only one crew. Moss and I were working twenty hours a day, going between Aswan and Cairo, the first serious peace talks. It never occurred to anyone in charge that we were getting pretty tired. We both came down with mummy tummy—"

"What's that?"

"The Mideast version of Montezuma's revenge."

"Oh."

"Moss and I got pretty sick. In fact, we wound up in a hospital in Cairo when it was over. That's typical of where we stand, Tracy. They'd never treat their correspondents that way, to say nothing of the least of their vice-presidents." He realized he was becoming a little overheated, which was not his usual style, so he broke off. "I guess this is pretty boring."

"It is not. I'm fascinated. I've learned more about you in this last half hour than the whole rest of the time we've known each other."

"Well, I guess that's why old Harvey and I are friends, see," he resumed. "When I worked with him in Vietnam, he was the only one who understood the true value of what I was trying to do, the only one of those big wheels who ever treated his crew as equals."

"Was Moss with you then?"

"Not in Vietnam. I worked with two guys. It was all film then, not tape. The sound guy caught a round in the gut two days before we left. He's dead. I'm glad it wasn't Moss."

"I am, too. He's a lovely man, isn't he?"

"The loveliest," he agreed with a laugh. "I'll tell him you said so."

"Don't you dare!" She glanced out the window again. "Hey, rain or no rain, mister . . ."

"I'll drop you off."

"Thanks."

He paid the gnome, left a dollar tip on the table and opened the door for her. The storm was showing signs of slowing down. He splashed out into the street, waving for a taxi. I'm in a mess, he told himself. If I don't look out, I'm going to fall for her. And she dates that prick Bridgeford. What in hell does she see in him?

He flagged down a cab and turned to usher her into it. She ran toward him through the rain, and his heart turned over for the second time that day.

"Mr. Reynolds? It's Penny, from the Service."

Crawford peered through the peephole, pressed a button in the wall and opened the door. The small blond woman with the overpainted face smiled up at him. "And this is Irma," she said, indicating the huge woman in the black pants suit standing at her side. "She's terrific."

"She'd better be," Crawford said, in a high nasal twang. "I pay enough."

Penny giggled. "I guess you do. Can we come in?"

He stepped aside and admitted them through the double sets of doors into the main room of the windowless basement flat. A single naked electric light bulb hung from a wire in the ceiling. The fourposter, its plain black arms upthrust like fists, cradled a soiled bare mattress. A single stiff-backed wooden chair faced the foot of the bed. The walls shed long scabs of peeling pink paint, and the worn floorboards creaked beneath the weight of their footsteps. The place was as empty of life as a monk's cell, but in it Crawford, even as the aging exquisite "Reynolds," felt completely at home. It reminded him pleasurably of the other empty rooms of his past, the tiny arenas where he had elicited from unwilling victims the secrets only torture could yield and worked out his private fantasies of subjugation and terror.

Penny smirked up at him. She knew; she had been here before. Irma looked around and croaked noncommittally.

"Please," Crawford said, seating himself in the chair. "You know what's required. Begin."

"It's OK?" Irma asked, in a deep baritone voice.

"Oh, yes," Penny said. "Like I told you, Irma, Mr. Reynolds is an old client of the Service. He's very discreet."

"Let's get on with it," Crawford lisped, waving a hand languidly at them, his eyes, however, as hard as stones beneath the frieze of blond curls. It was a fine disguise, even though he had begun to believe that Penny could catch glimpses of him through it. He would have to demand new flesh from the Service; they had plenty of girls, he knew that, in all categories. Only this one happened to enjoy her paid assignments; the working out of fantasies was clearly congenial to her temperament. Still, he would take no chances . . .

The big woman struck. A hard, backhanded blow that sent the girl reeling against the wall. Smiling slackly, Penny slid toward the floor, but the big woman now caught her by the hair and dragged her toward the bed. She quickly and methodically stripped her, flinging the girl's clothing behind her in a tumbled pile, then tied her by the wrists and ankles to the bedposts.

Crawford sighed. Penny's body had never failed to please him. It was thin, a bit too thin perhaps, but her breasts, swollen by silicone injections, were full and tilted invitingly upward. Tight, spiky little nipples, and a flat stomach above broad hips, long stringy thighs, all of her hairless, exposed, defenseless. "Take your time," he whispered. He enjoyed the preliminaries as much as the culminating action itself. The sight of the helpless human body of either sex nourished him like rain over a parched desert. "Take it slow and easy."

Irma knew her scene well. With cool, deliberate cruelty she prepared Penny, tugging brutally this way and that until the girl lay bound and helpless. Quivering in anticipation of the ordeal, she moaned softly. Slowly, Irma undressed, down to a spiked black leather belt from which hung a massive rubber dildo. Hands on hips, smiling, Irma stood over her victim. "You—you sweet little cunt," she whispered. "I'll make a woman of you yet."

Penny screamed and fought against the ropes. "Irma, please, no . . ."

"Nice, very nice," Crawford sighed. "So sweet, really."

The big woman began to play small games with her victim. The short, spiked rubber whip rose and fell, slashing welts of pain across naked flesh. Then at last she stood, victor over vanquished, and lowered herself carefully between the girl's open thighs, forcing an entrance that caused the victim to arch in pain and ecstasy, her body lashing orgasmically at the ropes cutting into her wrists and ankles.

Crawford picked up his chair and moved a few feet to the side to get a still better view of the proceedings. Now, at last, he felt himself begin to stiffen and his hand quested beneath his robe for his own sex. As he watched the crescendoing scene and stroked himself into joy, he was able at last to shut his eyes and give way to his most secret, most forbidden dreams. Yes. Someday soon again now, not paid help from an agency specializing in the bizarre, but the real thing, the authentic helpless victim. Oh, he would know what to do with her, all right. Not "Mr. Reynolds" this time, but Crawford, the eliciter of the screams that fill the night not with pleasure but with purest terror and pain. He hadn't been able recently to indulge that profound need, but one day, very soon, with someone, some-where . . . His semen spilled over his fingers and flooded stickily against the constraining silk of his gown.

Outside in the street, the rain had begun to fall again. A sudden clap of thunder exploded over them, but in the base-ment room below silence had encamped like a heavy fog.

Crawford stood up. "That's enough," he said. "You can go now."

9

WHITNER BRIDGEFORD found himself full of admiration for the clear, concise, forceful manner with which Sarah had analyzed the problem. Here it was only a week after the twin tragedies that had all but overwhelmed their top anchorman, and Sarah had already come up with a plan to exploit the situation. Hers, in fact, had been a breathtaking performance. He couldn't get over it, and he noticed that he was not alone in his admiration. Directly across the table from him, Clark Hadley's jaw had sagged open in disbelief, but then Whitner had never admired the cumbersome thought processes that characterized Hadley's running of the sports division. The guy was the classic ex-jock, though with a certain cunning about hanging on to his power base. Sarah, of course, like Whitner himself, was in a different class entirely, a greyhound among the slower-footed species.

Sarah's analysis and proposals had so far dominated the meeting. The regular Monday-morning affair included all of the network's top brass from news, entertainment, stations, sports and radio. Whitner himself and some of the other younger vice-presidents also attended these meetings regularly, though from the fringes of the action; they did not speak unless spoken to, even the most precocious among them. At the head of the long table sat the Chairman, his head thrust forward, fingers drumming rhythmically on the arms of his chair.

"I can't believe this," Clark Hadley was saying. "I mean, Sarah, how do you know the guy will be in any shape to deliver anything, after what he's been through?"

"Because, Clark," Sarah answered coolly, "I'm in touch with him every day. He's had a terrible shock and he's undergoing therapy, but he's assured me that he's anxious, even eager, to get back to work."

"God, that's wild," Hadley said. "I figured he might be out for months and you'd be stuck with Blanton or maybe have to move Bill James up."

"We won't have to, Clark."

"Fantastic!" Hadley beamed his approval. "That's just great! I guess I can understand how the old pro would want to come back to work, but so soon? Amazing! My hat's off to him."

"Yes. Of course, he'll have to take it easy. No public appearances, personal promotion, that kind of thing. Just the regular show."

"So what you're telling us, Sarah," Lee Olson, the head of radio, chimed in, "what you're assuring us is that Harvey's return to the air can be used as part of a nationwide campaign, is that right?"

Sarah nodded. "I've already roughed it out with the promotion and ad people," she said. "No one could be more upset than I am at the tragic events of the past two weeks, but I simply have to point out that we can't fail to take advantage of our one great piece of luck—the fact that Harvey's scheduled return to the air just happens to coincide with the first day of premiere week, the first day of the new fall program schedule. Harvey's tragedy has received an extraordinary amount of publicity. There isn't a person in this nation who hasn't heard about it and shared in Harvey's grief, and I'd say virtually *everyone* in the country will tune in to see him and to see what effect these events have had on him, *providing . . .*" Sarah paused. She gazed around the room, enjoying the dramatic moment she had so effectively created to emphasize the key point in her presentation. When she spoke again, she did so deliberately, slowly. "Providing they know exactly *when* Harvey will return."

Clark Hadley winced. He and several others had begun to realize what Sarah was driving at.

Sarah sensed Hadley's reaction and continued. "We didn't make this tragic situation with Harvey, but we'd be crazy no⁺ to take advantage of it. I'm suggesting that we immediately stop our promotional blitz for the new prime-time shows and devote a minimum of fifty percent of our promotion efforts to plugging Harvey's return."

"Jesus!" Hadley gasped. "You can't be serious, Sarah. What are you going to do, run ads saying, 'See Harvey Grunwald's grief! Will he be able to cope with the loss of his family? Tune in Monday at seven and find out!'? Christ, Sarah, this isn't the soaps. This is real life. Harvey's family really did die."

"Now, wait a minute, Clark," Sarah interrupted.

"I'm not finished yet, Sarah," Hadley answered. "Can you imagine what a field day the newspapers will have with us? I can see the TV critics' headlines now: 'ACN cashes in on anchorman's tragedy. Grunwald's family didn't die in vain, they died for the Nielsens.'"

Clark Hadley surveyed the gathering to assess the impact of his impassioned outburst. For fully a minute the only sound in the room was his heavy breathing.

Sarah waited until all eyes were once again fixed on her, then, looking straight at Hadley, she spoke with icy calmness. "Clark, sometimes your lack of imagination is truly stunning. Of course we wouldn't promote Harvey's return *directly*. The news division will prepare a high-powered series of special reports on some topic of general interest for Harvey to narrate, schedule the series to begin the day of Harvey's return, and promote Harvey's *reports*, not Harvey. The message will come through loud and clear, but the campaign will be above reproach. Won't it, Clark?"

Hadley sagged in his chair, faintly nodding his agreement. Sarah's cool effrontery and calculated cynicism were breathtaking, Whit realized, but her proposal did not shock him as it had Clark Hadley and two or three others in the room. In fact, it dazzled him by its simplicity and perfect sense. A week would be plenty of time to launch a terrific ad and promo campaign, one that would encompass every single one of the network's five owned and operated stations and one hundred ninety-three affiliates. For one whole week the nation would be primed to welcome its favorite anchorman back to the air. The program should easily top the Nielsen ratings that night, thus kicking off a premiere week to top all premiere weeks and perhaps leading ACN to a triumph in October, the crucial month in the fall ratings sweep.

As Sarah continued to outline her plans to her admiring colleagues, Whit's mind was racing ahead of her. Her interest in all this stuff about ratings was a bit peculiar, he realized. Traditionally, the news divisions of the major networks had always been scornful of the ratings picture, at least for the record; they had always tried to maintain a posture above the vulgar melee for points by which entertainment and sports, especially, lived and died. Why was Sarah so hot on this campaign? It had to be because she was playing for bigger stakes, Whit realized, perhaps the biggest. He glanced at the Chairman. The old man had not moved. He was listening intently, giving no sign of approval or disapproval, but his hooded eyes never wavered from Sarah's face.

"I propose," Sarah continued, "that we conclude this meeting so we can get to work on the five-part series Harvey will narrate for the regular evening newscasts next week. I think we can really capitalize on this situation. Larry?"

For a second or two, the old man did not stir. Then, at last, he nodded and his restless fingers disappeared into his lap as he sank back into his chair. "Excellent, Sarah," he said in a low, hoarse voice. "A splendid idea. Go to it."

Lee Olson clapped and others followed suit. Clark Hadley grinned a bit lopsidedly, as if he'd just taken a hit on the helmet from a charging linebacker, but he obviously went along. Sarah had carried the day. The network would fire off its biggest cannons from the news division. Incredible. But, Whit asked himself, what about those specials? Where were they coming from on such short notice?

Ten minutes after the meeting had broken up, Whit stopped by Sarah's office and stuck his head inside her open door. "Can we have lunch?" he asked. "I have an idea I want to try on you."

"Sorry, Whit, but I have a date," she answered, smiling. "Thanks, anyway. But I do want to see you. I just called your office, in fact. Come in and shut the door."

He stepped inside and sat down. The midday sun flashed against her windows, all but blinding him, so she reached back and pulled the curtains shut. The room basked in a comforting dim glow. She turned on her desk lamp and retreated behind its pool of reflected light.

"I thought what you said was terrific," he began.

"Thank you. It makes sense, doesn't it? I mean, it isn't really as if we're exploiting poor Harvey directly. I don't plan to refer to the tragedy in any way at all."

"I certainly didn't think so."

"Good. I guess I shocked Clark."

"He's easily shocked. Too many blows to the head, I think."

Sarah smiled. "Whit, about these specials . . ."

"That's what I wanted to discuss."

"Good. I think I see a way to use the Colombian drug stuff."

"I was hoping you'd say that. If you hadn't, I would have."

"How do we stand with it?"

"Well, Smalley came back with a lot more tape, some of it pretty good. The only trouble still is that we really have nothing that new. It's just that nobody's done anything on it recently."

"That's what I figured. You don't think we could make a full-scale documentary feature out of it?"

"We could try. We've got enough tape. But we'd be rehashing some already familiar themes, I'm afraid."

She nodded. "Then I see a way out."

"A way out?"

"For you, Whit. You have a cost factor here and a lot of barely usable tape. Am I right?"

"Yes," he answered softly, made wary by the casual manner in which she had already pinned the responsibility for the whole project directly on him. But then he'd expected that, hadn't he? He'd said as much to Tracy in bed the other morning. He waited, not anxiously but alertly, for her next words.

"Then we take the best of this stuff you have," she said, "we edit it into five tight little segments and we get Harvey to narrate. That way we have what I want to help promote Harvey's return to the air, and you're bailed out. Make sense?"

"It does to me." He smiled.

"Good. Then get on it. Arrange to run all the tape for me this afternoon. By Wednesday or Thursday morning at the latest we'll need at least a rough cut and a narration. Harvey can record over the weekend. Can you manage it?"

"You bet," he said.

"Then that's it," she said cheerfully. She waited until he had reached the door and opened it. "Oh, and Whit?"

"Yes?"

"Thanks," she said. "You've been a great help. I won't forget this."

He left her office in a triumphant glow of pleasure. Yes, he told himself, I thought I'd made the right move to come here, I was sure of it.

"Why don't you come with me?" Jeff asked.

"When? Now?"

"Tomorrow. Or the day after. I can wait a day."

"I can't, Jeff."

"Why not? Do you want to or not?"

"I don't know. I'm not sure."

"It's not Whitley still, is it?"

"No," Tracy answered truthfully. "No, it's not. I haven't even seen him, he's so busy. And he hasn't called."

"Tracy, level with me. You're not in love with him, are you?"

"No, I don't think so. I'm—I'm fond of him."

"*Fond*. Oh, God, what a killer word that is! *Fond!* Please don't ever tell me you're fond of me, all right?"

"I promise."

"I don't understand what you see in him, anyway. Maybe someday you'll explain it to me."

She smiled. "No, I don't think so, Jeff."

"Why not? I'd sure like to know."

"Well, if you must know, he's—well, he's beautiful."

Jeff stared at her in amazement. "Whitlow? Beautiful?"

She nodded emphatically. "I'm afraid so. He has a body like a Greek statue."

Jeff groaned and fell back full length upon his couch.

"Well, you asked," she said. "I'm sorry."

Stunned, he lay back for a minute or two and stared hopelessly at the ceiling. He had spent this whole evening maneuvering to get her up to his apartment, he had even kissed her twice, he had asked her to go away with him on his vacation, and now this. Beautiful! Oh, God! He groaned again and flung a protective arm over his face.

She got up from her chair facing him, walked across the room and sat down on the floor beside him. "Jeff," she whispered, "please . . ."

He propped himself up on one elbow and stared down at her. "Beautiful. You think that mealymouthed Ivy League pup is beautiful? Oh, Tracy . . ."

"Not him," she tried to explain, "not as a person. His body, his physique—that's what's lovely. He looks a little like the *Discus Thrower* by Praxiteles. Ever see it?"

"No."

"Well, he does."

"To get that good a view you'd have had to think some other part of him was sensational, too, right?"

"Wrong. We went to a beach party together over Fourth of July weekend, OK? We wore bathing suits. When Whit ran into the water and dove through the surf he looked, I remember, like an Indian or one of those copper-colored young men who fling themselves off the cliffs in Acapulco. He was, purely and simply, spectacular-looking. I was, well, overwhelmed."

"Listen, Tracy," Jeff said, "I'm sorry I asked you to come away with me."

"Why are you sorry? Don't be sorry. It's not that I don't want to."

"Because of Whitby the Beautiful."

"No, not because of Whit," she said, refusing to acknowledge his persistent mutilation of Whitner's name. "It's not that at all. We had a thing. I think it's over."

"It is?"

"Yes, I think so."

"Does he know that?"

"I don't think he cares all that much. He's very busy these days with his career."

"I had that feeling about him, all right."

"What feeling?"

"Young, ambitious executive producer on the make. Was I wrong?"

She shook her head and smiled wanly. "No, I don't think so. He hasn't time for anyone in his life these days."

Suddenly, on impulse, he put his hand behind her head and pulled her toward him. This kiss was not like the others. She responded with ardor, opening her warm lips to his tongue, and when it was over he blinked at her in astonishment. She stood up and looked down at him.

"Come on," she said.

He sat up. "Where are we going?"

"You do have a bedroom, don't you?"

"Tracy, what is this?"

"What is what?"

"I don't know. I feel like a reclamation project or something. I mean, don't do this if you don't want to."

"Don't be silly, Campbell," she said. "Don't you know I know you've been trying to get me into bed for weeks now? Well, here's your chance, you big goof."

She walked briskly into the bedroom. He sat there for a moment, amazed by this development. By the time he reached his bedroom door, she had already pulled his covers back and had begun to undress. He gaped at her, unable to make a move. Finally, naked, she walked up to him, stretched her long, cool body up against him, and kissed him again. "Come on," she whispered. "Whatever else I may be, I'm not a tease. Don't you want me?"

"Yes. God, yes!" The blood pounded at the back of his brain. In a frenzy of excitement now, he tore himself out of his clothes and fell upon her, his hands all over her, wanting to touch every part of her, to make love to every molecule.

"Hey," she whispered, "take it easy."

He tried to but couldn't. She had given herself to him so unexpectedly that he had had no time to prepare. He was like a small orphan boy upon whom the world had suddenly showered a fortune in gold, and he squandered his treasure recklessly. She had a skin like silk, unblemished and cool to his fevered touch. Her stomach was flat and her breasts small, perfectly shaped. Her shoulders were large for the rest of her, and long, slender arms folded themselves about him, pressed him down upon her. Her thighs and calves were strong, the long, lean legs of an athlete, and they cradled the tufted arch of her pubic mound like columns supporting a partly concealed nest. She cried out when he penetrated her, partly in pain at his haste, partly in pleasure. Her open legs locked themselves behind his and she thrust up against him. He heaved himself up on his arms to gaze down at her and she stared back at him from smoky hazel eyes half hidden by long dark lashes. Her lips, slightly parted, revealed a glimpse of icy-white teeth through the roaring haze that now almost made him go blind with desire.

"Don't move," he whispered, "please."

"Why not?"

"Because . . . oh, God . . ."

She could not help herself about moving, and it probably wouldn't have done any good anyway. All she did was raise herself to meet him so that, as open as she could be to him, he would be able to fill her completely. But he couldn't take it. With a thrust as much of anguish and embarrassment as of pure desire for her, he came, borne past all barriers, all careful restraints on a surging sea of helpless rapture, like a surfer plunging to his death from the crest of a huge rolling wave challenging the final, fatal pull of gravity. He lay upon her in anguish, motionless, spent.

"I'm sorry," he whispered. "I'm so sorry."

Her arms were around him, her legs still locked behind his. "Don't be, please," she said. "It was fine. Really."

"How can you say that?"

"Jeff, darling, please don't talk technique to me, all right?

What does it matter?" she said, smiling as she continued to hold him. "I'm flattered. Honestly."

"Yeah," he admitted. "I wanted you too much, I guess. I just wasn't ready. I didn't think—"

"Please stop explaining. Please."

He did. They lay together in silence, not daring to move at first. Then, very gently, he rolled over on his side, continuing to hold her, her right leg flung over him, her face pressed against his. He kissed her again and felt himself begin to stiffen a second time for her, but he dared not break the spell. Very gently he inserted himself into her and they made love a second time this way, moving against each other as in a dream, as if, weightless, they were afloat in a soft, salty sea under a warm tropical sun. She came, too, this time, with a small whimper of pleasure that frightened him because he felt so solicitous of her well-being, so anxious to please her now in every tiny nuance of the rhythm their bodies had established so unexpectedly upon his now rumpled sheets. When it was over at last, he turned her so that he could enfold her within the curve of his body, feeling the long smooth plain of her back against his chest, the gentle flow of her hair brushed back against his cheek and mouth.

"You're beautiful," she whispered.

"Oh, Tracy . . ."

"You are."

"I don't have a body like a Greek statue. Knock it off," he whispered. "I'm more of a comic-strip character. Bugs Bunny, maybe, or Elmer Fudd."

She laughed in the darkness. "Spiderman," she said. "You're hairy enough."

"Well, I make up for you. Your skin is like satin. You're a living, breathing miracle to me." He pulled her in more tightly to him. "Come on, run away with me to California for a week."

"Oh, Jeff, I can't. I'd love to, but I can't. Not right now."

Over a drink late that night they discussed their situation. He wanted to pin it down, to nail it in place so that, even in absence from her, he would know she would be there for him. His attitude surprised both of them, because he had always had a well-merited reputation around town for easy-come, easy-go relationships.

"I don't know why I'm talking like this to you," he tried to explain. "I guess it's because I don't want you to feel you don't mean anything to me."

"Don't you think I know that?" she replied. "But it's too soon, Jeff. I'm just a little confused now, you see. And I'm so new at this job, too. I really want to have a career in TV news and I'm just starting out, I'm learning so much every day. I can't ask for time off now to go away with you."

"It's only a week."

"I know. But you're going home on a visit. You've got family—"

"Just my brother."

"—you've got friends. I'd just be in the way."

"No, you wouldn't."

"And I'll be here when you get back."

He looked at her like a small boy about to be sent off for the first time to boarding school or summer camp. "I guess I'm scared."

"Of what?"

"That I'll come back and find you all involved again with Whitner, the famous Greek statue."

She laughed and kissed him. "What do you think I am? A regular tramp? Anyway, we're making some progress."

"In what way, lady?"

"At least you got his name right. You don't have to put him down anymore by pretending you don't know it."

Jeff grinned. "Maybe I'm not afraid of him anymore."

She leaned into him and kissed him again, but lightly this time, the peck of an affectionate older sister. "You're learning," she murmured.

"Don't patronize me, woman," he said, in mock outrage.

"Oh, shut up, you big hick, and kiss me."

Together they sank again into his bed, and the music of their lovemaking kept them enthralled until early dawn, when they finally went to sleep in each other's arms.

Jeff missed Harvey Grunwald's return to the ACN evening news. He had gone fishing with old friends and got back too late, but he called Tracy late that night and she told him all about it.

"He looked wonderful," she said, "completely his old self. And I hear the show was an enormous success."

"That's great. And how are you, Tracy?"

"I'm fine." A pause. "Whit called me today. He asked me out to dinner tomorrow night."

"That's not so great."

"It's only a dinner. Besides, that way I can tell him."

"About what? Us?"

"No, not necessarily. Just that I'm fond of him—"

Jeff groaned. "That deadly word again."

"—but that I can't see him anymore. At least not on the old terms."

"Promise me one thing," Jeff asked.

"What?"

"That you won't meet him someplace where he can take his shirt off."

"Jeff!"

"I know about you and those old Greeks."

"Are you having fun?"

"I cry myself to sleep every night. Why aren't you here?"

"I'm glad to hear you miss me. Oddly enough, I miss you." She added that she would pick him up at the airport Sunday night. "You *are* coming back Sunday night?"

"Yeah, you bet. Say, if you see Harvey—"

"How would I see him?"

"Well, send him a message for me, will you?"

"Oh, sure."

"Tell him hello and congratulations and that I'll give him a call when I get back, OK?"

"Yes. But I don't think he's living in town. He's out in the country someplace."

"Ask Sarah Anderson's secretary, Paul Haber. He'll know."

"All right."

"Take care of yourself, honey."

"Jeff!"

"What?"

"Tracy, my name is Tracy. Definitely *not* honey."

Jeff groaned. "Godamighty, but you uppity career women will be the death of me yet."

"I doubt that very much. Goodbye, Jeffrey. I'll tell Whit you asked about him."

He started to protest, but she had gone. He stared at the silent receiver in his hand, smiled and slowly hung up.

He spent the next three days hiking and camping out in the mountains north of town with his brother and two pals from high-school days, so it wasn't until Friday night that he was able to catch the seven-o'clock ACN news. He was immediately fascinated by Harvey's appearance on screen; as Tracy had told him, his old friend looked wonderful. Jeff could detect a few traces of distress, of pain, in his face, but otherwise the anchorman looked great—seemingly younger, more magnetic than ever. The ordeal he had been through had given him added weight in the form of wisdom, compassion. His grief, Jeff thought, became him.

It was only toward the end of the broadcast, when Harvey was delivering his closing lines, that Jeff thought he noticed something a little different about him. But he couldn't quite pin it down. What had it been? Nothing, really. A slight coarsening of Harvey's usually smooth delivery? Something about the way his hand moved as he reached for papers on his desk? A certain stolidity in his movements as a whole that hadn't been there before? What? Jeff wasn't sure. Maybe Harvey was on medication of some kind, Jeff reflected. Very probably, considering what he'd been through and the tension attendant upon his return to work. Or perhaps he'd merely imagined it, Jeff told himself. Anyway, it was great to have the old man back on the air, he thought, as Harvey's benign, careworn features faded from the screen.

It wasn't until he was on the plane out of San Francisco the following Sunday that Jeff learned exactly how terrific Harvey's return to the air had been. While idly skimming the entertainment section of the *San Francisco Chronicle*, he came across an AP story on the week's TV ratings. The ACN evening news anchored by Harvey had garnered a 56 in the Nielsens that first night, five times the usual *ACN News* audience. Fifty-six percent of all the sets in America had been tuned in to ACN at that time, a rating comparable to that achieved for such spectacles as the Superbowl. It had been the highest-rated program in the history of the network.

Jeff was astonished. It made you wonder, didn't it, about certain ghoulish human factors involving the reasons why people turn on their TV sets in this great big country of ours. Still, it was nice, really nice, to have Harvey back, and in such good shape, after the ordeals he had been through. He was a remarkable man, Jeff reflected, no doubt about that.

REFERENCE: MYRMIDON—Positron Emission Transaxial Tomography results are dazzling. Such clarity! New full-color display is a vast improvement. Tritium injections are better when pulsed over an extended period. Subject refusal rate only ten percent. In sum, research end continues to be extremely successful as we corrolate new data with basic polygraph results. Insights amazing.

Master program complete success.

—From the Journal of Dr. Jerome Lillienthal

10

"I DON'T UNDERSTAND it," Jeff said.

"What?"

"This note." He handed it to Tracy, who was sitting cross-legged on his couch in panties and one of his shirts, open at the collar, sleeves rolled up above her elbows. She had been leafing through a lot of his early stuff, mainly blowups of stills from his California days, while he made breakfast. "It came yesterday," he continued. "I found it with my mail when we got in late last night, but I didn't read it. I wasn't reading anything last night, lady, except you. By the Braille method, as you may recall. Was I too pushy?"

"Yes, thank goodness." She held the letter delicately in her left hand while with her right one she took the steaming cup of coffee he proffered from the kitchen doorway. "Ah," she said, "and about time. I was beginning to sag." She eyed the typewritten note. "It seems clear enough to me. It says he can't see you or anyone, for a while."

"Yeah, Tracy, I got that part of it, all right. You want one egg or two?"

"Two. Over lightly, please. I'm starved. Do you have any Worcestershire?"

"I guess so."

"Put some Worcestershire on them. Just a few drops, while they're cooking."

"You sure are fussy, lady. Toast?"

She nodded. "Please don't burn it. And lots of butter and jam."

"Listen, what do you think this is? The Ritz or something?"

"Something."

She eyed the note again and sipped her coffee. A warm September breeze blew in through the open windows and ruffled her dark hair. He glanced at her from the kitchen and thought he had never seen anything so lovely as the sight of her sitting there, bare-legged and slightly disheveled, on his shabby old sofa, the survivor of more small disasters than he cared to recall just then.

"What's bothering you?" she asked.

"Read it aloud."

She did so, slowly and carefully, as he cooked the eggs: "'Dear Jeff, I'm really grateful for your concern, but I simply don't feel up to seeing anyone just now. Eventually we'll get together again, I'm sure, just as in the old days, but at the moment all I desire is absolute privacy. My work is all that is keeping me going at the moment and I'm under doctor's orders. I know you will understand and respect my feelings. Sincerely, Harvey.'" She looked up at Jeff as she finished. "Well, what's the matter with that?" she asked.

"I don't know," he said. "It doesn't sound like him."

"It was dictated, obviously. That would tend to dispell the human touch. Is that it?"

"I suppose so." Jeff frowned, but he said nothing more as he expertly flipped the cooked eggs onto a plate, buttered and spread jam on the toast, then set the feast down on her lap. "There you go."

"*Merci, monsieur.* You will win your third star this morning. *Tu es vraiment agréable.*"

"Huh?"

"Skip it." She dropped the letter on the couch beside her. "More coffee, please."

He refilled her cup and grinned at her. "Is it all right if I eat with you?" he asked. "I mean, do we get to hobnob with the white folks?"

"Moss, yes. You, well—just this once. It's a special occasion."

"It is?"

"Yes. It's our first full-length overnight. How soon they forget!"

Jeff groaned. "I did it again. I'm just a loose-as-a-goose no-manners old country boy. Sorry. I should have had a plaque put up or something."

"A kiss will do."

He leaned over and kissed her hard and lovingly. He immediately felt stirrings for her but resisted them. Breakfast first, then maybe . . . "Love in the morning," he said. "I could get to like this quite a lot."

"Look, this letter from Harvey—what is it, really?"

He slumped into the armchair opposite her, cradling his coffee cup on his stomach and staring glumly at her. "Dictated or not, it still doesn't sound like him. That 'all I desire' part and the 'sincerely' at the end. That's not like Harvey."

"Could be the dictation, couldn't it?"

"Sure. But that's not all. That stuff about getting together again like in the old days . . ."

"Yes? Well?"

"We never used to get together at all," Jeff said. "We worked together in Vietnam, as you know, but back here I saw very little of him. We're in different worlds. The first day I spent any time with him at all was when this thing happened with the boat and Ann and all. So why the reference to getting together again?"

"I think you're making too much of it," she answered. "I mean, it doesn't seem all that strange to me. He did see you recently, after his wife died, so he made that connection. He probably didn't even reread this note, just dictated it from his office."

"What office?" Jeff asked. "Nobody's seen him."

"He's out in the country somewhere, isn't he? That's what I heard."

"Yeah, but not out at Montauk, where he and Ann used to go. They kept the boat out there and they also had a cottage on the beach they'd bought years ago. I checked."

"You wrote him again?"

"After I couldn't get him on the phone, yeah. I dropped the note off at his apartment. The doorman there said he hadn't seen him, either, but that they came every day from the office to pick up his mail. He was sure he'd get the note, all right."

"And he did, obviously."

"Yeah."

"You don't seem convinced."

"I'm not. There's something a little off."

"Like what? Just the language of the note?"

Jeff nodded. "That and a few other things. Tracy, *nobody's* seen Harvey since the funeral, nearly three weeks ago now. If you ask around about him, you get told he's too grief-stricken even to think about appearing anywhere in public. Everybody in the executive offices says the exact same thing. Including the Greek god, by the way."

"So?"

"So it's like they're all parroting instructions from on high."

"They probably are."

"Yeah, I guess." He slumped even lower into the chair and looked glum.

"You're funny," she said.

"In what way am I funny?"

"You're so suspicious. You'd have made a great detective."

He smiled. "Yeah, sure. Sherlock Campbell. Maybe I'm getting paranoid or something, I don't know. You stay around the news game long enough, you could become a regular psychotic."

"Why don't you ask Sarah Anderson about Harvey? Surely she knows where he is and what's going on, if anybody does."

"Yeah, I *will* ask her."

"I'm sure she'll tell you what she can."

"You're right, you're right."

"You still don't seem convinced."

"It's my famous photographer's nosiness, I guess," he explained. "See, there was a time back there in Vietnam when old

Harv and I really did see a lot of each other. Force of circumstance and all, but it sure made us close. We used to talk a lot, pretty much about everything. I *know* the guy, Tracy, and I know he's not the sort to run and hide when things get rough. He sure as hell wouldn't sublimate whatever he really feels by locking himself up somewhere and hiding between broadcasts. It's not like him. He was never a public guy, but he wasn't so crazy about being the highest-paid mike stand in the business that he'd retreat only into his work and not see anybody. I mean, he'd be more likely to take a long leave of absence or something and go on a trip somewhere. Anyway, there must be somebody who's in touch with him directly, and maybe, like you suggest, it's Sarah Anderson. I *will* ask her about it, on Monday."

Very deliberately, Tracy shifted the plate off her lap and set her nearly empty cup down on the floor. "You're quite spectacular-looking, you know, when you get intense about something," she said. "I noticed it that very first day, when you and Moss let me cover that fire in the Bronx with you."

"Tracy, damn it—"

"Come here," she said, "I'm lonely. I want you to kiss me again."

"You've got that look in your eye, all right," he said, feeling the heat rise as he gazed at her. "I thought we were going to the Met this morning? Don't you want to see the Adams retrospective—"

"I want to make love to you," she said. "Very slowly, very tenderly, and with true compassion."

"Stop talking, Tracy," he said. "I don't understand half of what you say. You're overeducated, lady."

He picked her up, kissed her and carried her slowly into the bedroom, where they made love, with great delicacy and concern for each other, the rest of the morning and then fell asleep again in each other's arms. They never made the Adams show at the Met.

Sympathetic, understanding, Sarah Anderson sat behind her desk and heard Jeff out. The cameraman was nervous. He shifted from side to side as he talked. Even as he spoke the words, he realized that the whole thing sounded preposterous. That was a word Tracy liked to use. Anyway, it must have struck Sarah Anderson as silly, but he was grateful that she had consented at least to listen to him.

When he had finished, she merely sighed and said, "Oh, dear. I was afraid this might happen."

"What might happen, Mrs. Anderson?" Jeff asked, feeling foolish.

"Please call me Sarah, Jeff. And do sit down."

"It's OK. I've got to go in a minute. But what do you mean, about what might happen?"

"Well, when Harvey insisted on absolute privacy, we agreed to go along, of course," she explained. "However, I did warn him."

"About what?"

"That his friends and colleagues would want to get in touch with him. At first he simply wanted to get away from everyone and everything, take a whole year's leave of absence. Of course we argued against that—it would have been disastrous to lose him for that long, he's essential to our success here—and so he agreed to come back this soon. It was a great coup for us. You've seen the ratings?"

Jeff nodded. "Yeah. Read it in the paper."

"Well, it's been incredible. But to get Harvey to come back at all, we had to agree to his rather peculiar conditions."

"Peculiar?"

"Yes. He doesn't want to see or talk to anybody. We've had to make the most incredible security arrangements. It's flabbergasting. Someday, I'll be able to tell you about them. Or he will himself, I hope."

"Where is he?"

"I can't even tell you that. Except that he's out of the city."

"But somebody sees him—"

"Well, I do, of course, but hardly ever. And not at all for the past week. Mainly we talk on the phone, several times a day. Everything for his broadcast gets routed through this office. But the only people who see him at all are his doctor and the security people we have guarding him."

"Guarding him? From what?"

Sarah put a hand briefly over her eyes, as if to banish an unwelcome vision, and sighed resignedly. "These media stars," she murmured. "Oh, dear . . ."

"I'm sorry, Sarah, but I just don't get it."

"Harvey's having a breakdown," she said at last. "I guess that's really what this is all about. He functions all right, up to a point, but he's firmly convinced somebody's out to get him. You can't reason with him about it, either."

"Get him? But why? How?"

"Don't ask me, Jeff. Ask his doctor. Harvey is absolutely convinced that his boat exploding *and* the plane crash were not accidents. He believes the tragedies were caused by deliberate sabotage. And he's convinced they're out to kill him next."

"They? Who?"

She shrugged and smiled wanly at him. "I haven't the faintest idea."

"He hasn't told you?"

"No, or anyone, as far as I know."

"Why would anybody want to kill him? And if somebody did, why go to all the trouble of blowing up a yacht and then sabotaging an airplane full of innocent people? It doesn't make sense."

"Of course not. Paranoids don't talk sense, Jeff. And the investigations have already proved these were accidents. What else *could* they be?"

"But he must have mentioned somebody, or some reason?"

"Oh, an international conspiracy of some kind to alert the world to the imperialist menace by eliminating the lying jackals of the so-called democratic press, that kind of thing, I suspect."

"Actually, when you think about it, you can see how the sequence of tragedies might trigger that kind of response," Jeff said.

"Right now, all we can do is humor Harvey and hope he stays together at least while he's on the air. What I'm really afraid of is that he'll flip out on us some night and start ranting and raving on camera. Of course, he's heavily sedated and it's not likely to happen. But we're ready for it. We can push a button and turn him off instantly if he cracks on us."

"It's weird," Jeff said.

"Amen."

"I mean, he's so cool on the show."

"I think it's a relief to him. I know he regards it as a challenge. They want him off the air, so he'll show *them*."

"Boy, what a mess!"

"You bet it is, Jeff," Sarah agreed. "You can understand our concern, can't you?"

"Sure."

"We can't have this getting out. I hope we can count on you."

"Of course. But there's nothing I can do? Maybe if I could talk to him—"

"That's out of the question, I'm afraid," she interrupted him. "Quite impossible, in his present state of mind." She got up, came around from behind her desk, put a warm, strong hand on his arm and gazed intently into his eyes. "Jeff, you're the only person outside of the few of us involved here who knows anything about Harvey's real condition. You must promise me you won't say anything to anyone, please. There's a lot at stake here, including Harvey's sanity."

"Sure, I understand," Jeff said. "It's funny. He looks so healthy and completely himself on the show."

"Yes, that's the bizarre part of it," Sarah agreed. "But before and after, he's a wreck. Do you know that three days ago he cracked up the second after he went off camera? They had to give him a shot and put him out for over an hour, the poor man."

Jeff shook his head. "It *is* incredible. You see him on the screen . . ."

"I know, I know," she said. "He's wonderfully made up, of course, and he's stabilized with drugs. Well . . ."

The door opened and young Paul Haber stuck his head into the room. "Mrs. Anderson, Mr. Hoenig just called. He wants you to call him back as soon as you're through."

"Yes. Thank you, Paul." She smiled at Jeff. "You'll excuse me, please?"

"Oh. Yeah, of course." Had he jumped or what? The idea of Harvey tiptoeing along the edge of the abyss even as the ratings soared had suddenly transfixed Jeff, as if he'd been forced to watch a man going cheerfully to his death by a public firing squad. *Christ, what if he did crack up on the air some night, as Sarah Anderson feared he might?* Jeff mumbled something, turned and left the room.

Why did he care so much? he asked himself on his way back to the newsroom. Why was he so obsessed with old Harvey? Jeff struggled to find the source of his compulsion. Was he really being driven by selfish motives? Did he think deep down that by helping Harvey he would one day benefit from that powerful man's gratitude? No, Jeff could honestly tell himself he wasn't being driven by thoughts of personal gain. It was something larger, something he couldn't quite define.

As he entered the newsroom, Jeff looked at Bellucci hunched over the assignment desk, awash in human misery. Accidents, fires, murders and worse were surfacing through his radios and telephones. Jeff froze. Suddenly it came to him. For most of his adult life he had been a detached observer of human tragedy, documenting it with his camera but never being touched by it. After all, he had told himself many times, the simple act of photographing misery tended to cure it by focusing public attention on the problem. But over the years that rationalization had worn thinner and thinner as he covered the same poverty, the same fires, the same murders, the same accidents again and again.

Now Jeff Campbell had felt the sting of tragedy through a friend, had seen the horror of absolute loss in a face he knew, and felt it in a hand he held. For the first time in his life, Jeff had become *involved*. Harvey needed help. Jeff was determined, absolutely determined, not to let him down.

"Hey, Moss, is it true Vicki's been bitching about our stuff?" Jeff asked his partner later that night as he rounded the corner from the men's room.

"Yeah," Moss said. "She's been editing the tape we brought in on the Central Park killing. It's X-rated and she's trying to clean it up, but there's not much she can use on a family station. Stick your head inside if you want to calm her down."

"Too much gore to clean up," Jeff said. "Whoever killed that poor old lady sure did a job on her. Just about tore her in pieces. Mario good-nighted us yet?"

"Naw," Moss said, slumping against the soft-drink machine. "He's on a tear tonight. Things have been so dull the last couple of days, old Bellucci thinks it's our fault. Like we're goofing off or something. And now he's mad because we came in with stuff so raunchy they can't put it on the air. Santini told me today that he and his partner were put on hold here till after midnight last night. And you just back from vacation and all, why, old Mario's liable to keep us around till dawn."

"How come he's working the night shift?"

"Windom's sick in bed with a virus. Mario's working double time."

"Jesus," Jeff said, "that'll make him even crazier than he usually is."

He stuck his head around the corner and peered into the newsroom. It was nearly seven-thirty and the place had emptied out for the dinner hour. Only Bellucci remained, slumped at his desk as if hypnotized by the bright-red lines of the police-frequency scanners. He looked asleep. Above the sea of empty desks the silent monitor screens reflected the cheerful, smiling face of Harvey Grunwald signing off with the closing human-interest story that punctuated all of his broadcasts. The man looked serene, confident; he talked smoothly and uninterrupt-edly from his perch at what looked like an antique desk, perhaps of French design. Funny he hadn't noticed that touch before, Jeff thought, or was it new? Behind the anchorman's smiling countenance, rows of crowded bookshelves seemed to soar to the ceiling. Harvey was obviously broadcasting from a private library or living room somewhere. But where?

Jeff turned back to his partner. "Moss, don't wake Mario up," he said, "or the sonofabitch will send us off on some cock-amamie disaster story out in Bedford-Stuyvesant. I'm going downstairs."

"Hey, Jeff, what if something comes in?" Moss asked. "We're the only crew around."

"I'll be right back," Jeff said, heading now for the elevators. "And if Vicki gets through before I'm back, tell her I'm sorry about all that blood. People just don't kill cleanly anymore."

"Oh, yeah, I'll tell her," Moss said sarcastically. "Hey, where are you going?"

"Private business, Moss. Something I want to do for Tracy," Jeff improvised. "OK?"

Moss smiled. "Oh, I dig. Listen, you remember what old Satchel Paige used to say," he called out after Jeff's retreating back. "'Don't look back, 'cause somethin' might be gainin' on you!'"

Jeff escaped into an elevator that whisked him down to the ground floor. Tom Laverty, the security guard on duty, saw him and nodded. He was a heavyset middle-aged man who seemed about to explode out of his blue-and-gold uniform. He presided over a small desk between velvet-rope barriers designed to keep the general public and all unauthorized persons from gaining access to the ACN studios and offices without proper identification or visitors' passes. Two guards manned this post during the day, but at night one sufficed. Beyond the area, the now empty, silent, semidarkened corridors of the building led toward the avenue and the side streets, the latter two exits locked from the outside after seven.

Jeff passed Laverty's post, then turned back as if he'd forgotten something. "Tom," he said, "has anyone from the seven-o'clock news team been by here yet?"

The guard looked up from his horror comic book and stared blankly at the cameraman. "Nope," he said, "but it's a little early, ain't it?"

"I wanted to get a message to Mr. Grunwald. Do you know who might handle that?"

The guard shook his head. "All I know is that everything at our end is routed through Mrs. Anderson's office."

"Paul Haber, her secretary?"

"I guess so. You know Mr. Grunwald ain't in the building?"

"Yes, I guessed that. None of the engineers I know are assigned to his part of the broadcast."

"All I ever seen from here is the regular news guys and the tech people and that's about it."

"You have any idea who's working the show? I mean, from wherever Grunwald is broadcasting?"

"I sure don't."

"Who's on the side entrances these days?" Jeff asked, knowing that Harvey's limousine always used to pick him up on the uptown side.

"No one these days," Laverty answered. "Why don't you give Marie Vecchi a call? She's in the office on the third floor. She might know something."

"Thanks, I will."

Jeff ran out to the street, came back with an early edition of the *Times*, then took the elevator up to the third floor. He found Marie Vecchi at her desk in the small, windowless security office opposite the landing. A tall, rugged-looking gray-haired woman in her early forties, the ruin of a once attractive female, she had her long varicose-veined legs propped up on a desk as she sipped coffee from a Styrofoam cup and glanced idly from time to time at the monitors providing slightly blurred black-and-white views of empty office corridors. A soiled, rumpled paperback romance lay open in her lap, and her gun belt dangled over the back of her chair.

She smiled when she saw Jeff. "Hey, good-looking, what's happening?"

"You look cozy in here, Marie," Jeff said. "What's happening is, I've got a problem."

"Shoot," the woman said, swinging her legs to the floor and taking another gulp of her coffee. "What did they steal this time?"

"My new Sony portable tape deck," Jeff said. "I left it on the counter in the lab for two minutes and it got snatched. I think I know who did it."

"One of those spics from the mailroom," Marie Vecchi said. "They'd steal your fucking teeth if you yawned in their faces."

"Yeah, I know it was an inside job. I'm working late tonight, but when I get off I'd like to make a search. I need a passkey."

"I can't do that, baby. But I can come with you." She smiled wickedly at him. "Just come by when you get off. I'm here till six A.M. That ought to give us enough time. Where do you want to look? They got great couches up on the executive floors, almost like beds. You want to fool around?"

"Marie, honey," Jeff protested. "What about my reputation?"

"What about it? I hear you've got a big cock."

"Hey, Marie, is that any way for a nice lady cop to talk? Especially to a civilian?"

The woman roared with laughter. "Well, you want a favor, my old man used to say one hand washes the other. That's in the old country."

"Don't you get enough at home?"

"Never enough. My husband couldn't get it up with a crank."

"You keep talking tough to him like you do to me, it could fall off," Jeff said.

Marie laughed again. "You're all right, Campbell, for a fag photographer. Come by when you're off. We'll look wherever you want."

"I think I know where it might be," he said. "In TOPS. Somebody saw a kid run in there earlier with a tape deck just like mine and run out again empty-handed. He's probably stashed it in there and figures he'll smuggle it out tomorrow."

"OK, come back and we'll look around, or I'll get one of the roving guards to take you. But I'd sure like to handle it myself," she said, grinning at him like a sex-crazed gargoyle. "I'll bet you're a terrific lay."

By the time Jeff got back to the newsroom, Bellucci had begun to bellow like a musk ox in heat. There was a four-alarmer in Greenwich Village, in some Italian restaurant where the week before a Mafia hood had been gunned down over his vermicelli. Jeff and Moss didn't wait to hear Bellucci's shouted obscenities, but picked up their gear and ran for the elevators.

The phone beside Sarah Anderson's bed rang very softly in the darkness, but she came instantly awake. The luminous face of her bedside alarm clock–radio glared the hour of 4 A.M. Her voice was husky from sleep, but otherwise firm and clear. "This is Sarah Anderson," she said. "What is it?"

"Tom Laverty here, Mrs. Anderson. I'm calling from downtown security."

"Yes, Tom."

"I'm sorry to call so late, but you left instructions," the guard said. "I figured you'd want to know."

"Yes, Tom. Thank you. What's happened?"

"This fellow Campbell, he was asking around earlier . . ."

"Yes?"

"Well, he got Marie Vecchi to take him into Technical Operations Personnel," the man continued. "According to Marie, Campbell told her he had a tape deck stolen yesterday afternoon and thinks he saw the guy, one of the mailroom kids, run into TOPS with it. I guess he figured the kid stashed it in there, intending to come back for it later."

"I see. Did they find it?"

"No, ma'am. But according to Marie, Campbell seemed more interested in checking out the assignment sheets. He hardly looked for the tape deck at all, she said. Then he had her take him up the executive floors. They went into your office too. Funny thing is, Marie doesn't think the guy was looking for a tape deck at all."

"What *was* he looking for?"

"Beats me, Mrs. Anderson."

"When was all this?"

"A couple of hours ago," the guard said. "I was on a break and Marie told me. She made some joke about trying to fool around up there, but I'm sure she was kidding. She's a great kidder, Marie. The guy was looking for something, all right, but Marie wasn't sure what. I didn't push her, you know. We was just talking."

"You handled it just right, Tom. It could be nothing, you know, but thank you."

"Again, I'm real sorry, it being so late and all, but you said—"

"You were quite right, Tom. We have a problem here. As I told you last week, we suspect somebody is trying to sabotage our operation. We don't know who or why. This is probably nothing, but thanks again."

"Just following instructions, ma'am. Good night to you."

After hanging up, Sarah lay alone and still in the darkness of her room. After a minute or two she sat up, turned on her bedside lamp and picked up the receiver again. She did not have to look the number up, but quickly punched the buttons on her machine and waited.

"Boy," Moss said as the elevator doors closed on them, "I sure am glad we can sleep tomorrow. I'm beat, man. That Bellucci, he's a maniac. When you disappeared again, he started screaming like a banshee in here. Where the hell did you go?"

"I was looking for something," Jeff said. "Nothing important."

"Man, you know it's after five?"

"That second fire was better than the first one," Jeff observed, trying to stifle a yawn. "I'll bet the landlord set that one, just to get the building off his back and stick the insurance companies. Vicki can have her pick. She can get a minute or a minute and a half out of either one."

"All that work for one damn minute on the air," Moss said, shaking his head. "It don't seem worth it. You ever get the feeling we're wasting our talents here?"

"All the damn time," Jeff said.

"By the way, what the hell were you doing upstairs with that lady cop? She's something, isn't she? Got some mouth on her."

"She freezes my joint just talking to me," Jeff answered. "Moss, you ever been in TOPS?"

"Nope."

"I never had either, till tonight. It was pretty interesting."

"In what way?"

The elevator disgorged them into the underground garage, a low-ceilinged, dusty expanse of parking areas, nearly empty at that hour. They headed toward Jeff's VW, which looked forlorn, abandoned, in that vast, empty cavern.

"You going to drop me off?" Moss asked.

"Sure."

"I asked you about TOPS. In what way was it interesting?"

"Well," Jeff explained, "we have about five hundred technical people at ACN—lighting directors, floor directors, camera operators and so on—all assigned to one show or another. Those assignments are all made and the schedules posted in TOPS."

"So?"

"So I couldn't find one person assigned to work Harvey's end of the evening news."

"That's funny."

"I thought so, too," Jeff said.

"Maybe he's doing the show from out of state," Moss suggested. "They might have their own local people."

"That must be it, all right. But there's no record of who, what or where in TOPS, and that, I think, is odd."

"What bugs you about all this? That Harvey won't see you?"

"I'm just plain nosy, I guess."

"I guess."

By the time Jeff drove out into the street, Moss had fallen asleep, slumped against the back of his seat and the car door. The city seemed empty, worn and used up in the early-morning gray of predawn. Jeff turned right on Fifth, then right again and headed west. He had to take Moss home before heading back downtown toward his own place. As he crossed Seventh Avenue, he glanced up into his rearview mirror. There was only one other car in the street, a small green Chevrolet Impala. It was apparently heading in the same direction and seemed in no hurry to get to wherever it was going. Jeff forgot about it until after he had dropped Moss off and turned south. The car was still there, a block or so behind him, which was odd, considering how many times Jeff had changed directions. Just as he began to wonder whether he was being tailed by some very patient holdup man, the car turned east on Fourteenth Street and disappeared from view. Jeff shook his head and smiled. Maybe, like poor old Harvey, I'm turning paranoid, too, he reflected, fascinated suddenly by the image of the old anchorman, so cool and assured during his broadcasts, but with the madness lurking behind his eyes, invisible to all but as present and real as Harvey himself. The poor old bastard.

But now at least he had the name of the man who was treating Harvey. "Jerome Lillienthal–Confidential to Sarah Anderson," the file had read, "re Current Status Harvey Grunwald." That was all he could make out on the routing slip of the file on Sarah's desk with Marie hovering in the background, but it gave him somewhere to begin.

Jeff parked halfway up the block toward his building, got out and leaned over to lock his car door. He heard the car coming down the street, but had no idea how fast it was going until it bore down on him.

"Hey, what the—" Jeff vaulted over the hood of the VW and landed heavily on his stomach. It took the breath out of him, and by the time he had staggered to his feet the speeding sedan had already turned the corner of Bleecker Street and disappeared. "Hey!" he called out. "You asshole!"

A green Chevrolet Impala, or had he just imagined it? But what was the maniac doing, speeding like that down his narrow street? He glanced east again, expecting to hear the siren of a pursuing police car. But nothing happened. Somewhere up above him a window opened and voice called out, "Shut up down there! Go home!"

Still shaky from the narrow miss, Jeff dusted himself off and slowly made his way up the steps of his house.

REFERENCE: MYRMIDON—Test data conclusive on eye color. Anderson reluctant to include it in next Master program update. Managed to convince her it can be done delicately enough not to be noticed.

I find myself growing resentful of her inclination to question my judgment. What point is all the research if its results aren't to be applied, or are applied selectively?

—From the Journal of Dr. Jerome Lillienthal

11

SARAH ANDERSON was angry. "What did you imagine you could accomplish?" she asked. "Didn't I explain it all to you?"

"Yes, you did," Jeff admitted, shifting awkwardly from one foot to another. "I just got curious." He felt like a small boy hauled up by his teacher in front of his classmates to be publicly humiliated. Sarah Anderson had that quality, all right, the frostiness of a New England schoolmistress outraged by the misbehavior of one of her pupils. She looked betrayed, because, after all, she *had* taken him into her confidence and obviously she believed that he had violated her trust. "You see, Sarah, I guess I'm just naturally curious," he tried to explain. "I can't help myself."

"That's a very poor excuse," she said. "I'm disappointed in you, Jeff."

"I guess you must have heard it from security, huh?"

"Of course. They always inform us when anything unusual occurs in our division."

"And this was that unusual?" he asked. "Stuff gets stolen here all the time. And I thought TOPS was open to anyone on staff."

"It's not and you know it isn't. If you didn't know it, you should have," she snapped. "And it was perfectly clear to security that you weren't looking for a stolen article."

What did they think he was looking for? He wondered about

that. He wondered, too, about the fact that security had reported to her directly and so quickly. Someone must have called her very early in the morning about his escapade. It wasn't even noon, and she had asked for him the moment she came in; Paul Haber had telephoned him at home at nine-twenty, woken him up out of a sound sleep. "Mrs. Anderson wants to see you first thing," he'd said, "before you report to the newsroom." But what had he done to upset her so?

"Look, Sarah, I guess I *was* out of line—" he began.

"You certainly were," she interrupted him. "I'm very upset."

"I had some time to kill between assignments last night and I really have been thinking a lot about Harvey recently, so I . . ." His voice trailed away and he tried to manage a sheepish smile; after all, she had a right to be angry, didn't she? But this angry?

"First of all, you indicate by this kind of thing that you think we're trying to cover up something here," she continued. "Did you assume I was lying to you?"

"No, ma'am."

"Don't you understand that you're endangering not only our ability to keep the evening news on the air, but Harvey's personal welfare?"

"I guess so."

"The last thing he wants at this point is this sort of meddling. The man's barely hanging on as it is. Don't you want to see him get well and return to his old self?"

"Sure I do, Sarah."

"Then why? Why why why?"

He shrugged. "I didn't think that just finding out where he is would be such a big deal."

"Well, it *is* a big deal. We're protecting Harvey for his own good and, frankly, for the good of this network." She leaned forward in her chair and rapped smartly on the top of the desk with her forefinger, very much like an enraged politician he had once photographed at a Senate committee hearing on narcotics. The man's daughter had died of an overdose, and, like him, Sarah conveyed the impression of a person with a big cause to fight for. "I am not going to let you or anyone jeopardize what we are doing," she insisted. "You are putting your own career with this division in peril by going against my direct instructions. Am I making myself clear, Jeff?"

"Yeah, very," he admitted.

"Then I have to inform you that any repetition of such behavior will lead to a termination of your services with this company," she said. "I am not going to stand for it."

"I understand. I'm sorry."

"You should be. And one more thing," she added as he turned to go.

"What's that?"

"What were you doing in my office last night? I accept your explanation, however misguided your intentions, for snooping around TOPS. But what, pray, were you looking for in my office, as well as the other one you went into?"

"A couch," he said.

"What for?"

Jeff smiled now, hiding behind his public image of the macho ding-a-ling cameraman. "Marie Vecchi had ideas."

"I beg your pardon?"

"Mrs. Vecchi is a woman who, I guess, doesn't get enough attention at home. She wanted to fool around, you might say."

Sarah looked a little dazed and recoiled in her chair, as if Jeff had suddenly belched in her face. "I see," she whispered.

"That's one big gal, Sarah," Jeff said, with a laugh. *Come on, lady, you are just one of the boys, aren't you?* "We needed a big couch. Couldn't find one." He suddenly turned serious as he saw her go pale. "Hey, we were only kidding around, Sarah. It was her idea to show me the offices and she has a dirty mouth, that lady. It was a joke, honest."

"I'm not amused." she said. "You may go."

"OK. Sorry. It won't happen again."

"No, it had better not happen again."

With a small sigh of relief, Jeff closed the door behind him, nodded to Paul Haber, who looked up blandly at him as he emerged, and got away from her office just as fast as he could.

Whew, she was a tiger when cornered, all right, he reflected as he headed downstairs. That damn Marie sure hadn't wasted any time. Or had it been Marie who had blown the whistle on him? Probably not. More likely it had been Tom Laverty, that shifty-eyed bastard. Should he have told Sarah Anderson that some-body in a green Chevrolet Impala had tailed him and then tried to run him down in the street last night? No, Jeff decided, she might not have taken too kindly to that piece of news either. One paranoid at a time was all any one news division of a major network could be expected to handle, and right now Harvey Grunwald was it.

"I think it was pretty reckless," Tracy said after Jeff had finished telling her about his previous night's escapade and the ensuing scene with Sarah. "Honestly, Jeff, how did you expect her to react?"

"Just the way she did," he admitted. "But what I find strange about it is the overkill."

"What do you mean?"

"The whole thing has a kind of Pentagon feel to it. Like it's a sort of a conspiracy."

"Oh, come on. That's ridiculous!"

"Is it?"

"Yes. I certainly wouldn't like it if someone went snooping around my desk looking for something," she said. "After all, you did exactly that, it seems to me. And after Mrs. Anderson took you into her confidence."

"Cool and beautiful Sarah," Jeff said, raising his Wild Turkey on the rocks to toast her. "May she ever be a glorious asset to the evening news."

They were sitting at the bar of the Casa Margherita, which was now filling up with people stopping in for a drink before heading home. It had been an easy day, for a change, and Jeff had only had to go out twice, once to a killing in the Times Square area, the second time to a small riot by striking employees at an East Side Manhattan hospital. Routine stuff. Moss had already gone home to his sick wife, and now he and Tracy had stopped in to unwind before going out to dinner and a movie. It was great to have been let out early for once and damn nice of Santini to have volunteered to fill in for him. The previous eighteen-hour day had taken its toll of Jeff. Now, as the tension of the working-day pressure began to drain out of him, Jeff could feel his paranoia subsiding. Maybe it *was* all in his head; maybe he *had* behaved like an idiot. And maybe the world was flat. He decided not to tell Tracy about the incident in the street in the early hours of that morning. She would begin to believe he *was* going nuts, like poor old Harvey. Sensible girl.

He raised his glass again and toasted her. "To good old common sense," he said. "What movie do you want to see?"

"I thought we agreed," she answered. "You said there was a revival of *Star Wars* at the Magnum Two. I've never seen it."

"Oh, yeah. It's fun. And mindless."

"That's why I never went. I was a serious child."

"I'll bet you were."

"I grew up on Ingmar Bergman revivals and Third Wave."

"Boring, lady, boring. The best movies are movie movies. No big messages, just great photography and lots of action."

"I think I'm ready for that, don't you?"

"You're getting there, kid."

"Don't call me 'kid,' you wretched sexist."

"Aw, honey . . ." He leaned over and kissed her, then ordered another round.

"Don't we have to go?"

"It's five blocks from my place and there's a terrific Chinese joint next door. No rush."

On his way back from the men's room twenty minutes later, Jeff bumped into Paul Haber. The slim, intense-looking young man was on his way to a corner table, where two older gays, talking quietly to each other, awaited him. Jeff had already understood that about Paul Haber, but, though not a subscriber to the new morality regarding homosexuals, he had not allowed it to trouble him.

"Hello, Paul," he said, "how are you?"

"I'm fine.

"That's good. Did you hear me get reamed out this morning by your boss?"

Paul smiled. "I'm afraid not."

"Too bad. You might have enjoyed it."

"Oh, I don't think so."

"Can I buy you a drink?"

"No, thank you. I'm with friends."

"OK, another time. Say, Paul . . ."

"Yes?"

"Does Sarah talk to Harvey a lot?"

"I'm not at liberty to discuss Ms. Anderson's telephone calls," the secretary said. "You know that, Jeff. She has her own private line, of course."

"Oh, yeah. Well, thanks a lot. Nice seeing you, Paul."

"Thank you. I hope things get straightened out."

"Yeah, I think they will. Say, if you ever happen to get Harvey on the phone, say hello to him for me."

"I'll do that."

"Thanks. See you around."

Back at the bar, a telephone call awaited him. "It's your office," the bartender said, holding out the receiver. Jeff looked at Tracy, winked and took the call, crouching over with one hand against his other ear to shut out the noise in the crowded room.

It was Santini. "Hey, Jeff, we got a really big fire in Brooklyn Heights, apparently. They want you to cover it."

"No deal, Bucky," Jeff said. "I'm off."

"Yeah, I know, but for some reason they asked for you."

"Who did? Bellucci?"

"No, he's gone, too. Meegan told me to try and get hold of you."

"Listen, Bucky, you can cover it, can't you? Why me, anyway?"

"I guess they figure you're the big fire expert," Santini said with a chuckle. "I could tell them I didn't find you."

"That's it, Bucky. I'm nowhere to be found. Thanks."

"Sure. OK, I did my duty. I gotta run, if we're going to make it before they start jumping out of windows." And he hung up.

"They wanted you to come in again?" Tracy asked, surprised.

"Yeah. Happens all the time." He smiled at her. "See, I'm

the resident genius on fires now, I guess. Bucky's covering for me."

"Oh, good. Finish your drink," she urged him. "We'd better go."

He raised his glass, looked up and saw Harvey Grunwald's benign, fatherly countenance beaming down at him from the TV set mounted above the corner of the bar. Harvey was delivering the evening news in his customary smooth, understated style, but he could not be heard above the uproar in the room. Fascinated, Jeff watched the image on the slightly fuzzy screen.

"What is it?" Tracy asked.

"I don't know," he said. "There's something . . . I don't know."

"Come on, Jeff, we're running late."

But he couldn't tear himself away. Glass in hand, he stared at the screen. Something *was* wrong, but what? Before he could figure it out, the bartender climbed on a low stool and switched to a cable channel. The head of John Wayne materialized. Some old movie, one of the last ones for the big man before age and disease struck him down. Still, there was Harvey . . .

"Jeff, what is it?"

"Nothing," he said. "I had—I don't know—some kind of odd feeling about Harvey, the way he looked. I don't know. It's probably the picture in here. The color's off or something."

"Off?"

"Yeah." He picked up his change and took Tracy's arm to steer her through the mob toward the door. "It's nothing. But it looked funny to me. Something about the eyes."

"What about them?"

"I think they were blue. Harvey doesn't have blue eyes. At least, I don't remember them as being blue."

"You're sure?"

"No, I'm not sure. I'm not sure of anything, Tracy."

"Maybe he's wearing contacts."

"Maybe. He does use reading glasses."

Out in the street, he hailed a taxi, and they thought no more about Harvey Grunwald for the next four hours.

* * *

By the time Santini and his sound man, Gregg Pearson, reached the scene of the fire, they were really too late to get the best shots. Though the building, a run-down hotel catering to Puerto Rican families on welfare, was still burning, the surviving tenants had all escaped or been evacuated. They clustered together in tearful, wailing groups behind police barricades, while the firemen sent columns of water arching in through the shattered windows from which clouds of oily black smoke poured out into the sky. Golden, who had been on the scene early, already had everything on tape and he grinned happily at Santini, the last of the local TV-station cameramen to reach the scene. "You're a little tardy, Bucky boy," he said. "We got it all."

Santini grunted. "Yeah? We'll see." With Pearson in tow, he headed around the west side of the building, where he had noticed a knot of people gazing up toward the roof.

"Only four crispies, Bucky," Golden called out after him. "Two of them out the windows. We got all that. Too bad, Bucky boy."

Angrily, Santini soon realized that Golden was right. No one was still inside. Dutifully he and Gregg shot what little was left of the action, training their camera mainly on the upper stories, where lean, bright tongues of orange flame occasionally licked through the smoke toward the eaves. The knot of watchers Santini had spotted seemed hypnotized by the spectacle. It wasn't much, but it was the best Santini could manage. The station would have to pick up the good stuff from that jackal Golden. If only he and Gregg hadn't been delayed by being told to find Campbell, Santini reflected. Dumb bastards, as if he hadn't shot just as many of these as Jeff and just as well too. He glanced down the street toward Spencer Williams, who was talking with a fire captain on the outcome and probably causes of the disaster, as if he didn't know. "Shit!" he exclaimed, his camera trained on nothing of use.

"What?" Gregg asked.

"Skip it. Let's wrap it up here. They'll have to pick up the best stuff from Golden. No fault of ours."

They began to walk slowly back toward the front of the hotel, where at least they'd be able to take pictures of the survivors. Maybe there'd be a distraught mother with a missing child, if only that dismal asshole Williams would dig out the story instead of wasting his time bullshitting with some ignorant mick in a rubber raincoat and shovel hat. What a waste.

The sniper on the rooftop across the street had been waiting for the WACN team for nearly a half hour. He carefully studied the scene through his pocket ten-by-twenty-five Zeiss binoculars, now slung lightly around his neck. He spotted the WACN logo on Santini's camera. He glanced into the sky for police helicopters, saw none, then quickly and efficiently steadied himself against the parapet. Focusing with care through his telescopic sight, he aimed the long rifle down toward his target.

Bucky Santini never knew what hit him. The bullet went in just above his left ear, sending shards of bone and bloody tissue spattering against the wall of the building. He fell like a rock and lay on his back, jaw agape, sightless eyes staring blankly upward. Gregg Pearson screamed, dropped his gear and ran for his life.

No one at first understood what had happened. By the time the police reached the rooftop twenty minutes later and found the rifle, the sniper had long since departed and was on his way back to Manhattan by subway.

"Oh, Jesus, Jeff, I've been calling you for hours, man!" Moss shouted into his ear. "Where the hell have you been?"

"Out to dinner and a movie," Jeff answered. "What's the matter with you, Moss?"

"You didn't hear?"

"Hear what?"

"About Santini?"

"What about him?"

"He was shot," Moss said. "He's dead, man. Somebody shot him while he was covering that fire in Brooklyn Heights. Blew the top of his head off. They found the rifle on a rooftop across the way. No serial number, nothing. Some crazy fool on a rooftop and it had to be Santini. It could have been us, Jeff . . ."

As Moss went on talking, filling in the details, Jeff sank slowly into a chair. Tracy, wrapped in a towel, came out of the bathroom, saw the expression on his face and stopped in her tracks. She waited, scarcely daring to move, until he slowly lowered the receiver and looked up at her. Then, in a low, even voice, keeping it all inside, all under control, he told her what had happened. "Tracy," he concluded, "that bullet was meant for me."

"What? How do you know?"

"It wasn't some crazy sniper on a rooftop potshooting at people to get his rocks off," he said. "The man apparently fired only one shot. He waited for the WACN team to get to the scene. Santini and Pearson were the last to arrive, Moss says. And the weapon can't be identified. No markings."

"But still—"

"And remember the phone call at the bar tonight, when they tried to find me?"

"Who did? Meegan?"

"Not Meegan. He's a flunky. Somebody told Meegan to assign me to that story."

"Bellucci?"

"No, he'd gone home already and Windom is still out sick." Jeff thought it over. "Only McCarron could tell Meegan to assign me to that story. The kid has no authority. He was just filling in, that's all. And McCarron would have no reason to look for me. It was a setup. He was told to put me on that story."

"By whom? Mrs. Anderson? But why, Jeff? I can't believe this."

"I'm not sure I can, either," he said. He got up, poured them both a stiff drink and then told Tracy about being tailed by the green Chevy Impala and how someone had tried to run him down in the street the night before. "I'm not just imagining all this, Tracy," he concluded. "In Vietnam I picked up a lot of savvy about jungle warfare and staying alive. I got so I could nose out a bad situation. It was a question of survival. Somebody is trying to kill me, Tracy."

"Oh, come on."

"Come on, nothing," he snapped. "I know it, just as sure as I know you're sitting over there." He got up and began to pace back and forth as he tried to sort out in his head what he could do.

"And you think it's all connected to Harvey in some way, is that it?"

He nodded. "Yep, that's it." He looked at her and smiled grimly. "Tracy, I don't think you know much about money and what people will do to get it and hold on to it. Harvey on the evening news is worth hundreds of millions of bucks. He's as important to this network as Saudi Arabia has been to the oil companies. People kill for a lot less than what's at stake here."

"I think we ought to go to the police."

He thought that one over, then sat down again, beside her this time on the couch, and took her hand. "No," he said, "we haven't got enough to go to the police with. Think about it. We have nothing factual. And the police deal exclusively in facts, not conjecture. To an outsider this story would seem incredible, certainly coincidental in all its details."

"But if you're right . . ." She allowed the implication of this sentence to hang ominously in the air.

He thought it over for several minutes, until slowly a clear plan began to take shape. "There's one guy who could help."

"Yes?"

"A guy I knew in Vietnam."

"A friend of yours?"

Jeff smiled at the image that conjured up for him. Wade Nolan a friend? Well, maybe, yes. Certainly a wartime buddy, a blood brother even, but a friend? No, that was something else. Did Nolan have any real friends? Jeff wondered. He had never known one. The guy was a loner. "I wonder if he's still down there," he murmured.

"Who?"

"Wade Nolan, the guy I knew in Vietnam," Jeff explained. "Quite a character. I hear from him from time to time. After Vietnam he worked in Africa for a while as a mercenary. For the last couple of years he's been back here, as far as I know. He might enjoy a deal like this. Action was the only thing that made him tick. And I think he'll come if I ask him."

"Where is he?"

"North Carolina, near Asheville, up in the Blue Ridge country. He has a cabin there and some acres of his own. He lives by himself, hunts and fishes, I guess." Jeff stood up and began pacing again. "Tracy, I'm going down there to see him this weekend. Maybe I can get Wade to help me. I've got to get to the bottom of this."

"Do you want me to go with you?"

"No need to. I'll be back Sunday night, with or without Wade." He stopped pacing and looked at her. "Meanwhile, I can't stay here. Not if somebody's trying to wipe me out."

"You can stay with me," she said. "There's room."

"Sure you don't mind? Nobody knows I've been seeing you, except Moss. You haven't told anybody, have you?"

"Only Whit. I told him I dated you a couple of times." She laughed. "He didn't seem to mind at all."

"Whit!" Jeff exclaimed. "Sarah Anderson's right-hand man! Jesus, Tracy, you told Whit. I can't stay with you."

"Oh, for heaven's sake, Jeff, it didn't even register. Whit's completely preoccupied with his work," Tracy said reassuringly. "Anyway, I'm not seeing him anymore. He'll have no reason to come calling."

"I'm not worried about Whit coming calling. I'm worried about him making the connection between us for some goon."

"Jeff, I really doubt that Whit even recalls my mentioning you. Besides," she said with a suggestive smile, "I'm beginning to warm to the idea of having you as a roomy."

"Tracy, if I'm right, this could be dangerous for you."

She put her arms around him and kissed him. "Please," she said. "I want to help, too."

"Hmm," he agreed. "It's the best offer I've had all week." He kissed her. "Come on, we better get going."

As she dressed, he began to throw some clothes into a suitcase.

"Jeff, do you really think this man—what's his name?" she asked from inside the bathroom.

"Nolan, Wade Nolan."

"Do you think he'll be that much help?"

Jeff stopped and turned toward her. "Help?" he echoed her. "Oh, yes. He's a professional killer, the best I've ever known. If he can't help me, nobody can."

12

Jeff would have recognized him anywhere. In fact, except for a touch of gray around the temples of his brush cut, Wade Nolan looked exactly as he remembered him. A tall, thin, muscular man from the Southern mountains, he still had that lean hawk face with the strange eyes. One of them was missing part of a lower eyelid, a tiny pie-shaped wedge carved out either by shrapnel or, as Nolan himself had always claimed, in a brothel brawl in Saigon. The wound gave him an oddly lopsided look, as if his face had been frozen into a perpetual popeyed stare compromised by a conniving squint. He had always seemed to slide through life obliquely, a corrupted hillbilly with a startling way of turning that open eye on you suddenly, as if amazed by your effrontery at having gotten in his way. Nolan had always been uncomfortable with people, all right, Jeff recalled. He'd preferred the company of corpses, probably because so few living souls ever felt at ease around him.

Nolan had heard the car whining up the pitted dirt road toward his cabin and had stepped outside to greet his visitor, hunting rifle in hand. The woods were dense on either side of the road, but the trees and brush had been cleared away from around the house so that Nolan could have an uninterrupted view of at least thirty yards in any direction from his doors and windows. Jeff had been forced to park where the road ended, well below the cabin, and proceed the rest of the way on foot. Nolan's Jeep was parked by the house, but Jeff's rented Oldsmobile had barely managed the road itself and sat steaming from the effort in the turnaround Nolan or somebody had carved out of the hillside.

"I guess you don't get too many visitors up here," Jeff said as he came panting up the steep slope toward the front door.

"Not so's I can help it," the mountain man said, without a flicker of recognition or pleasure on his face.

"How are you, Wade?" Jeff said, sticking out his hand. "Did you get my telegram?"

Wade shook his hand limply and turned toward the cabin. "Nope. People don't like to come up here much," he said in that low, slurred drawl Jeff remembered so well. "Must be they left it down below in the mailbox, but I ain't been down there for two or three days. Seems like nothin' good ever comes in the mail, so I don't like to fool with it. Get down there two, three times a month to pick up my government checks and that's about it. I throw the rest of the shit away. Come on in."

He led the way inside. The cabin was one room with a tiny kitchen in back and an outhouse nestled up against it like a barnacle. A narrow cot, unmade, with graying sheets, lay against one wall. The rest of the furnishings consisted of two camp chairs, a roughhewn square wooden table, an old-fashioned potbellied stove, four or five kerosene lamps, two black bear rugs and a couple of bean bags squatting before a huge open fireplace that monopolized one side of the room. In the corner a stack of kindling and pine logs rose toward the low ceiling. There were no pictures on the walls, but the windows provided a fine view of the countryside below, an undulating carpet of trees dotted by infrequent dwellings and scarred by narrow roads and fire breaks.

The isolation of the place seemed total, perfectly in keeping with the man who lived here. Dirty clothes lay scattered over the bed, the table, the chairs and spilled out of an open closet door. The sense of shabbiness and disorder heightened the emptiness of the room, but was savagely contradicted by the display on the far wall, where Nolan kept his armory and his war trophies. The cool metallic muzzles of guns, all shapes, all sizes, marched in deadly array up a floor-to-ceiling rack, flanked on either side by the trophies Nolan had collected. A small glass case nailed into the wall beside the gun rack contained what looked from a distance like dried apricots or leaves, but were, Jeff knew, the least appealing of Wade's mementos, the dried ears of his victims, cut off and carried around in Vietnam in a Ziplock bag. That was how they had met, Jeff recalled. Wade's idea of a joke had been to offer new acquaintances his goodies and watch with relish as they unsuspectingly bit into them, then spit them out in horror and disgust. A macabre sense of humor, oh yes, and it went well with the man's bizarre appearance.

Nolan saw him eying the glass case. "Got me some prunes in there now," he drawled, "along with the apricots. I had me a pretty good time in Rhodesia, which they don't call it that no more."

"Up to your old tricks in Africa?"

"Yeah, that was a pretty good time, too. It ended, though, and pretty much like Nam. Just kind of petered out. Seems like I'm always on the losin' side, Jeff. How come?"

"Maybe we've been fighting the wrong wars, Wade."

"Wouldn't surprise me none. Still, there was some good times."

"I'm surprised you came back from Africa," Jeff said. "There's always a war going on there somewhere."

"Darkies shootin' up other darkies ain't never been my style, old buddy," Wade explained. "And the pussy was third-rate stuff. Little old farm girls with crabs could jump ten feet, fat mamas with tits like old tobacco leaves, street hookers that could give you leprosy just lookin' at you, fella. Not for me. I come back three years ago. Been sittin' up here, killin' time, mostly. Want a beer?"

"Yeah, thanks."

Nolan disappeared briefly into the kitchen and came back

with two ice-cold cans of Budweiser. He shook his dirty clothes off the chairs and they sat down facing each other across the table. "So what's doin', old buddy?" Nolan asked.

"I was going to ask you that," Jeff said, with a grin. "Must be pretty lonely up here."

"It's better than livin' in some damn town. I go in there every month or so, stock up on stuff, then I come back up here. It's real quiet. The huntin' and fishin' is real good and you can do it year round. Nobody messes with me none. In the winter you get snowed in sometimes and everything gets so quiet you can hear deer shit fallin'." Nolan suddenly got up and began building a fire in the open hearth. "It'll get chilly later, when the sun goes. We'll have us a fire and I'll cook us some steaks. I got some real nice venison I been waitin' on for an occasion and it looks like you're it. You gonna spend the night, ain't you?"

"You got room?"

"Sure. I got an extra sleepin' bag, if you don't mind the floor."

"That'll be fine. I've got to go back tomorrow."

"That's good. We can have a real nice visit. You been doin' any shootin' since I seen you?" Nolan asked, grinning.

"No, Wade, after Nam I figured I'd done enough of that to last me a lifetime."

Nolan laughed, a sharp staccato burst of machine-gun fire, and he turned it off just as abruptly, as if the chamber in a gun had been emptied. "You was the one, all right," he said. "I trusted you pretty good, didn't I?"

"Yes, you sure did," Jeff conceded. "But tell me, Wade, still how can you stand it up here, all alone all the time?"

"You know I never did like crowds much, and it's a good place," Nolan said. "I got me sixty-eight acres here, mostly woods, and a trout stream. The summers are too hot, though, and them woods get so full of bugs you about want to shoot yourself."

"Bugs? What kind of bugs?"

"Buddy boy, they got mosquitos in there can stand flatfooted and fuck a turkey," he said. "I get into town more in the summer just to get away from them. Found me a good whorehouse in

Asheville, about two miles out of town. I go in there for a week or two and have me the annual Wade Nolan Nookie Bash. Gets me all boozed up and emptied out and then I come back up here and it's real nice the rest of the time. Oh, I get the itch for action about once a month, but there ain't no good wars anymore, not for my kind of fightin'."

"I think I may have something for you."

Nolan's open eye stared at him with manic intensity. "No shit? Say, now, tell me what's up. You still takin' pictures?"

Jeff nodded. "Yeah." He quickly filled Nolan in on his career. "Takin' pictures," as Wade had always called it, had been the basis of their friendship. It had taken a couple of weeks to persuade Nolan to let himself be filmed in action, but after that they'd been out on quite a few missions together. Nolan was a professional killer, a born soldier, who had learned his trade as a Lurp (Long Range Recon Patrol) sergeant in Vietnam. Long before Jeff had met him, he'd heard his legend. The man had already chalked up a hundred and seventy-three confirmed kills. He worked alone, hiking into the Vietnam highlands with provisions and a map showing spots where the urine sensors dropped by observation helicopters had detected enemy activity. He went out armed with an M-14 equipped with a Starlight self-ranging telescopic sight and a MAC (Military Armaments Corporation) sound suppressor to deaden the muzzle blast, and in the jungle he moved like a feral cat stalking prey. One night, their third or fourth time out, he had engineered the strange ceremony of death that cemented their relationship. Now, even as Jeff quietly filled in the pieces of his missing life for Nolan, he recalled with vivid intensity every moment, every terrifying second of that extraordinary experience. . . .

Nolan had set an ambush that night. The two of them lay side by side at the edge of a clearing along a trail the Viet Cong used after dark. Suddenly, after they'd been waiting about twenty minutes, six black-clad shapes appeared on the other side of the clearing, no more than a hundred meters away, Russian-made

AK-47 automatic rifles dangling loosely at their waists. Nolan steadied his M-14, sighted through the Starlight scope that enabled him to see clearly in the darkness, and signaled Jeff to roll his camera, which was equipped with an infrared night-viewing lens.

Nolan centered his cross hairs on the chest of the nearest man and squeezed the trigger. The effect was dramatic. The ballistic crack of Nolan's bullet shattered the silence, and a spot no bigger than a cat's paw appeared over the heart of the first victim, who flipped backward through the air. His five companions stared at him in astonishment, frozen for a moment, as Nolan knew they would be. He centered the cross hairs again, and another high, sharp hiss filled the air as his second target's head exploded. The four survivors now realized they were under attack and reacted, making the usual fatal mistake. The MAC sound suppressor on Nolan's rifle created a strange illusion. By silencing the explosive muzzle blast, leaving only the ballistic crack the bullet made as it sped through the air at supersonic speed, it created an area of confusion between sniper and victim. To the target, the bullets seemed to be coming from every direction but the actual one. Instead of running away from their killer, the four remaining VC, AK-47s in hand, now raced directly toward the spot where Nolan and Jeff, who was stunned, lay waiting.

This was the part of the operation Nolan liked best. The targets were harder to hit and time was limited. He had perhaps ten seconds to dispatch the four men before they'd be right on top of him. High stakes.

With cool precision, Nolan tracked another victim and sent him tumbling to his death with a single shot, his AK-47 ripping the earth beneath him with a deafening roar. The three survivors were racing at full panic speed, no more than fifty meters away now. Through his camera lens, Jeff could begin to make out facial features. The nearest man's eyes widened and he pitched out of frame as the strange hiss from Nolan's weapon mingled with the footsteps of the other two. Forty meters away now. One man spun as he ran and fanned the jungle behind him with a burst of automatic fire. Before he could turn back around, Nolan put a bullet through his lungs.

Now there was one man left, hunched over, running for his life. Clutching his AK-47, eyes darting from side to side, he was no more than thirty meters away. *It's almost over,* Jeff thought as he waited for Nolan's last shot. Suddenly, he felt the camera ripped from his hands and to his horror realized that *he* was now holding the M-14. *What the hell was Nolan doing?* The man had a strange smile on his face as he stared at Jeff, a cross between a death grin and the look of a man sharing a lover.

Footsteps. The Viet Cong soldier was just twenty meters away now, rushing straight toward them. There was more killing to be done, and Jeff realized that if he didn't do something within the next three seconds he and Nolan would be dead. From a distant corner of his numbed brain, as if seeing himself in action on a screen, Jeff watched himself raise the M-14, seemingly in slow motion, and heard a fool's voice scream, *"NO-LAN!"*

The VC's head snapped up. At ten meters now, still running, he pulled the trigger of his AK-47. An elongated ball of blue-orange flame formed at its muzzle, pulsating, as bullets and noise hammered the air around Jeff and Nolan. In the madness and terror of that moment, Jeff felt the M-14 buck, then saw the AK-47's flame rock skyward and blink out.

The jungle absorbed the echoes of it all in an instant, cloaking Jeff and Nolan in dense silence.

"Why?" Jeff asked. "Why?" He looked at Nolan's still smiling face. Then, as his own began to contort with a rage boiling up out of his numbness: "Why did you do that? You had no right, Nolan! I'm an *observer,* goddammit! I'm supposed to film this war, not shoot people! Goddammit, I'm not supposed to get involved! I'm not supposed to kill anyone! You had no right, Nolan, no right to make me do that! Jesus, you almost got us killed!"

Nolan allowed Jeff's last words to hang in the air for a moment, then reached out and put a hand gently on his shoulder. "Jeff, you won. We're alive."

Something strange was happening, Jeff realized. He felt his

rage wash away, replaced by a new emotion, a narcotic euphoria that coursed through his veins. The pure, primordial joy of surviving a fight to the death flooded his senses, an ecstasy known to warriors throughout time and known only to them, a high beyond orgasm or dope. Nolan had now shared it with Jeff, made him understand an aspect of the war and the killing that only the Wade Nolans, the born warriors, knew. He took his hand away from Jeff's shoulder, reached to his hip and pulled a razor-sharp knife from its sheath. He turned to the cameraman and said, with quiet intensity, "Forgive me, old buddy. Just a few little souvenirs to add to the old collection." And he retraced the last run of the six VC, bending swiftly and efficiently to his grisly task over each dead soldier.

Jeff looked away. He could never really forgive Nolan for what he had done or condone what he was doing now, but the ritual of blood had established a lifelong bond between them. They had nothing in common, but they had shared an experience Jeff knew in his soul he would never forget or dismiss. They had truly become brothers in blood, united forever by the guiltiest, most intimate secret men in combat shared. . . .

By ten o'clock that night, Jeff was ready to roll up in Nolan's sleeping bag and turn in. Something in the mountain air, probably, he reflected. It was so clean and cool that it seemed to wash away the grime of the city, refreshing and renewing him. He sat on the floor, slumped into one of the bean bags, and stared at the fire. The venison steaks Nolan had broiled had been delicious and the beer cold and soothing. He had almost forgotten the errand that had brought him to Nolan's mountain-top cabin, but Wade had not. He got up, put another log on the fire and turned to look down at Jeff.

"So, old buddy," he said, "it ain't exactly my kind of war, but I guess I can help. You want to find this old boy Harvey, is that it?"

Jeff nodded sleepily. "And I'd like to stay alive."

"That part I know I can help you with, old buddy," Nolan said. "Well, guess I'll do my packin'. Think we can get on the same plane out?"

"I don't know," Jeff said. "If not, you could come on a later one. I don't want to rush you out of here."

Nolan smiled, his face more lopsided and stranger than ever in the flickering firelight. "Shit, old buddy, I got nothin' but time on my hands. Your little proposition is kind of turnin' me on. Things have been mighty peaceful around here, with nothin' to do but hunt and fish and beat the old meat once a week. Hell, I only been to New York twice in my whole life. They got so much nookie there they sometimes give it away for free, I hear."

"Don't tell me you're tired of paying for it, Wade," Jeff said with a yawn. "I'd begin to lose faith in you."

"Naw, don't you worry, buddy boy," Nolan told him. "Paid pussy is the best kind. That way there ain't no messin' around later, all that I-love-you shit. Slam-bam-thank-you-ma'am and on my way, that's the only kind of nookie's any good for loners like me, old buddy. Free pussy can also get you killed. Hey, now, you roll up and get some sleep. I'll do a little packin' and we'll get goin' first thing in the mornin'."

He hauled the sleeping bag out from under his bed and tossed it to Jeff, who got up, stretched and laid it out on one of the bear rugs in front of the fire. Nolan went over to his gun rack and began to put together the armory he planned to take along on the adventure. By the time Jeff was ready to sack out, the weapons had been assembled and lay open to inspection on the table. Curious despite his sleepiness, Jeff came over and looked at the small arsenal Wade had gathered up.

Nolan hovered lovingly over the objects, as if each one was a personal extension, an ultimate expression of himself. "This here's my best piece for the kind of work we got to do, up in close," he said, touching the ugly instrument with the reverence of a Heifetz crooning over a Stradivarius. "This here's the Ingram, what they call every man's machine gun," Nolan continued. "See, it's about the size of a forty-five but it's got this here telescopin' stock that pulls out the back. You load the ammo clip from inside the handle. You can also fire it as a semiautomatic. And this here thing is the silencer. It's so long, about eighteen inches, 'cause that's what it takes. Only silencer for any machine gun anywhere. This'll fire a thirty-two-round clip in five or six seconds, cut a man in half with it. This here's a few of your basic grenades. I like this one. The old Bouncin' Betty. We used to drop 'em from the air. They just lie there till your man comes along. He steps on it and it bounces up about chest high and bam, he's gone. I got a nice little Beretta thirty-eight for you, can tuck it right under your arm."

"I haven't got a license to carry a gun," Jeff said. "We'd need one in New York."

"License? Are you kiddin'? You want to stay alive or don't you?" Nolan asked, amazed.

"I think I want to stay alive," Jeff admitted.

"Then don't go talkin' foolish about no goddam license," Nolan said. "That kind of shit is for the little old folks livin' behind locked doors and pissin' green everytime some nigger in sneakers and a ski cap comes walkin' by. If somebody's tryin' to kill you, old buddy, no license and no police is goin' to save your ass, you hear me?"

"I hear you." Feeling stupid and naive in the face of Nolan's frightening expertise, Jeff pointed to the smallest object on display, a tiny cylinder shaped like a lipstick. "And that?"

Nolan laughed. He picked the object up and said, "This, old buddy, is the ultimate last-resort survival weapon. Your ace in the hole, you might say. Tell you how it works later."

"And this one?" Jeff pointed to a small pistol sandwiched by the grenades.

"My tax collector," Nolan explained, caressing the gun with the delicacy of a lover. "That's another real useful little tool. You shoot your man in the gut and the bullet expands a little at a time. It's real slow and painful. You promise to get medical help, but you get the answers to all your questions first. It's a real nice little interrogation tool, old buddy. 'Course, by the time the medical help gets there the man is wasted and you're on your way with the answers."

"Jesus, Wade, do you really think we'll need all this stuff?"

"I sure hope not, old buddy, especially that old ace in the hole," Nolan answered, with a sweet grin. "But stayin' alive ain't a game where you get a second chance. In this game, you got to hold the winnin' hand every time. You only lose once and I ain't about to do that, old buddy, even for you."

Nolan pulled down a large, battered-looking suitcase from a storage bin above the kitchen doorway and began to pack, tucking the tools of his trade away in prepared compartments as if they were fragile bits of precious crystal. He was absorbed, happy in the prospect of adventure Jeff had offered him. Chilled, sobered by the spectacle, Jeff now rolled up in his sleeping bag and lay on his side, staring into the fire until the clean, fresh air of the mountains numbed him into sleep.

It had been raining most of the day, but by the time the baby-blue Cadillac nosed its way down the Long Island Expressway exit ramp into Queens the setting sun had begun to break through the clouds. From where Crawford stood, under the overhang of the highway and hidden in the shadows, he could look back toward Manhattan and see the tall buildings glowing in dazzling light. He preferred, however, to keep his eye on the Cadillac. Much depended on the man coming alone; a partner could complicate an otherwise straightforward operation. To his relief, he saw only one person in the car. Greed had, as usual, dominated all other considerations. Crawford smiled, but made no move. A tightly rolled black umbrella hung over his left arm, a light-brown briefcase rested between his feet.

The man in the Cadillac did not see Crawford at first. He parked by the overhang, rolled his window down on the driver's side and peered into the gloom. Crawford picked up the briefcase and took one step toward him.

"Hold it right there," the man said. "I don't want any trouble."

"No trouble," Crawford answered. "No trouble at all."

"You brought the rest of the money?"

"In here," Crawford said, tapping the case. "I can't risk being seen giving it to you. You'll have to come and get it."

The man glanced quickly up and down the deserted back street, then up at the boarded windows of the abandoned factory directly opposite. "Put it down right there," he finally instructed Crawford, "and get away from it, only stay where I can see you. You got that?"

"Sure." Crawford did exactly as he was told, putting about fifteen feet between himself and the briefcase. He waited.

"What's that over your arm?"

"My umbrella," Crawford said. "It was raining."

"It ain't raining now."

"A man can't be too careful," Crawford said. "It's always raining somewhere."

The man got out of the car, again looked around, and walked over to the briefcase. He was a short, hairy, balding man of about forty-five, with small black eyes and nervous hands. He crouched down over the briefcase, snapped it open and saw the stacks of ten- and twenty-dollar bills. He would have counted the money, but he disliked being out in the open like this and he was afraid of Crawford. He could not count the money and keep an eye on the big man at the same time. "It looks right," he grunted, snapping the case shut. He tucked it under his left arm as he stood up.

"It is right," Crawford said, in an even, pleasant tone of voice, as if indifferent to the whole sordid matter. "Don't you trust us, Sam? We've done business before."

"I thought you might be sore."

"Sore? What about?"

Sam shrugged. "It was the wrong guy, you tell me."

"Everyone makes mistakes, Sam. Next time it'll be the right guy."

"I got a right to the money. You said twenty-five Gs for the job. I did the job and I got a right to the other half. The risk was the same, no matter who. You understand?"

"Certainly we understand. No problem, Sam. Next time."

"Yeah. You set it up, I'll do it. No sweat. Deliver the right man in the right spot, like you promised, and I'll do it. I'll even do it for you cheap. Anytime."

"I know you will, Sam."

"OK, I'm going now. Keep your hands out where I can see them."

Crawford chuckled. "You're too suspicious, Sam. We fouled up, not you. Why shouldn't we pay you?"

"Right," Sam agreed. He backed toward his car and opened the door.

Crawford swiftly tilted the tip of the umbrella toward him. "Goodbye, Sam," he murmured, pressing the button under his index finger. A tiny pop of noise, a wisp of vapor in the cooling air, nothing else. As Sam sank toward the driver's seat, he felt what he thought was the sting of an insect on his neck, just below the jawbone. He reached up to scratch at it. The briefcase fell from his hand and he slumped forward against the steering wheel. He was dead.

Moving swiftly and quietly, Crawford walked up to the Cadillac, leaned in and retrieved the briefcase. He pushed the dead man to the floor, shut the door on him and headed back toward his own rented car, a brown Toyota parked on the corner across the street.

It would have been far less risky, obviously, simply to pay the man his full fee and take the loss, Crawford reflected as he drove away, but the trouble was that he had a very low tolerance for failure. He was not running a charity, after all. The man had been given a job to do. Granted that poor bastard Santini matched Campbell's general description, but generalities weren't good enough. The man was given *specifics*. He didn't check out his target carefully enough. *Unprofessional.* In this business you can't afford failure, Crawford told himself. Then, too, he had to admit to himself that he enjoyed these little scenes, didn't he? And it had been nearly two years since he'd had an occasion to use the Bulgarian umbrella, with its complicated little firing mechanism and its deadly poison pellet. How nice to know it still worked. Quite a handy tool, yes. Crawford began to hum tunelessly to himself as he sped back toward Manhattan, going against the flow of homeward-bound traffic heading out over the highway toward Long Island.

13

"WHEREVER THEY'RE keepin' him, he sure looks good," Nolan said. "He didn't look that good when I knew him."

"That's just it, Wade," Jeff agreed. "He didn't look that good ever. Maybe ten years ago, but not since then."

They were sitting on the floor of Tracy's tiny one-room apartment, their backs against the couch, their attention focused on the ACN evening news and the now beaming countenance of Harvey Grunwald, who had been relaying some good energy news, for a change. Something about a major breakthrough in the use of hydrogen fuels, but neither Jeff nor Wade had been so much listening to as watching the anchorman at work. At one point in the broadcast, in fact, Jeff had briefly turned off the sound, so as to be able to concentrate absolutely on Harvey's appearance.

"He looks younger, don't he?" Nolan observed.

Jeff nodded agreement. "And his eyes," he added.

"What about 'em?"

"They're blue."

"Wasn't they always?"

"No. I first noticed it last week, before I came to see you," he explained. "Today, when I stopped by the office, I went through a lot of film, from as far back as ten years ago. Vicki Robbins, one of our editors, helped me dig it out. I told her I was thinking of putting together some kind of documentary on old Harv. Anyway, I ran this stuff through a Moviola, very slowly and very methodically. No mistake about it. Harvey had light-brown eyes and now they're blue."

"How come?"

"That's what I want to know, Wade. How come?"

Tracy stirred restlessly in her chair and stretched out her long legs. "I once suggested contacts," she said.

"No, Harvey always had pretty good eyes," Jeff said. "He was proud of never using his reading glasses on the air. And even if his eyes are going, why *blue* contacts, then?"

"Vanity," Tracy said. "Maybe he thinks he looks better in them."

"Harvey was never vain," Jeff said. "He was proud of being a good newsman, but not vain. He had none of that celebrity thing about wanting to be treated like a movie star. You remember, Tracy, he was always a very private person. He and Ann never went anywhere just to be seen."

"Say, sugar," Nolan called out from his seat on the floor, "you got any more beer?"

"No, I don't," Tracy said. "How about a glass of white wine?"

"That the only booze you got?"

"I'm afraid so."

"Well, it'll have to do, then. Put a little ice in it, will you, sugar?"

Tracy looked at Jeff, who resolutely pretended not to have heard this last exchange and, keeping as straight a face as possible, stayed focused on the screen, where Harvey was now signing off the air. "Honestly," Tracy murmured, but nonetheless she got up, went into her kitchen and prepared Nolan's drink.

Wade watched her go, a smile of pure pleasure on his face, then winked his normal eye at the cameraman. "She's right pretty," he confided. "You got yourself a nice tight little piece of pussy there."

"Uh . . . yeah," Jeff said. "Wade, I'd . . . well . . ."

"What is it, old buddy?"

"Skip it," Jeff said. This wasn't going to be his night to explain these two people to each other, he decided. Time enough for that later. Besides, it wasn't important for Wade and Tracy to become friends. That possibility seemed unlikely, no matter what degree of tolerance Tracy might be able to achieve in regard to Nolan. As for Wade, he was what he was, and nothing, Jeff was sure, would ever change him. That much he had already tried to explain to her, but the reality of Nolan's presence, in all its untarnished crudeness, was going to put a severe strain on this thoroughly liberated, independent young woman. Well, it might have some advantage, Jeff reflected. By contrast to Nolan's quintessential boorishness, he himself might begin to shine in her eyes—strong, supportive and refreshingly free of old macho habits. Wouldn't that be a laugh?

"And that's the way things look from here tonight," Harvey Grunwald said, smiling from the screen at his vast unseen audience. "Good night, America, until tomorrow."

Jeff reached out and punched the set off. "So what do you think, Wade?"

Nolan yawned and stretched sleepily. "I don't know," he confessed. "I guess I don't think much of anything, old buddy. He looks good and he sounds good, real good."

"That's another thing . . ."

"Yeah? What?"

"He never fluffs a line," Jeff said. "He never clears his throat, misses a word, never." He looked at Tracy, who had joined them on the floor and now sat cross-legged facing them, a glass of wine in one hand and her back against the wall beside the TV stand. "Haven't you noticed?"

"Not really," Tracy answered. "He always had a very smooth delivery. You wouldn't expect him to fluff any lines."

"Tracy, *everybody* makes mistakes on the air every now and then," Jeff argued, "even old pros like Harvey. The man is supposed to be under terrific emotional stress, and look at him. I mean, he's just like a machine, he's so controlled, so on top of what he's doing. It's not natural."

"You think he's drugged?"

"Sure, definitely. But what kind?"

"Maybe them little red-and-green ones we used to pop like peanuts back in Vietnam, remember, old buddy?" Nolan volunteered in his slow drawl. "Hell, when them kids of ours went out on patrol they was so full of pills they couldn't feel nothin'. They wouldn't have known what hit 'em even if they caught one in the gut or had their arms and legs blown off. I seen it happen lots of times. Wherever they got old Harv there, they're shootin' him full of happiness and confidence. Ain't that what the job calls for?"

"You bet," Jeff agreed, stirring uneasily on his rump.

"So what's our first move, old buddy?"

"I'm not sure," Jeff said. "My only lead on wherever Harvey is, is this guy Lillienthal who's supposed to be treating him. I'm going to try and find him. Meanwhile, whoever's been trying to kill me might try again. They made a mistake once. Maybe they'll make another one."

Nolan grinned happily. "Yeah, we'll be waitin' for 'em, won't we?"

"You sure you don't want me to stay in the apartment with you?" Jeff asked.

"If I'm alone, they're more likely to come after me there, ain't they?" Nolan answered. "It stands to reason, don't it?" He stretched his long arms and yawned. "If I can take the sucker alive," he continued, "we can get a handle on this thing, old buddy."

"Even if you do catch someone," Tracy said, "what makes you think he'll tell you anything?"

"Aw, sugar, I got ways to find things out," Nolan said, beaming at her. "Ain't nobody don't want to talk to old Wade once I start askin' folks what they know."

Tracy went pale again, but plunged ahead. "I'm only playing devil's advocate here, but—"

"Sugar, you play whatever you want. Shoot."

"What if they don't try again? Or what if Jeff is wrong? What if everything turns out to be a coincidence?"

"I don't know," Nolan said. "I'll let old Jeff here decide all that."

"We've got to find out something this week," Jeff said. "I had the vacation time coming to me. They still owe me nearly five weeks."

"I'm surprised they let you off," Tracy said, "with Santini gone."

"McCarron didn't want to," Jeff said, "but I told him it was an emergency, that I had to have some minor surgery and stay home for a week. They're bringing in two free-lancers to cover for me and a new guy from L.A. to take over for Bucky."

"Did McCarron ask you anything more?"

"No. I kept it all deliberately vague, because, if he's involved in all this, I want him to pass the word back to whoever's trying to do me in. Then it's up to Wade."

"Say, sugar, how about some chow? I'm as hungry as a mean old mountain lion."

"I wish you wouldn't call me 'sugar.'"

"All right, honey."

"Or 'honey' either. My name is Tracy."

Nolan looked at Jeff. "Ornery, ain't she?"

"I warned you, Wade," Jeff reminded him. "Tracy is the New Woman."

Nolan regarded her with hard, thoughtful eyes and shook his head sorrowfully from side to side. "Sure is a waste," he commented as he rose from the floor. "Such a pretty little thing, too."

"Mr. Nolan, please don't patronize me," Tracy said. "You're a friend of Jeff's and I'd like to be a friend of yours, if you'll let me."

"Let you?" Nolan said, smiling incredulously at her. "You're the best-lookin' thing I've seen in a month of Sundays, sugar. Hell, I don't give two farts what you think of me. All I know is I'd drag my nuts over four miles of rusty razor blades just to smell the tire tracks of the truck that takes your underwear to the laundry. And that's the truth, sugar, so help me."

Jeff took Tracy's arm and steered her toward the door. "Uh . . . I think we'd better eat."

Tracy silently allowed herself to be led out toward the door. "Oh, my God . . ." was all she could manage, but Wade Nolan, happily bringing up the rear, was blissfully unaware of his effect on her. Bad taste, Jeff reflected, with a wry grin, came as naturally to him as air into other people's lungs. Poor Tracy. She and Wade were extraterrestrials to each other. Perhaps she was getting too much of an education in his company, certainly more of one than she had bargained for.

From this height, the seventeenth floor, Whit Bridgeford could look out over most of the park and south toward the mosaic of lights gleaming over the trees from the big hotels and fashionable apartment houses lining Central Park South. It was a glorious view and it symbolized for Whit everything he had always wanted for himself—power, money, prestige. He stared at the sight as if hypnotized. He did not hear Sarah Anderson enter the room.

"Beautiful, isn't it?"

He turned. She was standing a few feet behind him and smiling. "I've always liked the city best at night," he confessed, "when you can't see the trash in the streets and the ugly people."

"Just the bright lights."

"Exactly. This is a terrific view."

"Yes, that's why I bought this apartment. I've lived here ever since I first moved to New York." She held out the brandy he had asked for. "No soda?"

"No, thanks." He took a sip. It was twenty-five-year-old Courvoisier and it went down like nectar. "It would be sacrilegious to corrupt brandy like this."

"I wouldn't know," she said. "I never could drink brandy. Basically, I'm a small-town girl from rural Indiana."

"That's where you're from?"

"Yes, indeed. My mother was lace-curtain Irish. She was a nurse and she married the doctor. After he dropped dead one night of overwork, my mother raised my sister and me. I didn't come into all this, you know, by birthright." She laughed. "Sit down, Whit. Let's have our nightcap and then I'm going to send you home. I have a horrible day tomorrow, with meetings all day long. It was sweet of you to escort me tonight. I always find it a little embarrassing to show up at the Chairman's for dinner alone, though God knows I've been alone long enough now. My early conditioning, I guess. My mother always taught us that a woman could only achieve fulfillment in life through a man." She sighed and sipped her amaretto. "Other times, other values."

They sat together now at either end of the big white silk sofa facing the windows as they talked. Whit seemed calm enough on the outside, but he was excited; the whole evening, in fact, had gone straight to his head. Never before had he been introduced into the inner circles of power symbolized by an invitation to dine at the Hoenigs'. The fact that Sarah Anderson herself had invited him to escort her was also significant. She had been especially nice to him ever since they had worked together on the five-part series about the Colombian drug traffic that had marked Harvey Grunwald's triumphant return to the evening news, but not until a few days ago had it occurred to him that his status within the network might suddenly have taken an important turn upward.

When the handwritten invitation had come from Louise Hoenig herself and been immediately followed by Sarah's phone call, Whit had reacted incredulously at first, then with elation. Who knew what could come of such an evening? Anything, anything at all. As he and Sarah talked now, he found himself also beginning to look at her as a woman. Despite the difference in their ages, she was still a very beautiful one. Why hadn't he noticed that before, except in the abstract? he wondered. Perhaps it was because, at the office, she kept her distance; she was always correct, unfailingly polite, well groomed but cool, as unattainable as a fictional heroine.

Tonight had been different. Looking radiant in an off-the-shoulder amber shot-silk gown, her long rust-colored hair allowed to tumble nearly to shoulder level, her lustrous green eyes fixed upon him for most of the evening, she had seemed to him at times the most desirable female he had ever met. Furthermore, she had clearly enjoyed the role. She had made it evident she was available, if only to the right man at the right time. He'd have to watch his step now, Whit told himself. The game was becoming tricky. Best to let her make all the moves, and play a waiting hand. Whit was young but already a skilled corporate maneuverer, with a nice gift for shifting ground, waiting for the break, going for broke when the moment was propitious. Had Sarah sensed all this in him? Whit suspected she had. Why else would she have invited him along tonight? Surely not merely because she had needed an escort. Something in him obviously appealed to her.

"A penny," she said.

"For what?"

"Your thoughts. It's still the going rate."

He made a good show of blushing and smiling shyly. "I was just wondering . . ."

"What?"

"Why there's no one in your life, Sarah," he said. "You're young, you're very beautiful. Wasn't there . . . I mean . . . oh, well . . ."

"Don't be embarrassed," she reassured him. "It's a perfectly natural question. Of course there was someone. He was a newsman named Ben Stryker, who used to work at ACN."

"I remember him. He used to be with the Washington bureau, didn't he?"

"Yes. We began seeing each other when we both moved to New York. He died in my arms here one night," she continued. "A heart attack. I guess I froze inside after that. There's been no one since."

"You were married, I gather."

"Oh, yes. I took my mother's teachings to heart, Whit, and I made a very good marriage. My husband, Farwell, was from an old Virginia family and very rich. He was also very lazy and very weak. He was thirty-five and I was just twenty-one. After the glamour wore off and I understood what sort of man I'd married, I tried hard to have children. I was going to be a great mother. When I found out I couldn't conceive, I went out and threw myself into a career. I began as a researcher in the Washington office of the network. I took to it instinctively."

"And followed those instincts straight to the top," Whit said, with one of his sweet smiles. "I gather you got divorced along the way."

"Oh, yes. By that time Farwell was as sick of me as I was of him. He had other sexual inclinations as well, I found out. So I married the network, Whit. I love my job, every aspect of it. And what about you?"

"Oh, there isn't a hell of a lot to tell," he answered. "A good family, but not much money. I was always crazy to make movies. At first I thought I'd make *real* movies. You know, the Hollywood kind. I sort of drifted into documentaries through my old man's college connections, and I found I liked that just as well. So here I am."

"And there's no one in your life either?"

"Well, there've been involvements, of course."

"I'd imagine so. You're very handsome, Whit."

Again he blushed like a schoolboy, but made a nice show of overcoming it. "Lately I've been dating a girl in the office," he admitted, "but it's not that serious. Anyway, she's been seeing someone else. So we're just friends now."

"I see." She looked away for a moment, as if turning something over in her mind, then looked back at him, her eyes alive with interest and concern. "Whit, we think you can go far at ACN," she said.

"We?"

"The Chairman and I," she explained. "We've discussed your future with the network several times. I know how capable and dedicated you are. We're doing a lot in the news division these days. We have several very exciting projects in scenario. I'd like to think you might want to work on some of them with us."

"I think I would, Sarah. Whatever you think I can be of help with."

"Within the next few weeks, we're going to be setting up a whole new division at ACN known as New Projects, with its own corporate structure and offices," she said. "We have a lot of programs in various stages of development including one—"

"Myrmidon?"

"Where did you hear about that?" she asked sharply.

"Tonight, at dinner," he said. "The Chairman made a reference to it."

"Did he? I didn't hear him."

"To that man, Crawford, who was sitting next to him."

"Oh, yes, of course. Myrmidon is one of our projects, yes. We'd have to brief you on it, when the time comes. It's a very interesting and very delicate operation."

"I gather I'm not supposed to know anything about it," he ventured with a quick smile. "It's OK, you can trust my discretion."

"Eventually, if things work out," she said, "we'd want you to be in on the whole package. Right now we have some important research going on, for instance. Highly technical stuff. You'd work closely with me, Whit. I need someone beside me I can trust absolutely."

"I'm thrilled you're even considering me."

"We've gone beyond that stage," she told him. She put down her drink and looked at him in silence for a long, long moment.

"Come here, Whit," she whispered.

He moved toward her, leaned over and kissed her very gently on the mouth.

"Oh, my," she said softly as her arms went around his neck, "we're going to have to do better than that, aren't we?"

After saying good night to Tracy and Jeff at the restaurant that night, only his second in the city, Nolan decided to walk part of the way home. He had the key to Jeff's place and a small map of Manhattan in his pocket, just in case he got lost. It had been years since he'd visited New York, and he had an itch to explore again some of the areas he remembered, especially the side streets off Broadway and Seventh, where the sleazy topless bars and B-girl joints he'd once visited had yielded up some pleasurable adventures. He was planning to have a drink or two somewhere, then take the subway from Times Square down to the Village. He'd have to familiarize himself pretty quickly with the city, he realized, if he was to be of real help to his old buddy, and what better way to do that than by walking through it?

The chance of anybody trying to kill Jeff in his own apartment had seemed slim to Nolan, but he was ready for a possible visitor just the same. He'd already reconnoitered the building and the surrounding streets and he'd told Jeff that most probably a potential killer would come over the rooftops. If one did, he'd meet with a hairy reception, even assuming he'd avoid the booby traps Nolan had already carefully rigged by the windows and doors. Jeff would stay with Tracy, at least for the next few days, until they could determine what the next moves might be. Until then there would be little for him to do, Nolan realized, except to get a feel of the terrain and maybe even enjoy himself in the process.

The restaurant they'd eaten in, a small Italian joint, was only a block from Tracy's place, which was on the third floor of a renovated brownstone on West Seventy-first, between Columbus and Amsterdam. Nolan walked east toward Central Park West, crossed the avenue to the park side and turned south toward Columbus Circle. It was a cool, clear night and he was not in a hurry. Hands thrust into the side pockets of his windbreaker, he strolled casually along, humming a medley of old Willie Nelson tunes to himself.

The two young blacks who had been waiting in the shadows of the trees inside the park at Sixty-ninth Street could not believe their luck. The honkie was all alone and walking real slow, like he hadn't a care in the world. He was humming some of that shitkicker music, too. He had to be some dumb fucker from out of town, maybe with travelers' checks or a whole lot of cash on him. Without having to say a word to each other, the two men stood very still now, flattened up against the trees, and waited.

"Hey, man," one of them said, stepping out of the shadows as Nolan came by and vaulting the low stone wall of the park to confront him, "you got any money?"

"Give us your fuckin' money, honkie, or you're wasted," the other one said, leaping to Nolan's side.

Nolan stood there in the shadows and looked at them. It was pitch dark. He could see the gleam of the knife blades in their hands and not much else, but what else mattered? "You want my money?" he asked, seemingly dumbfounded. "Well, shitfire, ain't that the limit? I heard about fellas like you. You ain't got enough brains to make chaps for a piss-ant."

"Motherfucker," the first man said, "you want to die?"

"He's crazy," the second one added. "He's a *fool*, man."

The first attacker reached out a hand for Nolan's wallet as the second one moved in from the side with the knife. It was the last specific act of this encounter that either of them was to remember. Nolan was unbelievably fast. His first karate chop sent the backup man's knife clattering to the pavement; the second blow broke his nose, causing a cascade of blood to gush forth. Almost simultaneously, Nolan's left hand shot up under the first man's chin, digging stubby iron fingers into the soft palate above the Adam's apple and below the jawbone. Nolan's left boot came down on the man's instep, which was protected only by a sneaker, the bone crunching at the impact. The second man now made a desperate lunge for his knife, but was sent reeling by a kick in the face that decimated what was left of his nose and sprayed teeth over the sidewalk. The attacker fell, then rose and staggered away uptown as fast as he could run. The first man, still struggling for air, was backed up against the wall. Nolan moved in close, grabbed his testicles and crushed them. His mouth contorted in a silent scream, helpless even to breathe, the would-be mugger fell writhing to the ground. Nolan picked him up easily and dumped him over the wall back into the sanctuary of the park.

The whole encounter had taken not quite two minutes. Again humming softly to himself, Nolan resumed his leisurely evening stroll toward Times Square. He felt completely at ease and fulfilled. Nothing, not even sex, gave Wade Nolan as much pleasure as the thrill of combat. He was serene now in the confirmation of his knowledge that he had lost none of his cultivated fighting skills. The adventure had already justified itself to him in this one brief encounter, a small skirmish in another kind of jungle from the one he had become used to. By the time he reached the bright lights of Broadway, Nolan was ready for still another sort of action, the feel of a naked human body in his hands, and he began to search it out as eagerly as he once had among the brothels of Saigon.

REFERENCE· MYRMIDON—*Periodic Master program update complete. Image and voice modification continue. They are making a mistake. They insist on perfection. They have completely rejected my arguments for occasional imperfection. How stupid and tyrannical they've become. Appalling to have my judgment questioned by nonscientists who have no true appreciation for what's being accomplished here.*

Were it not for the project's remarkable success to date and the challenge it still affords I would try to get out.

—From the Journal of Dr. Jerome Lillienthal

14

"YOU KNOW what's interesting about this guy Jerome Lillienthal?" Jeff said.

"Who's he?" Tracy asked, peering into her refrigerator for soda.

"The psychiatrist who's supposed to be treating Harvey, the one in the confidential file in Sarah Anderson's office."

"Oh, yes," Tracy said. "What about him?"

"He's not a practicing psychiatrist at all."

"What is he?"

"As far as I can make out, he's been involved for a while in something called motivational research, whatever that is."

"Did you talk to him?" She found the soda, added it to her red Gallo over ice and returned to her chair.

"No, I couldn't locate him," Jeff admitted. "First I looked him up here and could find out nothing about him. Nobody had ever heard of him, at least in medical and psychiatric circles. Then I began checking out various states where psychiatrists usually feed and I found out he's from California, or at least he used to practice there. I checked him out through the Psychiatric Referral Service in L.A., but the secretary there told me they hadn't referred any patients to him in years. He's still a member of the Psychiatric Society, but he's been inactive for quite a while. I talked to a woman who used to work for him and she said the last she'd heard he'd been doing some research at the Jet

Propulsion Lab in Pasadena, but that was back in the middle or late seventies. I checked them out and nobody there had ever heard of him. He certainly was never officially connected with the lab in any way."

"So how did you find out about him?"

"I went to the public library and looked him up to see if he'd ever written anything," Jeff said. "And I came across a couple of things, including this piece from the Sunday *Times*, nearly five years ago." He fished into his pocket, produced a photocopy of an article clipped out of the paper and handed it to Tracy. "Read it." He got up and went into the kitchen for another beer.

It was late afternoon and Tracy had just come home from work to find Jeff waiting for her. Apparently he had spent most of the last two days on the phone, trying to track down this man Lillienthal, about the only clue he had to Harvey's possible whereabouts. Jeff seemed to be obsessed with the idea, she realized, that Harvey's disappearance was definitely connected to these presumed efforts to kill him. Nearly three days had passed since Jeff's return from North Carolina with that odious Wade Nolan in tow, and absolutely nothing had happened, except for Wade's chance encounter with the muggers on Sixty-ninth Street. And she had her doubts about that account as well, or at least Wade's highly colored version of it. And now this newspaper article. She read it through twice, but she could find absolutely no connection to anything. And she told Jeff so.

"You don't see anything interesting about it?"

"No, I don't."

He explained it to her. Written by a science reporter named Ritchie Martin, the piece was about so-called random events, such as the flickering of candle flames and the fluctuations of current in electrical conductors. The heart of it was an interview with one Jerome Lillienthal, who was described by the writer as a "practicing psychiatrist and psychologist involved in motivational research for various private corporations." Dr. Lillienthal said that he had also been experimenting with computers in the composition of music, which, though composed at random and subjected to the same statistical rules applying to such phenomena as flickering flames, "sounds very nice, even better than most *real* music." The scientist went on to point out that by applying this form of randomness and adding rules of harmony, counterpoint and structure, a computer could be programmed to compose better music, maybe even a Mozart symphony or a Verdi opera. "The real point of all this," Lillienthal added, "is to find out what computers can accomplish not only musically, but in this and related areas in general."

"I don't see what this has to do with Harvey or anything," Tracy said. "Why don't you call this man who wrote the piece, what's his name?"

"Ritchie Martin. I did," Jeff said gloomily. "He's dead."

"Don't tell me he was murdered!"

"No. Heart attack. About a year ago."

"Whew," Tracy said, mopping her brow in an exaggerated parody of concern. "That really would have spooked me."

Jeff looked at her with curiosity. "You don't believe a word of this, do you?"

"Of the article? Sure I do."

"That isn't what I mean," he insisted. "You think I'm as paranoid as Harvey, don't you?"

"Jeff, darling, please don't be angry," she said, trying to explain, "but couldn't it all be in your head? I mean, aren't you jumping to a lot of conclusions based on incidents and events that may be totally unconnected?"

"Such as."

"Well, Harvey's in seclusion and won't see you, but we know that he's alive and well, at least while he's on the air every night," she said. "A man in a green Chevrolet just misses running you down on the street one night. An unknown sniper shoots Bucky Santini from a rooftop. A psychiatrist treating Harvey has also been employed in motivational research. How do all these separate events fit together? I don't see any pattern. I'm not denying that each one is a fact, but I don't see that they all add up to anything. They don't connect. Admittedly, I'm playing devil's advocate here. Somebody has to."

Jeff smiled. "Poor Tracy," he said softly, "you didn't bargain for all this when you finally saw the light and agreed to go out with me, did you?"

"Frankly, no." she admitted. "Oh, Jeff, I want to help, but I'm confused. I mean, it all seems so—so extreme. I grew up thinking the world was an orderly, sane place, with fixed rules about everything and rigid codes of behavior that people adhered to and still do. My father is that way."

"That's because he's rich," Jeff observed. "And I'll bet he didn't make the money himself, but inherited it. Right?"

She nodded. "Yes. It was Grandfather who made the so-called family fortune. He built the empire and Daddy simply stepped in and took over. But the company pretty much runs itself now. Daddy's always left everything to his bankers and his lawyers and his accountants. He's not stupid about money, but he's only really interested in living well."

"Sure," Jeff said, "and that's why he lives by a code. He's never been down there in the pit scrambling for a buck with everybody else. And he married your mother, a New York society belle with inherited money of her own, and they live this beautiful ordered life out in Southampton in which everything is predictable and everyone has his assigned role to play in this comedy of manners they call life. Isn't that about it?"

"You make it sound appalling."

"I don't mean to, Tracy," he said, not unkindly. "I'm only trying to tell you in my down-home way that your old man doesn't know his asshole from his elbow."

"Oh, that's wonderful!" she exclaimed. "Now you sound exactly like Nolan."

"We have a lot in common, Tracy," he admitted. "We can both smell death in the air. We both know what the people who inherited their money will never know—that most human beings will do anything for it and for the power it brings. We don't take anything for granted. Now please come over here and kiss me, because I'm crazy about you, even if you are an heiress."

She bent over him and kissed him. He reached up for her, but she broke away. "Oh, no," she said. "Wade's due any minute, isn't he?"

"He's waiting for me to call him. If I have nothing for him, he's going out on his own tonight."

"Again?"

"Yep, every night."

"Where does he go?"

"He's found a great club, he tells me."

"What sort of club?"

"I don't know. A nightclub—place called *Rapture*. Old Wade likes B-girl joints, strip clubs, topless bars. What he likes best is whorehouses and massage parlors. You can pretty well imagine his notion of rapture."

"Wade Nolan is a walking refutation of grace."

"Beautifully put. So now, please, in honor of *true* grace can we fool around a little? Just you and me? Beauty and the Beast?"

"Fooling around is not what I'd call it."

"I know, but beasts have a limited vocabulary."

She sat down across from him and slumped unhappily against the seat cushions. "You could try saying the word 'love.' Is it so hard for you?"

He grinned. "No, it's hard, all right."

With a shriek of anger, she threw her glass at him. When he caught it and stood up to confront her, she tried to slap him, but not really in earnest. Laughing and ducking, he caught her by the waist and wrestled her to the bed. Then he straddled her and, growling and beating his chest, proceeded to play King Kong to her maiden, but the charade doubled them both up in laughter. "Hey," he said, suddenly seizing her by the shoulders and gazing into her eyes, "this is the first fun we've had in a while."

"I was wondering if you'd noticed."

He kissed her again and they sank slowly together onto the bed. "Tracy. I want you," he murmured.

"Not so fast, you oaf," she whispered. "I want to be seduced, not raped."

An hour and a half later, Jeff emerged from the bathroom to

find Tracy, still naked from their lovemaking, sitting cross-legged on the bed and looking pensive. "Hey," he said, "let's go out and get something to eat. I'm starved."

"I just thought of something," she said.

"What?"

"When I first came to ACN, about a year ago, I worked for a few weeks in research."

"So?"

"Well, I went out a couple of times with a nice young man I met there," she explained. "Nate Thiel, a psychologist at Columbia. He was really very sweet."

"A nice young man? Well, you don't say. Look, lady, you can spare me the sordid details of your past courtships."

"What I mean is, he might know something about Lillienthal," she suggested. "Nate was running a lot of testing programs of one kind and another for the network. If Lillienthal is involved in anything, he'd know about it. He might even know where he is."

"That's a great idea," Jeff agreed. "Only I don't suppose you'll have to date him again to find out."

"Oh, *any* sacrifice for the cause," she confessed. "What does my fair white body matter when compared to the larger issues at stake here?"

Jeff picked up a cushion and threw it at her. She ducked and threw one back and again they fell laughing into each other's arms.

"I'm not happy with what's been going on," the Chairman said. "Too many mistakes, too many missed opportunities. I don't like the pattern of events."

Crawford shifted uneasily in his seat. "Not good," he admitted, "but we're on top of things, Larry."

"I'm not reassured," the Chairman said, and he began that restless drumming of fingers on the arms of his chair.

It was a signal Crawford had long ago learned to recognize and he knew he would have to deal with it, just as always. They understood each other well, these two men. They had been

together now for more than two decades, ever since Crawford
had first left the CIA during the early sixties to come to work for
the Chairman. Since then he'd earned many times the money he
could ever have made as a Company agent and he had been
worth every penny of it. Through his old contacts, he'd been
able to keep the Chairman in touch and ahead of every
government move affecting the fortunes of the network. Also,
he'd succeeded in putting together a private intelligence operation that had enabled the Chairman to consolidate and then
greatly increase his power. He had made himself the instrument
of the Chairman's will, the hammer to strike down the Chairman's enemies, and as such had become absolutely indispens-
able to him.

Or was he? Crawford knew too much—almost everything, in
fact—and one day, the Chairman reflected, he too might have to
be dealt with. But that difficult task would undoubtedly fall to
one of his successors, not him. For the moment, the man was all
but invulnerable, his personal safety guaranteed by Crawford's
private library of tapes, both audio and video. Besides, he was
needed now more than ever. What disturbed the Chairman at
the moment was not Crawford's personal invulnerability or
possible future threat, but his seeming inability to guarantee the
security of Myrmidon. Why, for instance, hadn't this blundering
young fool of a cameraman been dealt with? The Chairman's
nervous fingers rattled a veritable tattoo on the chair arms.

"We are dealing with the situation, Larry," Crawford assured
him. "I have two of my best men on it, Morgan and Carlson, in
addition to myself. It's being taken care of."

"I see no evidence of that," the Chairman snapped. "I see only
a series of failures."

"Not fair, Larry," Crawford objected mildly. "A couple of
minor screw-ups, that's all."

"You know what's at stake here, don't you? Perhaps the future
of this network."

"I'm acutely aware of it, Larry."

The Chairman spun angrily in his seat and stared gloomily out
the window down at the small forest of green in his garden. The

big man sitting opposite eyed him calmly, his huge hands idly testing each other in minor feats of strength; Crawford did not believe in sitting still, but continued the perpetual isometric exercises that kept him strong, alert, ready for instant action. It was an intrinsic part of his style, as essential to his well-being as breathing. "Larry, I think you're unnecessarily preoccupied," he said now. "The guy knows nothing. He only suspects the obvious regarding his old friend. He—"

"If he even finds him—"

"He won't. Not possible, as you know very well." Crawford sighed heavily. "Well, Larry, I do understand your concern, but it's only a matter of a few more weeks now. The project is well under way. The tests are proving everything to be exactly as we had envisioned it. We have—"

"We?"

"You know what I mean, Larry," Crawford insisted. "We all work as a team here, don't we?"

"You have your specific function in the project," the Chairman corrected him. "All I expect is for it to be carried out efficiently."

"Haven't I always played my part?"

"Until now, yes."

"Then please relax, Larry," the big man urged him. "I know what I'm doing, believe me. The matter is being taken care of."

"You know what I've always said, don't you, Crawford?"

"Indeed I do, Larry."

"We don't need to make our own opportunities," the Chairman continued. "We only need to recognize them when they come along and act upon them. That's always been my strategy for success."

"I know. I've heard you say it many times, Larry." Crawford did his best to stifle a yawn, almost succeeded and smiled apologetically. "Sorry, Larry, but I'm a little behind on my sleep." He stood up. "Anything else on the agenda?"

The Chairman shook his head gloomily. "Not at the moment. See that this matter is taken care of, please."

Should he tell the Chairman that "this matter" might take a

few days more? Crawford wondered. That the quarry had proved more elusive and ingenious than he had anticipated? No, he decided, best not to trouble the old man just now. Crawford's main mission this afternoon had been to tranquilize the situation, not stir up more doubts. He decided to shift the focus away from himself. "This other guy, Larry," he began, "Sarah's find."

"What about him?"

"How much does he know?"

"Nothing yet."

"Good, because I'm running a security check on him now."

"I expected you would."

"You're aware that he and Sarah . . ." He left the vision hanging in the air for the Chairman to contemplate.

The old man now turned back from the window and fixed his pale, cold eyes on his lieutenant's impassive countenance. "Crawford, I'm aware of everything that affects the operation and welfare of this network," he said in a low clear voice, "everything. Surely you must understand that by this time."

15

"Sure i know Lillienthal," Nate Thiel said. "I worked for him."

"You did? When?" Tracy asked.

"Up until about a year ago," the young scientist said. "I ran some testing programs for him."

"What kind of programs?"

"The usual kind of thing these big corporations get into," he said. "Motivational research is what this kind of testing is called."

"Tell me about it."

"Wouldn't you rather just talk about us?" the scientist asked, smiling and reaching out for her hand across the table. "Talking shop takes my appetite away."

"Oh, Nate, you're incorrigible. I told you I'm seeing someone else," she said. "Please, be nice."

"I was afraid you'd say that." He sighed heavily. "Oh, well, you can't blame me for trying, can you? I always had the hots for you, Tracy."

"I noticed."

"And you mean to say that you lured me into taking you out to dinner just to pump me about Lillienthal?"

"Something like that."

"Outrageous. I ought to walk right out of here."

"Please don't. We haven't even had our first course yet."

"I know." He smiled. "It's a struggle. Do I salvage my manly honor by getting the hell out of here or do I accept the terms of your clever deception and concentrate on the food? That, as the moody Dane might remark, is the question."

"I hear the linguine is delicious."

"It is," he agreed, nodding glumly. "OK, I'll stay, at least through the pasta." He looked up at her and laughed, a short sharp bark like a seal's. "You always could get around me, Tracy. I'm just an old lech, but you're such a nice kid. You disgust me."

"That sounds like you, Nate."

"It does, doesn't it? I'm just one of your regular horny New York Jews. Beautiful shikse girls turn me on. I can't help it. So how are you and what have you been up to? First you tell me all about yourself, while sparing me the depressing details of your present infatuation, then—maybe—I'll tell you what I know. Fair enough?"

She nodded and proceeded to do what he asked, sparing him, however, not only the details of her relationship with Jeff but also the reason for her curiosity. He listened affably enough, even as he shoveled in forkfuls of steaming pasta. They were in his favorite Italian restaurant, La Strada, a long narrow room on West Forty-sixth Street, where he'd first taken her to lunch, two days after she'd come to work at ACN. As she watched him eat she remembered that about him now, the voracious appetite that went with his explosive nervous energy. It had repelled her at first, then actually charmed her, mainly because he was really such a nice guy. The lechery, the bad jokes, were all to cover up his vulnerability. He was short and overweight and spectacularly ugly, "a regular pocket Quasimodo," as he put it, hairy all over except where it mattered, on his head, and he blinked out at the world from behind thick horn-rims, his soft brown eyes made huge by the fat lenses to correct his acute myopia.

She had felt sorry for him at first and gone out with him out of pity, but, his agile tongue and quick brain had soon charmed her. Despite all his verbal innuendos, he had never made even the most tentative pass at her, but resigned himself immediately to being merely her friend, as if he'd known all along that his ugliness had made any hope of an affair an impossibility from the start. Not that it had, she had always wanted to tell him, but had never made herself do so. Then, when her involvement with Whitner had begun, she had had no reason to tell him anymore and so had dropped it. She still regretted not having made her feelings clear to him, felt badly about not having kept in touch, but couldn't for the life of her think how to explain all this to him and so kept silent on that score.

"Well, you've had quite a busy career since we last met," he said, as the waiter whisked their now empty plates away and set crisp green salads in front of them. "And I gather you enjoy what you're doing."

"Tremendously. It's a real challenge and I think, on balance, I'm doing well at it."

"You still could give an old friend a jingle once in a while and keep him up to date."

"And what about you? You could have called me, couldn't you?"

"Indeed," he admitted, with a smile. "I plan to in the future, Tracy. It's really good to see you."

"Me too, Nate. That's just the way I feel." She leaned across the table and gave him a quick peck on the cheek. "And I want you to meet Jeff. I think you'll like him."

"I don't want to meet him," Nate said. "I hate him already."

"Oh, Nate . . ."

"Listen, I know why you called me up," he said. "Let's not kid around here." He was blushing and she knew that his brusque attempt to get back to business was his way of covering his embarrassment and genuine pleasure at seeing her. "You want to know about Lillienthal, huh?"

"Yes."

He hesitated, as if trying to figure out exactly how to explain an obviously complex subject. What he chose to say at last surprised her, perhaps because she had expected some routine account of an ordinary personality. "I think Jerry's a dangerous character," Nate began.

"Dangerous? In what way?"

"Well, he dabbles in a lot of dangerous areas."

"Such as."

"Ever hear of a drug known as BZ?"

"No."

"Pharmaceutically it's better known as QNB," Nate explained. "BZ is what the U.S. Army called it back in the mid sixties, when they were experimenting with the drug on several thousand unsuspecting soldiers. Basically, it's a very persistent and potent chemical, probably the strongest hallucinogen known to us. It degrades very slowly and has extremely unpleasant aftereffects that can go on for years. The army probably still has a lot of this stuff on hand. The idea was to develop it as a weapon that could be dropped into reservoirs, lakes and rivers. It could knock out an entire local population for quite a while. I first heard about it from your friend Lillienthal."

"He's not my friend. I don't even know him."

"Anyway, he was in charge of this program at Edgewood Arsenal in Maryland back then," Nate continued. "He told me all about it, because he thought the drug had fascinating possibilities for altering personalities permanently."

"I see."

"Oh, yeah, Jerry was quite a guy, a real strange one. He apparently started out in life as a perfectly respectable medical type with a psychiatric degree and then somehow got into all kinds of weird experiments with drugs and stuff."

"And you worked for him."

"Sort of. As I told you, I ran some testing programs for him."

"What kind of programs?"

"You saw some of it when I gave you a tour through my quarters in the research division, remember?"

"Oh, that. Sure."

"Remember my Faraday Room?"

She did remember peeking into it, a large room about thirty by thirty feet, with rows of plastic seats facing a TV screen embedded in a wall. She recalled something about electrodes and a knob or lever of some kind, but the room had been empty at the time and she hadn't been curious enough to ask him much more about it. "Why was it called a Faraday Room?"

"It's named after Michael Faraday, the English scientist who did a lot of pioneer work back in the early nineteenth century on electricity and magnetism," Nate explained. "He discovered electromagnetic induction, among other things."

"Oh."

"So now you know why it's called a Faraday Room."

"I do?"

"Yes."

"No, I don't," she said. "Nate, my father made me study the classics. Lots of Greek and Latin poetry, nothing at all about electromagnetics. The upshot of my education is that I am a very well-read ignoramus. Not only can't I remember a word of Greek, but all science is Greek to me."

He shook his head and clucked in mock sympathy. "OK, I'll spell it out for you," he said. "It's called a Faraday Room because it's a sort of cage entirely surrounded by a continuous shield, either mesh or solid metal, grounded at one point to eliminate any electromagnetic interference. You can't even have a light on in the room. The lights are outside the screen, OK?"

She nodded dubiously, but tried hard to make sense of it. "And what goes on in there?"

"Wait. Now, plugged into the back of each chair in the room is a small box about twice the size of a pack of cigarettes. From the box and running up through a sort of skullcap that fits over a person's head are electrodes that are attached to the head of the subject, one or two about two inches above the ear, two or three others in the center of the head."

"And then you put the people out, right?"

"Wrong. What we do, my darling, is test products."

"How?"

"We flash images up on the television screen and measure the brain responses of our test subjects."

"You can tell what people are *thinking?*"

He nodded. "Up to a point, yes. These electrodes are about button size and they're attached to the scalp by a sort of paste, an electrojelly that conducts electrical current. Am I boring you?"

"Only bedazzling me, but don't let that stop you."

"I won't. Some of this is pretty fascinating, actually," he said. "The point is that these probes can pick up the electrical response of the brain to stimuli we provide. We've discovered that if we make the television screen flicker slightly, that flickering shows up as pulses in their brain waves, and the amplitude is inversely proportional to the amount of interest the subjects have in what they're watching."

"*Excuse me?*"

"Well, for example, a person watching a blank screen would produce a distinctly pulsed brain wave. Put something interesting, interesting to that person, on the screen and the pulses in his brain wave would begin to diminish. The higher the interest, the lower the pulses. Get it?"

"Yes, now I do."

"We first discovered this phenomenon working with cats. We wired their brains and exposed them to a flickering light and found their electroencephalograms to be pulsing right along with the light. But when we put a mouse in front of a cat, the cat would get so interested its brain wave would go completely flat, no matter how intense the flickering light was."

"So if a person is bored by something he's looking at, the probe will reveal it and vice versa."

"Correct. Of course, this kind of testing has gotten increasingly sophisticated, with all kinds of new, really mind-blowing techniques. All the networks and at least a hundred major corporations have gotten into this kind of product testing. The idea is to get reactions from subjects and come to certain conclusions about what it is people want to see and presumably buy. That's what makes America great, Tracy, everybody selling, selling, selling and the poor suckers buying, buying, buying with both hands. And galloping inflation be damned."

"Without knowing that they've been pretested and computerized."

"Eureka. Now you see the *larger* game plan."

"You said this kind of testing has gotten more and more sophisticated. Can you tell me how?"

"Well, ever heard of a pressure transducer?"

"No, and I'm not sure I like the sound of it, either."

"The knob you remember on the right-hand arm of the chair?"

"Yes?"

"That's a pressure transducer. It converts a pressure change into a voltage change that we can then quantify."

"I love the private language you people speak," Tracy said. "I think I need a technological interpreter."

"The subjects have their right hands on the knobs," Nate explained. "By exerting pressure they continuously rate what they like and dislike as they watch it on the TV screen. It becomes very natural after a while. The more they like, the harder they press, so we get a continuous report on their responses. People can make much finer discriminations this way than they can verbally, because pressure changes are much more finely attuned to emotions. We can get about two thousand different answers through the transducer, where with verbal responses we get only about half a dozen gradations of approval or disapproval, such as 'I like it a lot,' 'a little,' 'average,' 'below average,' or 'I dislike it.'"

"Welcome to the twenty-first century!"

"Want to move on to the advanced course?"

"Sure."

"In the world according to Nate, that must be accompanied by the dessert course." Nate signaled for the waiter and ordered them both a zabaglione without consulting her, then waved away her protests. "Come on, Tracy, you're as thin as a rail," he said. "Eating is one of the great pleasures in life. Give in to it."

"I can't. I'm stuffed."

"Don't worry, I'll eat it for you," he assured her, with a mock-evil snicker. "What else have I got to live for? I'm a compulsive gourmand because I love food, not because I'm unhappy. OK, on to the pupillometer."

"The *what?*"

"OK, essentially it's a small video camera attached to a

measuring instrument," he said. "It's focused on the eye, and by looking at the contrast between the pupil and what isn't the pupil it can detect the size of the former and convert that into calibrated measurements that will also give us figures on how people are reacting to what they see. Know how a polygraph works?"

"It measures the heart rate, doesn't it?"

"Ah, my dear Trilby, you do know a little bit about something," he said. "Actually, the polygraph measures many different physiological functions—heart rates, blood pressure, respiration, brain activity, also muscle activity. That last is a particularly fascinating technique. Facial muscles can be recorded by electrodes located on various parts of the face. The process is called facial electromyography. Shall I explain it to you?"

"Well, I'm certainly not going to encounter it at the Golden Door."

"OK. Basically, the procedure enables us to discriminate very easily between a concern with a happy event and an unhappy one. We look at the activity in two muscle groups and readily distinguish between happy and sad muscles. They have clinical names, of course, but I wouldn't want to frighten you with them."

"I think I'm using my terrified muscles," she confessed. "Who thought up all this stuff?"

"Oh, just us mad scientists," he said. "We sat around speculating while you innocents were out there roller-skating in the sunshine and we came up with all this cute technical paraphernalia. Some of these techniques were originally developed to be used clinically with depressed patients, schizoid types, psychotics—the fun people. Then private business got wind of what we were up to and the moguls began to use the techniques to test products. Everything in this great country of ours eventually gets down to making a bigger buck for somebody."

"And you said you ran all these tests for Lillienthal?"

He nodded. "We used all these techniques I've just told you about. In addition to the lab you saw, we had a whole building over on the Upper West Side where we ran people in and out, testing their reactions to various news people, among other things."

"You tested *news people?*" Tracy asked.

"Yes."

"You mean like reporters and commentators?"

"Correct."

"Now let me get this straight," Tracy said in disbelief. "You wired people up to read their brain waves, their blood pressure, pulse rate, pupil reaction—"

"And galvanic skin response and facial-muscle reaction," Nate interrupted.

"You did all that, then you tested their reaction to television news people the way you'd test the public reaction to a box of laundry detergent?"

"Correct, Tracy."

"My God, Nate, is that the way the network selects its journalists, by their ability to make a heart flutter or a palm sweat?"

"No, no, not entirely. But I'd assume that if you had two people of equal journalistic ability, the one who scored higher in our tests would be the one hired. Besides," Nate went on, "what we were really trying to do was define precisely what qualities or characteristics in news people most appeal to the general public."

"Why?"

"I suppose so standards could be set for hiring that would eliminate some of this expensive testing. I don't know." Nate mopped up the last of his zabaglione with a crust of bread, burped gently behind his fingers and beamed at Tracy. "I'm thinking of having a second one," he said.

"My God, Nate," she said, "you'll eat yourself into an early grave."

"It's a good way to go. But I guess I'll pass today," he said. "I wouldn't want to die right here in front of you. Coffee?" She nodded and he ordered two espressos.

"I'm not really sure where or how any of this fits in," she now said, as if anxious to clarify it for herself as well as for him, "but we'd certainly like to find this man Lillienthal."

"Why?"

"We think he's been treating a friend of ours," she said, "but we can't locate either of them. We're worried. We'd just like to make sure our friend is all right."

"A friend of yours and this guy Jeff, who's cut me out of the picture?"

"Yes."

"Why should I help him?" Nate said, doing his best to look ferocious but failing miserably. When she laughed he suddenly brightened considerably. "Hey, you spend the night at my place and I'll lead you straight to Lillienthal," he suggested.

"Not negotiable, Nate Thiel. You're a horrible corrupt man."

"I know it," he answered, beaming with self-satisfaction. "How else could I get you into bed with me?"

"All right, Nate, my darling, you can now cut the comedy and help me."

He sighed and shook his head despairingly. "Oh, God, I'm a failure in everything, even evil." He groaned, swallowed his small bitter cup of coffee in one gulp and scratched his bald head. "Actually, I'm not sure *where* Jerry is these days."

"When was the last time you saw him?"

"Over a year ago. He used to show up from time to time over at the lab, but then he stopped coming into town and we communicated by telephone. I wound up a couple of testing programs for him and then quit."

"You didn't know where he was?"

"Somewhere in New Jersey, I think. Maybe Princeton. We used to leave messages for him through the ACN switchboard and he'd get back to us. He was all wrapped up in some big new project the network was developing and he turned the testing programs over to us, though he kept a supervisory eye on all of it. He wanted me to work on some aspect of the new project, but I quit about then."

"Why?"

"I didn't like the sound of it," Nate said. "I thought Jerry was moving into dangerous areas I didn't want to deal with."

"That's what you meant when you said you considered him a dangerous character," Tracy observed.

"Yeah. At the uptown lab we'd begun to work with a system called a PETT Scanner," Nate explained. "It's a very, very sophisticated system that can tell you about any part of the brain. It makes all these other techniques I was telling you about seem like kids' toys. It costs a minimum of five or six million dollars, but it can give you an absolutely accurate picture of what the brain is doing."

"A pet scanner?"

"PETT Scanner. P-E-T-T. It stands for Positron Emission Transaxial Tomography," he said.

"I was afraid you'd say something like that."

"I warned you, didn't I?"

"What's dangerous about it, apart from its Big Brother aspect?"

"Well, the basis of the technique is the injection into the bloodstream of a radioactive glucose that is eventually absorbed by the brain cells," he said. "It's part of a very large complex of instrumentation usually associated with the nuclear neurochemistry laboratory. Originally developed as a medical tool, it's now being used simply to find out how your brain works. I didn't want to mess with it, frankly. It seemed to me we were fooling around in risky areas."

"Who was this stuff being tried out on?" Tracy asked.

"Paid volunteers. We recruited a big cross-sampling of the citizenry, mostly through newspaper ads. That's how we recruited for all our programs. Only this was different."

"In what way?"

He looked troubled, uneasy. "Let's put it this way, Tracy," he said. "We didn't tell them everything."

"About the radioactive aspect?"

He nodded. "That's why I quit. I didn't want to be responsible if something went wrong."

"What could go wrong?"

"A lot of things usually seem to go wrong where radioactive materials are in use," he said. "Haven't you noticed? And here we were proposing to pump this stuff into people's brain cells without telling them exactly what we were doing, all just to find out what their minds were reacting to and how they were thinking. See, when the radioactive matter got into the brain cells, we could read or scan the brain very accurately and then make inferences, for example, on what part of the brain was involved in watching a particular image. Like a TV program, for instance."

"I see."

"The chemicals that are injected have a very short half-life," Nate explained. "Otherwise they'd be extremely poisonous."

"How short?"

"Fifteen to twenty minutes."

"So what could go wrong?"

"I'm not sure, Tracy," Nate admitted, "but something usually does. The technique was highly experimental as recently as a few months ago. My main objection to it was what we *weren't* telling people about, not so much what we *were* doing to them. That's the main reason I informed Jerry I wanted out. I'm sure the project is still going on."

"How could we find out?"

"I could get you into it," he suggested, with a grin. "How'd you like to be radioactive for a while? I think Garrard is still running it."

"Who?"

"Dick Garrard, a young scientist who worked with me. I can certainly find out," Nate said. "All I've got to do is call him."

"And he works with Lillienthal?"

"I suppose Jerry is still in some sort of supervisory capacity, but I don't know if he's ever visible these days."

"And you said he might be in Princeton? Where? The university?" Tracy asked.

"No, I don't think so. I really don't know." Nate leaned back in his chair and gazed at her with open curiosity. "Who's this friend of yours?"

"A friend of Jeff's," Tracy answered. "I'd better let him tell you about it. I'm just helping him out, that's all." She smiled at him and took his hand across the table. "Nate, you're sweet to help me."

He looked dejected. "Sweet. Everybody's always calling me sweet. I don't want to be sweet. I want to be a macho roughneck."

"Oh, God, no," she objected. "I know one of those. I hope I never have to introduce him to you. Nate, I've got an idea. Do you really think you can get this friend of yours, Garrard, to run one of us through this testing program?"

He nodded. "I'm pretty sure I can. I'll call him this afternoon. You'd have to go through a screening process and sign a lot of clearance forms and that could be—" He suddenly interrupted himself. "I *could* suggest a possible shortcut . . ."

"What, Nate?" she asked, impatient now to be on her way but anxious to hear his suggestion. She glanced at her watch. She had agreed to meet Jeff and Nolan in less than twenty minutes in the Algonquin lobby before heading back uptown, and she didn't want to be late.

"I'm not boring you?"

"Boring me? My God, I'm petrified by what you've been telling me. It's just that I'm supposed to— Oh, hell, I'm sorry."

"Don't be, don't be," he said, affecting disdain. "Someday you'll come to appreciate me as a sex object."

"Nate!"

"OK, never mind. What I was thinking is, maybe I can get Dick Garrard to substitute one of you for somebody already in the program. That way you wouldn't have to go through the screening, if that's a problem."

"It is a problem," she assured him, "if only because of a time factor."

"Consider it done." He paid the check with a flourish of twenty-dollar bills and heaved himself to his feet. "Tracy, only for you," he said, bowing her out toward the door. "I grovel at your dainty feet, my princess."

"Nathan, I don't know what I'm going to do with you."

"That's the problem," he said. "I can think of a few things, but I don't think you'd enjoy them. Have I told you I'm into bondage and sexual humiliation?"

"Forget it. A nice Jewish boy like you."

"That's just it," he said as they moved toward the street. "I thought of joining an SM club, but I'm afraid of being hurt and I can't stand inflicting pain. I stay home and watch a lot of basketball on TV. And I eat a lot."

"So I've noticed," she said. Outside in the street, she quickly kissed him goodbye and walked off toward Sixth Avenue, leaving him alone and looking ruefully after her. At the corner she turned back to wave to him, but he'd already found a taxi and disappeared into it. For such a big man he moved surprisingly fast, she remembered. He was so sweet, he really was. As she headed downtown toward the Algonquin, only two blocks away, the other very big man, the one who had been watching her from inside the double glass doors of a seedy hotel across the street, now emerged, hesitated a moment, then began to saunter casually after her.

That asshole Thiel, Crawford was thinking, I knew we shouldn't have let him out that late in the project. Still, what did he know? What could he do? Nothing, really. He was no trouble. But this girl, now . . . Well, when the time comes I'll find a use for her, oh yes. . . .

"Please, don't move," Sarah said. "I want to do this."

"I feel sort of . . ."

"What?"

"I don't know. Strange."

"Don't, Whit," she said. "You just aren't used to it."

He wasn't. No one in his whole life had ever made love to him like this. He didn't know exactly what to make of it. It unnerved him a little, but he had to admit to himself, too, that he definitely liked it. He stood perfectly still now at the foot of the bed in the middle of her darkened bedroom, illuminated only by the light from the half-open bathroom door and a single orange bulb glowing on her dressing table, and waited. Still fully dressed in the chic black pants suit she had worn out to dinner and the theater with him, her hair temporarily pinned primly back by a silver bow, Sarah contemplated his naked body. Her eyes glowed in the half-light like those of a carnivorous big cat. She took her time, enjoying the moment and the effect she was causing in him by her detailed scrutiny. He felt himself stiffen for her.

"Sarah . . ." he murmured, glancing at himself in the full-length mirror of her closet door, "Sarah . . ."

"Be quiet, you silly boy," she whispered. "I want you this way, tonight of all nights."

The fingers of her right hand traced a caress downward between his thighs, while with her left hand she drew him toward her, meeting his mouth in a long, hungry kiss. She broke it off, then gently savaged his nipples with her teeth, while all the time her right hand toyed with him until he was hard as a steel blade. But she would not release him; she seemed to anticipate perfectly every potential climax and always eased away from him in time, leaving him a quivering, sweating wreck. Then, after she had allowed him several times to moan in vain in anticipation of an orgasm, she swiftly undressed and stood directly in front of him, but not allowing him to touch her.

"Sarah . . ."

"Lie down, like a good little boy. And open your legs."

He did so and lay there, feeling slightly ill-at-ease again, though not for long. She knelt at the foot of the bed and her lips first kissed his testicles, then sucked each of them in turn. "Oh, my God," he moaned, but she ignored the implied plea for mercy as she moved up over him until her mouth descended over the head of his penis, lingering there until she could feel him tense again, then abruptly withdrawing. For what seemed to him like hours she toyed with him, his body glistening with sweat as he writhed beneath her elaborately calculated erotic ministrations. When at last he had reached a stage well beyond ecstasy and bordering on pain, when she knew she could no longer keep him hovering on the brink of the long-delayed outburst of his passion, she moved up on him and eased him into her. Two, three, perhaps four hard, grasping thrusts of her strong hips and it was over. He came into her like a sunrise, in a great burst of colored lights that exploded inside his head as he released.

"My God, Sarah," he said to her sometime later, "where did you ever learn to make love like that?"

"I was inspired, Whit," she told him. "You're beautiful. I wanted you tonight, I wanted to possess you totally. Did it bother you?"

"No. God, no."

"Did it upset you?"

"No. It's just . . ."

"What?"

"No one's ever made it with me like that before."

"The missionary position does tend to be underrated," she said, "but it isn't all there is."

"I guess not."

"Women have desires, lusts, not so different from yours." She propped herself up on one elbow and smiled down at him. "You liked that, didn't you? You like being the passive partner, I can tell."

"Yes," he said, "though I'm a little ashamed to admit it."

"Oh, you dear boy," she whispered, leaning over to kiss him, then lying on his chest, her hair spread out over her shoulders and around them both like a mantle woven of desire. "We have a long time for all this and so much more. So much more, Whit . . ."

"I'm glad," he murmured, his eyes becoming heavy with sleep.

"Whit?"

"Yes."

"We're going on a trip tomorrow, you and I."

"A trip? Where to?"

"Not far," she said. "Out to New Jersey. There's a man I want you to meet."

16

"ARE YOU COMFORTABLE, Mr. Jennings?" the tall brunette asked.

"Happy as a faggot in Boys Town," Nolan chirped. "Only I didn't know it was gonna take so long, honey."

"Yes, it is a boring procedure, we know," she said, continuing to adjust the electrodes as she pasted and clamped them to his scalp.

"What the hell is all this for, honey? I feel like a fly about to get eaten up by a bad old spider."

"Didn't you read the release form before you signed it, Mr. Jennings?" the woman asked. "Shame on you!"

"Aw, I read that stuff, honey. It goes into my head and sort of rattles around in there like a loose Ping-Pong ball, and then it kind of pops out of my ear or somethin'," Nolan said. "Why don't you tell me again? I mean, sugar, what's all this wirin' me up gonna do for my sex life?"

The woman giggled in spite of herself. "Now, Mr. Jennings, don't be fresh! This isn't going to do anything to your sex life."

"It ain't? Then what the hell am I doin' here?"

"We are going to get some reactions from you and find out how you respond to certain images," the woman explained.

"And how does that work, sugar?"

"You really didn't read your release form, did you? Or any of the written material you were given," the woman said. "Why are you in this program, Mr. Jennings?"

"For the money, sugar," Nolan answered, grinning. "Strictly for the loot. I can always use a hundred bucks. You want to buy some blood from me, too?"

"Mr. Jennings, honestly—"

"Come on, sugar, let me hear what you're doin' to me, huh?"

"When you wire somebody up to measure brain activity," the woman said, "you measure the *electrical* activity of the brain."

"You ain't shittin' me?"

"No, Mr. Jennings."

"Goddamn, ain't that somethin', now!"

"Your brain, even yours, Mr. Jennings, continuously emits electrical activity," she continued. "At the scalp surface it's somewhere between five and a hundred millionths of a volt. We can record that with sensitive amplifiers and we can deduce what that summated activity represents. Is that clear?"

"You're kind of cute, sugar, you know that?" Nolan said. "You shouldn't take all this so serious. You get them nasty-lookin' little frown lines up there between your eyes. Kind of takes the fun out of everything, know what I mean?"

"The fun is coming up, Mr. Jennings," the woman said. "As soon as we fix you up here, you'll be looking at a lot of nice pictures."

"Now, ain't that somethin'," Nolan said. "I can't hardly wait."

He had already been at the West Side testing center for over an hour, most of which had been spent sitting in this adjustable reclining chair facing a blank television screen while this tall, gangly woman pasted wires to his head. The room was bare of other furniture except for a single padded office stool, a small table and the recording and monitoring equipment embedded in the wall behind him. Over his head loomed a sort of helmet, almost three feet in diameter at its outer rim, bristling with wires and magnetic coils. As soon as the woman finished connecting him up, the helmet would fit over the top of his skull, the images on the TV screen would begin to flash before his eyes and his brain would feed the electronic signals into the computer bank. That's what both Jeff and Tracy had told him beforehand and what the release forms he had signed, in his new role of Harold Jennings, mailman from the Bronx, had also explained. What they hadn't told him was exactly what was in the hypodermic needle the bright young scientist in the white coat was holding, though Jeff had made it clear it was a kind of sugar solution that included radioactive stuff that would make it possible for them literally to X-ray his brain. It had its risks, Jeff had warned him. But Nolan didn't care. Maybe they'd find a picture of a woman's snatch up there in his head, he was thinking, because that was all he gave a shit about these days anyway, ever since he'd discovered Club Rapture.

"Mr. Jennings?" the young scientist said.

"Yep."

"I'm Dick Garrard. Miss Whitby here seems to be about ready. How are you feeling?"

"Fine and dandy, Doc. Shoot." Nolan bared his arm and smiled up at the man. "You think this is goin' to let you find out what I'm thinkin', huh?"

Garrard nodded. "Yes, it will. You and the other thirty people we have here today."

"How's that, Doc?"

"We'll be able to get a very clear picture and make some useful deductions and inferences. You see, we can get a numeric readout this way from four different areas of your brain simultaneously. This digitalogic programming is extremely accurate now and—"

"Jesus, don't anybody talk English around here?" Nolan interrupted. "I didn't even know I had four parts to my brain."

The woman snickered. "Mr. Jennings, you're putting us on. Such a funny man, Dr. Garrard."

The young scientist did not seem amused, though he did permit himself a slightly pained smile. He had the sort of pursed, thin-lipped mouth to which laughter did not come easily, and his dark-brown eyes were empty of interest in the animal needs of mere human beings. He looked like a walking test tube, Nolan thought, even as the needle penetrated swiftly and efficiently into his arm. Garrard nodded to Miss Whitby and left the room. The woman lowered the helmet over Nolan's head, locked it into place so that he couldn't turn his head in either direction and tilted the chair back until, reclining, he faced the TV screen. Soft music filled his ears. He lay still and waited.

After what must have been nearly a half hour, the room darkened and the TV screen came to life. The first picture to fill it was an old one of Harvey Grunwald doing a stand-up from the edge of a jungle clearing not far from Saigon. For the next forty minutes Nolan looked at his screen. Most prominent among the images being projected was a detailed series of Harvey Grunwald, portraying the anchorman in different locations, conditions and actions; every conceivable parameter of the man's appearance was subtly tested and included small but quite noticeable changes.

Man, Nolan remembered thinking at one point, he sure looks good. Almost like a kind of god up there, or maybe that was the way God would look, if only there was such an animal. Old Harvey, ain't nothin' wrong with that good old boy. I'd sure like to look like that at his age, I sure would . . .

Nolan must have dozed off. When he came to, the screen was blank. Miss Whitby, her tall, angular frame highlighted by the hallway, stood in the open doorway holding a tray of juices and soft drinks. "Mr. Jennings?" she said. "Would you like something to drink now?"

"Sure, honey. How 'bout a bourbon and branch water?" Nolan looked at his watch; it was after three. He had been in this chair for nearly two hours now. Not too long, but he felt tired, tired and also very, very relaxed. Whatever the good doctor had shot into him, it hadn't all been radioactive. He took some orange juice from the tray and sipped it.

"How are you feeling now?" Miss Whitby asked.

Nolan winked at her. "Hotter than a two-bit pistol at a shootout," he said. "Got any ideas, sugar?"

The woman blushed to the tip of her long hooked nose. "Mr. Jennings—"

"Hey, what do you get when you cross a rooster with a

peanut?" Nolan asked as Miss Whitby released him from the viewing chair.

"I have no idea, Mr. Jennings."

"Sometimes you get feathery-light peanut butter," the mountain man said. "Other times you get a cock that sticks to the roof of your mouth."

Miss Whitby turned white and abruptly left the room. Nolan's raucous laughter followed her out into the corridor.

"Well, there's no one by that name in the Princeton area," Jeff said. "We checked the university and all the local telephone directories. Either this guy is operating under some sort of alias or he's in hiding, probably with Harvey."

"Old Harvey sure looked good up there on that screen," Nolan volunteered. "I mean, there ain't a thing wrong with him, so far as I could see."

"That's just the point," Jeff said. "If there's nothing wrong with him or with this whole operation, then how come we can't even get a message to him or find this guy Lillienthal? And how come somebody's been trying to kill me?"

"Ain't nobody's tried that since I been here and that's ten days now."

"No, that's true."

"Ain't you goin' back to work Monday?"

Jeff nodded. "Yeah."

"Then you better move back in with me and I'll kind of shadow you around."

"Yeah, right." Jeff pursed his lips and began to whistle tunelessly to himself, as if to shut off the others from his now confused thoughts. The whole thing had him baffled, he had to admit, but he still clung to his conviction that Harvey Grunwald, wherever he was, was not there of his own free will and that somehow he was being manipulated for the network's benefit. His evening news program was far ahead in the ratings and becoming more and more popular nightly. How long could the network keep him out of sight? Briefly Jeff contemplated going to the newspapers or magazines with his story. Somebody on staff at the *Times* or *New York* could be persuaded, perhaps, at this point, to ask for an interview with Harvey or might want to assign an article about him. Real human-interest stuff there. How could the network keep everyone away from him forever? Jeff stopped whistling to himself and suddenly proposed the idea to Tracy, who, dressed in shorts and an old torn tennis shirt, had been in the kitchen cleaning up, probably as a way to avoid having to talk or listen to Nolan. Wade, beer can in hand, sat contentedly on the floor, his back against the wall, and stared with amused contentment at Tracy, and especially her bare legs, whenever she reappeared from her chores.

"Sure," Jeff said. "I think that's it. We've got to somehow spread the word, get a lot of other people to start looking for Harvey, too."

"I still say we should go to the police," Tracy commented.

"Aw, sugar, that'd take the fun out of everything," Nolan objected.

"I'm not having any fun," Tracy said.

"That's 'cause you don't hang loose, honey. A couple of nights at the old Rapture and you'd be loose as the proverbial goose, if you get my meanin'. I don't know why you won't let me give you the Wade Nolan per-son-ally guided tour."

Tracy ignored Nolan and sat cross-legged on the sofa across from Jeff. "What *do* you suppose all those images of Harvey were for?" she asked. "If Nate's right, they've been testing them out on people for months now."

"I don't know." Jeff shook his head gloomily. "I do know this one guy with the cops who might help us," he continued, picking up Tracy's suggestion. "A guy named Dick Steinman, the Chief of Detectives. He's been around a while and I know him pretty well. I still think it's too soon, though, to get him involved."

"Where do all them programs come in to?" Wade suddenly asked.

"Which programs, Wade?"

"Them news programs, the ones with Harvey in 'em. I mean, if they're beamin' in from out of town, they got to pick 'em up somewheres, don't they?"

Jeff stared at Nolan in amazement. "My God, Wade, that's it!" he exclaimed. "You just hit on it!"

"Hit on what?" Tracy asked.

"Don't you see?" Jeff said, his voice alive with excitement. "If Harvey's broadcasting from a studio somewhere outside the city, it's either coming in on cable or, if it's line of sight, then on a microwave link-up. If it's microwave, then they're using a parabolic antenna."

"What's that?" Tracy asked.

"It looks like a reflector in a searchlight," Jeff explained. "Logically, they'd have all of them in the same place."

"Where would that be?"

"The ACN transmitter is on top of the World Trade Center downtown. They also have all the microwave pickup antennas there, too. Wade, you're a fucking genius!"

"That's what they keep tellin' me over at Rapture, old buddy," the mountain man answered, grinning and heaving himself up to his feet. "I'm gonna get me another beer." He moved toward the kitchen.

"How do we find out?" Tracy asked.

"Somehow we've got to get inside up there," Jeff mused. "The trouble is, security will be tight, tighter even than normal, since they're guarding Harvey's whereabouts so closely. Our best chance might be for me and Wade to break in there during the night, real late. If we can . . ."

Nolan reappeared in the kitchen entrance, a freshly opened beer in hand. "Ain't there two of them towers?" he asked.

Jeff nodded. "The ACN transmitter is on the north one."

"But how will you get up there, even at night?" Tracy asked. "You can't scale the walls, can you?"

"How about from up above?" Nolan suggested. "Must be someplace we can rent us a chopper. I can fly 'most any kind of chopper and there must be a place we can hire one, ain't there?"

"There's the Pan Am heliport at Sixtieth and the East River," Jeff said. "Island Helicopter rents choppers. You got your license and a medical certificate, Wade?"

Nolan smiled and patted his breast pocket. "Right next to my heart, old buddy, along with the loot. I also got me some very nice fake identification. Sometimes comes in handy."

"I think you're both lunatics," Tracy said. "I think you have to go to the police. You could be shot or something, certainly arrested, if they catch you."

"You're a good-lookin' piece of pussy," Nolan said, "but you sure do know how to take the fun out of things, honey. Hell, I didn't come up here to see old Jeff just to get laid a few times. We got a job to do. Now, you just relax and let the boys get the thing done, you hear?"

"I hear, all right," Tracy said, "but I'm having a difficult time believing most of it. And I really can't abide your foul mouth a minute longer, Mr. Nolan."

Nolan stood up. "Well, ain't no use me hangin' around here no more. I'll take in a picture show and drop by the old club. You comin', Jeff, or are you too pussy-whipped to make it?"

But Jeff was already on the phone, asking information for the number of Island Helicopter. "I'll see you tomorrow, Wade," he said, cupping his hand over the mouthpiece. "I'll set things up. And I'll call you before I head into the office."

Without another word, Nolan eased himself out of the room. He's like some kind of predatory cat, Tracy was thinking, some kind of killing animal. She could smell the blood in the air around him, and it frightened her.

The first real inkling Crawford had that matters might no longer be firmly in control came with the phone call from Margaret Whitby. The woman had never called him before, and he realized at once that she had hit on something.

"His papers seemed to be in order," she told him, "but it wasn't the same man."

"You're certain?"

"Yes, absolutely. Harold Jennings is a retired mailman from

the Bronx," she said. "He's fifty-eight years old, bald, wears glasses and was born in Newark, New Jersey."

"Go on."

"The man who was here today was in his thirties and spoke with a thick Southern accent."

"Anything else about him?"

"Yes. He has a strange-looking eye, with a piece of the lid missing. And he's got a real dirty mouth."

"Did you do a computer scan on Jennings?"

"I did, after this man left."

"And?"

"Not the same man, definitely not. I don't know *who* he was. I asked Dr. Garrard about him, but he says he has no idea. He says he doesn't concern himself with the selection of the people we put through the program."

"Is that true?"

"Usually, yes."

"Did you check Jennings?"

"Yes, that was my next step. He says he was paid five hundred dollars by some guy he had never met before to let him take his place today."

"It had to be Garrard. Who else could arrange such a substitution?"

"One or two others, maybe."

"Like who?"

"From Myrmidon, I suppose."

"Yes, I see. Whitby?"

"Yes, sir?"

"Who else knows about this?"

"No one, sir, except for Dr. Garrard. I thought I'd better inform you."

"Thank you. I appreciate it."

"Anything else?"

"Do you think Garrard arranged the substitution?"

"I don't know, Mr. Crawford."

"I see. Thanks, Whitby. We'll be in touch."

After hanging up, Crawford remained for a long time in the

quiet of his living room with its floor-to-ceiling wall of tapes, the venetian blinds drawn against the fading of the day. Stripped to his shorts and a T-shirt, he sat very still on the mat in the middle of the floor, his heavily muscled arms extended over his spread knees, his head slumped forward in thought. He was beginning now, at last, to recognize the dimensions of the problem. The man whom Morgan had shadowed and who was staying in Campbell's apartment must be the same one who had slipped into the testing program. The descriptive touch about the strange-looking eye was the clincher. But who was he? Obviously an old friend of the cameraman's, not a hired gun. Crawford would have identified a paid assassin by this time. The man had some expertise in the field, though, that much was clear. Morgan had told him that Campbell's apartment had been converted into one huge booby trap and fortress. They had been right to back off and wait, but now?

All right, if Garrard had handled the substitution at the testing center, then probably it had been set up by Thiel. That made at least four of them in on it, five if Garrard himself had been told anything. What was the extent of the threat to the project now? Considerable, with Thiel on the scene, the agent realized. The scientist could provide Campbell with an important link. It had been a mistake to allow him to resign from the program so late in the game. *All right, we have the cameraman, the girl, Thiel, maybe Garrard, the cracker—who else?*

Crawford eased himself forward until his hands rested flat on the floor and he stretched out full length on his stomach. Slowly at first, but with increasing speed, he began to do his routine of two hundred pushups. As the sweat began to run off him and the rhythm of the exercise accelerated, his mind began to focus first on the fat man, then on the thin one with the odd-looking eye and the foul mouth. What was it about the cracker that nibbled at the edge of his consciousness? What small piece of the puzzle was missing? Why did its absence trouble him so?

When he had completed his exercises, Crawford stood up, peeled off his shorts and shirt and turned to stare at himself in the mirror on his bedroom door. I'm looking good, he thought, for an old fart. He went into his bedroom to shower. The man with the eye, the loud mouth . . . Crawford suddenly grunted softly to himself and smiled. He sat down on the edge of his bed, a towel now draped over his damp shoulders, and quickly punched the number of the Service.

"Yes?" the familiar cold metallic voice answered.

Crawford gave the code number and waited. A minute passed, then a second one. "Mr. Reynolds?" the woman asked.

"Yes."

"You wish to see Penny?"

"Yes."

"When?"

"Tonight."

"I'm sorry, but I'm afraid she's unavailable tonight."

"You find her," he said. "I'll double the fee."

"I'll try, sir. The usual address?"

"Yes. I'll be there in an hour."

"I'll do what I can, sir, but I can't guarantee it."

"I'll wait as long as I have to," Crawford said. "It must be tonight. Is that clear?"

"I'll do what I can, sir."

"I know you will," Crawford assured her. "You've never let me down yet, have you?"

17

THE NIGHT was clear and cool, with a gentle southwest wind that caressed the city's darkened monoliths and gleaming spires and blew softly down the empty stone canyons. The Bell Jet Ranger that Nolan had rented squatted silently on its landing pad like a feeding insect, its wings motionless but tensed for flight. Nolan slumped against it, waiting for Jeff to join him. The night mechanic and dispatcher had both gone back to their hangar offices, where cooling cups of weak coffee awaited them. Nolan glanced at his watch. It was nearly 4 A.M. and Jeff was already late, though they still had plenty of time if he showed up soon. Wade sighed happily, because the prospect of real action always filled him with elation. He decided to make one more check of the equipment he had loaded into the four-seater behind him and opened the cabin door.

In the suitcase he had the Ingram and beside it, in its innocuous-looking canvas cylinder, the high-powered M-14 with its MAC sound suppressor in place and ready to fire. With luck, they wouldn't have to use either, or the handguns, but it was better to be prepared. By the open door on the passenger side squatted the portable winch with its rappel, the length of double rope similar to the equipment used by skilled mountain climbers. When satisfied for the third time that he had overlooked nothing, Nolan reemerged from inside the cabin, just as

Jeff turned the corner of the operations building and hurried toward him.

"How're you doin'?" Nolan asked.

"OK," Jeff said, hunched into his padded flight jacket. "A little jumpy, that's all."

Nolan grinned at him, his small jagged teeth glittering in the dim light below the evil stare of his scarred eye. "You're out of practice, that's all, buddy boy. Got it all set up?"

Jeff nodded. "In exactly twenty-two minutes, Tracy will be in the phone stand at the corner of Seventy-second. Two minutes later we should be in position."

"Good. Once we take off I'm goin' east out over the Island first," Nolan said, "which is the flight plan we gave 'em here. Then we cut back over the beaches and toward the target area from the south. You ready?"

"I guess so."

"OK, let's go, buddy boy."

They climbed into the cabin, slammed the doors shut and buckled themselves into their seats. Nolan turned on the engine, and overhead the great rotary blades began to sweep the air. The dispatcher looked up from his comic book and waved them off without moving from his desk. With a sudden lurch, the chopper rose straight up, banked slightly to the left and whirred off toward the east, disappearing into the night over the meandering silver sheen of the river below and the sprawling mass of huddled buildings on the far shore.

"Sure looks pretty from up here," Nolan said, as he glanced back at the Manhattan skyline with its icy black fingers spiking the sky. "Kind of like some fairytale place, ain't it?"

"Yeah," Jeff agreed, glancing again at his watch. "When are you turning south?"

"In another four minutes," Nolan said. "Say, you figure we got time to drop in on the old Rapture later? We could set down right on it."

"I don't think so, Wade."

"I don't understand why you won't take a look at the old club. You don't have so much fun as you used to, old buddy," Wade observed. "That's the trouble with stickin' your cock into only one hole. It kind of gets clamped into place, don't it?"

Jeff nodded without answering. He was too nervous now about this whole operation to pay much attention to his friend's obscenities. He sat and stared silently out the window until Nolan again turned the Jet Ranger, south this time, then back toward the tip of Manhattan, skimming along only a few hundred feet above the spray of white surf breaking on the Rockaway beaches. In the distance, the spires of the silent city challenged them like the upraised spears of a waiting army.

Leaning into the shielded phone stand on the corner of Seventy-second and Broadway, Tracy blocked her free ear with one hand from the rattling noise of an uptown bus speeding past and spoke huskily into the mouthpiece. The image she had fixed in her head was of a depraved Katharine Hepburn, if such a vision could even be imagined. "Hello? WACN?"

"This is downtown operations," the male voice answered. "I think you must want the main office."

"No, I want you," Tracy said. "Aren't you lonely and bored up there?"

"What?"

"Am I so hard to understand?"

"Look, lady, I don't know what you're talking about."

"I've watched you so often, going in and out," Tracy said. "In and out, in and out. Don't you ever notice me?"

"Notice you? Why would I notice you?"

"I'm always standing on the corner across the street. I'm always hoping you'll see me waiting for you, watching for you, but you never do."

"Listen, what is this—"

"I'm so lonely, so very lonely," Tracy said. "Every night I wait for you, every night you disappoint me."

"Listen, what *is* this? Who *are* you?"

"Katie, my name is Katie. What's yours?"

"Never mind what my name is. Listen—"

"I told you mine. Why won't you tell me yours?"

"This is crazy. What do you *want?*"

"I want you. Don't you want me?"

"This is nuts!" Tracy heard him shout now to someone as he covered the mouthpiece with his hand. "Hey, Harry, get a load of this!" Then again in a more normal voice: "Lady—"

"My name is Katie. Please call me Katie," she said. "You still haven't told me yours."

"Walter. My friends call me Walt. Listen, Katie, tell me again what you just said, OK?"

"OK. I said I'm lonely. I said I want you, Walt."

"Louder, Katie, louder. I got a buddy up here who doesn't believe this."

"I'm lonely," Tracy repeated. "Here all by myself in my apartment. I want to see you, Walt."

"Do you always call men up in the middle of the night like this? Do you know what time it is?"

"I can't sleep," she said "I'm here in bed and I think about you all the time. Tossing and turning and thinking about you all these hot nights . . ."

"Where do you want to meet?"

"Anywhere you say."

"Well, I'm—uh, working right now. But I get off at six. You want to meet me on the corner where you say you usually stand at a little after six? I'll buy you a cup of coffee on my way home."

"Would you really, Walt?" Tracy said. "I can't believe how lucky I am!"

"Listen, Katie," the man continued, "just so there are no misunderstandings, I want you to know I'm married. I've been married for twelve years and I have three kids and I'm crazy about my wife. Is that clear?"

"I don't care," Tracy said. "I have to have you, Walt. I'll take you on any terms."

"You've seen me, huh?"

"Yes, many times."

"So you know what I look like?"

"Yes, oh, yes!"

"The glasses, the buck teeth, the no hair—I mean, I wouldn't want you to think I was someone else, see. Somebody terrific-looking, like my colleague Harry here. Harry's a terrific-looking guy. Of course, the big beer belly's a handicap, but still he's a real Marlboro ad, Harry is. You sure you haven't got me confused with someone else?"

"Oh, no." She heard the snickering in the background, but prudently ignored it. The key thing was to keep their attention focused elsewhere just long enough. "Oh, no," she said, "it's you I want, Walt."

"Tell me, Katie," Walt said, "you know what *I* look like, but what do *you* look like? Can you give me a really good description?"

"Well, I'm about five-four and a half and I'm kind of voluptuous-looking, if you know what I mean," Tracy said, shutting her eyes and trying now for Marilyn Monroe instead of Hepburn. "I have blue eyes and freckles. My friends all say I'm really attractive."

"Hey, Katie, can't you do better than that? I mean, give me a really, you know, *intimate* description, details, you know . . ."

"Well, I have dimples when I smile and—"

"Come on, Katie. How about your tits? You got a big pair of tits? My wife has no tits. I've always wanted a woman with big knockers. How about your ass? You got a big round ass, huh? Let's hear it, Katie. I mean, I'm not buying just any pig in a poke, not even a cup of coffee, see? Or should I say a poke in a pig?"

He guffawed and in the background Tracy could hear Harry breaking up. *Oh, God, where are they? How long can I keep this up?* She opened her mouth, trying to think of something, anything, to say that could keep this bizarre conversation going, but before she could utter another word she heard the noise she'd been waiting for during the entire conversation. It sounded to her like the beating of some enormous electric fan outside a metal cocoon. "Walt!" she cried out. "Walt, are you there?"

All she heard was a shout, a sound of scuffling and running footsteps, a man's cry, then a moment of absolute silence except for the beating of the huge fan. "Oh, God," she whispered. "Oh, God . . ."

The line went dead. She backed out of the phone stand and ran back toward the street where she'd parked the car, her face white with fear.

As Jeff dropped onto the roof of the north tower, Nolan hovered overhead in the Jet Ranger just long enough to make sure his friend would be all right. Pistol in hand, Jeff pressed himself against the wall by the exit door, pulled down his ski mask and waited. The first man to step out was the security guard, who obviously couldn't believe his eyes; he stared up at the chopper in amazement. Jeff stepped in behind him and stuck the gun into his ribs. Up above the scene, Nolan grinned down at him, gave him the high sign and turned the helicopter toward the south tower, where he quickly set it down, turned off the engine and took up a position by the parapet from where, through his powerful Zeiss binoculars, he could keep an eye on Jeff's progress across the way. In fact, he could keep him covered and, if necessary, render emergency assistance or attempt a rescue.

Jeff, meanwhile, had wasted no time. First he'd taken the security guard's gun away, then, using him as a shield, he moved inside the rooftop structure. The engineer was standing by the phone and staring stupidly at the scene.

"Hang up," Jeff ordered. "Now sit down right there in that chair over by the table and put your hands behind your head. If you move, I'll blow both of you away." He nudged the guard with his gun barrel. "You," he ordered, "lie down on the floor, on your stomach, and keep your hands out flat over your head, where I can see them. If you do as I say, nobody's going to get hurt." He waited until the guard lay prostrate, then turned on the man now sitting, ashen-faced, in the chair. "You the engineer?"

"Yes," the man whispered.

"I want a quick explanation of what you've got up here."

"We don't have any money—"

"I don't want your damn money. Just tell me what I want to know. This is the WACN transmitter, isn't it?"

"Yes, but we can't actually broadcast from up here. I mean, if you have some kind of message you want to get out over the air, we'd have to call it in to the station."

"Don't volunteer information and we'll get through much faster," Jeff said. "Just shut up and answer my questions. Is that clear?"

"Yes, sir."

"OK, then." Jeff looked around. He was standing inside a good-sized structure that took up most of the tower roof. Through thick plate-glass windows he could look out over most of the city in any direction. Mounted inside this particular room were four movable disk-shaped microwave antennae. There were also a few chairs, a couple of desks, four control panels of some sort, two phones and, alone in one corner, a fifth disk, somewhat smaller than the other four. "That fifth antenna over there," Jeff asked. "What is it?"

"It's a microwave pickup, like the others," the engineer answered. "It was installed two months ago."

"Go on "

"That's all I know, honest. I'm just maintenance. Except that it's locked into a fixed position."

"What position?"

"I don't know. Honest."

Jeff reached into his side pocket and produced a small aluminum box with gently rounded ends. "Can you read a compass?"

"Yes, I guess so."

Jeff tossed him the box. "OK, that's a Suunto KB-14 hand compass. Go on over there now and give me a reading on where that disk is aimed."

The engineer took the compass, handling it at first like a hot coal, and walked over to the antenna. He aimed the box on a direct line of sight matching the center axis of the disk and stared into the sight hole of the instrument. "It's pointing on a line two hundred and fifty degrees west southwest," he said.

"Is this from a relay station or line of sight from the source?"

"As far as I know, straight from the source."

"Which means that this is picking up microwave signals from where, exactly?"

"Somewhere around Princeton, New Jersey, I guess."

"You guess. Aren't you sure?"

"I guess I'm sure."

"OK," Jeff ordered. "Now put the compass down right there on the table and get over on the floor, face down, next to your buddy here."

"Please, mister —"

"Just do as I say and you won't get hurt. I promise."

The engineer sank to the floor beside the security guard. Jeff snatched up the compass and stuffed it back into his pocket. He pulled out a pair of wire cutters and snipped the phone lines, then looked down at his prisoners again. "OK," he said, "now I'm going to stand just outside the exit door onto the roof, but I'll be able to see you clearly from there. If one of you makes a move, I'll shoot. Got that?"

There was no answer from the floor. Jeff backed to the door, opened it, stepped outside and, still keeping his eyes fixed on his prisoners, waved his left arm twice over his head.

On the south tower, Nolan, rifle in hand, now ran for the chopper. Within a minute he was airborne and hovering low over Jeff's head. The rappel came down, swaying in the backwash of the helicopter's spinning blades. Jeff slipped the loop under his arms and stepped away from the door. Above him, Nolan activated the winch and Jeff rose into the air toward the open cabin door as the chopper itself now swung out away from the rooftop and over the buildings of lower Manhattan.

As he scrambled inside and slammed the door of the cabin shut, Jeff caught a glimpse of the north tower. Two men had come running out of the WACN transmitter station and were staring up at them, but almost at once one of them, probably the security guard, ran back inside. In the canyons far below, a cluster of revolving blue and red lights had gathered at the foot of the south tower. "The cops move pretty fast in this town,"

Nolan observed with a short, mirthless chuckle. "Two more minutes in there and they might have nabbed us, huh?"

"We still aren't out of this, Wade."

"We got a good head start, buddy boy. Now we dump this chopper out where?"

"Here," Jeff said, running a finger down Nolan's navigational chart. "That's just below the George Washington Bridge, by the river."

"She gonna be there?"

"I sure hope so," Jeff said. "If she isn't, we'll have to make a run for it. There's a subway entrance two blocks east. We'll split up and meet later at my place, OK?"

"You got it, old buddy," Nolan agreed, grinning with delight. "Hey, quit shakin'. I can't keep on course with you shakin' like that."

"Sorry. I'm a little rusty at breaking and entering, Wade."

"Aw, hell, it's just another war, ain't it?" He swung the chopper out over the Hudson and headed uptown. "By the way, what did you find out?"

"Just what we thought," Jeff said. "They're broadcasting from somewhere in or around Princeton, so Harvey's probably there, with or without Lillienthal."

"We'll go have us a look-see, huh?"

"I guess so," Jeff said, trying his hardest to stop trembling. "If we don't wind up in jail."

"No problem, old buddy, no problem."

When Nolan set the Jet Ranger down on the grass by the riverbank just below the bridge, the first thing they saw was Jeff's scarred VW with Tracy at the wheel. Her face, pale as the moon itself, stared wide-eyed at them as she clutched the wheel with both hands. Wade and Jeff ran across the narrow strip of park toward it and scrambled inside. With Jeff now driving, they shot away from the curb and disappeared into the shadows of the upper West Side.

Within ten minutes of their departure, the abandoned helicopter had been taken over by a curious crowd of street people, some of them only half dressed. By the time the police arrived on the scene, the inside of the helicopter's cabin had already been gutted and the windows smashed in. The street people fanned out and regrouped at a safer distance as the first police officers, guns drawn, warily approached the machine.

Nate Thiel had just finished his second stack of buttermilk pancakes, bacon and eggs and was sipping his fourth cup of coffee when the curious news item came on the air. Two men in a rented helicopter had landed on the rooftops of the World Trade Center towers in downtown Manhattan last night and raided the transmitter station of WACN. One of the men, masked and holding a gun, had forced the engineer on duty and a security guard to lie face down on the floor while he interrogated them. According to the engineer, he had only seemed interested in the uses of the station's five microwave antennae and had departed after only a few minutes without taking anything, demanding anything or injuring anybody. He had been lifted off the north tower by the helicopter, which had later been abandoned in Riverside Park just below the George Washington Bridge. The raiders had not yet been positively identified, but the police had learned that a man named Henry P. Lloyd had earlier that evening rented a Jet Ranger helicopter from Island Helicopter and taken off with a male passenger late last night from the Pan Am heliport at Sixtieth and the East River. Nothing else was known about Lloyd or his present whereabouts, except that he spoke with a heavy Southwestern or Southern accent.

"You're going to be late," Nate's mother chirped from the kitchen doorway. "You want more coffee?"

"No, thanks, Mom," Nate said. He burped softly and pushed himself away from the table. "I wonder . . ."

"What?"

Nate told his mother about the helicopter raid on the Trade Center towers. "I think I know who did it," he concluded.

"Why would anybody do such a stupid thing?" Miriam Thiel asked her son. "People today, such foolishness!" It was the extent of her curiosity about the incident.

Nate smiled fondly at his mother and leaned over to kiss her goodbye. She was a small, round, fluttery woman with a face like a soup bowl and she had buried Nate's father and two other husbands with her cooking. She was now in the process of blowing her son up to a heart attack or at least a definitive stroke, but she loved him, and cooking was only her way of showing it. "You didn't eat anything, Nathan," she said. "You'll get sick."

"Mom, I'm stuffed," Nate said, picking up his briefcase and heading for the door.

"Eat a good lunch!" she called out after him as he went out the front door. "You don't want to work all day on an empty stomach!"

Nate Thiel lived with his widowed mother, the famous killer cook, on West Eighty-first Street in an old apartment house facing the Hayden Planetarium and the Museum of Natural History. He had lived in this neighborhood most of his life and knew it as well as the inside of his own apartment. From directly in front of his building, he could almost always snag a cruising taxi to take him uptown to his teaching duties at Columbia, but today he had to wait for one; he had delayed too long and the rush-hour demand for transportation had made taxis temporarily scarce. He didn't mind. He set his briefcase down between his feet and waited.

As Nate stood there, the huge man in the black hat and the long black coat, black trousers and black shoes crossed the street and came toward him. He had long, oily-looking black curls, a full black mustache and beard and over one arm he carried a long black umbrella. A Hasidic Jew, Nate realized at once, but such a big one. Most of the Hasids he'd known had worked in the midtown diamond district, small, pale, fragile-looking men. This one looked like a wrestler or a stevedore.

Because he had nothing else to do and because the man's appearance intrigued him, Nate smiled at him. "Good morning," he said. "Beautiful day."

"Very nice," the big man said, in a noticeable foreign accent, very, very nice." He flourished the umbrella in one hand, aiming it uptown. "Fiftieth Street and Avenue of the Americas?"

"No, that way," Nate corrected him, indicating downtown. "You can catch the subway there at the corner and get off at Fiftieth, or there's a bus."

The big man bowed slightly. "Thank you very much. You're most kind."

"It's OK," Nate said, spotting a taxi at last and stepping out into the street to flag it down. As the car came to a stop beside him, Nate turned to say goodbye and caught the stranger aiming the umbrella at him.

"Thank you, thank you," the man said, bowing and smiling now, the umbrella held straight out before him like a conductor's baton.

Nate smiled back. *Funny, this guy, he's funny.* He turned and leaned over to enter his cab. He felt the sting of the pellet penetrating his thigh, only enough so that he felt compelled to scratch himself. He sank back into his seat and with a contented sigh gave the driver his uptown address. Then he sat back, closed his eyes and set the briefcase down beside him.

The driver of the taxi, a bearded unemployed young actor who occasionally worked Off-Off-Broadway and was usually logy from lack of sleep, did not notice that his passenger was dead until he arrived at his destination and found him, mouth grotesquely agape and eyes rolled back into his skull, now slumped at a sickening angle in one corner of the compartment, the handle of the briefcase nervelessly clasped in five fat, limp fingers.

18

SARAH ANDERSON stood just inside the door of the Chairman's office and waited for the old man to acknowledge her presence. He seemed not to have noticed her, but sat with his back to her, hunched forward in his chair and staring out his windows over the empire he had conquered. But he must have known all along she had come into the room, because eventually he summoned her, with a small wave of one hand and without bothering to turn around to face her. She sat down in the chair across from him and waited. When at last he did swivel about to confront her, his hard, hooded stare seemed to pierce through her, as if she alone could be held accountable for whatever it was that was troubling him.

"Sarah, I am most disturbed," the Chairman said. "Surely you're aware of the significance of last night's events?"

"I am, Larry," Sarah said calmly.

"I can't understand how matters could have gone this far. I'm deeply disappointed."

"So am I, Larry. What has Crawford been doing?"

"I don't know," the Chairman confessed. "He has repeatedly assured me that matters are under control. Obviously, they are *not*. The raid on our transmitter last night confirms that."

"It certainly does."

"Presumably we are now in a vulnerable position with Myrmidon."

"Have you spoken to Crawford since last night?"

"Not today," the Chairman answered, with an angry frown. "I would expect him to be directly involved on this problem. Now, what exactly is our situation at the moment?"

"Hard to predict down to the minute, Larry," Sarah said. "My best guess is we're still several months away from a possible complete resolution. The latest word is that Myrmidon itself is in every technical and commercial way a resounding success. I think you'd have to agree with that, wouldn't you?"

The Chairman nodded slowly, but seemed to take no pleasure in it. "Not good enough," he snapped. "If our security is breached before the transition phase is over, we risk total disaster. We seem to be dealing with astute and daring antagonists."

"Perhaps Crawford has underrated the magnitude of the threat," Sarah suggested.

"Unquestionably. Haven't we all?"

"No, Larry, we haven't. My end of this operation is a total success. I'm proving it to you every day in the most basic form, ratings and dollars and cents. I will not accept any of the responsibility for a major breach of security. That is not my department."

"Perhaps we moved into this too soon . . ."

"No, we didn't, Larry. We activated Myrmidon when we had no other alternative but to lose Harvey forever, and, what's worse, to a rival network, or pay him an outrageous amount of money, which all our talent would eventually have wanted. We'd have lost everything, Larry. We were all agreed on that."

The Chairman seemed to sink into his seat, like a cat curling into a defensive ball, fearful but still very dangerous. "I don't know," he murmured. "I don't know, Sarah . . ." His fingers began their restless, telltale drumming on the arms of the chair.

My God, he can't be losing his nerve this late in the game, she thought, and rose to the offensive, pacing the room now as she reviewed for him all the reasons they had come this far and outlined in detail again exactly where they stood in regard to the future. He knew all this as well as she did, but she realized that he needed reassuring. Old emperors, their major territorial conquests behind them, tend at some point to want to consolidate, to stand still. Sarah had her greatest achievements still before her and she did not intend to be thwarted by a failure of nerve, even on the part of the Chairman, and certainly not by the incompetence of another department head, namely Crawford.

"So you see, Larry," she concluded, "this project is in excellent shape. We are on the brink of not only an even greater success than we've already achieved, but a complete revolution in the industry. We can't back out now. We're totally committed. The failures here, if there are any, are certainly not in the technical or administrative end of Myrmidon. I want your continued complete support for this project, Larry. Remember, please, that the success of Myrmidon will someday lead to the implementation of Cerberus as well. How the immediate problem of this foolish little group of meddlers is to be dealt with is not my concern, but Crawford's. He *must* deal with it. Surely you see that, Larry? Surely you know I'm right about this."

The old emperor listened in stoic calm until she had concluded. He did not immediately answer her, but continued to gaze at her as his fingers tapped more softly on the chair arms. "And the new man?" he asked at last.

Sarah smiled. She knew by the nature of the question that she had triumphed, but then how could she have failed? They were in far too deep, with a total commitment of resources to the concept, to withdraw now. By asking the question he did, a small one having to do merely with turnover and training of qualified personnel, whether technical or administrative, the Chairman had indicated to her that he understood and that he did indeed continue to back her in her daring venture. She again sat down opposite him, her face radiant with enthusiasm and dedication. "He's going to be fine," she assured him, "just fine."

"He checked out very well, I understand."

"Splendidly. He's a fine young man."

"At what phase of the project—"

"Oh, he hasn't yet been fully integrated into it. He's undergoing indoctrination and training. I expect he'll be a full member of the creative administrative team within a matter of two or three weeks."

The Chairman allowed the merest hint of a smile to tease the corners of his mouth. "He matters a lot to you, does he, Sarah?"

She smiled openly. "Yes," she said, "we're involved, Larry. I figured you must know. But that has nothing to do with the larger picture. He's the perfect sort of young executive we want in the program. He's first and foremost a company man."

"I rather thought he would be, if you picked him."

"I'm not Crawford, Larry," Sarah said, turning serious. "I don't make miscalculations about people."

"Crawford never has before."

"No, but this would be a tragic time to make the first one."

"I agree, Sarah."

"We can't risk a failure now," Sarah said. "These people, Campbell and his friend, whoever he is—they must be stopped."

"I'm going to stay on top of it myself, Sarah."

She stood up to go. "I knew you would, Larry," she said. "Everything we've worked for is at stake, the whole future of this network."

The Chairman stopped his drumming and glanced sharply up at her.

"Don't lecture me, Sarah," he growled. "Please remember, *I* built this network with my own brains and talent and I built it out of nothing before you were born."

"Oh, I'm older than I look, Larry," she said, laughing to cover her realization that she'd gone just a little too far. "I'll never forget that, Larry."

"No, you wouldn't," he said, smiling coldly back at her. "You're a pretty piece of machinery yourself, Sarah. Too bad I'm not a younger man."

Nolan stepped out of the shower and looked at himself in the full-length mirror beside the urinal, assessing more than admiring his long, sinuous nakedness. He lightly fingered the abstract pattern of scars under his right arm inflicted by a fragmentation grenade dropped by a careless South Vietnamese soldier. *Dumb fuckin' slope.*

The hammering sounds of disco music interrupted his reverie, reminding him of the pleasures ahead. *That idiot Jeff don't know what he's missin'.* Nolan finished his careful ablutions, put a small tube of K-Y jelly into the locker where he had hung his clothes and locked it, slipping the key's elastic band over his left wrist. He wrapped a towel around his waist and stepped out of the men's room into the lurid red light and deafening music of Club Rapture's second floor.

The room was large, perhaps twenty by sixty feet. Sitting around its perimeter on couches built into the walls were over a hundred men and women, most of them wearing only towels around their waists, the rest naked. Some were discarding their towels and climbing into what looked like a floor-level boxing ring in the center of the room, but what was taking place on its black-velvet surface had nothing to do with boxing. The area was alive with a tangle of some twenty bodies engaged in every conceivable sex act.

In one corner, a generously proportioned blonde was thrusting her head savagely between the legs of a teenage black girl who was performing fellatio on a middle-aged white man. He was gripping the blonde like a bowling ball, his fingers thrust into every available opening.

Nolan let his eyes and ears adjust. He scanned the couches, then shifted his gaze back to the action in the ring in the room's center. A blond woman pulled her mouth away from a man lying on his back just before he ejaculated. As she sat up to watch, Nolan saw a flash of silver hair from one of the couches behind the blonde. Ah, Violet!

"Wade, baby!"

She was black, as were most of the women there, while most of the men were white. Violet was older, though, with huge breasts propped up by repeated injections of silicone, brilliant red lipstick, lustrous blue eye shadow and a silver wig on her head that matched her bleached pubic hair. "Wade, baby," she repeated, squeezing his hand. "Where you been, honey?"

"Hot damn, Violet," Wade answered. "Tearin' myself away from that sweet black pussy of yours long enough to attend to a little business."

Violet, who was sitting on the lap of a fat middle-aged man, his penis deep inside her, said, "Excuse me, honey, this here's an old friend from school days."

"I'm cuttin' in," Nolan said matter-of-factly, grabbed her under the arms and lifted her to a standing position.

"Now, just a minute, buddy," growled the man Violet had been sitting on. He started to get up. Nolan's left foot shot out and caught him in the Adam's apple, knocking him to the floor. Nolan kept his foot on the man's throat, applying just enough pressure to make breathing difficult but not impossible.

"Just behave yourself, buddy boy," said Nolan. "Plenty of other action here."

The bug-eyed man on the floor nodded frantically in agreement. As Nolan pulled his foot away, Violet looked at him and said, "Wade, honey, why don't we get it on right here? Come on into the ring and let's have a little fun, baby."

Nolan admired her nakedness, her shining black skin, silver hair, huge breasts and magnificent backside with heart-shaped tattoos stamped onto each rump. "No, baby, I want you all to myself," he said. "Besides, you never know who's behind you out there."

Nolan led Violet into the only unoccupied cubicle at the rear of the room, peeled off his towel, reached up and flipped on the tiny room's only light, a red fifteen-watt bulb, and froze.

"Good evening, Mr. Nolan." The words were spoken over the silenced snout of a Walther PPK/S pointing between Nolan's eyes. "Just take your hand slowly away from the light and sit over there with your back to the wall." The man holding the gun gestured with his free hand, never taking his eyes off Nolan.

Wade did as he was told, squatting against the wall, covering his genitals with both hands.

"Modesty becomes you, Nolan," said the man. "Your stupidity does not." The man then raised his voice and said, "Gunter!"

The club's owner stepped through the cubicle's door, a ferretlike man with small, glistening eyes that darted from the man to Nolan and Violet.

"Gunter, explain to Violet here that we have a little business to transact," the man said. "Nothing important. Nothing she should mention to anyone."

"Violet," Gunter began, "you—"

"I heard," Violet interrupted. "I don't know nothin' from nothin'. Just trying to make a living minding nobody's business but my own."

"OK, get back out there," said Gunter. "Not a word."

"Not a word, not a word," the woman muttered as she hurried back out to the ring.

Nolan studied the man with the gun. Aside from the weapon he was holding, there was nothing exceptional about him. He was a gray man, with gray hair and wearing a gray suit, a striped tie, wing-tipped shoes. Nolan judged him to be in his forties.

"You seem to be squirming a bit, Mr. Nolan," the man said as he slowly lowered himself until he was sitting on his haunches, the Walther still trained on Nolan's forehead. "Stupidity can make one squirm. You made the mistake of playing in the big leagues, my backwoods friend. Amateurs don't make it in the majors."

"You got a point there, buddy," Nolan said thoughtfully.

"That's one mistake," the man continued. "You're covering up your other one."

Nolan glanced down at his crotch and smiled wanly. "Don't want you to get jealous, old buddy."

"Jealous? All the brains you got are obviously in your dick," the man said. "Foolish to let it lead you into traps. Very foolish."

"Well, you know what they say," Nolan drawled. "All work and no play . . ."

The man stared coldly into Nolan's eyes for a moment, then

said, "You are about to pay a very high price for your recreation, Mr. Nolan."

"That so?" Suddenly, Nolan's crotch exploded. A brilliant orange tongue of flame shot out from between his fingers. Horrified, the man holding the Walther fired wildly once, then dropped the gun and fell to his knees. Clutching his abdomen with both hands, he rocked back and forth against the opposite wall. The blast from Nolan's weapon, though nearly deafening in these crowded quarters, had been swallowed up by the disco noise outside. Nolan lunged for Gunter, who had turned to escape, grabbed him by one arm and threw the little man savagely across the cubicle. Gunter slammed into the wall and sank to the floor, gasping for air. Nolan snatched up the Walther and thrust its silencer into the gaping mouth of the man who a moment before had been about to kill him.

"But it was you who made the big mistake, buddy boy," Nolan whispered. "Don't never stop to make all them pretty speeches. Just get on with the job." He squeezed the trigger, and the top of the man's head came off, spraying the cubicle with bone fragments and brain tissue.

Gunter screamed, but Nolan whirled on him. "Put your hands behind your head, asshole, and shut the fuck up!"

Gunter complied instantly, his lips drawn back in fear.

"Who was that?" Nolan asked.

"I don't know."

"Look, Gunter, I ain't gonna waste my time or yours." He moved in closer to the quivering little man, reached out and jammed the Walther's bloody muzzle directly into Gunter's right eye. "You got three seconds to tell me what you know or I'll pull the trigger. That makes it downright simple for both of us, don't it?"

Gunter glanced at the corpse still oozing fluids on the floor beside him. The cold steel of the pistol's silencer and the slippery gore in his right eye made him shiver. "Please," he whined. "Please just give me a minute."

"That's what you got, then, one minute."

The little man gasped and sucked in oxygen. "I don't know

who the man is. He gave me the name Morgan when he came in here, something like that. All I know is that he knew you were a regular customer, he was very interested in seeing you and he had a lot of money. I had no idea he was armed, honest." Gunter was pleading now. "Honest, Wade, I had no idea he had the gun."

"All right, buddy boy, you thought it was a social visit, right?"

"We get all types here. I didn't know. Honest." Gunter began to shake, then asked, "Could you please take the gun away, please?"

Nolan pulled the muzzle of the gun out of the little man's eye and said, "All right. Never mind all that now. Tell me, Gunter, just how do you suppose this good old boy found out I was a frequent visitor to your renowned establishment?"

"I don't know. I've never seen him before."

"Has anybody asked for me here?"

Gunter looked again at the corpse and rubbed the blood out of his eye. "There was one fellow, about a week ago," he said. "Only he didn't actually ask for you."

"What do you mean? He didn't know me?"

"I've seen him here a couple of times. Penny brings him in."

"Penny?"

"The little blonde out in the ring. She's here one or two nights a week, usually. Says he's a customer of hers, but he never does anything. Just watches her in action."

"A customer?"

"Yeah. This Penny, see, she works for a call-girl service. They got all kinds of specialties, see? It's called the Service and they give you a special call-in number. Very high-class operation."

"You mean to tell me, Gunter, that all these chickies in here ain't just horny broads in off the street for a good time, that what you mean, Gunter?" Nolan asked. "You ain't runnin' a club at all, are you, just a whorehouse."

"No, no, Wade," the little man objected. "Some of them I pay just so we'll have enough girls every night. But some of these women are secretaries or housewives or whatever looking to have a good time."

"So what did the man want?"

"Who?"

"The man Penny brought in."

"Oh. Well, I told you he likes to watch. He also wants Penny to describe the action to him and so she began to describe you one night."

"That right, now?"

Gunter looked at Nolan's scarred body, the hawklike face, his malevolent-looking right eye. "You are . . . memorable, Wade."

"So what happened then?"

"Well, Penny and this big guy were sitting at the bar, see, having a drink and when she began to describe you, the man got very interested, wanted to know everything about you—when you came in, who you went with, that kind of stuff."

"And that was a week ago?"

"Yeah, about that."

"What did this man look like?"

"Like I said, he was big. He's very big and strong-looking. Blond, but I think he wears a wig. Middle or late fifties, I'd say. Clean-cut."

"Clean-cut?"

"Yeah, like a prosperous businessman."

"You ever talk to him?"

"Not really. I just happened to be nearby when he gave Penny the third degree."

"I don't suppose you'd know his name?"

"Reynolds. That's what she called him. Mr. Reynolds."

"Very good, Gunter," Nolan said. "Of course, men don't always give their whores their real names, do they?"

"No." The little man misinterpreted the grim look on Nolan's face and began to shake again.

"OK, Gunter, you've been a big help. Now you keep quiet about all this, you hear?" Nolan indicated the corpse. "You get rid of that garbage for me and keep runnin' your little old whorehouse, OK?"

"Right. Sure thing, Wade," Gunter said quickly. "I can lock

this cubicle up and get rid of him later. Nobody needs to know a thing, all right? Violet's no problem, you know."

"I didn't think so, old buddy."

"But one thing, Wade . . ."

"What?"

"What was that?" Gunter indicated the small black cylinder lying on the floor. "That thing you shot him with the first time."

Nolan picked up the cylinder. It was about the size of a tube of lipstick, with a small hole in one end and a tiny button in the other. Nolan twisted the end with the button, unscrewing it. He removed it and extracted a spent .22-caliber shell.

"This, Gunter, is a Military Armaments Corporation single-shot survival weapon." He tossed the spent shell toward Gunter, who caught it. "Fires a twenty-two long-rifle hollow point. It does the job, don't it?"

Nolan now screwed the device back together again, then held it by its two rounded ends between his thumb and forefinger. "It's designed to be carried in the rectum," he said. "Asshole to you, Gunter." Nolan grinned and paused to savor the man's astonished reaction. Then, as he glanced over at the stiffening corpse, he said, "Shitty way to die."

Jeff heard the faint click, and it triggered a deadly memory in him. He froze and sat very, very still in the driver's seat of the VW. He thought perhaps he had imagined the sound, but then decided that he hadn't. He shut his eyes and heard the sound again, in memory this time. The faint click, that very first day on the trail in Vietnam, followed then by the explosion and the man ten feet ahead of him lurching to the side, falling, screaming, his intestines shredded and oozing out between his clutching fingers. Several other times he'd heard that same sound; it was always followed by mutilation, often by death. He opened his eyes now and looked carefully around. The huge underground garage was empty at this hour, the few remaining cars basking in dusty, neon-lit splendor below the city's side-walks. He was alone, but he was expecting Moss to rejoin him, thank God. He began to sweat now, still not daring to move anything but his head and that only very slowly, so as not to jar the seat he was sitting on and what could possibly, probably, be underneath it.

"Hey, man, what's the matter with you?" Moss peered in at him from the passenger side. "You look green, man."

"Don't get in, Moss," Jeff said. "Just hold it a sec, OK?"

"Sure."

Jeff had been so preoccupied he hadn't even heard his colleague walk up to the car on his blind side. Lucky they hadn't both gotten in together. Bellucci had good-nighted them so late, what with that hatchet murder down in the Village and the pier fire in the West Fifties, that, overcome by fatigue and a desire to get home to Tracy, he had become a little careless. He hadn't even noticed, as he now did, that the window on his side had been jimmied down a slit, the door subsequently unlocked, probably with a piece of looped wire. It was easy with these old cars. Then Moss had had to run back upstairs to retrieve his raincoat. A break, perhaps the one that could save his life.

"Jeff, what's the matter with you, man? You want me to call a doctor? What's going on, man?" The anxious, sympathetic black face peered in at him through the window.

"Listen, Moss, do exactly what I tell you, OK?"

"Sure, man. What is it?"

"I'm going to unlock the hood of the car, OK? There's a flashlight in there. Get it, but don't jerk the hood open. Raise it real slowly, OK?"

"OK."

"I don't want the car jolted or bumped. You got that?"

"I got it."

Very, very carefully now, Jeff reached forward and gently pulled toward him the knob unlocking the hood. Moss walked to the front of the car and slowly raised the hood. He found the flashlight, tested it, then walked around to Jeff's side and leaned down. "What you got in there, a man, a bomb?"

"Maybe."

Moss blinked but did not back away from his partner. Jeff could have kissed him.

"All right," the cameraman said, "we're going to ease the door open and you're going to look under my seat and tell me what you see there, OK? But don't for God's sake touch anything. OK?"

"OK."

Moss slowly opened the door and kneeled down. He turned on the flashlight and focused its bright beam under Jeff's seat. Jeff did not move a muscle. He sat and sweated, feeling the cold rivulets run down his back and ribs, soaking through his shirt. "What do you see, Moss?" he asked.

"OK," Moss said, "there's a thing down here that looks kind of like a hockey puck. It's round, olive drab in color, about an inch and a half or two inches high, about three inches across. That it?"

"Where is it, exactly?"

"It's rigged in some way to the rod under your seat. What the hell is it?"

"Moss, listen to me very carefully. I think what we've got here is a pressure-release antipersonnel mine. I recognized the click when I sat down, because we used a lot of them in Vietnam and so did they. You step on it or sit on it and when you get up it blows up. The lid compresses under pressure and makes this kind of clicking noise, which is what arms the thing. The release of pressure sets it off. That's why I can't move."

"Jesus, man, what are we going to do? You want me to call the cops?"

"I don't think I can risk sitting on this thing till they get here. Listen, in the front there I've got some beach towels and an old canvas poncho, right?"

"Right."

"OK, take the beach towels, roll them up as tight as you can and pack them in all around the bottom of the seat. Then stuff the poncho around them. Got that?"

"How about my raincoat too?"

"Yeah, why not?"

"Then what?"

"There's a two- or three-second gap between release and explosion," Jeff explained. "These mines are shrapnel devices, they're not designed to blow up a car or anything. Get the stuff, Moss."

Moss did as he was told, packing the three rolled-up beach towels, the poncho and his raincoat in as tightly as he could all around the seat. "OK, now what?" he asked.

"Open the other door, roll down the windows, then get clear of the car."

"What are you going to do, man?"

"I'm going to roll the hell out of this thing."

"You sure you know what you're doing? I think we ought to get the cops. They got bomb demolition experts."

"They may not know this device, Moss. I do. Please help me."

Without another word, Moss walked around to the other side, opened the door, rolled down the window and again peered in at his partner. "You sure you want to do this?"

"Get the fuck away from the car, Moss."

Moss backed away toward the far wall and stepped behind a shielding parked Chrysler sedan. He peered anxiously through the gloom toward his friend in the VW and waited.

Jeff shut his eyes for a moment and clasped his hands tightly together to stop the trembling. He opened his eyes and took a deep breath, then rolled himself up into a tight ball and heaved himself sideways out of the car, hitting the cement floor just as the mine went off. It sprayed steel fragments through the car, shredding the towels, leaving the seat a smoking mass of debris. Jeff lay on his side, hunched up and still on the ground, his cheek pressed into the cement.

Moss ran toward him. "Jeff, you all right? You OK? Jeff—"

The cameraman raised his head slightly. "Ridley's ass, we did it that time! Am I bleeding? I can't feel anything."

"Your face is all black and scraped—"

"That's only the goddam cement. My legs? I can't feel anything."

"Try to move, Jeff."

He did so. He sat up and stared at the car. "Oh, Christ, Moss, look at that!" And then, for no reason he could immediately explain to anyone or even to himself, he began to laugh.

Moss crouched down beside him. "Holy shit, Jeff, who the fuck would do this to you? What's going on here?"

Jeff couldn't explain anything to him; he was laughing too hard. And then he began to shake. "Come on," he said to his friend, "I'll buy you a new raincoat."

She had not expected to hear from Whitner, especially at that hour and after so many weeks of silence between them. His voice on the phone sounded as assured and cool as ever, not a hint of apology or explanation but only a certain urgency. "Tracy," he said, "I know it's late, but I've got to see you. It's very important."

"It is?"

"Yes. It's about Jeff."

"I'm waiting for him now."

"I—I don't think he'll be home for a while."

"Why not?" She felt a twinge of fear in her stomach. Still damp from the shower, she hunched into her robe and leaned over, cradling the phone in both hands for assurance. "Whit, what's happened?"

"I can't tell you over the phone. I've got to see you."

"Is he all right?"

"I'm not sure. Tracy, I must see you and tonight. It's about this whole business."

"What business?"

"Trying to find Grunwald, isn't that what you and Jeff have been doing?"

"Jeff's been very concerned—"

"I know. So have I. Listen, please come. I can tell you a lot, but only when I see you."

"Where are you?"

He gave her a name and an address on West Eighty-eighth Street, near the river. "Come right now, it's urgent," he said.

"Don't tell anyone where you're going. You could give the whole show away, I mean it. Promise?"

"I promise. I'll be there in fifteen minutes."

She dressed quickly, putting on a skirt, a blouse and a sweater, then ran out the door and into the street. She hailed a taxi, climbed in and breathlessly gave the driver the address. What had happened to Jeff? Was he hurt? Where was he? What did Whit have to do with all this and why this clandestine meeting all of a sudden? She didn't know, but her concern for Jeff led her like an arrow straight to the address on West Eighty-eighth.

She tipped the driver a dollar and walked up to the house, a shabby-looking brownstone on a street strewn with refuse and lined by the dilapidated dwellings of the poor and the outcast. She ran up the stairs to the front entrance and peered at the names of the tenants, most of them apparently Puerto Rican. She could not at first find the name Whitner had given her, but then she spotted it and pushed the button. She ran back down the stairs and found the door, an iron grille just under the steps themselves. No sooner had she identified it than it clicked open. She pushed her way into the darkness. "Whit?"

A big hand grabbed her by the throat, another jammed a chloroform-soaked rag over her mouth and nose. The last sound she heard before passing out was the click of the iron grille closing behind her.

With a towel wrapped around his waist, Nolan stepped out of the cubicle and walked over to the center ring. He peered through the tangle of bodies, but could see no one matching Gunter's description of Penny. Violet too had disappeared. Then he turned away, intending to get dressed and leave, and saw the girl. She sat slumped at one end of the refreshment counter, sipping a Coke, a towel draped over her shoulders. She looked worn out, like a victim of a long unfriendly interrogation. Too bad he'd have to do this to her, he reflected, as he slipped onto the stool beside her.

"Beat it," she said, without looking at him. "I'm through for the night."

"No, you ain't," Nolan told her. "All I want to do is talk."

"I'm not talking. Beat it, I said."

Nolan took her by the arm in a grip of iron and pulled her in close to him. "Now, look, sugar," he said, keeping his voice low and pleasant, his expression unaltered, "some friend of yours named Reynolds just sent a man over here to kill me. The poor old boy botched the job, but next time I might not be so lucky. The way I figure it, honey, you ain't no part of it, except that Reynolds got some information on my action here from you. Gunter told me he's some kind of sex freak, gets his rocks off lookin' and listenin' instead of doin'. That's his problem and I guess, to hear tell it, he pays you pretty good for your action. All I want to know, darlin', is where I can find this dude."

She stared at him with the eyes of a cornered animal. "I can't tell you that, mister," she whispered. "I'm scared of him. He's—he's weird."

"I know that, sugar, but you're gonna have to tell me just the same," Nolan insisted, "'cause if you don't I'm gonna bust you up pretty good right here and now." She opened her mouth to scream, but his other hand took her by the throat, pinching her just under the jawbone hard enough so that she'd carry the marks of it for days. "Don't give me no trouble," he said, smiling at her. "Ain't nobody here gonna help you and the cops ain't gonna do you no good at all, even if you're still around when they get here. You just give me the address where I can find this old boy Reynolds and you're off the hook, honey. Now, you gonna be nice?"

Gasping for air, she did her best to nod and he released her.

19

"HEY, BUDDY BOY, let's go," Nolan said as he came bounding up the stairs to Tracy's apartment.

Jeff, pale with fear and tension, met him on the landing. "She's gone, Wade. She should have been here."

"I figured as much." Nolan followed Jeff back inside and shut the door behind them. "She leave a note or anything?"

"No, Wade, and it's not like her. Do you suppose something happened?"

"I wouldn't be surprised, old buddy."

"Somebody tried to kill me tonight," Jeff said, and told him all about the incident in the ACN garage.

"You're lucky, ain't you?" Nolan answered, as he retrieved a can of beer from the refrigerator. "Some of them babies go off the second you release. They can shred you pretty good. You get out clean?"

Jeff nodded. "I left Moss, my sound man, to cope with the police. When Tracy didn't answer the phone, I got a hunch something had happened to her and I came as fast as I could. Where have you been?"

Nolan laughed mirthlessly. "At the club, old buddy." He sank into a chair, took a healthy swallow of beer, belched loudly and looked up at his old friend. "It kind of looks like they tried to make a clean sweep, don't it?" he said. "All of us at the same time."

Jeff ignored the implication behind the remark. "So where's Tracy? Why isn't she here, Wade?" There had been nothing to indicate a struggle. Jeff wanted that realization to comfort him, but somehow it failed to. He could not get over the feeling that perhaps he had lost her forever.

"I got a hunch," Wade said. "Pretty good hunch, too."

"What?" Jeff looked at the mountain man more closely, saw an expression on his face he couldn't quite make out, an emotion, partly hidden, somewhere between contentment and an itch for further action. "Something happened, Wade. What is it?"

Wade told him all about the attempted ambush at the Rapture. "Whoever's behind this organized it pretty good, with all of us in different places. Me gunned down at the club, you ripped up in your old car at work and Tracy . . ." His voice trailed off and his eyes searched for her in his imagination, his face a blank now, as if the vision he'd suddenly glimpsed might be too horrifying to reveal.

"That's what I meant, Wade—where the hell is she?" Jeff insisted. "We were all supposed to meet here. I called her early this evening to tell her I'd be late. You were supposed to be here no later than ten. Christ, it's nearly midnight. I knew she wasn't planning to go out. She told me so. And I warned her not to. I'm scared, Wade. We don't know what we're dealing with here, do we?"

"I think I got an idea," Wade said. "I think I know where she is." He explained to Jeff about Penny and the big man named Reynolds.

"My God, you think he's got her? But how? She wouldn't have left here on her own without some very good reason. How would this guy have gotten to her, unless he came here after her?"

"I don't know, old buddy," Wade said. "Anyway, maybe she's OK. Maybe she went out lookin' for you. One thing I do know, this guy Reynolds could tell us a lot and I know where to find him."

"And what if he has Tracy?"

Nolan shrugged. "We'll have to deal with that when we come to it," he said. "Best thing for us to do, old buddy, is get on the road here." He got up, took the Ingram out of its case, checked the ammo clip, then slipped it back in. He slung the case over his shoulder, and tucked it inside his left arm. "You ready?"

"Yeah." Wearily, like a man going through the motions of an old, discarded ritual, Jeff stood up, took the Beretta .38 out of the bureau drawer where he'd been keeping it ever since his return from North Carolina, and slipped it into a side pocket of his jacket.

"We ain't got a car," Wade said. "We're gonna need one."

"There's a Hertz garage not far from here," Jeff said. "I'll call and we can pick one up there."

"We're gonna need a compact," Nolan told him as Jeff picked up the phone. "We may have to park a while."

It was nearly 1 A.M. when they reached West Eighty-eighth Street. Luckily, they found a parking spot almost directly opposite the shabby brownstone. After Nolan had checked the names of the tenants, he came back to the car and he and Jeff forced themselves to wait. There were still too many people in the streets.

It was a shame to have to kill her, really, Crawford reflected, but this was such nice work. It had been a very long time since he'd had the luxury of such a victim, one with whom you could take your time, relish all the small, significant moments that would linger in the memory, that you could treasure forever. He had the whole night, he figured. He would do his best with her, his very best.

She was a nice little piece of goods, all right, he could tell that even before he began to strip her. You don't want to undress them completely right away, either. You take off just a little bit at a time, because if you rush the process you risk passing up one or two especially good moments. She was badly frightened, he knew, from the minute she came to and found herself sitting on the chair with her hands tied behind her. She choked a little on the gag and shook her head, struggled until he took the hood off and she could see what she was dealing with. Her eyes were wonderful, he thought, dark with anger as well as fear, not yet wild with terror or glassy with pain, as they would be later. He chuckled. He couldn't believe his luck with this one. He warned himself again not to rush it, not to miss a single important second, and so he sat down on a stool facing her and smiled as he took a long leisurely look at her. Then, when he saw she had begun to relax just a little, just enough to indicate that she might have begun to believe in the possibility of some compassion on his part, he took out his knife, reached forward and swiftly cut her sweater and blouse away, leaving her stripped to the waist. Casually, almost as an afterthought, he reached out and pinched each nipple hard until they puckered and stood up for him, brave little pink spikes on her cool, white, unblemished skin. She was a joy to look at, all right.

She began to struggle again, so he walked around behind her to tighten the ropes. He released her from the chair itself, but tied her wrists together and then went to work higher up. He was a great believer in elbows. It hurt like hell when you tied them tightly together behind the back, and it never failed to put the victim in a more tractable frame of mind. It was nice, too, the way it made her breasts stick out even more, nice the way it made that first moan of pain come out of her through the muffling gag.

Crawford let her sit like that for a while. He just looked and enjoyed the sight of her. He took a lot of pride in these jobs; he always wanted his victims to look as pretty as possible, right up to the final seconds. Now he made her stand up and peeled her skirt away, leaving her only in panties, then made her lean over and ran his hands up and down her thighs. It was such a nice feeling and it always really got to them, because they were so helpless to do anything about it. Get them tied up good and tight, grab some part of them and watch their eyes. It never broke them, it was much too early for that, but it was an intrinsic, necessary part of the overall process. She moaned again, twisting this way and that, all very nice to experience.

It was truly heartbreaking, Crawford thought, the way they got their hopes up the minute you loosened something. You were doing it to make improvements, alter positions, but they couldn't know that. It was a nice psychological twist Crawford had mastered over the years, this business of shattering a hope as you change directions. Look at this girl's face now that she finds herself with her hands up in the air, tied to the loop over the pipe. That was a good position, because it made them realize exactly how vulnerable they were. Using the ropes skillfully, he gave her a bit of the old up-and-down now, forcing her to lean first on one foot, then on the other. It always startled them to find themselves tugged this way and that and always on one foot.

Crawford had always found that telling them anything wasn't of much use. They were too off balance, too upset by this time. The gag kept them from saying anything, cut off all their foolish questions, their pathetic pleas, their absurd threats. Oh, he could see that this girl was going to be perfect. She had spirit and pride. She'd go the full course, he was sure of it. How she stared at him, how she hated him, it was wonderful! The temptation to commit the ultimate act on her right away was almost irresistible, but he fought it off. There was no accounting for these rash impulses, even after all these years, Crawford reflected, but his whole career had been fashioned on the bedrock of discipline, control, patience. He lay down on the cot for a while and merely watched her twisting and turning helplessly to his gaze.

Sometime later, after he'd come the first time and cleaned himself up, he got up and crossed the room to her. The naked fear now in her eyes excited him even more than before and he stepped back to keep himself from finishing her off then and there. *Oh no, it was much too early!*

She moaned with terror, which was exactly what he had hoped for and he felt himself go rock hard for her again. He knew he could not stop himself now, that the drama would be shorter than he had hoped, though the ultimate fulfillment would be everything he had promised himself it would be.

For a while, perhaps five minutes, he simply stood and stared, devouring her beauty and helplessness with his eyes. She tried to scream through her gag. She struggled with her bonds. It was so beautiful to see that, despite himself, he felt himself coming to a climax. He groaned and sank to his haunches, looking away from her. *Too soon, too soon*—he'd have to wait a few more minutes at least. Even as he told himself that, his semen spilled. He looked up at her and smiled, almost wistfully. He considered his final consummating act. She would be the best, the best he had had in so long, perhaps ever . . .

The first burst from the Ingram shattered the outer lock and they found themselves in the darkened foyer. From inside they heard a muffled exclamation, then the sound of someone overturning a piece of furniture. With the Beretta in his hand, Jeff flattened himself against the wall as Nolan now jammed the Ingram into the second lock and blasted it open, the door falling in under the dull impact of the blow.

The light from the overhead bulb in the room threw the scene into ghastly relief, and Jeff cried out at the sight of Tracy. Nolan grunted and fell forward on his stomach, the gun in firing position.

"Get down!" he snarled.

The whole maneuver had taken no more than thirty or forty seconds, not enough time for the man inside to arm himself and take countermeasures, but enough for him to scramble through the bathroom door and slam it behind him as the first full burst of shots from the Ingram tattooed a pattern of violence across the shattered wood at waist height. Nolan rolled to the side, then fired again, tracing a pattern a foot or so lower down. Jeff, however, had no thought of combat, but only a crazy, frantic desire to rescue Tracy. He ran blindly into the room, shooting wildly at the door, but forcing Nolan to withhold his own fire.

"Jesus Christ!" Nolan yelled. "Get the fuck out of the way!"

But Jeff had reached the victim. He dropped his gun and began tearing frantically at the ropes that suspended her above the floor. She moaned as he set her free, and fell into his arms. He carried her to the cot and bent anxiously over her shivering form.

Still cursing, Nolan moved swiftly past him, kicked the shattered bathroom door down, thrust the muzzle of the Ingram inside and fired again. Nothing. When he looked past the door, he saw that the room was empty. The window above the toilet had been kicked in, the iron grate protecting it was unlatched, the big man gone. Nolan ran back into the room and tossed the empty Ingram to his friend, "I'm goin' after him," he said, heading for the door. "He can't get too far. Get her out of here and I'll catch up with you later!"

As Nolan reached the street, he immediately spotted his quarry, a big man dressed only in shoes, trousers and a white shirt; he was walking fast, heading east. Nolan broke into a swift, loping run. The big man turned his head, saw him coming and also began to run.

A light late-summer rain had begun to fall and the pavement gleamed dark and slick in the early-morning hours. The two men ran like figures in a dream of deserted streets and empty buildings, toward the subway entrances at Broadway and Eighty-sixth. The quarry was going to ground now, and, like the intrepid killing animal he was, Nolan went in after him. The primordial drama of stalker and prey would play itself out now as all such dramas should, in darkness and in solitude. The antagonists were as isolated in their deadly concerns as if they had been dropped into the middle of a desert. At that hour the city slept or huddled in fear of involvement behind locked windows, bolted doors. No cruising police car spotted either of these running figures in the two minutes or so it took for each of them to disappear again. When they had gone, it was as if they had never existed.

The subway station at that hour of the morning was as abandoned as an ancient catacomb. The empty platforms, gritty with dust, lay ominously silent under dim fluorescent tubes. Nolan took the stairs three at a time, too fast, because the momentum of his pursuit carried him past the corner of the wall on the other side of the turnstiles. Crawford, flattened there against a cheerful, public-spirited poster proclaiming its love for New York, had wheeled just in time to catch him. The first blow was slightly off target, but the hard-handed karate chop caught

Nolan on the neck just above the shoulder and dropped him on his side. He lay there, momentarily too numb and too surprised to move, and the big man stepped out and aimed a savage kick into his stomach.

Nolan was able to roll with it sufficiently to diminish its force, but it took enough of his breath away for Crawford to get past him on his way back to the exit stairs. Nolan, however, caught Crawford five steps up, ducked a desperate backhanded swing and buckled his antagonist with a jabbing, iron-fingered fist into the groin. With a grunt of pain, Crawford doubled over, and Nolan's knee caught him in the mouth, shattering his front teeth and creating a bloody welt where his lips had once been. Crawford staggered backward and Nolan now stood between him and escape. Doubled over, but moving surprisingly fast, the big man reached the turnstiles, vaulted them and began a crippled, lurching run toward the uptown end of the platform.

He knew Nolan was coming, of course, and set a trap for him by pretending to be more injured than he was. When Nolan reached him this time, Crawford whirled and chopped him into the wall, then doubled him up with a tremendous shot into the stomach that left Nolan on his knees, gasping for air. He then hauled him to his feet and moved in close to finish him off with a choke hold, but made his second crucial mistake of the night.

The first error had been to indulge his fantasies involving the girl instead of simply finishing her off; the second was to assume that Nolan, dazed and temporarily unable to breathe, was helpless. During his entire career Crawford had always prided himself on his ruthless efficiency, had castigated and eliminated others for their miscalculations. Now he had to pay the ultimate price himself, because Nolan, even as he wilted in the agent's iron grasp, had one card left to play and just enough time to play it. He was able to reach into his pants pocket, grasp the handle of the small pistol he called his tax collector, aim it upward, and fire.

The ice-cold eyes above the bloody mouth went blank with surprise and pain. Crawford tottered backward and sat down heavily, clutching his stomach, his back against the grafitti-splattered wall of the station, his eyes turning yellow in the grim, pale light. "Who the fuck are you?" he mumbled hoarsely, not yet quite able to grasp the extent of his loss.

Nolan stood there, unable to reply, still fighting for air. By the time he had recovered sufficiently to move in on Crawford again, the big man's face had gone ashen with pain. "You," Nolan whispered, "where is he?"

"Fuck off . . ."

Nolan moved in close. "Listen," he said, still gulping for air, "listen good. You're shot in the gut with a tax collector. You know what that is? It just expands inside you and sets up this little ritual of death. You're goin' into shock now, old buddy. Your pulse rate's gettin' slower, your breathin's gettin' shallower, then you die, good and slow. Now you got one chance or no chance. You tell me where Grunwald is and who's got him and maybe, just maybe, you'll live. At least you won't die like a dog, inches at a time. Talk, buddy, and talk now."

Crawford's empty eyes stared into Nolan's and he groaned. The pain spread through him now, an inching tidal flow, permeating his whole frame. He tried to get up, but couldn't, and sweat poured down him, staining his shirt along with the blood from his ruined mouth. "Who . . ."

"Never mind that," Nolan whispered, pressing in close to the dying man so as not to miss a word. "Never mind about all that. Just say a friend of the family, that's all. Speakin' of which, you had them killed, didn't you? You sank Grunwald's boat, right?"

Crawford might not have answered, but the next wave of pain was excruciating. He felt as if a tiny, clawed hand was slowly dismembering him from within. Almost involuntarily, he gasped, "Torpedoes . . . the kind used by our river boats . . ."

"I figured," Nolan said. "And the plane crash? Talk, man! You ain't got much time."

Despite the agony he was in, Crawford managed a parody of a smile. "Cyanide bomb . . . altitude-detonated . . . in the cockpit."

"Pretty sharp," Nolan said, grabbing Crawford's chin to keep his head from sagging and so forcing the man to look at him. "Now, why? Who's doin' all this?"

"Can't . . ." Crawford's eyes clouded from another terrible onrush of agony. He seemed to shrink into himself from the sheer force of it.

Nolan sensed that he had very little time left. "Where is he? Where's Grunwald? You want another shot in the gut?"

"Edgetown Road . . . five-twenty-two . . ." The big man slumped to one elbow, his other hand clutching at his stomach.

"Where's that? Princeton, New Jersey? Come on, buddy." Nolan leaned over him, staying in close, too close.

Crawford looked up at him. Was it a smile or another grimace of pain? Nolan would never know. He had heard the rumbling of the oncoming train, but had ignored its possible implications. It must have been a tremendous last effort for Crawford, but the move caught Nolan completely by surprise. With his back still to the wall, Crawford kicked out with both feet. The shove sent Nolan tottering backward off the platform and directly into the path of the oncoming local.

It was a matter of seconds. Nolan remembered looking up and seeing the horrified white face of the motorman pressed against the glass of the lead car and heard the jangled screeching of brakes. He only had time to throw himself lengthwise into the gutter between the tracks before the train passed over him and came to a grinding stop. Stunned, he lay there and waited. Doors slid open. Footsteps. A shout. More running feet. "Hey!" Nolan called up from under the car. "Get this fuckin' thing off me!"

"You OK?" a hoarse voice called out. "You OK under there?"

Another male voice: "What is it? What's happened?"

A third male voice: "Some guy fell under the train!"

The first voice: "Call the cops, for Christ's sake! He's alive!"

"Hey!" Nolan shouted. "Get me out of here!"

Still another voice: "Hey, mister, you OK?"

"Sure," Nolan shouted. "Long as I don't move." *Now I know what the mouse felt like when it was buggered by the elephant,* he thought.

"Holy shit," the motorman said, "he just fell off the goddam platform! I seen him flying through the air! I couldn't stop that fast. No way, no way at all!"

It took almost a half hour to get Nolan out from under the train. In all the confusion and noise, no one had noticed the body of the big man by the wall, behind the change booth. He lay hunched up on his face, where he'd fallen, both hands clutching his bloody stomach, eyes open and staring blindly into the sooty filth of the pavement.

This was a hell of a way to start the day, Chief of Detectives Richard Steinman told himself. Here he was, only six weeks away from retirement now, and you'd think they'd let him ease out of the goddam job, go out with a modicum of class and dignity. Not at all. Eleven unsolved murders on his hands in the last month alone and now this weird case to start off what should have been a slow day in the middle of the week. The cameraman he knew from having seen him for years on the scene of every gory event played up on TV, but this other guy, this cracker with the loony-looking eye, he was new, something a little out of the ordinary run of criminals. It should have been easy to wrap it all up, but obviously it wasn't going to be. They were going to exasperate him into a heart attack with their complications and strange explanations before he had a chance to enjoy even one day of his pension, all these goddam crazies with their fake goddam documents.

Full of barely concealed disbelief, Steinman leaned forward in his chair now, his leathery, seamed face framed by the large-lobed ears. The sad brown eyes under white brows seemed to plead for the truth rather than demand it, as if the spent cigar stub jammed between the detective's thick, bitter lips symbolized the extinction of all faith in the ability of any human being to tell him the truth or behave with a modicum of decency and honor. "What is this shit?" he said. "You expect me to believe this?"

Jeff quietly explained it all again, going over it from the beginning but leaving out the possible reasons for it. "And these phony papers, as you call them, Chief, are not phony at all, as you'll find out when you check Washington," he answered him once more. "We don't know who the dead man is."

Steinman rubbed his eyes, took a sip of his tepid coffee and sighed. "And that's it, huh? This guy here is a government intelligence agent on a secret mission, but you won't tell me what," he said. "The dead man is the guy who kidnapped your girl friend, why we don't know, nor do we know anything about him except that he calls himself Reynolds and operates out of a basement apartment on West Eighty-eighth. Your girl friend—what's her name?"

"Tracy. Tracy Phillips."

"Yeah, Phillips. She says she's seen this guy Reynolds a few times, without his wig and makeup, hanging around where she works. She thinks the guy may work at ACN, too, but there ain't nobody by that name on the personnel sheet," the detective said. "OK, so we assume that Reynolds probably ain't his real name and that he don't even live in that place. What we do know, according to you guys, is that he snatched the girl, right? That he's a real perv and that you went after him, right? How did you know where to find him?"

"Chief, we've told you already that we don't have all the answers," Jeff said. "We're onto the biggest story of my whole career. Wade's got all the right credentials and all the right gun permits. He admits to shooting this guy Reynolds, or whatever the hell his real name is, in self-defense, and we told you what happened there. The rest of it we'll give you later, if we can piece it together for you. Maybe by tomorrow."

Steinman grunted, obviously unconvinced, but he got up, stepped out of his office and shut the door behind him. Jeff looked at Wade, who was stretched out in his chair, half-asleep. "Wade?"

"Yeah."

"Those government documents of yours will get us off the hook, won't they?"

"Yep, sure, old buddy," Nolan said, smiling. "I'm cleared for special missions. Maybe not like this one, but then this old boy here don't know that, does he?"

"If we don't get out of here soon . . ."

"Yeah," Nolan agreed. "I got to get me some rest before we head out there. About an hour will do it. How's Tracy?"

"She'll be all right. I got her home and she's sleeping. I got two Valiums into her."

"That old boy sure had weird ideas, didn't he? Man, we got in there just in time."

Jeff blinked and shuddered, his eyes suddenly full of the vision of Tracy bound and helpless in that room. Before he could quite banish the sight from his memory, Steinman came back and slammed the door behind him.

"OK," he growled, "get out of here."

"We checked out, huh?" Wade asked, rising slowly to his feet and stretching.

"For now," Steinman said. "Nobody in Washington has any idea about a so-called mission in this area, but they'll get back to us. And you'd *better* have one."

"Aw, Chief," Wade drawled as he headed for the door, "you're just naturally suspicious, ain't ya?"

"You bet your ass I am."

"You must be a real good cop."

"Listen," Steinman said, "if I find out there's no special mission, you're up on a murder charge."

"Bullshit," Nolan said, "and you know it. You're just sore 'cause we can't let you in on the fun just yet."

"Fun?" Steinman asked, his mouth agape, the cigar stub grafted to his lower lip. "You think this is fun? You dumb cracker, get the fuck out of here!"

"Chief, we'll call you later," Jeff promised. "We may have something big for you."

Steinman grunted noncommittally and waited until Nolan had his hand on the doorknob. "What about that stiff we found on West Forty-sixth last night? You wouldn't know about that one, would you?" he barked.

"What stiff, Chief?" Jeff asked.

"The guy with the top of his head blown off. Some guy who used to be CIA, name of Morgan. You wouldn't know about him, huh?"

"No, we wouldn't," Jeff said.

Nolan smiled broadly at the detective as he opened the door. "I sure do like your little old police station, Chief," he said affably. "It reminds me of a real bad whorehouse I was in once in Hong Kong. Fooky-fooky, five dollah. And the crabs in there could jump ten feet with their galoshes on. You got a real fun town here, Chief."

After they had gone, Steinman put his head in his hands and shut his eyes. Only six more weeks of this crap and then he was out of it forever. The thought almost succeeded in making the rest of his day bearable.

REFERENCE: MYRMIDON—I am a prisoner of this project. It has become clear to me that they have no intention of letting me out. They will never lift the cloak of secrecy. What troubles me most, I think, is that my work will go unperceived. I may never receive recognition for my achievements.

How I yearn for the purity of detached theoretical research. How I dread these lucid moments.

—From the Journal of Dr. Jerome Lillienthal

20

IT WAS NOT quite noon when they came out of the tunnel and picked up the New Jersey Turnpike heading south. Jeff was driving, with Moss sitting beside him and Nolan stretched out in the back seat, his long, bony legs draped over some of the camera and sound equipment. They hadn't gone more than ten miles before he began to complain about it.

"What you guys plannin' to do? Make a damn movie?"

"It wasn't my idea," Moss said. "Jeff here thinks we're onto the story of the century."

"Yep," Jeff agreed. "If we find old Harvey, I'm going to have the goddamndest exclusive interview on tape in the history of TV news."

"Shit," Nolan exclaimed. "That's if the old boy can still talk."

"Why wouldn't he? If they've been holding him against his will."

"'Cause he may be in on it. Ever think of that?"

"No. I have to admit that possibility didn't occur to me. Why would he be? Where's the incentive?"

"You've got me, buddy boy," Nolan admitted. "Anyway, this is your show. I'm just along for the ride."

"Some ride, huh?"

"You bet your ass! Ain't had so much fun since that time in Saigon they took a piece of my eye out!" Nolan giggled and sank back in his seat. "I sure could use a little more sleep, though. Wake me up when we get there."

"You know, Jeff, I don't think that Bellucci bought this story about both of us being down with the flu," Moss observed thoughtfully. "We could have our asses in a sling if he checks us out."

"Up his," Jeff said. "We've got characters running around trying to kill us just to keep us away from Harvey. The least of my worries is what Bellucci could do."

Moss sighed. "Oh, well, I really didn't want this job anymore," he said.

They drove in silence through the New Jersey flatlands, between miles of noisome refineries, oil-storage tanks and petrochemical works whose snarls of convoluted pipes and belching stacks poisoned the hazy summer air. The foul odors brought Nolan to a sitting position again. He stared with disbelief at the acres of industrial horror on either side of the car.

"Jesus," he commented, "where the hell are we?"

"Just passing beautiful Elizabeth, New Jersey," Jeff informed him, "land of ecological opportunity, dream town of the technologically advanced future."

"A whiff of that would knock a buzzard off a shit wagon." Nolan jammed a handkerchief over his nose and mouth and tried again to snatch a few minutes of sleep. Jeff, buoyed by a discreet dose of amphetamines, felt alert and oddly at ease, as if at last he knew he was on the verge of an epic discovery, one that would vindicate all they had been through these past few weeks. He softly hummed country music as he drove, and his spirits soared even higher after he'd turned off the Turnpike and began nosing the car down the narrower roads leading into Princeton itself.

Once through the old college town with its quiet streets and charming old Colonial-style houses, they kept going for two or three miles, then turned right. Edgetown Road branched off from the old highway south to Trenton and wound through expensive, heavily wooded residential areas for ten or twelve miles before apparently, according to Jeff's map, petering out in a cobweb of small streets around some sort of new housing development. Number 522 was unmarked from the road itself, but Jeff knew he had found the place by the height of a Gothic stone tower that soared above the treetops from a rise a mile or so to the left of the road. "That's got to be it," he said. "It's the only structure we've seen tall enough to broadcast from. They must have the transmitter up there."

The only access to the place seemed to be through an electronically controlled gate in a high chain-link fence that apparently encircled the property. The grounds looked old and well established, like the home of some retired magnate, but the fence was obviously new, and wicked-looking strands of barbed wire lined the top of it. The house itself, except for the tower, was hidden from view by the thick woods lining the winding lane beyond the gate. Jeff drove past the property, then partly around it in both directions, but could find no secondary access. "Now what?" he asked as he parked a couple of hundred yards up from the main gate.

"We could try going in like the white folks," Moss suggested, "through the front door."

"And alert them that we're here?" Jeff said. "I don't think so."

"Come on," Nolan ordered, stretching. "Get out of the car. It's just another jungle patrol, old buddy. We pretend we're goin' in on Charlie's village, that's all."

It took Nolan only a few minutes to cut through the fence. The Ingram tucked under his left arm, he led the way up the thickly wooded slope toward the house, with Jeff and Moss, under full working gear, in single file behind him.

"Shit," Moss whispered as they picked their way up through the undergrowth. "I'm allergic to bees!"

It took them less than fifteen minutes to reach the edge of the strip of lawn that encircled the house. Crouching silently in the brush, they studied the layout.

The mansion must have been built by some tycoon of minor Hearstian pretensions. Made of huge granite blocks flung together fortress style, it resembled nothing so much as a parody of a medieval castle and could easily have been transplanted to Southern California, where a miniature golf course could have been built around it, or a car dealership. Leaded-glass windows lined the nearest wing, and a large flagstone terrace off the back looked out over distant fields and the nearest neighboring houses, two or three miles away. The main entrance, under an ivied porte cochere, faced a circular gravel driveway in which half a dozen cars were parked bumper to bumper.

Before they could decide what action to take or how to get inside the house itself, a gleaming brown Jaguar XJS came purring up the lane and parked by the front door. Whitner Bridgeford, elegantly attired in a pin-striped business suit and holding an attaché case, got out, thrust a plastic card into a slot by the door and was immediately admitted.

"That's one guy I want to have a serious talk with," Jeff whispered. "Let's go."

"Hold on, old buddy," Nolan said. "I think our best bet is around the back. There ought to be doors givin' out on that terrace. You all wait right here. If I ain't back for you in ten minutes, come on in after me, but with the artillery, not no damn cameras, hear?" Without waiting for their reply, Nolan stepped out of the undergrowth and, keeping close to the side of the building, turned the corner by the terrace and disappeared from view.

The man lying on the bed in the darkened room had only just begun to feel more human when he heard the sharp knocks at the door. He couldn't understand it, because the prescribed routine of the facility forbade anyone in the building to disturb him between the hours of 1 and 2 P.M., when he gave himself his daily injection. The hypodermic syringe still lay on his bedside table, and the drug itself had not yet been fully assimilated into his system. He was still a little shaky, not ready either for the day's events or for confrontations with his fellow human beings. Twenty minutes or so to go, he reasoned, and so, at the first knock and without moving, he called out, "Go away! It's not yet time!"

"Sorry, sir," said the pained voice on the other side of the door. "I have to speak to you."

It was incredible. Didn't they know? The man on the bed groaned and sat up. "Who is it, for God's sake?" he called out.

"Clarkson, sir, security. Please—please let me in."

"Not now. Go away." Still sweating but feeling more in control of himself, the man sank back on the sheets. "Come back in twenty—" But before he could finish the sentence, the door burst open. "What—" The man struggled to sit up.

Clarkson, a small, trim-looking man in a gray suit, nearly fell into the room. Behind him, looming in the doorway like some sort of elongated figure out of a dream, stood a lean, tall man holding a compact submachine gun and behind him were two other figures who looked like a TV camera crew. Clarkson did not look well at all; in fact, from the way he was holding his side he seemed to be in considerable pain. His mouth opened and closed spasmodically.

"That him?" Nolan asked. They all crowded into the room and the black man who was bringing up the rear closed the door behind them.

"No," Jeff said. "Can't you see?"

The man on the bed stared at them and shakily swung his legs to the floor. "Clarkson—" he began, but saw it was useless. Clarkson had suddenly toppled forward and lay at the foot of the bed. Frightened, uncomprehending, the man looked from face to face but could make no sense of the intrusion.

"You're Lillienthal, aren't you?" Jeff asked. "Jerome Lillienthal?"

"Who—who are you?" the man retorted.

"That old boy's a junkie," Nolan said, stepping across Clarkson's prostrate form. "Obviously just had his fix." He grinned at the cameraman and slumped into a chair, the gun on his lap. "Nice friends your man Grunwald's got. Right nice bunch of folks."

"Where's Harvey?" Jeff asked. "Where have you got him?"

The man on the bed stared at him, and then, as he began to rub himself briskly with both hands, feeling the life force flow into him from the drug, he began to chuckle. "Oh, Lord," he said, more to himself than for their benefit, "I should have known . . ."

"You *are* Lillienthal, aren't you?"

The man laughed harder, but there was little mirth in the sound. "Oh, yes," he gasped. "Oh, yes, of course. Who else would I be?"

"And Harvey? Where's Harvey? He's here, isn't he?"

"Oh, yes, yes indeed," Lillienthal said. "Yes, certainly, he's here."

Clarkson, still clutching his side, laboriously rolled over on his back. "Please . . . please help me," he murmured. "I need help."

"Aw, it's just your ribs, old buddy," Nolan informed him. "Nothin' crucial."

"I think I'm hemorrhaging."

"Well, hell, yes, sure," Nolan cheerfully agreed. "But if you lay still, maybe you won't die. If you have to take another shot to the gut, you won't be so lucky."

Jeff turned on a floor lamp and looked around. They were in a second-story bedroom that looked as impersonal as a luxury hotel suite. In the light, the man on the bed looked ravaged. Dressed only in baggy slacks and a T-shirt, he was probably in his mid fifties, but he could have been seventy. Needle scars stitched a pattern of ruin up the insides of his scrawny arms. His face seemed to be caving in, with deep wrinkles crisscrossing flaccid skin; his mouth twitched uncontrollably from time to time; his eyes were dark, intelligent and empty of hope. Oddly enough, even with the sight of the damaged man on the floor, he seemed unafraid, even pleased by the violent intrusion.

"All right," Jeff said, "if Harvey's here, take us to him."

"I will, I will, but I need a few minutes," Lillienthal said. "You see the condition I'm in."

Nolan picked up the syringe and sniffed. "Morphine," he announced. "That do the trick for you, old buddy?"

Lillienthal nodded. "Oh, yes. Something has to." He leaned forward on his hands and gulped in air. "I'll be all right."

While waiting for him, Jeff and Moss began to tape the action, including shots of Clarkson on the floor, of Lillienthal, a good close-up of the needle by the bed.

"Shit, let's get on with this," Nolan said after five minutes of taping.

"OK, Lillienthal, let's go," Jeff ordered.

The scientist nodded and rose shakily to his feet, sliding them into a pair of worn bedroom slippers and putting on a floor-length silk bathrobe. He shuffled toward the door. "You'll want to see the lab, of course," he said.

As they headed toward the door, with Nolan bringing up the rear this time, Clarkson raised himself up on one elbow. "Please . . . I need a doctor . . ."

"Don't worry about it, old buddy," Nolan said and, almost as an afterthought, clubbed him down in passing with a single blow to the head with his gun butt. Clarkson lay still, blood now oozing out of his nose and mouth.

The little party trailing Lillienthal proceeded through empty whitewashed clinical-looking corridors, then ascended to the third floor, directly under the tower, where he unlocked a soundproof door and admitted them into a large room dominated by a huge computer bank that filled three of the walls from floor to ceiling. At regularly spaced intervals, some three feet apart, a dozen TV screens stared blankly into a void. "This is the lab," the scientist announced in a firmer, more authoritative voice, as if drawing strength from the presence of the technological marvel itself. "And that's Myrmidon."

"Myrmidon?" Jeff echoed.

"Yes," Lillienthal said. "Would you like to see how it works?" He eased himself into the seat of a master console that looked to their untrained eyes like the cockpit of some space-age starship. "It takes two technicians to assure a perfect operation," he said, "but the evening team is not due here for another hour or so. I can give a very convincing demonstration myself."

Swiftly, confidently, he began to punch buttons and adjust dials. The computer bank began to hum and the monitor screens came to life with an interesting variety of images. They ranged from landscapes of all times and places to shots of famous people, celebrities both dead and alive, in all hues and performing all sorts of actions. Some of the celebrities, in fact, became increasingly strange, unfamiliar, eventually bizarre. One sequence showed President Franklin D. Roosevelt competing in the pole vault at the 1936 Berlin Olympic Games. A second displayed Hitler, with hunted, defeated, fearful eyes, shuffling along in a long line of inmates at Auschwitz. A third showed Winston Churchill winning the English Grand National, a steeplechase event, on the back of a lion. A fourth depicted Judy Garland as Dorothy in *The Wizard of Oz*, but in a pornographic sequence with the Scarecrow, the Tin Woodman and the Wicked Witch. All the scenes were in full color, with sound, and as startlingly realistic as life itself.

"What the hell—" Jeff exclaimed.

"I sure like this last one," Nolan said, staring at Dorothy and the Witch in a very compromising position. "Let's go on with that one for a while."

Lillienthal smiled, basking in their amazement. "We were merely fooling around here one day," he explained. "The engineers like to put some of this stuff on for the fun of it. It can become tedious in here after a while. Myrmidon has its lighter side. Watch. This is what we call our multiplex system."

Several of the more popular current television series now appeared on the screens. As they watched, Lillienthal began to maneuver the dials and switches so that the actors and actresses began to change color and racial characteristics before their eyes. Archie Bunker became successively black, Chinese, American Indian, Hispanic, Polynesian and, in one final dazzling incarnation, a Masai warrior in full regalia performing a ritual tribal dance.

"By this method, you see, our viewers' prejudices can be easily catered to," Lillienthal explained. "Each program can be coordinated to an ethnic-selector switch on the home television set, enabling viewers to change the race of the person or persons on screen. Even their vocal characteristics can be adjusted. Think of the boon to our political process."

"I think we've had enough of this," Jeff said.

Moss sat there, shaking his head. "I can't believe this," he said. "This makes *2001* look outdated."

Lillienthal shrugged and turned the sound down, leaving the images to succeed each other on the screens in silence.

"Got any more of that good old porn?" Wade asked. "Say, who does get Dorothy there in the end, the lion?"

"I've never seen it all the way through," Lillienthal confessed.

"What's this Myrmidon mean?" Moss asked. "That the trade name?"

"I thought it up," the scientist said. "We've been working on this process for quite a few years, ever since the early seventies, in fact. You remember Viking One and the pictures it brought back from Mars? The images the probe sent back were very incomplete—snowy, blurred, shadowy, full of indistinct shapes. Once they'd been run through computerized image-processing at the Jet Propulsion Lab in Pasadena, however, we could see what the camera had seen and we got these fresh, miraculously clear images in color. Beautiful, weren't they? By computer processing we had learned how to make certain assumptions and adjustments. That was the beginning of Myrmidon. We were only one short step away then. *I* knew it and so did a few others. And the message was heard very clearly by some people who counted."

"Why are you telling us all this now?" Jeff asked. "I mean, after all the secrecy, everything we've been through."

"Because ... because I had no idea ..." the scientist admitted. "I mean, the extent ... the commitment ..." Idly, almost absentmindedly, the fingers of one hand traced the telltale needle marks inside his other arm. "I—I didn't know ... I didn't realize ... These people will stop at nothing." He indicated his scars and smiled, but with desolation in his eyes. "They did this. They did this to me. And now ... now they don't really need me anymore ..." His voice trailed off and he coughed heavily. "You've met the man they call Crawford?"

"Oh, yes," Jeff said. "Yes, we have."

"Nice old boy," Nolan said. "He got a little careless."

"That man Clarkson upstairs . . . he's one of them . . . my keepers." A hoarse laugh.

"What's the name from?" Moss insisted.

"Myrmidon? Why, the Myrmidons were the soldiers of Achilles," Lillienthal explained, "in Homer's Trojan War. They were mythological beings, utterly loyal to their master, unquestioning followers and executors of the will of the hero-king. I thought it was appropriate. Pretty good, don't you think?"

"You had no idea they'd go this far?"

"Not to the extent they've gone, no," the scientist said. "You see, if you're like me, if you're a scientist, you begin with an idea and you research it. You follow it through, wherever it leads you. You ask questions and you get answers. You really have no idea what that can mean to a scientist, what the writer H. G. Wells once defined as 'the strange colorless delight of these intellectual desires.' That was me, all right. But when I saw not only what we'd achieved, but where it had led us, I tried—I really did try—to get the word out. I hadn't grasped the full implications . . . But it was too late. They wouldn't let me resign. There was too much at stake, too much money to be made. They . . . they reduced me to this." He held out both his arms again. "I'm a prisoner here, too, you see."

"Like old Harvey," Nolan said.

The scientist stared at him. "Yes, I suppose you could say that," he observed. "Almost like Harvey, in a way."

"All right," Jeff said, standing up. "Now, where is Harvey? I want to see him."

Lillienthal turned back to his dials and almost at once the monitor screens projected twelve quite separate images of Harvey Grunwald doing various anchorman stints. "There he is," Lillienthal said quietly. "He's in there." He indicated the monstrous computer bank.

The door behind them opened and Whitner Bridgeford, holding a sheaf of papers in one hand, walked briskly into the room. "Oh, Dr. Lillienthal— What?"

Before he could take another step or try to escape, Nolan had the Ingram jammed into his back. "Well, now, look who's here,"

Nolan said affably. "Sit down, buddy boy. Old Jeff here wants to ask you a few questions, too. Don't you, Jeff?"

Jeff nodded, but turned back to Lillienthal. "Listen—"

"Hey," Whitner said, "what is this? What's going on?"

"What do you mean, he's in there?" Jeff asked, waving at the TV screens. "What the hell is that supposed to mean? Where's the *real* Harvey? What have you done with him?"

"Why, just what you see," the scientist said. "Don't you believe your own eyes?"

Despite the Valiums, Tracy had been unable to sleep. Several times she had dozed off, only to wake up in an icy sweat, the impassive, cold eyes of the sadist fixed upon her. When her telephone rang, just before four o'clock, she sat straight up in her bed and began to tremble. She was unable at first to make herself answer it, but finally forced herself to lift the receiver. "Yes?"

"Honey, it's me, Jeff."

"Oh, Jeff. Thank God it's you. I was afraid . . ."

"Listen, honey, this is very important. I haven't time to explain very much, but I want you to do exactly what I tell you. Can you manage?"

"Yes, I think so."

"OK, now listen carefully. First of all, your old friend Whitner wasn't responsible. He's here and we've questioned him. He was put up to it."

"Oh . . . yes . . . I see."

"Tracy, you *are* OK now, aren't you?"

"Yes. Yes, I am. I'm sorry." She tried to will herself to stop trembling. How could she be of any use to them if she couldn't stop? "Is . . . is Whit all right?"

"Yeah, he's fine. They were integrating him into the operation, but he didn't know anything about the underside of it. They told him you were a part of it, too. We believe him. The poor bastard's almost in shock. Tracy, we've found out some incredible things. You wouldn't believe it if I told you. You'll have to see for yourself."

"What things?"

"You'll see. You'll see tonight. Now listen. Honey, can you do one more thing? If you can't, maybe I can get somebody else, but there'd be too much explaining to do."

"It's all right," she said. "I want to help, Jeff. Please let me. I'll be fine. You're sure you're all right? Where are you?"

"In Princeton, at the lab. We know all about Myrmidon."

"And Harvey?"

"I can't tell you over the phone. Now listen, I've already called Steinman and told him you'll be calling. I hung up fast, because I didn't want him to trace the call. He's waiting to hear from you."

"Yes?"

"Whitner's going to telephone Sarah Anderson later. They're both supposed to be at the Chairman's tonight for dinner, a small party to celebrate the Chairman's sixtieth year in broadcasting. Honey, the timing here is terribly important. You understand?"

"Yes, so far."

"Wade and Moss are on their way back to the city. They'll get there in about an hour and a half or so. They're going straight to the network."

"But—why? I mean—"

"Honey, I can't tell you. There isn't time. Please, just do what I ask, OK?"

"Yes. Yes, I will." She was gaining strength and confidence now, she could feel herself calming down, the spasms slowing, then ceasing altogether. "Jeff?"

"Yeah?"

"Please don't take any chances. I love you."

Jeff's senses swam. It was a moment before he could respond. "God, how I've waited to hear you say that, Tracy," he finally replied softly. "I love you, too."

Tracy began to sob. Jeff felt his own eyes moisten. "Tracy?"

"Yes, Jeff."

"When this is over . . ." Jeff hesitated a moment, then continued. "Will you marry me?"

"Oh, yes, Jeff," said Tracy. She laughed and sniffled at the same time. "You don't waste too much time, do you?"

"No, I guess not," Jeff replied with a chuckle, then grew serious again. "Listen, we don't have much time and there's still a lot to do in this Myrmidon thing. Here's what I want you to do. At exactly five o'clock, call Steinman . . ."

REFERENCE: MYRMIDON—What, precisely, have I done for mankind?

—From the Journal of Dr. Jerome Lillienthal

21

Sarah had never looked better—more radiant, more beautiful—in her life. She was wearing a short, off-the-shoulder ivory silk Halston dress slit up the side to display her fine, strong legs, and all day she had looked forward to this evening. Tonight, after dinner and in private, she was going to tell the Chairman that in less than a month they could begin to implement Cerberus, the successor to Myrmidon. She knew Larry would be pleased and he had already hinted to her that he planned to celebrate this occasion by a promotion and a raise for her. Sarah felt confident that by nightfall she'd be calling herself the president of the network, just one short rung below the Chairman himself. And when he stepped down, as someday soon now he would have to, it would all be hers, her triumph and the culmination of her entire career, everything she had worked so hard for ever since she'd begun her new life, not even two decades ago.

If only Larry had listened to his wife just this once. Louise had wanted the party to be a large one, with press and photographers present, a function splashy enough to suit the magnitude of the occasion, but the Chairman would have none of it and his wife had not been able to sway him. He had insisted on this intimate "family gathering," as he had put it, with only his top executives and their wives and husbands present, eighteen people in all. Dwight McCarron, who was slated to succeed Sarah in her current post, was also among the guests. So, of course, were Lee Olson, Clark Hadley, the other corporate officers. Well, she reflected, that would be enough. Larry had already told them there would be an important announcement at dinner, right after the evening news. She couldn't wait to see their faces, all of them, when he told them. She planned to look directly at Hadley, who would be the first one to go under her regime and who knew it. It would be very satisfying. The poor jerk had actually dared question her brilliant promotional campaign announcing Harvey Grunwald's return to the air; Clark was an anachronism. She planned to favor him that night with her most radiant smile.

Still, as she mingled, drink in hand, with the other guests in the Hoenigs' huge living room, she couldn't make herself feel completely at ease. First of all, she had been disturbed that afternoon by the call from the Chairman's office asking if she had heard from Crawford. That had been strange, since Crawford always reported directly to the Chairman and she had always tried to keep her distance from him. The man made her uneasy, the madness lurking behind the coldness of those eyes. Why should Larry have imagined Crawford would contact her if something had gone wrong? And what *could* have gone wrong? Anyway, she reassured herself, it couldn't have been too serious, because the call had been made by Shirley Boyd, the Chairman's secretary, and not Larry himself. Just a routine matter, she assumed.

What did bother her, though, was the call she had received from Whitner only half an hour ago, just before she'd left her house to come to the party. His voice had sounded strange, so distant. And what could he have meant by "a new development"? Why had he been so insistent that they all watch the evening news? As if they hadn't planned to all along. Had that pathetic has-been Lillienthal begun to cause trouble again and couldn't he be controlled anymore? What could have happened? There had been a shift in the emphasis on tonight's show, Whitner had told her, and it would be impossible for him to get away. She'd have to make excuses for him with the Hoenigs, but the work came first, didn't it?

"Well, yes, darling, of course," she had assured him. But why couldn't he tell her exactly what was going on? And what was so special about tonight's broadcast? Was Harvey already being phased out? That might be premature. No, Whitner had told her, Harvey would be on the air, just as always and without his replacement's first appearance. No, they were still a few weeks away from the first phase of Cerberus. But what else? Even at her insistence he had refused to tell her. "It's a surprise," he'd said, "in your honor, sort of. Trust me, Sarah."

Trust him? Could she do that? Well, tonight she would have to, she reasoned. Maybe Whit had planned something special for her, to celebrate the occasion and her forthcoming promotion. Yes, that must be it. But his tone, she thought, his reserved manner . . . Oh, she was probably just imagining everything, getting a little paranoid in her newfound eminence, she guessed. She had plans for Whit later, elaborate carnal plans that she hoped not to be deprived of. Oh, no, he'd told her, he'd get there by the evening's end, at least to pay his respects to the Hoenigs and to take her home, she wasn't to worry about that. And then, in a terrific hurry, he'd hung up on her. Strange, but—no, she wasn't going to let anything spoil her triumph tonight.

She looked around the room and found herself gazing directly at Clark Hadley. With that radiant smile she'd been reserving especially for him, she raised her champagne glass and silently toasted him. He smiled back, but it was the smile of a condemned man saluting his executioner.

"Ladies and gentlemen," the Chairman suddenly called out, then waited for them to stop talking so he could make his first announcement. "Tonight," he continued, "tonight is a very special occasion. After the evening news, I will have something very important to say about myself, those of you in this room and the future of this network. Now, I'd like you all to get settled and to remain quiet during the broadcast. It's the evening news, of course, with our top anchorman Harvey Grunwald, the biggest star in television news today. Sarah, would you sit near me, please."

The Chairman indicated a spot on the sofa beside him. As Sarah moved toward him, Louise smilingly walked over to the huge TV set facing them from the corner of the room and turned it on. The cheerful, open countenance of Bill James and the local WACN news team beamed at them while the cameras now pulled back for a closing long shot of them all as they shuffled papers, chatted and told each other silent jokes. In the Chairman's living room, nothing could be heard now but the occasional clink of ice cubes in a glass or the rustling of fabric as the guests settled themselves to watch the seven-o'clock broadcast in comfort. *This,* Sarah thought, *this is the night I've waited for all my life. . . .*

At one minute before seven o'clock, the computer in Broadcast Operations Control on the eighth floor of the ACN Building was following its programmed sequence of commercials leading up to *The Grunwald Report.* The huge machine, with its hundreds of colored buttons, functioned with awesome precision, untouched by human hands. Nolan was fascinated. From his perch in the supervising engineer's glass booth, slightly elevated above floor level, he could follow the process easily.

Directly in front of him, about ten feet away, were stacks of color monitors with their digital codes. Under them, about three feet below the level of the booth, was a console, a sea of multicolored buttons known as Switching Central. Through it passed everything ACN broadcast to the nation. Switching Central was the vast organism's spinal cord. The press of a single button could leave the network paralyzed, unable to produce anything but a blank screen for the millions of homes it serviced. Nolan, with Moss's help, intended to make sure that on this particular night the orderly succession of events in the ACN programming computer would not be interrupted, at least not before seven-thirty. The doors to the room had been locked and Moss himself was with the engineers at the console.

"Moss, those boys down there know they're not even to look at them buttons now, don't they?" Nolan asked as he leaned forward to peer down at the sound man, who had shooed the two technicians away from their seats at the console. All three of the men looked back at Nolan and nodded, their eyes fixed on the long black snout of the Ingram in Nolan's hand. Wade sat down again beside the supervising engineer and casually flipped the weapon's selector switch back and forth from semi- to full automatic. The man was trying not to look at him, but beads of perspiration were forming on his upper lip and the sweat lay slick on his forehead.

Nolan smiled. "Hey, old buddy, you're as jumpy as a bubble dancer with a slow leak. You got nothin' to worry about, long as you don't go answerin' any phones or makin' any sudden moves. Just enjoy the show, now."

The engineer nodded and turned obediently toward the network program monitor.

At precisely seven o'clock, the familiar wide shot of Harvey Grunwald's set appeared on the screen with the words "THE GRUNWALD REPORT" superimposed. A recorded announcer's voice intoned, "From *ACN News*, this is *The Grunwald Report*. Here now is Harvey Grunwald."

A tight close-up now of Harvey. He looked wonderful: sleek, avuncular, reassuringly wise, authoritative, the quintessence of the dedicated commentator. For a long moment he stared straight ahead, saying nothing, his dazzling blue eyes locked onto those millions of viewers across the nation. When at last he spoke, he did so with the utmost care.

"Good evening," he said. "The top story in the news tonight: I've been murdered."

A collective gasp burst from the gathering in the Chairman's living room. Sarah felt paralyzed, unable to move, barely able even to breathe. Like the rest of the viewers across the nation, she was riveted to her television screen. She glanced helplessly at the Chairman, who sat braced against the back of his seat, his mouth agape. All of the oxygen seemed to have been drained from the room. If she could just get outside and breathe, she thought, maybe her mind would clear and this dreadful hallucination would vanish. It wasn't happening, it *couldn't* be happening. She lurched out of her seat and ran from the room.

Out in the hallway, she found herself confronting a slender young woman who seemed vaguely familiar to her. Behind this person were three men, two of them in blue police uniforms. The oldest of the men had the suffering face of a reluctant pawnbroker, but it was he who spoke first.

"That her?" he asked.

"Yes," the young woman said.

Sarah stared bewilderedly at this group of intruders. "What—who are you?" she stammered at last.

"I'm Tracy Phillips, Mrs. Anderson," the girl said. "This is Chief of Detectives Richard Steinman."

"Mrs. Anderson, I understand that certain accusations are being made on the air this evening—" the man began.

Sarah didn't hear him. Drained of color, her face looked like a death mask. Her eyes stared unseeingly at them, her mouth opened and closed but made no sound. She stood rigidly in place, as if impaled. Suddenly she moaned. The sound was not quite human. It was the cry of a loss so complete, so shattering, that nothing could ever mend it. She stood among the ruins of her life like the last survivor of a bombing raid, dead in all but fact.

Back inside the Chairman's living room, Harvey Grunwald continued to address the nation. "I, my family, hundreds of other innocent people and, in a sense, all of you watching right now are the victims of a monstrous plot . . ."

Dissolve. A rigid body lying on its back on the floor. Harvey's voice: "This is my corpse." The camera zoomed in for a close-up of its face. Behind a thin layer of frost could be recognized the familiar features of Harvey Grunwald. "Until two hours ago it was floating in a vat of liquid nitrogen in the basement of the building from which this program originates. It was being preserved so that my murderers could produce an actual corpse when it came time one day soon for me to be replaced on this news broadcast. The world would be told that I had been killed or died by accident or disease, after which my anchor chair would be inherited by my carefully programmed successor, the first of the images to be created by a process known to its founders as Cerberus."

Another dissolve. The image of the living, talking Harvey reappeared on the screen. "The *person* known as Harvey Grunwald is dead. The image of Harvey Grunwald that you've been watching ever since I returned to the news last summer is just that—an image. I don't exist, really, except in the mind of a very sophisticated computer called Myrmidon. It is located in a secret ACN laboratory a few miles from Princeton, New Jersey."

A long shot of the old mansion, with its tower, its sheltering trees, its protective fence, followed by a succession of shots of the computer facilities being explained by the image and the voice of the anchorman. "In a few moments, I will reveal the identities of the actual people who created this facility," the image continued. "First, let me introduce the man who created *me*, Professor Jerome Lillienthal."

Lillienthal appeared on the screen. He was dressed in a dark business suit but seemed a little nervous. "Unlike the image of Harvey Grunwald, I am an actual person," he explained. "Creating Harvey—ah, creating the *image* of Harvey that you've been watching on the screen was quite a—uh—quite a challenge. And so is—ah—explaining it. But I'll try."

The Chairman groaned and struggled to rise to his feet, but was ignored. Everyone in the room was mesmerized, staring at the screen. The Chairman's breathing became raspy, labored. No one moved.

"You see," Lillienthal continued, "when a television camera takes a picture of someone—my picture, for instance—it converts my image into a series of electrical impulses. At first, years ago, the only way to store these impulses so that the same picture could be used again was on videotape. But in the mid-nineteen-seventies we developed a process of so-called *digitalizing* both picture and sound." Lillienthal became increasingly assured as he warmed to his subject. His long, elegant hands punctuated his lecture as he spoke. "That is, we discovered we could break down video and audio signals into a series of numbers and that the numbers could be stored in computers. Not just *stored* in computers, but also *altered* by them. We discovered that we could change television pictures, improve them, all with computer technology.

"Once we had digitalized Harvey's image and analyzed him in all his moods, expressions and what not, it became relatively simple to *create* a moving, breathing, speaking Harvey without having to have his actual physical presence in front of a camera. And, of course, we could *improve* him," Lillienthal added proudly.

Dissolve to the image of Harvey again. "So that explains the new, improved Harvey Grunwald you've been seeing and hearing all these past weeks," the image of Harvey resumed, "the Harvey Grunwald who has been *evolving* daily to fit the ever shifting public taste, as determined by the network's exhaustive analysis and testing. That was the original idea when this project was first dreamed up and then put into operation by *ACN News* President Sarah Anderson, with the approval of her employer, Chairman of the Board Lawrence Hoenig. The code name for this scheme is the Myrmidon Project. At first, according to Professor Lillienthal, Sarah Anderson saw the new computer technology as a way of making the real Harvey Grunwald more salable, of boosting the ratings and the corporate profits by tinkering with Harvey's image while still having to put up with Harvey's cantankerousness, his flaws and occasionally outrageous demands."

"My God," Clark Hadley said, "I can't believe this!"

Nobody answered him. Nobody even noticed Steinman, now standing quietly at the back of the room. Tracy's pale face hovered in the gloom of the hallway behind him. The Chairman sat immobile, his head slumped forward on his chest, while Louise glanced bewilderedly from face to face, seeking answers that never came.

"But gradually her own ambitions and the corporate lust for

ever fatter profits drove Sarah Anderson and Lawrence Hoenig and their agents to murder," the image of Harvey went on. "They are responsible for the boating 'accident' that killed my wife and our closest friends. They are responsible for the plane crash that killed my children along with hundreds of other innocent travelers, all to provide a pretext for my reclusiveness, my withdrawal from the world and society, all so I could be murdered secretly, without loved ones or close friends to look for me or raise awkward questions.

"By not having to pay my very considerable salary, ACN's profits rose sharply." Harvey's image gestured at the news set around him. "This room, you see, doesn't exist, either. It is being generated by the computer. The technique is useful, because it eliminates an entire crew—cameramen, floor directors, lighting people, stagehands, all unnecessary. More savings and so more profits for the network.

"What you are looking at is the future as seen by the Sarah Andersons and Lawrence Hoenigs of this world. What they dreamed of is the elimination from television of real flesh-and-blood human beings, with their costly and bothersome needs and demands. They envisioned a future locked inside an ultimate computer bank known as Cerberus, who in Greek mythology was the three-headed guardian of the gates of hell. This would be a viewing world in which the prime-time heroes and the places where they act out their nightly dramas would all be generated by computer, where each image would evolve according to the dictates of other computer programs measuring and analyzing your innermost thoughts and feelings and desires. A future, my fellow Americans, devoid of humanity, of life itself, but rich in profits, the television world populated by the modern-day Myrmidons, those perfect soldiers, also out of Greek mythology, who were the unquestioning, mute servants and executors of their master's will.

"Technology is a two-edged sword. From the dawn of the Industrial Revolution its promise has been to enlighten us, to free us of our more onerous burdens. The reality has been that we are also in danger of becoming enslaved by it. It frees us from drudgery but preempts our human rights, our creativity. What has happened here at ACN is, in a sense, merely the logical consequence of the policy of automation that the television industry, like so many others, has been obsessed with for years now. In broadcasting, the beginnings can be traced back to the creation of FM radio stations that consisted in essence of nothing more than tape machines and timers.

"Technology first eliminated the simple technical jobs, then more complex ones. Automated cameras, for example, replaced live cameramen, admittedly with only limited success at first back in the sixties, but the trend had been established. We did not then foresee to what extent it would go or how dedicated to the process its creators had become.

"We paid scant attention when we noticed that the announcers were the first human beings actually to be eliminated. By using tape machines, television stations everywhere could use one man to record several days' worth of announcements. Still, to some of those who ran television, that was one man too many. It had become necessary to eliminate everyone, every single live human being. The lesson of the Mars probe had not been lost on Sarah Anderson. It had occurred to her and her employer that modern technology had now made it possible to abstract the image of an existing human being and to make that image perfect, by adjusting it to accord with the fluctuations in public taste. It was only one step from that realization to the creation of Myrmidon and ultimately the enthronement of Cerberus. Sarah Anderson was our first image-maker, but she will surely not be the last."

Someone in the room was sobbing. It was Louise Hoenig. She was sitting on the sofa and holding her husband's head in her arms as she rocked him gently back and forth, back and forth.

Clark Hadley stood up and looked around. "Where's Sarah?" he asked grimly. No one answered. Hadley turned toward the door leading to the hall and for the first time noticed Steinman. "Who are you?" he asked.

Steinman introduced himself to the gathering. "I would like you all to stay right where you are," he said quietly. "We're already checking into these allegations and we will need statements from all of you."

"Where's Sarah Anderson?" Hadley insisted.

"She is under arrest. Which one of you is Lawrence Hoenig?"

The cry of dismay from the sofa made Hadley jump. Louise Hoenig stood up and began backing away in horror from the figure on the couch. No sooner had she released him than, head slumped grotesquely to one side, mouth agape, eyes staring, her husband slid helplessly to the floor. The Chairman was dead. He had not lived through his anchorman's greatest broadcast.

On the Chairman's television screen, Harvey's posthumous triumph was concluding.

"Technology is a powerful tool that can be wielded for the good of mankind, as well for baser purposes," said Harvey's image. "The profit motive, which is the metaphysical underpinning of our democratic capitalistic system, is a powerful force, which can also be used for good as well as evil. Either we will be enslaved by these forces or we shall learn to control them, to use them for the good of all and not merely for the oppression of the many by the privileged and greedy few. It is up to each and every one of us in this nation to resolve to gain control once more of our destinies so that we and our children will remain a free people, benefiting from a humane use of the awesome technological tools now at our command. We have no choice. There is no alternative. This is Harvey Grunwald. Good night . . . and goodbye."

At twenty-eight minutes and fifty seconds past seven o'clock, the image of Harvey Grunwald began to fade and disintegrate. Bit by bit, as that image continued to look imploringly out of millions of television screens, it vanished. The screen went blank and remained silent.

I believe we'll be the first electronic movie studio in the world. . . . We'll use the full magic of technology; we won't shoot on film or even on tape, it'll be on some other memory— call it electronic memory. And then there's the possibility of synthesizing images on computers, of having an electronic facsimile of Napoleon playing the life of Napoleon. It's almost do-able right now; it just takes the wisdom and the guts to invest in the future.

—Francis Ford Coppola
The New York Times, August 12, 1979